"I think of you as my good angel," said Gilles.

Afraid of his reaction, Veronique's voice was a whisper. "Is it what you wish me to be?"

He continued to study her as if to fix her face in his memory. "I want you to be as I see you. Alive, enchanting, with everything possible for you."

"I am not your good angel, monsieur. I am very much of this earth."

He pulled her against him. Veronique tried to protest, found herself more closely enmeshed. But in that first feather touch of his lips all her very earthy imaginings about him took hold of her. The woman who existed in her body responded to him now, and for a breathless few seconds she had no sensation that was not involved with him. When Gilles finally let her go, she was so lightheaded she could only say what she honestly felt. "If this is gratitude, monsieur, I am grateful for it. . . ."

Fawcett Crest Books
by Virginia Coffman:

MISTRESS DEVON

THE DARK PALAZZO

THE HOUSE AT SANDALWOOD

HYDE PLACE

VERONIQUE

Veronique

A NOVEL BY

Virginia Coffman

A FAWCETT CREST BOOK

Fawcett Publications, Inc., Greenwich, Connecticut

VERONIQUE

THIS BOOK CONTAINS THE COMPLETE TEXT OF THE
ORIGINAL HARDCOVER EDITION.

A Fawcett Crest Book reprinted by arrangement with
Arbor House

ISBN 0-449-22964-5

Printed in the United States of America

10   9   8   7   6   5   4   3   2   1

Veronique

Prologue

July 28, 1794

LOOKING more like a witch than ever, Madame Turgot drew her hand over her moist upper lip and tried once more to make the girl see reason.

"Even here in the shop I feel the heat. I warn you, Veronique, you will find yourself fairly spit-roasted in that crowded square."

"I must go. You know that." As she spoke, the dark, slender young woman who called herself simply Veronique went on calmly removing the bloodstained pinafore in which she worked. Then she rolled down the sleeves of the faded, mauve-colored gown that was her day dress at Turgot's Waxworks when she was not called upon to guide visitors about the display room.

La Turgot watched the young woman scrub her knuckles and fingernails fanatically with a handful of cut-up broomstraws, as if she would tear the flesh itself. It was not flattering to the Turgot Waxworks, this suggestion that its filth must be scoured away before the young woman went out into the dirty Paris streets, but Turgot realized that an artist who produced waxen heads of the famous and infamous, working from life, must be tolerant of people with Veronique's religious background. All the same, did the girl know what lay before her today?

"Have you seen many of these out-of-doors entertainments?"

"None, since—" Veronique cleared her throat. "None at all. May I leave now, citizeness?"

"Have you thought of its effect on the child?"

Veronique said coolly, "My child will not be born for six months. It can hardly be marked in its third month."

"Humph. You certainly are thin enough. You should eat more." But La Turgot gave up. "Well then, go. One hour I will give you to see the business through to the end."

9

Veronique reached for the leghorn hat perched upon a faceless wooden bust. The big-brimmed straw hat was probably ten years old. It had not been new when it was bought for her, and its prerevolutionary style might have been her death warrant on the streets of Paris but for the *rosette tricolore* that now decorated the low crown.

It was annoying to find her fingers unsteady as they knotted the frayed mauve ribbons under her chin. . . . The result of Turgot's warnings, no doubt. Impatiently—or was it nervously?—Veronique brushed the disheveled dark strands of hair away from her cheeks, and saw that she was still being watched. She said, "Have I your leave to go now, citeness?" and was proud of the even tone she had taken.

La Turgot waved her away.

"Go! If you stand about much longer, you will miss the entire affair. Remember. One hour."

Veronique hurried out of the side door, avoiding the workshop laboratory at the rear of the building as she invariably did when possible. In that laboratory she felt quite a different horror from the feelings she had known while she attended the sick and dying in the great Paris hospital, the Hôtel-Dieu.

The July heat took her breath away. The alley enclosed within walls of huddled, medieval buildings appeared to sizzle under the worst wave of heat Paris had seen in this burning summer of 1794. She stood there a minute or two trying to decide how she might reach the far end of the Tuileries Gardens without encountering crowds until the last minute when they would be inescapable in the huge Place de la Révolution.

Reaching the eastern end of the former Rue St.-Honoré, Veronique was within walking distance of the bridge over which the carts passed from the prison on the Cité to the Right Bank. Though she had endlessly imagined herself following those tumbrils all the way to the guillotine in the great square, she found herself grateful now that she would be too late to catch the procession itself.

She inhaled deeply and then coughed, still fancying she could smell the vinegar and other preservatives in the vats of Citeness Turgot's laboratory. She hurried through the alley, out into the street which was now uncharacteristically deserted. It seemed clear that most of Paris had poured along the narrow, curving Rue Honoré toward the place where the last act of the drama would be played out.

In the great silence that gripped the area, a voice suddenly called to her:

"Sister! Sister Veronique!"

She stiffened. In spite of all her mental rehearsals, and all Gilles' stern warnings, Veronique looked back instinctively. No one seemed to have heard her addressed by this proscribed title, which could send her before the Revolutionary Tribunal. There was no human being in sight except the haggard, delicate-featured woman dragging a portmanteau up from the nearest Seine boat-crossing. She was incongruously dressed in striped blue, white and red sansculotte pantaloons and a blue workman's smock. One could make out her collarbone and shoulders, parchment thin. She wore no head covering and her pale, wheat-colored hair was a thin barrier against the blaze in the western sky.

As Veronique crossed the cobblestones to meet her, the woman sat down on the worn cloth side of her portmanteau, fanning herself with a fragile hand while she apologized.

"Forgive me. I hope no one heard that, but I was so very glad to see someone from the old days. I am the Duchesse . . . No! I *was* the Duchesse de St.-Aubans. I met you first at your Cousin Sylvie's house at the time the States-General were meeting in eighty-nine. Only five years ago. Can it be possible? Now I am a polisher of boots. And a seamstress. I sew on buttons, mend hose and rips in petticoats." She laughed, the same light, merry little tinkle of sound Veronique suddenly remembered having heard so long ago in Versailles. Marie de St.-Aubans had been one of the wealthiest heiresses in France. Surely that was an eternity ago!

"Yes, five years," the Duchesse said, reading her inevitable thoughts as they embraced. "Your parents and cousins were about to make you take your vows, and if I do not mistake, you seemed most unwilling."

Veronique smiled, remembering. "Now those vows could cost me my head. Where is your mending shop? When I am paid my wages I will come and see you."

The Duchesse fluttered her arms. "My shop? Wherever I set down this dainty bandbox." She indicated the sunken portmanteau beneath her. "But do not let me detain you. You are in a hurry?"

"It is a vow I made. Forgive me, your grace."

The Duchesse shaded her eyes and glanced westward toward the gray hulk of the Louvre and the Tuileries Palace beyond.

Then she looked up at Veronique. During their few seconds of silence they could hear a continuous, muffled roar in the distance, rather like faraway rolling thunder.

The Duchesse nodded. "I understand. Let me advise you. Do not go there, Sister Veronique, I know!"

But Veronique was already on her way. She waved once, then hurried onward, passing the narrow entrance to the Rue Honoré. This artery carried the lifeblood of the city's heart, never more so than during these July days. Now it was blocked by carts piled with boxes containing articles of all descriptions and sizes—used clothing, household items and furniture once priceless—now to be traded for a loaf of sour black bread. And at present prices, Veronique thought a loaf of bread would be considerably more useful than a polished escritoire that had once graced a Loire château.

By taking the Rue Honoré—the "Saint" had been expunged from its name—to the street that had once been the Rue Royale, she could reach her destination more directly. But there the mob would be—half of Paris, more than a quarter million of its citizens, crowded along that ancient street—the awful, hydra-headed monster that was the mob. . . .

There was a jumble of alleys and streets between the Louvre and Rue Honoré, and Veronique hurried along these uncertain little thoroughfares, so narrow between the jutting overhang of medieval buildings that she might almost have spanned the width with her outspread arms. Beyond the Palais-Royal, now the Palais Egalité, whose popular arcades were unusually deserted, she began to run, with the advantage of long practice in the flat-heeled sandals that had been part of her nun's habit at the public hospital—the great, gloomy Hôtel-Dieu. Those were the times before she returned to Gilles Marsan. Before her real life began. Memories spurred her.

By the time she had reached the Place des Piques—it was a crime now to call it the Place Vendôme—she changed her direction and cut into the Rue Honoré, joining the laggards among the crowd who pushed and shoved their way along the street toward the all-important Rue Royale, which emptied into the Revolutionary Square. Veronique was breathless now, but not yet sweating. The air was too dry, the lowering sun an open furnace in the west behind the thickly wooded Champs-Elysées. Her hands and face felt dry as old bones. But it was the attitude of the mob that held her interest. She

had never seen them more tense. The sounds in their throats
were not laughter and cheers, nor even the dread sound of
their hatred. The terror they had barely lived through was
still too close.

As she snaked her way along the Rue Royale, moving
through every shift in the rapidly tightening crowd, she caught
her first sight of the two slender uprights, stark against the
sky. The heat had blurred the sky to a pale gold and it was
difficult to make out the slanting blade at the height of the
uprights. The soldiers had formed a neat square, bordering the
scaffold on all sides, but Veronique could make out only
their bayonets gleaming red in the sunset light.

A scholarly looking gentleman of the middle years elbowed
his way past Veronique, calling out the question she herself
silently asked: "Can you see? Is the blade stained yet? Are we
too late?"

A woman ahead of him took up her apron, wiped sweat off
her arms and her comely if somewhat unclean throat. "Not
yet, Old One. You are in time. It would be a shame to miss
the greatest exhibit since the Crucifixion."

A grotesque comparison, Veronique thought. As for herself,
her body had begun to tighten with nervousness, especially her
stomach. She set her teeth and slipped through the crowd,
which further shifted until she reached the approaches to the
square. Directly opposite the parched foliage of the Tuileries
Gardens she was trapped behind the backs of two men, a
butcher and a furniture-maker from beyond the Bastille area.

During the last few weeks the guillotine had been set up
at the other side of the city, and it was said that as each
day's batch of condemned was delivered to the far east end
of the Faubourg St.-Antoine, all the householders along the
way had closed their shutters and the crowds on the street
were very thin. But today was different. Veronique made
out what appeared to be an endless series of heads covering the
Square as far as the trees and greenery of the Champs-
Elysées and the banks of the Seine bordering the square on
the south. There didn't seem to be a single empty area or
breathing space in all that massed humanity.

Activity was beginning at the foot of the scaffold. The
lesser figures in the drama appeared on the wooden platform.
There went Augustin Robespierre, the younger brother of the
man who had dictated almost every heartbeat in Paris for
the last four months, and close by on the scaffold stood
Antoine-Louis St.-Just, said to be the handsomest man in

Paris, when he was not referred to as the Angel of Death. Most terrible, Veronique thought, was the predicament of the third among those who supported the dictator. This was the paralytic cripple, George Couthon, who had to be carried up to his death. Couthon the humanitarian, Couthon whose ideas about the care and understanding of the insane were far ahead of those in any country with which Veronique was familiar. Couthon had once helped Veronique in the Hôtel-Dieu when she had needed surgeons and food, and more space for the endless lines of new and starving patients. But in spite of all his brilliance, Couthon had implemented his master's terrible plans to the last degree. And today he would pay the reckoning.

Veronique looked away. She hated these men for their betrayal of friends, their perversion of ideals, but most of all, because they had used every weapon of pen and oratory to enforce the actions of their leader.

The furniture man from the Bastille area boomed out at Veronique as he turned, "Open those big brown eyes, girl. The bastards have shed our blood long enough. Now it's their turn to bleed."

Behind Veronique, almost in her ear, a woman yelled, "I'm minded to dip my petticoat in their blood." She carried a pike taller than she was, but the pike's business-end dragged behind her, scratching the cobbles underfoot and earning her the curses of her neighbors. In spite of her words, she was not really of that fanatical breed that had used the pikes to such deadly effect in months past.

"The world, our world, *is* changing, almost hour by hour," Veronique thought, and for the first time in months silently prayed, "Dear Lord, thank you for this." The country had suffered an almost mortal illness, but no matter what these voices in the crowd boasted, everything else about them announced that today, on the Ninth Thermidor of the revolutionary calendar, this reign of terror would end when the head of Maximilien Robespierre fell into Sanson's basket.

Robespierre was such a neat, precise little man! As Sanson's assistants supported him up the steps to the scaffold he looked like a lawyer's clerk who had found a mistake in one of his briefs and couldn't understand how it had occurred. Veronique remembered that tight-lipped, humorless mouth as she and her friends had seen it at cafés on numerous occasions. She thought of it as a tiger's smile. His green eyes were sometimes masked by spectacles, but that mouth, the mouth of a man who is never wrong, had always chilled her. Now something had happened to it. A thick, white strip of cloth bound the lower half of his face. Throughout Paris this morning there was gossip that he had shot himself, or been shot the night before at the time of his arrest.

He had not yet reached the platform when Veronique heard the rattle of boards and the snapping of the *lunette* through which the paralytic Couthon's head was fitted. It had been necessary to lay him sideways, due to his crippled condition. The blade moved downward with a rapidity that caught Veronique unaware. She closed her eyes just in time. From the mob in the square rose a curious humming noise, none of the fierce, savage lust for blood that had once characterized these exhibits.

There were still one or two bystanders anxious to be heard. "The cripple!" a hoarse voice cried out then, whether male or female, no one could be sure. "Couthon will dance now with a head as free as his feet."

Veronique backed away. No more, she thought. Please, God, let it be over soon. . . . Yet she was astonished, and pleased, when others in that silent throng apparently shared her revulsion and hissed their answer to the terrible joke. It was true. Paris was changing already. The blood lust had gone.

The blade did its work.

She did not see it, but the trembling of the wooden uprights as the blade fell could be heard the length of the square. The head was lifted from the basket, raised high above the waiting crowd.

A little pause, then a muttering sound gathered force, spreading like a stain through the waiting mob as something more interesting than the guillotine's first victims attracted them.

"There he is. The Incorruptible! Robespierre who thinks he is God!"

She opened her eyes. The little man was being dragged to the plank. His buckled shoes beat a tattoo upon the floorboards of the hastily erected scaffold. His face appeared curiously mottled, thanks to the bloodstained bandage that held his broken jaw in place. Veronique watched in fascinated horror, aware of a feeling so intense it had managed in sixty seconds to burn away months of vengeance-filled dreams. The feeling was pity.

To be the last of those condemned, to see before one's

last sight in this world! Even the blade itself, now dulled from so much use today, would not be so terrible. Yet how many thousands had this quaking little man sent to that death?

As the terrified lawyer was about to be laid facedown upon the wooden plank, the executioner Sanson reached out to him, jerked off the cloth which held the shattered jaw. The condemned man's shriek filled the entire square. The cry of unbearable human agony was so hideous that neither Veronique nor many present heard the blade fall a minute later. Veronique tried in vain to turn away, feeling as though her body had been pierced by that cry.

They were all correct, those who warned her not to come to this place today, but a pledge to herself, born of festering bitterness, had overcome her normal revulsion to such a scene, and so she had come. And further imperiled her immortal soul, which was not to be acknowledged in the France of 1794—indeed, there was much talk that souls, like belief in God, were about to be legislated out of existence.

. . . Did I lose my soul when I defied my church and took an oath of loyalty to the Revolution in order to work in the hospital? she wondered . . . or when Gilles and I became lovers. Or was it at this moment, when I felt the pull of vengeance so strongly that I let myself be a witness to this monstrous sight?

"The blood of Danton chokes him!" cried a voice in the mob, echoing what had been said of Robespierre in the National Convention the day before.

When the roar went up through the square, Veronique knew that Sanson was holding up like a trophy the head of Maximilien Robespierre, with its hanging, broken jaw. It would look like a waxen head, not real at all, except for the gouts of blood pouring out upon the cobblestones.

Veronique felt herself spun around, then thrust closer to the scaffold as the mob rushed forward. She shrank back, let herself be whirled about again as everyone passed her, plunging toward the foot of the guillotine. She was brought up hard and painfully against the base of the scaffold and had to push her way a foot at a time, making her way beyond the horror of that stench above her. . . .

She did not gain her equilibrium again until she had reached the northwest end of the square, thrust against what had once been the privately owned mansion built for a member of the Crillon family. Still confused, she looked up at the exquisite building designed by Gabriel, and at that instant had the most extraordinary sensation that its quiet, classic façade symbolized peace once more. Was it true that it had looked its last upon horrors like the one it had impassively witnessed today? She took another step, aware now that her sandals clung to the cobbles. A sticky, viscous substance remained on the soles. And then she saw the footprints she and the others had left as they crossed the great square. They had carried the blood of the dead over the cobblestones. The prints of the soiled sandals still marked her progress.

Sickened by this aftermath of the horror she had witnessed, she made her way up the tree-shaded lane beside the building toward the Rue Honoré which would take her back to her post at Turgot's Waxworks. In the effort to keep on her feet against the onrush of the mob, she had grasped so hard at the stone wall of the building beside her that she found her fingers numb, the flesh raw. She studied her fingertips, and one of the running mob, a girl who had just skimmed over the passage that bridged the moat bordering the square, stared at her in passing. The girl would never know that Veronique's abrupt laugh had been ironic. What were these drops of blood on her fingertips after the deluge that had stained the great square?

At this hour it was much easier walking on the Rue Honoré and she made excellent time until, near the east end of the Louvre she met the early evening traffic bound for the Palais-Royal arcades and the lively entertainment there. The females parading in the gardens of the Palais-Royal were superior in looks, more easily approached, and likely to take everyone's mind off the horrors of starvation, the guillotine, and the Austrian enemy at the borders of France. Yet already Veronique could see the difference even in that desperate gaiety as she crossed the enclosed gardens on her way out to the far side, past the entrance of the busy Café de Foy. Everywhere there seemed to be a feeling of lightness, of hope in the air. She stopped briefly in the garden as she was passing a window of the café.

The last time she remembered passing this exact spot she had been with Gilles Marsan. The realization struck her so powerfully she remained quite still, fancying his dark eyes watching her, their haunting, disillusioned quality warmed by his smile.

She closed her eyes, murmured his name. It was a conjuror's trick but for a minute or two her body knew exactly the sensation of exquisite happiness it had known during those days and nights of their love. When this slim, dark phantom was driven away by the sounds around her, the tinkle of glasses, the already drunken voices of the revelers, she was so shaken she found herself weeping.

"It is senseless," she reminded herself angrily and struck away these signs of weakness. "The dead are dead! They do not come back. In all of eternity I will never see him again."

She hurried out of the gardens hardly aware that two grenadiers of the National Guard tugged at her sleeve and wanted to know why she ran from an evening with two such likely fellows.

"You'll not find better citizens in the whole quarter, *chérie*," one of them boasted, and they laughed uproariously. Once such attentions might have made her nervous, embarrassed, or even angry, for her duties had often called upon her to cross Paris at all hours in her nun's habit. She hurried on. Of greater concern was an incident occurring on the street just after she had left the Palais-Royal.

A man called out joyously, "Sister!"

Old custom made her stop. Then she saw the man across the street, heavyset, still in his baker's apron. He was embracing a female who looked so very like him it was clear to see why he addressed her intimately. Veronique had been conceited in imagining that every "sister" must be Sister Veronique.

Children were dancing the Carmagnole in front of the waxworks, but without the obscene and bloodcurdling words they might have used a month ago. Veronique looked around, wondering if the frail Duchesse de St.-Aubans was still at the right bank of the boatlanding, weary but somehow cheerful, hoping to polish some soldier's boots or sew on buttons in order to survive. There was no sign of her now. Veronique hurried in through the side door of Citizeness Turgot's shop.

"You're late!" the old woman greeted her, predictably.

Veronique laid away her hat, took her pinafore off the peg in the wall and studied the fading stains down the front. Would there now be an end of blood-spilling? Gilles Marsan once said that man simply managed to exist through horrors until they went away at last. Life was an endless circle. Round and round. With no beginning and no end. But could there be no more?

She looked up. La Turgot was watching her. This artist in the production of busts and wax heads was not the kind of sympathetic soul in whom people confided; yet Veronique recognized something in that Medusa-face that made her say abruptly, "Do you believe in anything, citizeness?" She saw that she had managed to surprise her employer, not an easy trick.

"I believe in myself." As an afterthought, "And in France, of course."

"But when so many have died, do you think we may hope to know any happiness again? Do you believe in God?"

"What? And have my neck shaved by the national razor? You know the Incorruptible outlawed God. . . . You had best get on with the labels for the new exhibits. And that puts me in mind of immediate matters. Sanson's lads should be delivering the better part of the Incorruptible Robespierre at any minute, unless the Committee of Public Safety revokes my permit; so if you continue to be squeamish, you may leave when you've done with the labeling."

Enormously relieved at the prospect of dismissal before the shop's laboratory became a horror chamber of skull measurements, wax impressions and the odor of preservatives, Veronique got down the standish of ink, sharpened a pen and began to work upon the back of an old, rolling parchment with her careful printing. The light in the room was dim and the room itself surprisingly cold now considering the heat that blistered the flesh of those crowds who had poured through the narrow, serpentine streets earlier. As she worked, Veronique's thoughts went back to the events of the afternoon, those moments she wanted to fix in her memory. She tried to relive the magic seconds in the Palais-Royal gardens when Gilles had almost managed to come back to her from . . . the grave? But his was a communal grave. His bones rested in quicklime in the great Errancis charnel pit, along with those of his friends— Danton, Camille and Lucille, and the others.

She spoke her thoughts aloud to this woman whose very lack of sentiment made her easier to talk with.

"Citizeness, isn't it possible if we love anyone deeply enough—let us say a lover, a friend, even a parent—that the power of our love could bring us together in heaven?"

La Turgot grinned. "My loves do not go to heaven." She had moved over to the brazier whose fiery coals kept blowing scarlet and blue and which burned on even the hottest days. She had a bundle of finely honed sticks and the faceless bust she often used for reproducinng measurements. Apparently taking pity on Veronique, she said gruffly, "I do not believe in a heaven or hell beyond this life. It is quite enough, what we suffer here below."

"But think of our memories, the wonderful thoughts and feelings . . . they must return in different forms. Somehow."

"They return in your child. Your precious Gilles Marsan's child. There you will find the thoughts and feelings that you adored so much in that lover of yours. . . . But, child, I have handled the human brain. When the pulsebeat of life is gone, believe me, that fistful of bleeding guts we call a brain is dead."

Veronique paused in the act of dipping the pen into the standish of thickened ink. She raised her head and said, "I felt Gilles Marsan near me only minutes ago." She knew she had caught the fierce old harridan's attention and went on more firmly, "We are not done with each other, Gilles and I. Someday, in some future time perhaps, we will take up those unlived days together. I know it!"

The old woman scratched her nose. "My dear, you would meet, and pass, and never recognize each other, in those centuries ahead. That's the pity of it. Too many lifetimes would have separated you. Don't you see that?"

Veronique winced and straightened her body, aware of the deep, aching pain of her loss. She wanted to hold onto everything connected with past happiness. If she ever let herself become numb to the past, she would lose her last awareness of his presence near her.

But as Madame Turgot had reminded her, there was his child who would be born one day. For his child's sake she must fight to conquer her depression.

"Madame, I feel him near me many times, in all those places in Paris that we knew together. When I walk across the Pont Neuf . . . toward the Luxembourg Gardens. Or here on the Right Bank in the Café Parnasse. When I pass the café I sometimes think I hear Danton's booming laugh and see Gilles and Camille Desmoulins arguing over that wretched newspaper of Camille's while his wife Lucille and Louise Danton and I wait for our men to order dinner. . . . And of them all, I alone am alive today. Small wonder I live in my dreams."

She finished the labels, set the pen back and took off the pinafore again, but she couldn't help saying, "I would always know him. At any time. In any disguise. In faraway China, or in the heart of Africa, I would know."

"Where are you going tonight? Africa? Or China?"

"The Luxembourg Gardens. I want to think. And I think best when I walk."

"It's getting dark, child. Take care not to meet any of those ghosts you are always talking about."

There was an extraordinary difference in the atmosphere when Veronique walked out onto the street again. The blood-red sunset had burned itself out behind the woods of the Champs-Elysées and twilight lent a suggestion of cooling relief to the air, which perhaps helped explain the change in the people of all ages and classes who now thronged the streets. Some, like the children she had seen earlier, danced the Carmagnole, some sang the childishly simple "*Ça Ira!*" and all of the singing and shouting seemed so good-natured. An enormous load had been lifted from them and they could go to sleep tonight without wondering if, when they slept next, they would do so in two pieces. Neighbor had betrayed neighbor, child had betrayed mother, but now the terrible Incorruptible was dead and the Law of Suspects would be repealed.

Gilles and I would have been happy tonight, she thought. We would have strolled to the Café Parnasse, a step from the Seine, and joined Georges and Louise, Lucille and Camille, and then—she sighed with a wry laugh as the dream surfaced into truth—and then the men would have discussed newer, more humane laws to take the place of the old, and Danton's father-in-law Charpentier, who owned the café, would run to fetch more wine for the men while she and Lucille Desmoulins exchanged tolerant glances, with no hope that the men would recall them until hours had passed.

At the Pont au Change, which crossed the Seine from the Right Bank toward the dreaded towers of the Conciergerie, Veronique was slowed by a mob pouring over the bridge in her direction, singing that most blood-stirring of all marches, brought up to Paris by the soldiers of Marseilles, and called until recently, "The Song of the Army of the Rhine."

Suddenly terrified, besieged by old memories of the horror following in the wake of that incomparable march, Veronique shrank back against the bridgehead. She would have liked to make herself invisible.

It took a minute to realize that this mob did not mount bleeding heads upon their pikes. They waved torches, mob caps, rags and tricolor sashes, anything to show their happiness that a new day was ahead for France, a day in which there might still be a bread shortage, a meat shortage, a shortage of everything—except wine and life.

This much they assumed from the death of that virtuous little incorruptible, Maximilien Robespierre, the man who believed virtue was born on the blade of the guillotine. Veronique found the crowd's joy contagious. She began to believe in it as she crossed the bridge after this deluge had pressed forward, pouring onto the quais of the Right Bank. She did not look to her right as she passed the big iron gate enclosing the courtyard of the Palais de Justice and the Conciergerie.

Very shortly on her left the great square towers of Notre-Dame cast their shadow over her and over the village of hovels clustered at its base. She noticed that the stars were out. They seemed to have ringed the medieval giant in silver, and she genuflected furtively before moving on to the Petit-Pont, the bridge that would carry her to the Left Bank. Only yesterday the Committee of Public Safety and Robespierre's Jacobins had been debating whether to tear down the cathedral of Norte-Dame stone by stone, or to use it for storing ammunition.

"You are safe now, dear Mother of Paris," she whispered, and then remembered the girl she had been less than two years ago: Sister Veronique, vowed to chasity and obedience. Perhaps the events of 1794 which touched her had been God's judgment for the sin that gave her happiness? Presumptuous thought . . .

All the same, tomorrow she would go out to Meudon and walk under the trees there. It was easier in the Meudon woods to pretend she was once more the girl Veronique de Vaudraye, in those cool, green lanes so like the apple orchard around the Normandy château where she had been born.

In her mind's eye she saw flashes of those days in the spring of 1789 when the carefully planned and sanctified career of a nobleman's daughter was colored by a glory that would illuminate all the rest of her life. . . .

Book One

April, 1789

Distant Thunder

IN 1789 Paris was a city of 500,000 but still only twenty percent of France's twenty-eight million people lived in cities. Most Frenchmen were still rural peasants. Their life, centered around the family and the village, was traditionally conservative and generally hostile to change. They rarely traveled far from home and while they felt perhaps a personal loyalty to Louis XVI they took little interest in matters beyond the village. But by spring of 1789 even they had heard the sounds of change, usually from students and political activists that traveled about the countryside. They were told about the dreadful conditions that existed everywhere, and were offered a most extraordinary idea—that they were entitled to a better life than they had known.

And so in the spring of that year young men who were winding their way to Versailles for the meeting of the States-General carried with them the heady and subversive excitement of such new ideas. They had seen their ideals of liberty and equality come to life in the recently, and successfully, concluded American Revolution. Their own Lafayette had been a hero of that revolution. Now, they felt, the time for their revolution had also come, and no royal will could deny them. The modern age of Europe was about to begin. . . .

1

ON the morning of April 20th in the cold, bright spring of 1789, seventeen-year-old Veronique de Vaudraye was awakened by a gunshot. Waiting for further sounds, she lay there stiffly, muffled from the world of Normandy by the velvet winter curtains of her four-poster bed. She guessed that the shot had been fired by a poacher on the Vaudraye grounds, and dreaded the possibility that it may have been heard by her father's gamekeeper.

The Vicomte de Vaudraye was a man of liberal instincts, but he was adamant against theft of his property by poachers, no matter how desperate the provocation. She listened anxiously for the distinctive crack of the flintlock musket used by the gamekeeper, a Fleming named de Gleeb. He would not hesitate to kill an intruder caught with the evidence in his game sack.

After a tense minute she relaxed. The poacher must have gotten away with his catch, very probably a hare which would give at least one village family a full meal.

In northern France in 1788 the months of May, June and July had been excessively hot and the grain shriveled. On July 13th, just before the harvest, a severe hailstorm added to the extraordinary losses of most of the wheat farmers. From that bad harvest of 1788 were to come the bread riots of the next year. But to add to their miseries the people of the north provinces had suffered a winter that year that was the worst in a century, with the frozen rivers unnavigable, and roads a quagmire. But, though Veornique had spent many wintry days and nights helping her father attend the poor and sick of the countryside as any member of the privileged orders was expected to do, she found it hard to dismiss human despair simply by doling out grain and salt meat, with laudanum for hunger pains.

Satisfied that no one else had been awakened by the poacher's shot, Veronique sat up and parted the bed curtains. Even with the mullioned panes of the window tightly sealed, she fancied she caught the scent of blossoms in the apple orchard that spread eastward from the pink stone Vaudraye château. Her shoulders ached and she stretched her arms, which were still cramped. She had spent most of the previous day working at the pesthouse and asylum in the market town of Vaudraye, where scrubbing stone floors and changing shredded, ancient linen occupied most of her time.

The rasp of a door latch across the room distracted her from her concern over the poacher's safety. She sat with thin, faintly bronzed arms outstretched in mid-motion, staring at the door. A second or two later, realizing the identity of the intruder, she let her arms fall and her fingers bend into fists. She buried them in the bed coverlet. So long as she lived in her parents' house, there was little she could do to rid herself of this unwanted company. Only her recently appointed companion, Lise de Gleeb, the gamekeeper's wife, would raise the door latch in that odiously furtive manner.

Madame de Gleeb had insinuated herself into the Vaudraye household through her husband's usefulness to the Vicomte. It was her mission to report all of Veronique's less circumspect activities to the Vicomtesse, whose family had endowed the Convent of Ste. Veronique of the Holy Cloth and expected Veronique to take her vows in that order.

Veronique's own inclinations had early turned her toward the nursing sisterhood. With a semi-invalid mother and a volatile if well-meaning father, she began in childhood to exert authority where it was needed and to bring organization out of chaos. Considering the lowly state of the nursing profession outside the Church, she was fortunate in choosing— or having chosen for her—the only way left for her to exercise a genuine gift for improving conditions among the sick, as well as the aged and the orphans. Nevertheless, she intensely disliked having all her acts, even her thoughts, reported by Madame de Gleeb, this snooping wife of a man she detested for his cruelty.

She called out, "I am awake, Lise. You need not sneak about so. Tell Mama you found me still in my bedgown but about to say my morning prayers."

Carefully piloting her old-fashioned, elongated panniers into the room, the lank and lean Lise de Gleeb curtsied while reminding Veronique, "How delightfully you put it, to be sure, mademoiselle. Especially when one reflects that a few springs from now, you will be wearing hair shirts instead of silken bedgowns—" She giggled. "Wearing your little habit of Ste. Veronique, I should say. How proud you will be. It is not even necessary to be beautiful, you know, if one wears the coif of Ste. Veronique."

Aside from the observation that thin, brown-eyed Veronique was less than a great beauty, the woman's comment abused the dream Veronique lived with. Nonetheless she closed her eyes briefly and forced a smile, reminding herself that in the service of holy Ste. Veronique, who had cooled the sweating brow of the Lord on the road to Calvary, bad tempers held no place.

Lise bustled over to the red mahogany armoire, barely squeezing her heavily wired skirts between the two doors of the wardrobe.

"Shall we consider what gowns we may be requiring today, mademoiselle? And then I will send for your hot chocolate. That maid of yours is late as usual."

"Let me at least bathe my face and hands," Veronique protested. This concern for cleanliness always seemed to take Madame de Gleeb by surprise, so Veronique put her bare feet over the side of the bed, not troubling to use the two carpeted wooden steps, and took up the pewter carafe on the mahogany commode nearby. She had just poured water into the shallow ewer when the air was cut by a cry of pain outside her window. Without moving her head, Veronique glanced in Lise's direction, wondering if the woman had heard the sound.

Lise was holding up various gowns and undergarments, shaking out the panniers, and the frilled and ruffled underdresses. She did not seem to be interested in noises elsewhere. The ripple of taffeta covered many sounds. But the cry of pain told Veronique that the poacher had not escaped after all. He must have been caught in one of the snares artfully planted at the near end of the orchard by the Vaudraye gamekeeper, Lise's husband. Nor was this the first time de Gleeb's infernal machines had crippled some desperate villager or local peasant.

Veronique splashed water as noisily as possible.

"Lise, please bring me my chocolate."

To perform the errand herself was beneath the woman's household status, but, except for a stiffening of the spine, Madame de Gleeb made no protest. She curtsied at the door and went out.

Veronique took a deep breath and set the ewer back so quickly the water spilled out over the floor. The rugs, though well worn, were of excellent quality, imported long ago from the East, but she was in too great a hurry to use them as she ran across the chill floorboards to the window and pushed it open. Its little panes caught the sunrise and almost blinded her.

The scent of apple blossoms rose around her on the dawn breeze, and with it the groans of a man in agony. By the pale golden light sifting through the orchard she saw him, a gaunt peasant with a shock of white hair, writhing on the muddy ground in the aisle between two rows of apple trees. The teeth of the trap chewed ever more deeply into his bony ankle, and she knew the pain was excruciating.

Holding the ribbons that closed the neck of her bedgown, Veronique leaned out the window and studied the other windows in the east wing of the Vaudraye château. The morning breeze lashed dark strands of her hair across her thin, high-boned cheeks; she brushed them away impatiently. It appeared that neither the poacher's shot nor his agonized scream when he stepped into the trap had aroused any of the household, unless Lise had heard him from this room.

"That will give me a few minutes to free him," she thought, hoping against hope that one of the sympathetic servants would meanwhile go to his rescue.

She turned from the window, hurried to the armoire and snatched off its peg the old, deep-pink sprigged gown she wore when working in the local Hôtel-Dieu, the hospital of the town of Vaudraye. She stepped out of her voluminous bedgown, shivering a moment in the cold before she laced the bosom of her dress. The gown scratched her bare flesh beneath, but she hadn't time to concern herself with that.

It took a minute to find her wooden sabots, which would serve her best on the wet ground of the orchard. Still in bare feet, she carried the sabots out of her room, careful not to rouse the servants who would be up and about at any minute, kindling the various hearthfires for the day ahead.

Her bedchamber opened on the gallery above a delicate, curving main staircase, but the far end of that gallery would take her to the servants' stairs, which undoubtedly would also mean an encounter with Lise de Gleeb and the tray of chocolate. She hesitated, then remembered Old Mathieu, a former apothecary's apprentice, who slept on a straw pallet in front of the ancient kitchen hearth. It would not be the first time she called upon him to help her—once before he had sprung one of de Gleeb's traps with an iron bar. She made her way along the gallery to the main staircase and ran lightly down just as she heard the rustle of Lise de Gleeb's skirts at the opposite end of the gallery. With no time to lose, Veronique raced through the spacious salons on the ground floor until she reached the service quarters and ultimately the big country kitchen.

The room was empty. Mathieu had left and his pallet was carelessly stacked against the crockery wall. She had just reached the stillroom behind the kitchen pantries when a door slammed somewhere within the house. She stopped. Almost any of the kitchen servants would help her, but she knew the poacher was doomed if the gamekeeper or her father caught him. The previous November a young peasant had been shot by de Gleeb in similar circumstances, and all of Veronique's frantic efforts to treat the stomach wound, aided by Old Mathieu, who knew something of medicine and surgery, had not been enough to save the boy's life.

As a result of the killing there was a deal of muttering in the province and protests came from a political club of so-called radicals in the city of Rouen; but the Vaudrayes were considered to have acted within their ancient seigneurial rights, and local loyalties had been restored somewhat by the Vaudrayes' charitable work during the frightful winter that followed.

There were no more sounds. Veronique stepped out into the kitchen yard, among the soggy, stunted little plantings of herbs, and slipped her chilled feet into the sabots which in such soil were far more practical than a genteel young lady's slippers. She ran now along the eastern face of the château, between the apple trees. The morning wind showered her with blossoms, which she did not trouble to shake off.

Ahead she could see the huddled back of Old Mathieu as he knelt on the soggy ground. The body he knelt over was hidden by a thicket of wet grass and the trunk of a tree. In spite of Mathieu's age, he had excellent hearing and was aware of her approach. He looked back at Veronique over his hunched shoulder, his grizzled countenance without expression.

Veronique did not call to him, afraid as she was of being heard in the château. As she reached the thicket she found the poacher's body at her feet. It lay twisted, one leg heavily weighted by the closed trap, as though it had frozen in that agonized pose. The body was very still.

A shadow blotted out the rising light, and she looked up across the body to see the long face of Arnauld de Gleeb, with its pale, watery eyes and loose mouth, which was parted in his usual unconscious grin. He carried his well-used flint-lock musket under one arm. He was chatty today.

"Good day, mademoiselle. You may rest easy. As you see, it was not necessary to shoot the rogue."

Veronique found her limbs shaking and went down on her knees beside the body. It appeared to be quite true. The poacher had died of pain or shock, and the gamekeeper could piously claim innocence.

In a low voice she murmured to the old man kneeling beside her, "Did you reach him before he died?"

Mathieu shook his head. "The pain did it, mademoiselle. That and a bad heart. He is called Guillaume. He brought his wife home from the pesthouse in Vaudraye yesterday. She had a flux of the lungs. There was no food. A broth boiled from this . . . might have helped." His gnarled fore-finger indicated the sack beside the body. She caught a glimpse of the dead hare, which had half fallen out of the sack.

It looked as bony as the unfortunate poacher, she thought. Veronique was aware of bitter thoughts, un-Christian and certainly unworthy of the life that had been chosen for her. She wanted to seize de Gleeb's musket and fire pointblank at that flabby face with its eternal grin. At least this violent feeling saved her from the disaster of tears she felt welling up, the sight of which would only amuse the watching game-keeper.

She disappointed the fellow by ignoring him and saying to Mathieu, "Have Guillaume taken to his lodgings in town but give me a few minutes start. Someone must see to his wife."

Sibilant whispers, along with the shuffle of sabots and boots through the orchard, told her that the Vaudraye servants were gathering, and for a moment she felt alarm about the position of her father in this tragedy. But one-thing-at-a-time had been her successful motto since she first reorganized the asylum and the moribund Hôtel-Dieu in the province.

Arnauld de Gleeb cleared his throat with a grating sound that made her pulses jump, though she forced herself to follow Old Mathieu's admirable calm.

"If mademoiselle will be so kind as to report to his excellency the Vicomte what she has seen and heard—"

She paid no attention to de Gleeb's suggestion and gave her orders crisply: "You others—Jehan, and you, Henri—please wrap the body in something clean and follow Mathieu's orders. Mathieu, are Guillaume's lodgings in town opposite the church? . . ."

De Gleeb thrust the muzzle of his musket between the two men to get near Veronique. "Mademoiselle, let a couple of my lads take charge of the carcass. It will save you all this work, which need not concern you."

"It concerns all Christians," she said as she stood up. The men set about their painful task, but she was aware of something in their manners, in their almost total lack of emotion, and she was struck by it. An angry populace was one thing, but these faces were sullen, as if all emotions had turned inward, and for a moment it was difficult to tell one seamed face from the other, though she had known them all her life. They did not even exchange glances, which had become their way of reacting to the acts of the privileged orders when they could not speak out. She suspected that they did not find it necessary to exchange looks. Each knew quite well what the other was thinking.

We are in dangerous waters, she thought, though what turn the tide could take with these peasants who did not even speak the patois of the next province she couldn't guess. . . . But she sometimes thought if they should find leaders who could speak a language the whole of France would understand, they might be led to any disaster.

In spite of her faith, by nature she was, like her father, more of a realist than an optimist and she soon abandoned this reflective moment in her overriding concern for practical matters. Still with no acknowledgement of the gamekeeper, who rattled the musket under his arm and began to issue orders, Veronique quickly went back to the château's small door opening into the back of the ground-floor reception hall.

Mme. de Gleeb's long face greeted her over the balustrade above the great staircase, her lugubrious expression in contrast to the everlasting grin of her husband.

"Ah, mademoiselle, you are back. But your condition! Those dreadful wooden clogs . . . and no underthings! I shudder at your dear mama's feelings when she learns—"

"Then she must not learn."

Trying not to feel guilty, Veronique removed her muddy sabots which had clattered over the beautiful parquet floors, and carried them up to her bedchamber. Lise de Gleeb rustled after her, talking all the while. Veronique went about her business; there was much to be done. She shrugged out of the deep-pink gown which was encrusted with mud about the hem and had long muddy stains where she had knelt. She changed quickly to a shift, one unstiffened petticoat, and the least decorative of the elaborate gowns selected by her mother's seamstress, who had once been apprenticed to Rose Bertin, who designed for the Queen of France.

It was not a recommendation to impress Veronique, who had come to regard the queen as a silly useless female with too much pride. This opinion had so shocked her mother that the Vicomtesse suffered one of her migraines.

In spite of a normal healthy vanity, Veronique had nearly abandoned looking into the mirror the previous year when she knew that in the autumn of 1789 she would enter the Convent of Ste. Veronique. It especially did not matter now whether or not her hair was flyaway, or that there might be mud on her cheek. Besides, she was in a hurry, as usual.

She paid no attention to Mme. de Gleeb's peckish "what are you about? . . . where are you going? . . . not alone . . . you know how the dear Vicomtesse disapproves . . ."

Veronique had already left her bedchamber, trailed by Lise de Gleeb, when she heard her name called out in her father's implacable tones:

"Vero, you are not to leave this house! Do you hear me?"

Her father was an honest man and she disliked deceiving him or flouting his authority, so she equivocated, moving rapidly beyond his sight toward the south portico.

"What, Papa? . . . I will explain presently—"

But the short, stout Vicomte de Vaudraye knew his daughter well. His sturdy legs made fast work of the staircase and he reached the graceful twin doors opening out of a small salon onto the portico before she could get beyond hearing him. He was still in breeches, hose and bedslippers. His shirt was crisp and clean but he and his valet had not yet arranged the ruffles at his throat and his bagwig, that remnant of a fashion popular in his youth, had been too hastily set upon his head. He caught her shoulder.

"Daughter, I forbid you to go into the village today."

Despite his lack of height, he was a strong, fleshy man and his grasp was firm, but she removed his fingers by what appeared to be an unconscious shrug.

"Papa, please give me your permission. I am going to see Guillaume's widow. I am sure you will do the same when you are less—disordered."

"I am not disordered. I saw what occurred. I regret the poor devil's death as much as you do, and I intend to make some arrangement to provide for his widow. But he shot the animal in my enclosures. This is not free land. These are Vaudraye properties and my rights must be maintained."

"Yes, but, Papa—"

"It is all this agitation, these radicals screaming for the rights of the people. My people have the rights I gave them. And I am a fair man."

"There was no food in the house when Guillaume's wife was brought home yesterday."

His face began to redden but he controlled himself. He had been through this sort of thing before with his headstrong daughter, and he knew Veronique always hoped that his basic good intentions would win him over to her viewpoint.

"I am sorry to hear that. It shall be attended to." Like a mariner facing a contrary wind he tried tacking in a new direction. "But your conduct, Veronique, has upset your mother. At this very minute she is suffering tortures from another migraine."

Ashamed that she had once again been responsible for discomfiting her delicate mother, Veronique glanced up at the long windows of the Vicomtesse's suite, then across the grassy slope at her pony being hitched to the little cart she often used for her town visits.

"Papa, can't you convince mother that I am doing what Ste. Veronique would wish?"

"Ste. Veronique! It is because of your mother's precious Ste. Veronique that I am to have no heirs and Vaudraye will go to your Cousin Alexandre, almost a stranger."

"You know perfectly well Sylvie and Alex are on your side, Papa. I don't grudge them my inheritance. Why should you?" She saw he was going off on a tangent; so she added quickly, "I must go now, please, Papa. The stable boy knows our custom. He will have stored a little food and some wine in the cart. But if you can bring more"—she saw that he might thaw—"then there may be less trouble over de Gleeb and his traps."

She knew she had won when he no longer tried to stop her except with his disgruntled complaints. "I don't believe it. The *canaille* have no gratitude. After all we've done for them, they still insist on sending their bourgeois lawyer friends off to Versailles to pass laws against their betters. Call themselves a Third Estate. These damnable lawyers are responsible. Stirring up the peasantry who've always been our friends, whom we've always been friendly to."

"It did not start today, Papa."

But there was no purpose in pursuing the argument. Her father owed allegiance to the privileged estates, the nobility and the upper clergy. To him there was no understanding what the peasants, and worst of all, newly risen bourgeois classes, would want that the Vicomte de Vaudraye would not give them . . . if he felt they deserved it. After all, privilege had its responsibilities, he firmly believed.

Veronique kissed him on one flushed cheek and started running toward the country road into town. He called after her, "I will join you presently. I want to be certain this morning's business is recorded properly with the King's Lieutenant. And, Vero . . . take care." She waved back over her shoulder. He shouted then, "And watch for those seditionists in the village, the ones from the radical Jacobins and Cordeliers Clubs in Paris. They are due to arrive any day, babbling about a constitution and the rights of the Third Estate. Rabble rousers, I'd say—"

She waved again. She loved even his predictability.

Once Veronique had left, the Vicomte immediately called for a servant to say that he wanted to speak with his gamekeeper. "Tell him I wish to see him without delay."

A few moments later de Gleeb appeared in the Vicomte's drawing room with a look of easy confidence, which was soon dropped when he saw his master's mood.

"What in God's name are you doing? Last autumn you shot a poacher and caused all sorts of problems, and now this morning one of your traps kills a man from the village, someone I have known for years—"

"But, sir, I am only protecting the game on your land from poachers. This is why I am in your employ."

"We both know why you are still here at Vaudraye, de Gleeb. And while you remain I wish no more incidents such as these to occur. It is *not* necessary to deploy those iron traps so they seize my villagers as well. I do not like the notion of trapping for men, as much as you apparently do, even though they be poachers."

"I understand, sir." Then, as if to recover from the chiding, he added, "But in these troubled times, sir, it would seem politic to protect what is yours by any means against those who work to take it away."

"All right, de Gleeb, please do not make the mistake of patronizing me. Rather be certain you know what my feelings are about these matters because they are to be yours as well. Now to repair some of your damage I want you to go to the ice house and get a side of venison to take to the widow of the man who died this morning. And be quick about it. I'll expect you to be ready to leave with me within a quarter hour."

Veronique hurried to the cart, climbed onto the narrow seat, and snapped the reins gently across the pony's mane to follow the path taken by Mathieu in the tumbril containing the body of the dead poacher. As she was moving off, she was aware of the disturbing silence of the coachman, one of the garden boys and a footman from the château. Only moments before Veronique reached them they had been speaking with great animation. Now they were overly respectful, too polite, quite unlike the easy cameraderie she had always known among the Vaudraye people.

The cart rattled along muddy runnels, the pony trotting smartly. He knew the impatient hand on the lines. Veronique was relieved to note the attitude of the peasants in the Vaudraye fields. The men, already long at work that morning, bowed as she passed, and one or two answered her brisk, passing wave. They, at least, did not seem to be caught up in the somehow sinister, unnaturally formal hospitality she now felt among many of those servants and garden workers closer to the household. It was ironic that those who knew her father well should be most hostile to him, but then, most of them were educated, and there was no doubt education had begun to play havoc with old loyalties.

Veronique had nearly reached the Vaudraye churchyard at the river end of the village when she overtook the tumbril driven by Old Mathieu and bearing Guillaume's body. The covered body itself was not visible to anyone in passing, since the tumbril was deep and the sides high. All the same, Vero-

nique felt that the grim contents were known to some of the
peasants and villagers Mathieu passed. She was certain of
Mathieu's loyalty; yet the word had been spread. She heard
a shout from among several fishermen on the banks of the
River Vaudraye as she crossed the arching stone bridge.

"A hare, they say. A single, scrawny hare! And for that,
Guillaume must die. . . ."

"Quiet . . . There she is—one of them."

Veronique greeted the fishermen pleasantly as always and
without slowing the rapid pace of the little pony, but she
found herself unnerved. The town fanned out in a northerly
direction, lacking the precise southern boundary of the river.
The ancient gray stone church amid poplars and gravestones
was set back from the main High Road which wound away
toward the coast and the English Channel. Also on the
grounds was the one-time refectory which the local curé now
used as a pesthouse and hospital, a kind of miniature Hôtel-
Dieu. Only yesterday Guillaume's wife had been brought
across the High Road to her husband's lodgings. To a room
without food, and very likely without warmth.

Veronique drew up the pony cart across the High Road
from the church, immediately in front of the half-timbered,
two-storied house amid a half dozen others, all equally old
and in disrepair and all facing to the south. Mathieu and a
local man had gotten out the wrapped body of Guillaume and
were carrying it to the hospital's dead chamber across the
road.

The High Road itself, running beside these several houses,
seemed to be unusually busy, with knots of local townsfolk
gathered in front of each house. That too was unusual and yet
made her think of the most recent occasion when she'd
noticed such gatherings, at a time when the province learned
that the Kingdom of France was bankrupt. And this during a
period when the taxes to the Crown, the tithes to the church,
and seigneurial payments to landowners like the Vicomte de
Vaudraye had never been higher.

"One hope. One thing may save us." She had heard it
everywhere that bitter winter. They expected a miracle
merely from the calling together in Versaille of the three
estates—the Clergy, the Nobles, and the bourgeois Third
Estate whose deputies would be expected to represent all
classes below the privileged two. Veronique shared the general hope that this convocation of the States-General would
at least solve the awful problem of the nation's bankruptcy.

"Wait until May," she heard a man mutter now. "Our deputies will pass laws, and this won't happen again."

But Veronique had heard the other side discussed among her father's friends. Because the Nobles and Clergy could outvote the Third Estate, there would be no laws passed to save the nation's monetary system that would in any way touch the privileged orders.

"One more month," someone else said. "Wait until the States-General meet."

There were more comments in a similar vein, though some effort was made to silence them as the nearest man helped Veronique down from her seat. They shuffled back, leaving her a narrow path to the half-timbered old door. For about five seconds, as she raised the latch on the door, she wished profoundly that she could turn back. Or better yet, be forcibly turned back so that it would not be possible to enter and give Simone Guillaume the news of her husband's death. Only yesterday, in a warm glow of self-satisfaction that disgusted her now, Veronique had seen the Guillaume woman borne home by her relieved husband after a miraculous survival from the lung illness, and had never thought to consider what the sick woman would eat, her husband having been out of work since the failure of the fall apple crop.

The narrow passage that Veronique entered smelled of humanity and animals, both unwashed. There must be something done about cleaning the room, she thought, well aware of the inadequacy of such a solution to the problem of starvation. But the evidence of animals, a lamb, several geese, all long since dead and eaten, had to be washed away at once. Veronique knew from long experience that the presence of such offal would be fatal to the recovery of Madame Guillaume. At all events, its removal would give Veronique something to do after the painful news was relayed to the sick woman.

Veronique groped her way into a room on her right whose weathered shutters were closed and where the heavy paper that once served as a glass pane had long ago dissolved in soggy strips. Tallow candlelight flickered in one corner of the room and turned the faces of those present into sinister masks, all highlights and darkness. The only person she recognized was a village woman, Madame Faure. The two men she did not think were villagers. The other stranger was an exquisite, fragile-looking blonde, perfectly gowned in sky-blue sprigged muslin which matched her eyes.

It was now evident, from the enmity in the room, that the news of Guillaume's death had already been relayed to his widow.

Quite a different pair of eyes from those of the beautiful blonde now glowered at Veronique from the young man perched on the side of the sick woman's bed. He had Madame Guillaume's hand in his, and though his grasp was gentle, even caressing, to the sick woman, his dark eyes blazed at Veronique.

"We do not see your noble father, mademoiselle. But then, that is the custom of the privileged orders, as we all know. To vanish before they see the consequences of their cruelty."

She tried to ignore it. "How is Madame Guillaume? I came as quickly as I could."

Madame Faure a little uneasily murmured agreement. "The monsieur as only just arrived on a visit from Paris. He doesn't understand about you, it's not you we blame, mademoiselle. We know your goodness."

To which the young man said angrily, "These people don't want charity, they want land. If Guillaume could have bought and owned the ground he planted and tended for a lifetime, he would not be dead today."

However much Veronique might regret her father's part in the morning's disaster, she found herself resenting the stranger's attack. She recognized at once that no local peasant his age—he was under thirty—would be wearing neat buckskin breeches and top boots, plus a tailored jacket that accentuated a tall, muscular slenderness. On closer observation she noted that these garments were well-worn and frayed at the cuffs but they were from Paris. She did not doubt that he was one of the Jacobin troublemakers her father had mentioned who were spreading their sedition through the province, demanding that the deputies to Versailles work on a constitution—highly impractical for an absolute monarchy like France, but the fools dreamed on, thanks to just such hotheads. . . .

For the benefit of the others she answered. "The Vicomte is also bringing food and fuel and clothing for Madame Guillaume and the villagers."

The young man said stiffly, "Everything will be repaid, mademoiselle, I assure you. We are not beggars. I can pay at once for"—his voice failed just a little—"for a great part of it."

Veronique dismissed his offer as rhetoric for the benefit of his audience and crossed the room, wishing the young man would leave. A troublemaker, no matter what his pretense of interest in the unfortunate Guillaume's wife. She stopped beside the tumbled, stale-smelling bed.

"Madame, I beg you to believe how much we deplore what has happened."

The woman in the bed turned her head with an effort. She looked up at the dark-eyed, angry man. "Gilles, don't be rude to mam'selle." She took a deep painful breath. "She has been good to us always. Believe her, *mon petit*."

The lovely blond visitor said, "Your aunt is right, Gilles. The crimes of mademoiselle's ancestors are not her sins."

Veronique ignored her double-edged goodwill. She stared at the young man. "You are related to madame?"

"I am Gilles Marsan, a sketch artist with the Jacobins' Society of Paris. My friends and I came to my aunt's village to explain the workings of the new States-General. I had no idea things were so desperate with my aunt and uncle."

The sick woman explained weakly, "The public letter-writer. Very expensive. Three sous."

Veronique suspected that part of Gilles Marsan's anger was directed against himself for not having suspected the condition of his aunt and uncle. He went on bitterly, "It is just this sort of injustice that will turn the people to support the States-General with new laws."

To Veronique's father nothing was more dangerous than this political club of wild-eyed young men who were so strident in their demands about constitutions and limiting the royal power. It was possible her father now might believe that the Guillaumes were somehow criminals because they were related to this radical.

"Don't imagine that my aunt needs to live on your charity," Marsan assured her immediately. "My uncle's death was murder. It has happened before on your grounds, mademoiselle, but I doubt if the noble Vicomte Vaudraye will condemn his own gamekeeper to be broken on the wheel for murder, as would have happened to one of us. All the same, your gifts will be paid for." With his free hand he reached into various pockets, collected four pieces of silver and some sous, and tried to press the silver on her.

It was enough to make her smile at his pride, but her good sense prevailed. She said calmly, "You may pay my father. You think I am not needed here, but you are wrong. No one has changed Madame Guillaume's bed, and the hospital across the road will give you some wholesome broth at once if one of you will fetch it. They will have had three or four chickens on the boil for several hours by now. You, Monsieur Marsan, lift your aunt while I turn the sheets. Madame Faure, will you go across to the hospital and get a pan of broth and some tender white meat for her? Mademoiselle"—to Marsan's blond friend, who seemed slightly taken aback at being asked to share a servant's work—"we will clean this place meanwhile."

The blond glanced at Marsan, who was busy with his aunt. Then she smiled pleasantly at Veronique. "I am Yolande Berthelot. And that is my brother, Raymond. He and Gilles work together in the Club."

Veronique studied the other stranger briefly, a tall, cadaverous young man with a forbidding look and prematurely graying hair—Raymond Berthelot, another radical Jacobin.

"And you, Monsieur Berthelot, will you bring in the supplies from my cart? We can deliver what is left to others in need when we are finished here."

"I find it difficult to take orders. Especially from aristocrats." In his gaunt face was a fanatic's dedication, its cold, implacable quality a contrast to the fire she had seen—and felt—in Gilles Marsan. Yolande Berthelot, his sister, said hurriedly, "Raymond, you are not polite." The man shrugged and went to carry out Veronique's request.

The dingy little room was soon engulfed in activity. Having satisfied his honor by placing some silver on the one rickety old table in the room, Gilles Marsan lifted his aunt, trying to keep her thin bare feet covered by her inadequate nightrobe. With the help of Madame Faure he shrugged out of his coat, which was then wrapped around his aunt's limbs. Presently, when Veronique had remade the bed and Mme. Guillaume was returned to it, Veronique looked at Marsan, aware that he had been studying her, He still looked like a formidable opponent, but at least he was curious about her.

"Are you actually the daughter of the Vicomte de Vaudraye? Tell me, why does he keep that de Gleeb in his employ?"

"Because he . . . he is the gamekeeper. And you?"

"I am everything that you Vaudrayes hate and fear, mademoiselle—a free man. I don't belong to the Vaudraye land, as my unfortunate uncle did."

"A free man . . . then you are indeed unlike us. I belong to this land and so does my father, just as your uncle did."

For the first time he smiled. She thought the smile made him remarkably attractive. "Do I really sound so pompous?

I am sorry. Perhaps we had best begin our acquaintance again, mademoiselle. I understand the villagers call you their good angel. I see they are not entirely wrong."

This was so unexpected she looked away to find a less embarrassing subject and encountered a steady, unblinking look from Yolande Berthelot and a frown from her brother. Somehow, by responding to the warmth she found in Gilles Marsan, she seemed to have added these two to her rapidly growing list of enemies, first the de Gleebs, then her old friends, the peasants of the Vaudraye lands, and now two unknowns named Berthelot.

To counter this, it was pleasant to feel at least Gilles Marsan no longer found her impossible.

As he helped her up into her pony cart he thought how surprised she might be if he told her that he had seen her many times before this day. Well, she would learn so at another time, perhaps sooner than he thought.

2

UNTIL today Veronique seldom had doubts about her own ability to deal with people such as these radicals. Due to the weakness and delicacy of her mother, at an early age she had played hostess at dinner with the Vicomte and delegated to herself the task of handling the estate problems. Her success led her to assume that very little was beyond her grasp, until she found her old friends on the estate and in the town swayed by forces agitating from outside. And they were undoubtedly swayed by such revolutionaries as the Berthelots and Monsieur Gilles Marsan, who used his artistic talents to turn the minds of her father's people. "Constitutionalist" was almost as threatening a word to her father as "assassin," and perhaps even more dangerous to the privileged orders; for a constitution could threaten their present freedom from taxation, and their freedom to mete out private punishment, as well as other remnants of feudal custom. Her father, though, was a decent man; still, she knew others were not. . . .

In spite of her suspicions and her plain dislike of agitators, she got on well with the artist, partly because their political disagreements were diffused in the press of immediate problems. She was relieved when the Berthelots went off to preach their doctrinaire sedition at the local inn; they had been of little practical help, like so many other revolutionaries of her experience.

Meanwhile Mme. Guillaume asked if it would be possible to see her husband and to pray over his coffin.

"Perhaps later, Aunt Simone," Marsan told her quietly. "All of Vaudraye will be with us to hear the priest's words." He cleared his throat. "That is true, mademoiselle?" He looked at Veronique, who had just stirred the savory contents of the big black pot on the hearth. Veronique nodded, glad he had not mentioned the word "burial."

Work was a temporary panacea. With her palms wrapped in rags to protect them from the heat, she gave her attention to the food, shifting the hook from which the black pot was suspended. She knew Marsan was looking at her again and for the first time in a long while she felt her true age, a gauche seventeen. She did not like being ill at ease. She almost felt as though she were asking this tall stranger's approval of her conduct. Absurd . . . still, it would have been flattering if he had seemed to admire her as a young, feminine woman —and a pleasant change from the respectful admiration for her abilities rather than herself.

Gilles Marsan interrupted what she decided were inappropriate thoughts in this place. "You see, Aunt Simone, mademoiselle agrees. All Vaudraye will come. He was very much loved."

Simone Guillaume had taken the news of her husband's death with calm so often shown by those who are themselves critically ill. She asked only when the broth would be ready and whether her husband might be buried in the uniform he had worn with General Montcalm's army at Quebec.

Veronique was pouring the second ladleful of reinforced broth into a bowl when she heard her father's unmistakable footsteps in the passage outside the open door. She spilled a few drops which sizzled on the coals as she nervously hoped there would be no painful scene between her father and Gilles Marsan. She glanced quickly at Marsan, who had likewise heard the swift, booted steps punctuated by the squeak of leather which, for some reason, haunted all of the Vicomte de Vaudraye's expensive footgear. The Vicomte was apt to strut, though not consciously, his daughter thought. At heart he was a real cockerel.

Madame Faure, remaining with Madame Guillaume, sank in a deep curtsy, and flattered by the arrival of their seigneur, said, "The master visiting your very own lodgings, Madame Simone!"

Marsan took the bowl of soup from Veronique, pointing out the women's conduct. "Serfs in Russia could not be more subservient. He is their master only because four hundred years ago his ancestor led a crusade. Is that just?"

"In the first place, my ancestors did not go on crusade."

"Cowards?"

It appeared, she thought, that he might have a sense of humor after all. "Not at all. They felt they were much more useful at home, seeing to the crops and the feeding and protection of their dependents."

She suspected he wanted to smile, but at that moment the Vicomte addressed the women in his brusque fashion and Marsan, turning toward him, said, "Monsieur le Vicomte, you have courage. You do not hesitate to face your victims."

Startled, the Vicomte peered into the half-dark where he made out the faces of his daughter and his critic.

"What? Are you addressing me?"

"I believe Madame Guillaume owes you for the food your daughter brought. The money is upon the table near your hand. Whatever else is owing will be paid . . . very soon, with the proper interest."

To forestall this silly bickering Veronique interceded. "Father, this is Madame Guillaume's nephew, Monsieur Marsan. He came from Paris for a visit."

"I came," Marsan corrected her, "to explain what the deputies of these people hope to accomplish at Versailles next month."

"Yes, very commendable." The Vicomte waved him aside while taking up the widow's work-worn, reddened fingers. "My dear Simone, we are old friends, you and I. Why did not Guillaume come to me in his need? I would never have let you starve. Name of God, how I remember those days when you and I sat on the kitchen hearth at Vaudraye and licked the pastry pans. Your mama made the most delicious pastries in the province—"

"Too much honor, monseigneur," the widow murmured. "To think monseigneur remembers! Gilles, *chéri*, your grandmama—my mother—was the head cook at the château. Wicked to talk against Monsieur de Vaudraye."

"Aunt Simone, this man's gamekeeper is the very cause—"

"Hush! Forgive him, monseigneur. He doesn't know of

your kindnesses. You send your dear daughter to do a servant's work. Now you honor me in my lodgings."

Watching all this plus the helpless exasperation of Marsan at the Vicomte's indifference to his money, Veronique found herself pitying him. Such firebrands for all their good intentions would never prevail against her father. The man who held the bread controlled the people. It might not be quite equitable, but it was God's way of delegating His tasks and all the proud, indignant young men in the world would not upset God's immutable laws.

The Vicomte capped his highly successful behavior by saluting Madame Guillaume's hand with a light kiss that would have been applauded at Versailles. He won her over completely while her neighbor, Madame Faure, sighed in delight. Gilles Marsan, on the other hand, was disgusted and looked a little tired as he set a wooden tray with the bowl of meat-thickened broth upon his aunt's lap. Veronique sympathized with his mood, although she admired her father's finesse in dealing with the situation. Flustered by so much attention, the widow did not like to remove her hands from her seigneur's clasp; so the Vicomte managed the matter neatly, placing a wooden spoon between her thumb and forefinger and helping her to eat, while continuing to look up at him. He grinned his approval. Then he turned to Veronique and Mme. Faure.

"My man is bringing the carcass of a deer. I suggest you have some good fellow carve it for a fair distribution among yourselves and those you feel are deserving." He strode to the doorway and called, "Bring in the carcass, and the flour."

Marsan reached for the silver pieces as he walked after the Vicomte.

"Monsieur! You forgot your pay. The rest will be sent you within the week."

But Veronique's father ignored him as he ignored the money. "Arnauld, I am here."

Veronique heard Gilles Marsan catch his breath. Nor was she surprised. It had been a brazen act, bringing the hated Arnauld de Gleeb into town.

Marsan demanded, "Does that murderer dare to set foot in this house? The house of his victim!"

The Vicomte looked back, just a trifle on his dignity.

"What is this? De Gleeb did not lay a hand upon your uncle. Be sensible, young man, or you will find yourself in serious trouble. This is not Paris. I am the magistrate here.

And these are good people in Vaudraye. They do not welcome rattle-brained radicals."

"Father! Guillaume was killed in a trap set by de Gleeb. He should not be here. This gentleman is quite right."

"I do not need your defense, I thank you!" Marsan said to her sharply. "I can still defend myself."

"Of course you can. But you don't want to disturb your aunt, do you? Now, please, monsieur—and Father—" She thought her father looked relieved at her intervention. Not so with Marsan.

"Monsieur! You will not hide behind your daughter! You say you are a magistrate. Very well then. Condemn your gamekeeper, that murderer huddling there in the darkness."

The Vicomte was dumbfounded at this insolence from one of the *canaille*, and Veronique, who started to interrupt again, was almost swept away by Marsan's outthrust hand.

"If you please, mademoiselle! He is a magistrate. He should give us an answer."

At the same time the passage came alive with the long, loose-jointed figure of Arnauld de Gleeb, balancing the carcass of a deer upon his shoulders. He swung one end of the carcass like a flail in Marsan's direction. Veronique gasped and fell against the door frame to avoid this fantastic weapon still dripping wet from its storage in the icy stillhouse at Vaudraye. The Vicomte issued an order, garbled slightly by his shock at this behavior in a subordinate.

"De Gleeb! I'll have your hide for this! Stop at once!"

Marsan, the gamekeeper's real target, swerved, barely avoiding the huge carcass, and shot a fist under the gamekeeper's flabby chin with what sounded like bone-splintering force. The carcass dropped heavily to the floor, and as Mme. Faure rushed to the doorway, a hunting knife flashed between de Gleeb and Gilles Marsan, who luckily proved swift and light on his feet. He barely avoided the cutting edge and got in a hard, chopping blow across the gamekeeper's wrist. De Gleeb's knees buckled but he did not drop the knife. For a moment no one moved. De Gleeb fixed his stare on Marsan, his knife poised. Veronique rushed to the street door for help, since it was clear that the gamekeeper would not obey her father. But the sounds of the scuffle in the passage already had drawn a number of men and three of them now squeezed in from the street. One of the men wielded a rifle-bayonet, and another a gigantic steel-pointed pike.

Before they could get at the gamekeeper, as was clearly their intention, the Vicomte finally made himself heard.

"Arnauld, another move and I'll have you thrashed. You others, stop this. At once, I order you!"

Somewhat breathless, but wanting to get in another blow, Gilles Marsan backed into Veronique, begged her pardon, and then challenged her, "Now, we will see how much justice there is in your noble father."

True enough, the Vicomte made no effort to chastise his gamekeeper, whom he ordered to go outside, get up onto the tumbril and drive back to the château. There was an angry muttering at the door. The man with the pike thrust it out, but the Vicomte pushed it aside with a regal wave and nothing else was done. The gamekeeper came out, grinning to all around. To Veronique's relief, even Gilles Marsan made no further remarks that could have inflamed the situation, except to say, "You see? Nothing will happen. He will not even be dismissed."

"He will if I have anything to say in the matter."

Marsan did not look convinced.

Meanwhile the Vicomte went back into the room where Madame Guillaume was struggling to rise from her bed.

"They must not quarrel, Gilles, I beg you, take care. Monseigneur has been kind to us in a hundred ways. Monsieur le Vicomte, he is a good boy. Gilles worked very hard to become . . . what he is."

"Whatever that may be," the Vicomte muttered, but then assured Madame Guillaume that he paid no heed to "the young rascal's remarks" and took up the widow's hand.

Veronique assured Marsan, "De Gleeb will be punished, monsieur. My father does listen to me, you know."

"Your father will listen, perhaps. But if that gamekeeper remains at Vaudraye, my uncle will not be the last man he kills."

He was probably right, but she could not say so. As she tried to reassure him without lying, she found herself noting that his dark hair looked disheveled after all his exertions and she had an alarming impulse to reach out and smooth it. . . . She recalled there had been the eldest son of the Comte de la Jouvenet who fussed over her at his eighteenth birthday fête, and there were one or two scions of neighboring estates who had flirted with her. But her life's work had never been far from her thoughts and she was disturbed now at her deep awareness of this man.

She dared not view him as a vital young male. She dared

not, yet her feelings were not subject to her command. . . .

He surprised her by apologizing. "Mademoiselle, I have been thinking. Perhaps I expressed myself badly to you . . . to your father, that is to say. I am not always tactful." He smiled and Veronique again found that the effect of his smile on her was remarkable. She forced herself to avoid his eyes and to think about practical matters as he suggested, "I might speak to the Vicomte—very tactfully—and make him understand how important it is that there be some changes made when the States-General meet. If he deoesn't have any interest in the people, at least he must certainly care about our bankrupt country."

"No, no, please, monsieur! I doubt that any of your arguments could sway him today. I will talk to my father, and he will listen."

He did not agree but took up her hand, held it a moment as though he found it interesting. She had wiped her hands on a rag after dishing up the soup but she flushed with shame, thinking there must still be grease on her fingers. She felt a tingling sensation as he held her hand. His palm was warm, and she felt a hard, tensile strength in his hand, the knuckles of which she noticed were skinned and reddened. While she was acutely aware of what she considered her own unladylike fingers, he said. "What a small hand to be so capable!"

Which overturned her thoughts about her hand so that she could not think of anything to say while he raised her fingers to his lips and then went to answer a call from his aunt.

She went out to the street, where Arnauld de Gleeb had already driven off with his empty cart in the wake of the Vicomte de Vaudraye, galloping his enormous bay stallion. It was only then that she realized Marsan had slipped the silver pieces into her hand. Since it was clearly all he had been carrying except a few sous, she did not know whether to smile or cry.

A coach belonging to some elegant English milords on the Grand Tour rattled by, filling the crisp air with mud and pebbles as they made their way from the Channel ports to Paris. They were off to see the world of Continental Europe.

That's a life I'll never know, Veronique thought, and for a moment she felt regret. She remembered that as a child she would amuse herself with dreams of faraway places and people who would tell tales of wonder and romance. But those were things, she told herself, that should remain in one's childhood. The real world pressed upon her more and more each day and there such dreams had no place. For some time now Veronique felt that her own life must be spent as dearly as possible, offering her help where it was most needed. This could best be fulfilled as a nursing nun . . . Gilles Marsan would be like a passing coach in her life, making an overnight stop only. . . . Smiling to herself at the private thought, she wiped the palms of her hands on her skirt as if to remove both the imagined grease and the touch of Marsan.

In this case . . . an empty gesture?

3

"WHAT dreadful suffering!" Madame de Gleeb whispered to Veronique. "And for a lady of her station, her delicacy, how she endures it, I do not know. One should not add to her suffering, surely."

In the sunny bedroom of her mother's suite, Veronique watched the Vicomtesse and tried not to think of that other sick woman in the village. "I am sorry you expected me here, but there was trouble in town."

"Of course, dear, I do understand. More important matters must come first. At times I am rather selfish." The Vicomtesse Hermione de Vaudraye gracefully accepted a bonbon from the box extended by Mme. de Gleeb. The sigh with which she punctuated her gesture seemed a reminder of her daughter's thoughtless behavior. "But my child, you must remember your future. A sister of Ste. Veronique should not be out frolicking in the mud at dawn like a peasant child, riding off to town unaccompanied in a most hoydenish fashion. And now"—she slipped the pink bonbon between her lips—"now you cap your folly by lending support to a wild-eyed revolutionary against one of your own kind."

A murmur of sympathy from Madame de Gleeb encouraged her and she managed a small shrug, catching the early-afternoon sunlight on the gold tambour muslin of her dressing sacque.

Called into this airless white boudoir the moment she arrived home, Veronique was acutely aware of her own disheveled appearance by comparison with her mother's careful, almost immaculate toilette; but the Vicomtesse's last complaint stopped her at the lowest point in her respectful curtsy and she stood up rapidly.

"I beg pardon, madame, but I trust Arnauld de Gleeb is not my own kind." She ignored Lise de Gleeb's look. "It is my belief he enjoys cruelty for its own sake."

Before the de Gleeb woman could say anything in her husband's defense, the Vicomtesse raised her voice in one of her infrequent outbursts of anger. "Silence! You demean yourself with these *cant* expressions. I will not permit it in my presence. You forget that I depend upon my dear Lise in a hundred little ways and I will not have her husband maligned. I can scarcely believe it is my daughter who speaks so uncharitably. Where is your understanding of Arnauld de Gleeb and his problems?"

Veronique stood speechless. It was unthinkable that she should bandy words with her mother, yet it was the second time that day she found herself annoyed at her parents' defense of de Gleeb, a man she thought repellent.

"Madame, may I have your leave to retire? I should like to change for dinner."

The Vicomtesse exhaled heavily, glanced at Madame de Gleeb and composed herself. The red-blond beauty that in its time had brought a dozen suitors to their knees was still visible when the Vicomtesse lost her querulous, strained look. She suffered from migraine and, though her thin, fair skin was flawless, around her lips there was a network of wrinkles from the way she pursed her lips too frequently in discontent and pain. In a more relaxed manner she said, "Very well, my dear. And I am afraid you must take my place at dinner tonight. My head has been splitting all day, ever since that terrible disturbance that awakened me this morning. There is no consideration for others these days. However, I have no doubt you regret today's disgraceful affair."

Much relieved, Veronique curtsied, but as she reached the white-paneled double doors her mother added, "Now, Veronique, I am persuaded that the next time you meet Monsieur de Gleeb, you will make your apologies for your part in today's attack upon him."

"Attack! But Mother, he attacked Monsieur Marsan."

Lise de Gleeb said, in gentle reproof, "Oh, my dear mademoiselle! The young radical insulted my poor Arnauld in the grossest terms and then threatened him with a—a skinning knife. And not satisfied with that, he then summoned several of his wretched followers to attack my husband."

"What a lie, Mama! De Gleeb had the skinning knife. It was all the reverse."

"Veronique!" The Vicomtesse seemed to wince with pain. It was hard to say whether fragile nerves had produced the migraine or quite the other way around, but such encounters with her daughter, for whom she envisioned a saintly and obedient future, were always wearing upon her. Lise de Gleeb quickly applied a perfumed handkerchief to her forehead.

Veronique mumbled an apology and her mother roused herself to make a similar effort. "Dear child, remember always that you have a very precious destiny. . . . Now, come and kiss me like the good girl I know you can be."

Veronique crossed the boudoir and knelt beside her mother's satin-covered chaise. She was relieved that the painful scene had ended in a truce. The Vicomtesse brushed her forehead gently with a kiss, then waved her away.

"Go, now. And do try and show a little Christian charity to Monsieur de Greeb. I shall expect to hear that my little girl has apologized to him for her conduct today."

"Yes, madame."

She quickly left the two women. She raced down one flight of stairs into the gallery and toward her own bedchamber, her hair and skirts flying. But as she turned the corner in the gallery she stopped abruptly and gasped with alarm. It was de Gleeb standing there, arms akimbo, virtually blocking her path. She was sure nothing fed Arnauld de Gleeb's self-love like the knowledge that he inspired terror. His thick, moist lips seemed so near she looked away in revulsion.

"Please. My father is waiting for me at dinner."

"Only a moment, mademoiselle. All I wish to know is why do you oppose me so? I have been faithful in my service to your father for years and remain so. Yet I know that you speak ill of me to both the Vicomte and the Vicomtesse."

"You are a cruel man, Arnauld, you delight in having life-and-death power over others. . . . It seems important to you that others fear you like death. I really don't know why my father keeps you here, he must see this also." Her heart was racing now, as much from anxiety as from anger.

For answer he merely smiled, shook his head and finally stepped aside as she made her way quickly to her own bed-chamber and threw the bolt on the door.

She leaned against the door shivering. It took a minute or two to recover from the fear and loathing the man aroused in her. She thought if she reported to her father exactly what had occurred, she might be rid of de Gleeb; but there would be a terrible scene with her mother, who couldn't seem to feel entirely alive without the ministrations of de Gleeb's wife. After a moment she thrust herself away from the door as if it bore the gamekeeper's imprint, and went to ring for her hip-bath.

From her mother she had very early acquired a taste for baths. And on this April afternoon she scrubbed until her smooth flesh was flushed, and even then she was not quite sure she had scrubbed away the memory of the gamekeeper's look.

When her maid, Marie-Josette, brought out the pattern book of her gowns with tiny samples from the underdress and the overskirts, Veronique did not at once wave away the book as usual with the remark, "Anything. Whatever is simple."

This time, while the maid watched her curiously, Veronique turned every page, wondering what colors best became her. And in the midst of these musings she thought of Gilles Marsan and imagined that he must cut a handsome, imposing figure when dressed in one of those new fashionable frock coats. Not that his trim, athletic body would not look well in any covering. . . .

She looked at her fingers, turned her hand over and caressed her right hand with her left forefinger. How strange, and how wonderful, that he had admired her hand. . . .

Marie-Josette coughed. Recovering, Veronique handed the book to the maid. "Anything. It doesn't matter."

To Lise, Arnauld seemed more worried than she'd ever remembered him. She was sitting on a bottle-green sofa in their apartment while her husband paced the floor.

"Before Veronique leaves for the nuns and perhaps sooner I am afraid she may find a way to have me discharged. We must not let that happen."

"But the Vicomte is in your debt," Lise replied. "You've always said that. He won't let you go merely because his daughter dislikes you—"

"I fear that may no longer be true. The Vicomte sometimes places great store in his daughter's opinions. At any rate I've decided something must be done, and tonight."

Lise was alarmed by the tone of her husband's insistence. Surely they would not be turned out by the Vicomte and Vicomtesse. But it was what Arnauld had not said as yet that she feared most.

"This evening when you are preparing the Vicomtesse you are to get her out of her bed about the time the Vicomte and Veronique are finishing their dinner. I will signal you from the copse outside."

"But why should I do this? And won't the Vicomtesse think it strange?"

"Stupid woman, think of something. She loves the way you fawn over her. Tell her that she should walk briefly for her health or something."

"All right, but what are you planning to do?" She knew he would be angry with her prying but she had to ask.

"All you need know is that, after I signal, you be certain the Vicomtesse is *not* in her bed or near the window. Do you understand?"

Lise nodded, afraid to do otherwise.

Veronique was her calm self by the time she came down expecting to go in to dinner. Instead, she was surprised when she heard Gilles Marsan's voice, angry and full of bitterness, coming from the Blue Salon near the South Portico.

"You wonder that France has fallen to pieces when starvation and despair can lead to this?"

"By God! I am not to be held responsible every time some damned peasant's lungs fail her."

"You are as vile as the rest of your fellow aristocrats!"

She stepped into the Blue Salon in time to see her father shake his fist at Marsan.

"Vile, am I? You'll *not* say that again in my house. Now get out—"

"Papa, what are you doing? What's happening?" Veronique reached him before he managed to touch Gilles Marsan, who looked tense but in better control of himself. It was he who explained to Veronique coldly, as if they had never seen each other before, "My aunt is dead."

"What!"

The Vicomte began to shout again but was silenced in stupefaction by his daughter's impatient wave of the hand as she asked Marsan, "How did it happen?"

"I am not a surgeon. I cannot say. But it happened while I was with her. She began to cough. She seemed to choke, and suddenly . . ." he stopped, shrugged, once more in control, "she was gone."

Her father responded, "And he assumes the blame must be mine!"

"I am sure Monsieur Marsan does not—" she began but Marsan's answer startled her.

"Starvation, mademoiselle, killed my uncle. He was not a thief or a poacher. He shot that hare in order to save his wife and himself from starvation. It is a motive as old as man. Starvation caused my aunt to lose strength, to become ill, and ultimately, it kept her from recovering. Since the Vicomte claims his seigneurial rights over all these lands, and over all crops and all peasants who work his lands, then the starvation of the land, the crops and the people becomes his problem."

"I know my father deeply regrets your aunt's death," Veronique assured him, too anxious over this quarrel to concentrate upon the second tragedy to strike Marsan's family.

The Vicomte, who genuinely liked his peasant friends, spoke now but in a tone that suggested he genuinely needed to defend himself. "Monsieur, I regret this double tragedy that has come to you in this one day. I have known Simone all my life. I wish to appear personally at the burial and say a few words. You may tell the curé as much. But as to food— they had only to tell me. I never dreamed things were so bad with them. You may be certain I will have de Gleeb look into such matters frequently in the future."

Veronique bit her lip at that and was not surprised when Marsan said, in a voice full of measured fury, "If nothing else had shown me, I would know after today that our country needs an end of feudal privilege such as you enjoy in this province. I remind you of what happened when the Polish aristrocrats refused to give up some privileges not so long ago . . . it ended in anarchy and partition of the country."

In the silence that followed he went to the door, stopped a moment and added, "Monsieur, you are responsible for your political ignorance, if not for the continuance of these abuses. Don't you understand how demeaning the *corvée* is, that ridiculous requirement to work on the roads for ten days a year at the King's pleasure. And worse yet, during our terrible crop failure, that crazy prohibition against fencing in gardens or even hoeing them until the hunting season was over so that rabbits and other small game would not be disturbed and spoil the hunt! The King must come out of Versailles to become the king of France again or I assure you there will be a terrible bill to pay. I warn you, when the people avenge themselves, they may not stop with you and your kind. All those you love may suffer. Think about it, monseigneur." And he left.

The Vicomte stared at the empty doorway.

"Mother of God! He is mad. Now he threatens my family as well. Girl, where are you going?"

Veronique reached Marsan as he was crossing the portico on his way to the estate road.

"Monsieur, please wait. You must not go away thinking we care so little. My father grew up with your aunt and her mother."

He smiled his disbelief, but then said warmly, "I wish you were on our side, mademoiselle."

Lest he think he had flattered her out of her family loyalty, she said firmly. "I prefer people to politics." Still, pleased at his flattery—and frankly attracted by him—she added, "I wish you well, though. Please remember that."

Having taken one step down to the grassy slope, he remained still, as if torn by conflicting impulses. He raised one hand. She sensed that he was about to touch her face. She was too astonished to make a sound or to avoid his touch. Nor did she wish to; yet he was a stranger, and in a political sense, an enemy.

He lowered his hand. "I will remember, mademoiselle. I promise you." This time there was no sarcasm, no bitterness.

After he had gone across the lawn to the road, she remained there watching him until called impatiently by her father.

"Daughter! The servants are waiting dinner for us. You know how sullen they get these days if we put them to all this unnecessary trouble." As she did not move, he added, "If you have done apologizing for my cruelty and barbarism, come along."

She went with her father to the long crimson and gold dining salon. They took their places at the mahogany table whose top-heavy silver epergne and candlesticks were his prizes from a British general during the American War of Independence. Veronique sat with her back to the long windows that faced on the apple orchard. The flower scent was customarily pervasive that spring evening, and with all the disturbing events that day Veronique found it especially diverting.

Her father broke the unusual silence with a remark that startled her. "You are in quite a glow tonight, my girl. I don't suppose your indignation at that Jacobin can have been the cause." .

She dropped her knife with a clatter. "It probably is anger, Papa. This afternoon I had another meeting with that wretched de Gleeb—"

"De Gleeb has his rough ways, but he has his virtues as well. In fact I thing it is time I told you something of this man that you don't know. . . ."

"I can't imagine it to be very attractive."

"I think it best, Veronique, you listen a moment before you tell me again how loathsome you find my gamekeeper. . . . Some four years ago I was on a hunt with the Flauberts and some others, and de Gleeb was in charge. We were after quail that day and so the hired men were out beating through the high grass and lucerne driving the birds up. Now often when quail are disturbed they prefer to run and hide rather than fly, and so are difficult to see in the wild. We were strung out on line and I was at one end when I saw what looked lke a number of birds scurrying off to my left away from everyone else. I went after them, but after about fifty yards I lost sight of them and was about to go back when I saw two men, hunters I thought, as they were both carrying guns. . . . One of them shouted something to me and gestured that I should come over in their direction. As far as I could see, one of them favored his leg, but as I approached, the one who had motioned to me raised his gun and aimed it at me. It was only then I realized they were not hunters but probably roving bandits who had lured me away to rob and kill me. Before I could react a shot came from behind me and the one bandit fell while the other ran off, his leg suddenly quite healthy. That rescue shot was fired by your hated Arnauld de Gleeb. He had noticed that I had wandered off and decided to keep me in sight. Veronique, I owe him my very life, and that is a lifetime debt. And so now perhaps you better understand my feelings about 'that wretched de Gleeb.' "

Veronique said nothing. She was attempting to sort out her feelings. Her father had never been quite so confiding with her before over a matter he quite clearly, and for him naturally, saw as the business of men.

"I realize, my dear, that all this must be unsettling to you, but it was my wish for you to know this and understand. Loyalty among men is prized above all else. And therefore disloyalty is the mark of a scoundrel, no matter what his station. De Gleeb was loyal, his loyalty need never be tested or questioned again."

This was the closest to a speech Veronique had ever heard from her father. But she was torn between the nobility of his sentiments and the fact that they still were talking about Arnauld de Gleeb, a man she never could nor would respect. She remained silent.

"Now as for this M'sieur Marsan, he is a man without loyalties except to the spread of his villainous doctrine. And that makes him the most dangerous of all. He may be well-spoken and decent enough but his ideas of reform lead to anarchy and they have taken possession of him—"

"Father! Please don't exaggerate. I know that you do not agree with M'sieur Marsan's ideas, but you must admit these are strange times we are living in. Forces we can't always control are sweeping us along. Don't you feel it, Papa? If we are going to survive, we must adapt to these times."

The Vicomte stabbed his venison in a gesture no one could misunderstand.

"Not I! Not Claude de Vaudraye. And don't speak to me further about that Jacobin! He'd have slaughtered me for two sous—"

"Papa, that is nonsense."

But he went on, thoroughly warmed to his subject now . . . "The world may whirl around in all directions, but it will find us as it always has, not asking for what doesn't belong to us, defending at any cost what does. We are like that, we Vaudrayes, we take our stand and nothing will shake us. . . ."

Hearing her father speak in this fashion caused Veronique to consider just how much of a Vaudraye she was. Marsan did represent the world outside for her, outside her class and her Church. Her world had been ordered, predictable and re-assuring. But how long would it be so? The Church with its beauty and godly purpose was the only suitor she had ever really known, or expected. Yet understanding all this she was surprised, much to her pleasure, that she found Gilles Marsan's passage through her life causing such a rush of excitement. Somehow it seemed almost illicit. . . . In any case it was no surprise that her father should rage so about him. Everything the Vicomte held valuable, his lifelong understanding of how things were and were *meant* to be, was being challenged by Marsan, whose rhetoric seemed at once impudent and threatening. No, her father would probably never be able to understand a man like Marsan. Not that Veronique really understood him, and his politics were something she neither liked nor disliked. Politics was not something to be studied or much talked about. It was life itself, the life around her that she wanted to know and understand. And she sensed that it was this life that was changing for her, almost imperceptibly.

After a moment's silence Veronique asked, "Father, I don't think I've ever asked you when it was you decided I was to make my vows?" She asked the question with a casualness she didn't feel.

"Why, when your mother told me so. Even before you were born."

"And if I had been a boy?"

"In that case, my dear, your cousin Alexandre would not be the heir to Vaudraye. It is fortunate for your mother's wishes that your inclinations ran in the same direction as hers."

"Well, then, Father, you should not object to Cousin Alex and Sylvie as your heirs. According to their last letter, mama says, Cousin Alex is to represent the nobles in the States-General at Versailles."

"So. You see? You have nothing to reproach yourself with when you enter Ste. Veronique. It is lucky that things came about so well. That flighty wife of Alex's would wear a lesser man down, but I daresay he can handle Sylvie. You must see something of them for a month or so, before you enter the convent."

She brightened. "Yes. That would be wonderful."

Theobald, the old butler-steward who had served Veronique's grandfather, hovered discreetly behind the Vicomte's scarlet-cushioned chair and produced another bottle for the master. Veronique stifled a yawn. They had been at dinner nearly two hours and her father had managed to drink through both of them.

"Father, I forgot to say—" She had hoped to speak without the slightest sign of feeling and certainly before her father ordered in another bottle with his dinner. "I forgot to give you the silver pieces. Would you listen to me just a few minutes, Papa, before you open that bottle?"

"Silver? What silver? Theobold, hold there a moment. Is there some of the silverware missing?"

Veronique smiled. She suspected her father's first bottle must have been potent enough.

"No, Papa, not silverware. Silver pieces. I left them in your study. They are in payment for the food we took to the Guillaumes today. Guillaume's nephew tried to pay you, if you recall."

The Vicomte's mood darkened again. "Where would he get silver pieces? Held up a channel coach, very likely."

"Father! You are not very consistent. You always complain that charity weakens character. Well, this man doesn't accept charity, even from a Grand Seigneur."

"Veronique, you credit this rogue with virtues he doesn't possess. At this minute he is very likely preaching sedition to my peasants, the people who have belonged to Vaudraye lands for centuries. What can he have to say to my people? Theo—the bottle."

She might have left him to drink alone, as English gentlemen did, but she wanted to make one more effort to get him into some slightly more accommodating mood. As she pushed back her chair to approach him, he looked up, started to rise with the bottle in his hand, and then to Veronique's amazement waved it excitedly toward the big glass doors overlooking the eastern half of the estate.

"Someone is out there! I swear I see him. Theobald, call de Gleeb."

"No! Father!" Amid the rustle of petticoats and taffeta overdress, she reached for the steward's arm as the old man shuffled toward the hall. "Please, don't. It isn't necessary to send for de Gleeb."

The old servant did not know which way to turn. His master nudged him, waving the bottle, and it seemed discreet to obey him, or at all events to get out of his reach. Veronique swung around in time to see her father fumbling at the latches of the two doors across the dining salon. She managed to reach him, aware that a lock of her elaborately piled and powdered hair had tumbled down.

The Vicomte de Vaudraye stalked out onto the narrow walk, which had been flattered by the name of terrace. The long side of the dining salon paralleled the end of the apple orchard and a stretch of green park which, at this hour, was little better than a shadowy copse. Veronique seized upon this darkness to entice her father back inside.

"Where the devil—?"

"It is nothing, Papa. Just a deer wandering through the orchard. Come in now." They could not possibly see anything or anyone prowling through that underbrush.

A path of light suddenly cut through the dark of the orchard. Veronique glanced up apprehensively. The portieres of the suite occupied by the Vicomtesse on the floor high overhead were pushed aside and two women stood silhouetted against the candlelight behind them. Lise de Gleeb pushed the window open and leaned out.

"Lise, close the window. You will chill my mother. It is only Monsieur. We thought we heard something."

The woman backed away, said something to the Vicomtesse and closed the window while Veronique managed to coax her father back into the house. He still wielded the wine bottle like a club, and by the time they had returned to the table he finally noticed the bottle.

He held it up to the nearest candelabrum. "Afraid I've given the contents a bit of a jar. Better turn it over to the servants." As Veronique reached for it, from the direction of the terrace there was heard a crack like a tree limb breaking, and then the sound of breaking glass and a woman's screams.

Terrified, Veronique shouted, "God of heaven! It's mother!"

. . .

4

BY the time Veronique reached the top floor of the building, Mme. de Gleeb had run out of the Vicomtesse's suite. She called out for her husband who suddenly appeared on the east terrace far below with the steward Theobald and Old Mathieu immediately behind him. The three ran out into the darkness. Veronique was in terror at the thought of what she might find in her mother's bedchamber.

Mme. de Gleeb, wringing her hands, kept repeating, "While I decided to get a heavier robe for her, she stepped near the window. I should never have left her. Never! Oh, my God, I am sorry . . ." She seemed more terrified by far than even the Vicomtesse.

She led the way into the Vicomtesse's bedchamber, where Veronique found her mother—sobbing, huddled on the carpet, but unquestionably alive. All around her glass and slivers gleamed in the candlelight, which flickered because of the rushing air through the broken pane in the window.

The Vicomte muttered, "Dear God!"

"My arm . . . don't touch it," the Vicomtesse moaned to Veronique and continued to tremble with her sobbing.

Veronique was shocked but did not see any blood where her mother held the ruffles of her white sleeve. Very gently she suggested, "Mama, darling, let me raise you, just a little

. . . to get you out of all this glass."

But the Vicomtesse called, "Claude," who recovered somewhat at the sound of his name.

"Now, my angel, your Claude is here. Don't fret. Put your hand on my shoulder. Here we go."

Veronique rushed to pull down the bed's elaborate satin coverlet and sent Mme. de Gleeb after a basin of hot water and cloths.

"Name of God! Will she be all right?" the Vicomte murmured to Veronique.

Veronique said, "Don't worry. Just set her against the pillows. No, no! Sitting up. She is too near to fainting. Mama? Can you hear me? Try to keep your eyes open."

Marie-Josette, Veronique's maid, fortunately appeared in the doorway, holding up the half-fainting Edwige, an elderly woman who had been the Vicomtesse's personal maid since long before her marriage.

"Marie-Josette, fetch me mama's handkerchief there on the floor. Edwige, get control of yourself and bring some of mama's cordial."

While the Vicomte supported his wife against her satin pillows, Veronique searched her mother's blouse for any glass or cuts. She then motioned Edwige to put the cordial to her mother's lips and while the lady sipped, taking long sobbing breaths in between, Veronique very gently raised the sodden ruffles of the sleeve.

She decided to wrap the arm and shoulder into position in the event the Vicomtesse had wrenched it in her fall, but as she adjusted her blouse with great care to the wound, her mother jumped, pulling her arm away in a panic.

"Careful!" her father ordered. "This is not one of your patients in the Hôtel-Dieu—"

Biting her lip, she tried again, ever so gently, holding her breathe. This time her mother shivered but did not draw her arm away as Veronique managed to treat and wrap it. Once this was accomplished, the Vicomtesse, now fully composed, settled back contentedly with her cordial while Mme. de Gleeb, still terrified, and the elderly Edwige continued to make a fuss over her.

The Vicomte walked to the broken window and frowned down at the orchard, where everything but the blossoms was shrouded in darkness. He called out, "You, down there! Arnauld, have you tracked that damnable scoundrel?"

Veronique, having cleared away the debris from her

mother's bed, asked Marie-Josette to sweep the glass off the floor. At the Vicomte's shout, she glanced toward the window. She could have sworn a musket ball had broken the window. What man in the neighborhood of the Vaudraye lands hated her parents so much he would make an attempt on the life of the Vicomtesse de Vaudraye? No one had made fewer enemies. Indeed, the Vicomtesse had scarcely been seen outside the château in the past year. It was a bitter reflection that her innocent mother, who was not in the least responsible for the crimes of de Gleeb or the grand-seigneur attitude of the Vicomte, should be suffering now. Veronique's first angry impulse was to refuse any more help to the people of the town.

Marie-Josette motioned to Veronique, who squeezed her mother's fingers gently and then went over to examine the sweepings Josette had collected. A musket ball still preserving much of its original shape had been swept up with the shards of glass. She took it and examined it.

"Papa!" Even as she called to him she wished she had given the matter some thought first, but Marie-Josette was already gaping at the spent ball as was Mme. de Gleeb. Since Veronique's mother's rooms were three stories above the ground, with each floor containing unusually high ceilings for such a small château, this shot had required a powerful musket, not to mention an excellent marksman. Most muskets would not have sent a ball this far with this accuracy from the depths of the park unless weilded by an excellent marksman with an especially accurate weapon.

While she speculated about this, Mme. de Gleeb spoke up. "Those rabble preaching sedition all across the province! They tried to murder my lady." She hoped Arnauld would be proud of her . . . and forgive her for not carrying out his instructions more successfully.

Ironically, by calling attention to herself, the gamekeeper's wife brought her husband into Veronique's thoughts. Arnauld de Gleeb was the best marksman in this quarter of the province, with a weapon superior to those of the local peasantry. Was it only her dislike of de Gleeb and her sympathy with the townspeople that had planted a sudden suspicion in her mind?

Veronique kept the spent ball in her hand and listened as de Gleeb raised his voice, shouting up to the Vicomte from the orchard below.

"Excellency! We have footprints. Old Mathieu found them

in the copse, the marks of some peasant's clogs, and the wad of a spent cartridge."

The Vicomte leaned far out the window.

"Like something from the guns of those damned poachers, I dare say."

"Just so, excellency. It would seem to suggest—"

"I understand. Not satisfied with hunting down my game, they now hunt down my innocent family. Send Mathieu in with the evidence and see if you can collar the fellow. I will join you shortly. And to think those rogues actualy resented your carrying out your duties."

As the Vicomte turned from the window to arm himself for the search, Veronique touched him arm. "Papa, before you go, may I speak to you?"

He was stiff with anger and spun around, waving away her request. "Later, later. Don't trouble me now. We have serious business to discuss, Arnauld and I. I mean to make an example of the vicious scoundrel who tried to assassinate your mother."

From the bed the Vicomtesse said weakly, "Claude . . . you must not risk your life. Don't do something foolish."

"Yes, my sweet. Don't trouble your pretty head." He patted her cheek and went abruptly out of the room.

Marie-Josette swept the debris into her apron, tucked it up over her skirts and asked Veronique, "May I be excused, mam'selle?"

Veronique made a slight motion with one hand. The maid nodded and went out. Before joining her, Veronique instructed Mme. de Gleeb, "My mother must be moved to other quarters. It will be much too cold in here. The shutters will never serve tonight. The first thing tomorrow, the window must be repaired. Keep her warm. Will you be all right, Mama?"

"Yes, dear." Drowsily, the Vicomtesse closed her eyes, held her free hand out to her maid. "Edwige, another blanket, please."

Between them, the maid and Mme. de Gleeb covered her with robes from the chaise-longue, and the Vicomtesse went off to sleep, completely enclosed in satin and wool except for the wounded and stiffly wrapped arm, which surely would trouble her tomorrow.

"Poor mama," thought Veronique. "This world is not the gentle cocoon in which she was born."

Out in the passage Marie-Josette was waiting for her, still

with the apron doubled up over her skirts. "Mam'selle? You do not mean to tell His Excellency about the musket ball?"

"Presently," not adding that she had just tried to but had been frustrated by her father's refusal to talk and his abrupt departure to hunt down . . . hunt down *whom*? . . . and according to *whose* scheme . . . ? "Josette," she added, "have you a fondness for Arnauld de Gleeb?"

She looked at Veronique a trifle furtively, as if to read the thought behind her question.

"He is very capable, mademoiselle. He will not permit anyone to poach upon Vaudraye lands. He is as loyal to them as he would be if they were his own lands."

"I don't doubt it." Something in Veronique's dry voice caught the girl.

"Monsieur de Gleeb feels the same way about the people who belong to Vaudraye. Especially the women. I do not let myself be caught alone with him. I even seek the company of that skinny old gargoyle, his wife. At least he doesn't dare anything in her sight."

"I can well imagine. I told my father he took liberties but I'm afraid he has a man's answer."

Marie-Josette nodded. "They claim we must have tempted them."

Veronique remembered her father's easy, jovial reply to one complaint she had made: "Eh—well, he must learn his place, of course. But, my dear, I think you exaggerate. You are rapidly becoming an attractive young lady and until you wear the veil, you must expect hearty males to admire you. If he continues to be difficult, come to me and I will settle the matter."

Hearing the doors of her mother's suite open behind her, she whispered to the maid, "Say nothing about what we have found."

The grinding suspicion of the gamekeeper remained, and Veronique knew that if one of the local people was accused of de Gleeb's crime, an innocent man could be broken on the wheel and hanged. She was so convinced that it would be found that the musket ball had come from de Gleeb's musket, she carried it to her own bedchamber, rolled the ball in her handkerchief and placed it under one of the pillows on her bed. She had tried to show it to her father, but since he preferred charging off into the darkness she decided it might be a better idea to wait until morning when he, and she, were in a more settled frame of mind to hear her theory as to what may have happened.

Later that night as she climbed up into her bed it occurred to Veronique how providential that Lise de Gleeb had not been near the window when the shot was fired! Mme. de Gleeb was always at the side of the Vicomtesse when she wasn't hanging about Veronique on her mother's orders. Always there was that closeness, except for the lucky decision to go and get a heavier robe for the Vicomtesse. And why would de Gleeb fire this shot? To cast further blame on some troublesome peasant? Mme. de Gleeb had already done so tonight. Most logical of all, the gamekeeper might have done this thing to justify his own murderous activities against poachers. Those townsmen today had been dangerously aroused against him. But if it was believed that a poacher had actually tried to murder her mother, their sympathy might shift and de Gleeb's actions would be applauded, particularly by her father. As she lay there she heard voices under the windows and knew that her father, accompanied by the gamekeeper and Old Mathieu, was still examining the evidence of the attack on his wife.

Veronique decided to remain awake and speak to her father when he came in to go to bed. She felt under her pillows, found the handkerchief with the hard musket ball properly tied in, and closed her eyes.

Despite her intentions, it was the next morning when Veronique awoke to a brief knock at her door. When she replied, it burst open and her mother's maid rushed into the room.

"Mademoiselle! My lady is asking for you. She is troubled. There will be violence, she says. You must see to it at once, and stop them."

Veronique, who was still half-asleep, did not quite understand the panic. While she seized her dressing sacque and threw the too elaborate bit of silk and camlet over her bedgown she asked the maid what had happened.

"It is about the shot last evening. Monseigneur and my husband wish to go into the village and hang someone."

"What!" Before leaving the room she felt under her pillows, found the weighted handkerchief and went hurrying out to her mother's suite, with Edwige following behind her.

The household seemed to be up and about but hardly at its work. Even members of the kitchen staff were huddled around the newel post at the foot of the grand staircase and on the gallery floor Veronique saw, as she passed, the faces of various personal servants, including her father's valet. Evidently the entire household was aware of a crisis. Even the outside servants and peasants seemed aroused, though in a way that did not suggest a sympathy with the Vicomte. The men had gathered in groups of two and three, occasionally with a woman, on the wide tree-bordered park fronting the château.

"Father," she thought. "What disaster are you about to launch now?"

In her mother's bedchamber the scene was equally crowded and far more noisy. The Vicomtesse sat up in her bed and stretched out her uninjured arm, trying to reach the Vicomte, who was engaged in a heated discussion with Arnauld de Gleeb and, of all people, Veronique's personal maid, Marie-Josette. Mme. de Gleeb stood beside the Vicomtesse's bed, apparently composed and dignified but with a gleam of excited interest.

The gamekeeper first saw Veronique, eyed her disheveled condition from tousled head to her bedslippers, but was careful to behave with studied propriety.

"But here is the young mademoiselle," he said. "She will force the truth out of the wench."

"By all means." Veronique struggled to match that bland, unruffled manner of his. "Marie-Josette and I have no secrets, Papa. But we aren't accustomed to being quizzed by your gamekeeper, so you must pardon us for being a little surprised. What did you want to know?"

The girl had glanced at Veronique, obviously asking for help, as she added what sounded like a repetition of previous denials.

"I know nothing of guns, Monseigneur. Truly. Rifles and muskets and all. I swept away the glass and maybe a little dust." She looked so shaken, they must have been at her for some time.

The Vicomte was dressed for riding, in boots and jacket and buckskin breeches. His low square brow made a scowl look even more formidable and he must have appeared quite fierce to the young girl, which suggested to Veronique that he was more than ever determined to do something drastic.

Veronique said hurriedly, "She is right, Papa. I asked her to clear away the debris, and then I sent her to bed."

The Vicomtesse tugged at her daughter's sleeve.

"Dearest, don't let him go into the village to hang anyone."

Veronique was surprised at this uncharacteristic speaking

out by her mother in favor of the townspeople. She clasped her mother's nervous fingers in her own and assured her in low tones, "I'll take care, he won't kill anyone. Papa is too humane . . ."

Her mother continued, "No, dear! You don't understand. Claude will do what he thinks best. But you must not let them hurt your father. That is what I mean . . ."

While her father, hearing himself discussed, turned to listen, Mme. de Gleeb declared: "How very strange that the musket ball has not yet been recovered! Nothing seems to have been found . . . except, of course, mademoiselle's handkerchief. I remember seeing it in your hand, did I not, mademoiselle Veronique? And what could that matter? One could hardly conceal anything in a handkerchief, except a few glass fragments . . ."

The pointed comment was useful for Veronique's purposes. It set the Vicomte against the de Gleeb woman, and he said crossly, "What the devil has that to do with anything?"

Veronique opened her clenched hand.

"Why not find out? I wanted to discuss this with you last night, Father, but you were too busy searching the grounds. This was the musket ball that struck the window. Examine it, please, and tell me if you think it could possibly have come from one of the old rifles they use in the village."

Staring at her, the Vicomte took the handkerchief. Then he glanced down. He was puzzled, and it was plain that he did not like the interference of a servant in pointing out some shortcomings of his daughter. At the same time he was faced with evidence that, to Veronique's amazement, seemed to confirm for him his gamekeeper's story.

"Well? The musket ball. And a poor thing it is, too. Hardly worth the loading. Good God! How did that bastard expect— I beg pardon, Hermione—how did the fellow expect to do any damage from the center of the copse with . . . this?"

They all crowded around. The de Gleebs seemed mildly interested, hiding their triumph nicely. In fact, on Arnauld de Gleeb's brow was the trace of a puzzled frown.

"As you say, exactly the sort of musket ball that was well spent long before it ever reached a target."

It was Veronique who was stupefied. The musket ball was flattened, hardly recognizable, and certainly not a ball that would be used in the gamekeeper's good musket. Desperately, Veronique turned to Marie-Josette.

"That isn't the ball we found last night. It doesn't look remotely like the one we found——"

The girl stepped forward, rose on her toes and peered over the Vicomte's arm. "Y-yes, mademoiselle. That's the one. . . . I swept it up with the bits of glass. Very sharp they were."

She was too frightened to observe anything accurately, Veronique thought. She tried to encourage the girl.

"No, Josette. Don't you remember? It was not shapeless, not like that at all."

Even as she spoke she realized it was a mistake to warn everyone of her suspicions. She had left the handkerchief under her pillow last night while she and Mme. de Gleeb chose a new bedchamber for the Vicomtesse. But afterward she made up the new bed without the gamekeeper's wife; so Mme. de Gleeb might have changed the musket ball in the handkerchief during that period. And the gamekeeper was alone for some little time before her father reached him in the copse. Had his wife warned him about that handkerchief?

Marie-Josette became aware that she was the center of attention and shook her head nervously. "I do not understand, mademoiselle. We both saw what is there in Monseigneur's hand."

With satisfaction, the Vicomte pocketed the musket ball.

"At all events, I am satisfied. Come along, Arnauld . . . Hermione, do not trouble yourself. I will be quite safe. But by heaven, we will deal out justice to this assassin! They cannot attack my wife and live to boast about it."

He kissed his wife, who called his name anxiously as he left the room with the gamekeeper. Pursued by her mother's plaintive voice, Veronique hurried after the two men.

"Papa, you can't believe our own townsmen did this thing. I know every man in Vaudraye, and there isn't one of them capable of such a shot."

At the head of the stairs the Vicomte looked back. Veronique knew that stubborn expression. She had inherited it.

"Possibly not one of our own townsmen, my girl. But you forget that troublemaker who threatened my family in this very house yesterday."

Which aroused her to an unreasoning panic. Gilles Marsan, a stranger to her, yet she was startled at her own strong feelings at this threat to him. With an effort she managed to remain calm as she protested. "You don't know that. All you know of a certainty is what you have been told." Realizing immediately that this was the wrong approach, she tried appealing to his affection for her. "Papa, I swear by—by Ste. Veronique—that I told you the truth about that musket ball. You must know I would not lie to you."

As she had expected, he could not ignore this plea. He waited for her, took her chin between thumb and forefinger and said, "Last night you were tired. You took that musket ball for some reason. And you did not look at it again until this morning. A professional gamekeeper knows a great deal more about guns than my little girl does. And don't worry. Have I not always made fair rulings with my people? Vaudraye is not some bourgeois town, you know. Those upstart merchants have no municipality in my village. Not yet! But I promise you, this villain shall be heard. Afterward, of course—but the punishment of a wrongdoer is not fit conversation for a gentleman's daughter. Run along to your mother now."

She was furious with her father's patronizing dismissal, even though she realized that in the custom of the time the advice of women was rarely sought by men and when offered tolerated, at best. It was also in the fashion of the day that the Vicomtesse had been married at fifteen and given birth to Veronique by the time she was seventeen. At times the Vicomte encouraged his daughter not to allow emotions to rule her as they did her mother, and even looked to her for support when he found it difficult to cope with his wife. And yet at other times he seemed put off by the very assertiveness that he had encouraged . . . she found it frustrating and, indeed, annoying. Maintaining, or submitting gracefuly to, the charade of a little helpless girl was difficut for someone who already had worked among the sick and dying with the Sisters in the public hospital.

The Vicomtesse could be heard calling Veronique's name. But when Veronique reached the top of the stairs she shouted down to the two men who had nearly gotten to the entry way and the front doors.

"Papa, you must not make a judgment until he has counsel, whoever the man may be. You mustn't be swayed by anyone . . . not anyone. You do understand, don't you?"

He waved to her and disappeared.

Arnauld de Gleeb remained behind long enough to say, "Be assured, mademoiselle. I will see that he listens to no one."

Frustrated to the point of rage, she could barely contain herself when Mme. de Gleeb broke into her thoughts with

"Mademoiselle, your mother has been asking for you now these ten minutes." The insufferable woman even had the nerve to sound reproachful. . . .

5

"SHALL I read to you, Mama?"

The Vicomtesse settled back among the satin pillows with a sigh of contentment.

"How good you are, dearest. Read me some of those naughty rhymes about the queen. So shocking! Their author really should be flogged. Still, one can't help being amused."

Mme. de Gleeb added confidentially, "I've heard it said the queen's own cousin, the Duc d'Orléans, publishes them. What a delicious rascal!"

The Vicomtesse smiled. "Really, Lise! You are an incorrigible gossip. But tell me, do you think these dreadful stories about the Austrian Woman are true?"

"Madame, I had the story from the lady I formerly had the pleasure of serving . . . the Duchesse de St.-Aubans, the richest peeress in France, as Your Ladyship may know. And the Duchesse is a Lady of the Bedchamber to Her Majesty. She assures me the Duc d'Orléans publishes these lies about his cousin in order to win favor with the rabble *canaille*."

Veronique watched the two women with their heads together and decided she might safely leave her mother at least long enough to dress. Would there be time for her to send Gilles Marsan the warning to leave Vaudraye before her father's arrival? At least he must be warned. She could do no less than that . . .

"I am going to dress now, Mama. Then we shall have our chocolate here together and I will read your horrid gossip to you."

"Yes, dear. And have you made your morning prayers yet?"

Veronique remembered that she had not and promised to do so as she left her mother. Her prayers were made while she searched for her rosary and even while she dressed. At the same time she rang for Marie-Josette and asked the girl to locate Old Mathieu as rapidly as possible. When he made his way to her room, puffing from the exertions of the long staircase, she gave him her message for Gilles Marsan. Watching him, she observed a note of satisfaction in his expression and called his attention to it.

"If I am not mistaken, you would like to help Monsieur Marsan?"

He chewed one yellowing end of his great white moustache, and nodded a decisive yes.

"Then you must reach Vaudraye before my father and his gamekeeper."

"I know a way, much shorter."

"Do not tell him precisely who sent you. Just warn him."

"Yes, mademoiselle."

As he left, she became convinced more than ever that he was her best ally in her father's household.

She tried to remain calm, but by the time the morning had passed and her mother was dozing after a delicate luncheon suited to an invalid, Veronique was infinitely relieved to have Josette appear, making signs that she had a message which was not for Lise de Gleeb's alert ears.

Although Marie-Josette was clearly upset, she said nothing until they reached the gallery floor. "Old Mathieu rode one of His Excellency's stallions into town. He is back now."

"Thank God for that. Then he succeeded?"

"M'sieur Marsan was at the church with the curé about the burial service. His betrothed said she would give him your message."

"Monsieur Marsan's betrothed?" She hoped the girl did not her the surprise in her voice.

Marie-Josette said, "Mademoiselle Yolande Berthelot, I believe."

Veronique was brusque. "Yes and then?"

"Mathieu was hurt as he prepared to leave the village. Then M'sieur Marsan came out of the church, and found Mathieu. It was M'sieur Marsan who brought him home. They are in the stables now."

"Why did you not tell me sooner, in heaven's name? Marsan must be mad to come here." She turned and went rapidly across the dining salon to the east doors, while the shorter, less agile Marie-Josette followed, trying at the same time to answer her rapid questions.

"How was Mathieu hurt? It was good of monsieur to bring him home but Marsan has walked into a trap! Doesn't he know that?"

The girl shrugged. "He did not say. He said only that Mathieu was mounting to ride home. De Gleeb saw the horse. He recognized it as one of His Excellency's and shot at the rider."

"God of heaven!"

"But there was a tumbril between them, and de Gleeb did not recognize Mathieu. The villagers got in the way, and the old man escaped. M'sieur Marsan found him and brought him here. To the stables."

Of all places for Gilles Marsan to come! She turned her attention to immediate matters. "They need splints, bandages, powders—"

Marie-Josette looked over her shoulder anxiously. "Tregastel, the cook, he is so unfriendly. A Breton and quite radical, you know. But he is helping M'sieur Marsan to bandage the old man."

Veronique knew that the neighboring province of Brittany was a center of sedition, but she had not supposed that her family's food was prepared by a man who might be plotting the destruction of all that the Vicomte de Vaudraye stood for.

As Marsan stood over the wounded Mathieu in the Vaudraye stable he had time to realize fully how dangerous it was for him to return to Vaudraye, but the old man needed to get back and there wasn't any possible way he could have done so alone. Besides, Mathieu had placed himself in danger to warn him that the Vicomte had come to the village looking for the man who'd shot at the Vicomtesse—and apparently suspected him of being that man. Still, despite the Vicomte's enmity toward him, he was most concerned about his gamekeeper . . . so quick to shoot. It appeared that someone wanted blood, and before any explanations could be offered. Nonetheless, he tried to reassure himself that the Vicomte would not press any charges, that he would discover there were no witnesses available or in fact existing to testify to something he obviously didn't do. It seemed crazy that anyone should want to assassinate the Vicomtesse, though, thinking on it, he decided it was prudent to stay clear of this gamekeeper for the while . . .

The two girls reached the stables, and Marie-Josette pointed out the stall where Veronique's cousin, Alexandre de Vaudraye, stabled the black stallion, which was the only horse big and powerful enough to carry the weight of two men any distance.

As Veronique passed the lathered stallion she found two men kneeling over a third in the straw of an empty stall beyond. She knelt between the two men and saw Old Mathieu's eyes staring up at her, watery, without expression but at least he was alive.

"M'sieur rode the stallion back with me."

She tried to strain the anxiety out of her voice. "I did not tell you to play a hero at the Comèdie Française, Mathieu."

"No, mademoiselle."

Seeing her bending over old Mathieu, Marsan acknowledged to himself that it was she he'd most especially come back to see again. He remembered they were mere children when he'd first seen her, but then she was the unapproachable Vaudraye daughter, who only occasionally came to the village. It was years later, after living in Paris as a student, that he had returned to the village to find her a lovely and desirable young woman. In addition he learned that she spent many hours each day nursing the sick and the poor. It was this young woman of noble birth who virtually ran the infirmary at the Hôtel-Dieu. Even the rough-speaking nurses found her determined, skillful with the injured, gentle with the ill and intolerant toward the incompetent and negligent. Gilles thought her a most remarkable young woman. He could also see that the people of the village loved her and, though they were reluctant to approach her, he knew that it was a mark of their respect and gratitude for her service as well as her noble birth. He too didn't find it easy to make an opportunity to speak with the daughter of the Vicomte de Vaudraye. And he hoped often that it would be soon, he never imagined it would be the death of his uncle on her father's estate that would make it possible.

She looked at Gilles Marsan for the first time. His smile

was reassuring, which gave her hope. "He will do well, mademoiselle. The musket ball caught him in the shoulder. We have taken it out."

"Can you take care of him?" She glanced at the swarthy, muscular Breton, who nodded. She felt his dislike—a matter of politics, she assumed—but ignored this and made the obvious suggestion. "Then Monsieur Marsan ought to be on his way at once. Take one of my mounts. The gamekeeper will be here at any minute."

"Just so." The Breton moved away. "I will watch the estate road, monsieur. You must leave through the copse of the Rouen High Road."

Marsan got slowly to his feet. "It seems I'm in your debt again, mademoiselle . . ."

Veronique's own reactions to the sight of him disturbed her. In piecing together her memory of him it seemed strange that she did not recall his height or how attractive his dark eyes were. She concentrated upon Mathieu. When the cook had gone she returned to the danger Marsan faced.

"I trust, monsieur, that no one in the village knows where you have gone. Our gamekeeper is quite capable of making them speak."

His voice held an edge she'd not heard since that first hour of their meeting. "Yes, I know. In Paris I once saw a man publicly spread-eagled, his arms and legs broken by hammers before he was dispatched by a sword. They said he had attempted to kill someone. That was legal too."

Marie-Josette whispered, "You should not say such a thing to mademoiselle. It's not fitting."

Veronique brushed aside the girl's objection. "Since it is true, we should know of it, Josette. I only say, monsieur, that you are in even more danger than you imagine."

"There is no evidence against me. I happen to have been in the village yesterday afternoon an hour after I left this estate."

Old Mathieu laughed drily. Veronique repeated with hope, "The village? You have a witness?" Doubtless that would be his betrothed, the mademoiselle . . .

"The Berthelots were with me."

This would be disastrous as far as her father was concerned. "You cannot expect my father to welcome such witnesses. The first of their Jacobin demands will be to abolish the privileges of men like the Vicomte de Vaudraye."

"But these laws have to be challenged sometime, and since

I am innocent and can prove it, Mathieu's warning seemed providential. This matter perfectly illustrates the injustice in the so-called rights of your grand seigneurs."

"And you mean to see it through? An arrest and trial? You are a fool!" She hoped to shake him with her insulting frankness and make him escape while he could. Instead, he laughed at her.

"Probably, mademoiselle, you would be much appreciated at the Jacobin Society. They admire forceful argument."

Angry that her fears for him were not being heeded, talking here as if they were sitting leisurely in a salon, she tried once again—more bluntly.

"I tell you there is reason to believe that your only safety is in leaving immediately—regardless of your innocence. Now, will you take my cousin Alex's stallion and ride as hard as you can for Rouen?"

He did not immediately reply and when he spoke it was with such peculiar emphasis, she looked up sharply.

"Not quite yet."

When she heard Marie-Josette's gasp she knew what she would see when she turned around. Arnauld de Gleeb's loose-boned, lanky figure cast a shadow across the doorway. His musket was loosely tucked under his arm.

"Ah, there you are, Marsan. Luckily the gatekeeper saw you enter the grounds."

"Your good fortune appears not to be mine," Marsan said. "Mademoiselle, will you call your father? I wouldn't want the gamekeeper to think it necessary to take me out of my misery while caught in his field, at least without witnesses."

Anxiously, Mathieu pinched at Veronique's hand and she said, more brusquely than she felt, "There are witnesses this time, de Gleeb." She signaled to Marie-Josette. "Bring Tregastel. And when you see my father, ask him to come here at once. That should provide witnesses enough."

De Gleeb's grin wavered and his mud-colored eyes looked uneasy. As he began to lower his musket, suggesting action, his fingers nearly shaking with rage, Veronique moved toward him.

It was Marsan who stepped between her and the gamekeeper. "Don't interfere, mademoiselle. He's hoping for a diversion. Don't give it to him."

The gamekeeper laughed. "We need no tricks. We found the weapon you used. Your uncle's musket, with a scored barrel. The scoring mark is on the spent musket ball." Which, Veronique realized, was further reason for de Gleeb or his wife to change the ball she'd found!

"And where did you find my uncle's musket so conveniently?" Marsan asked.

"Mademoiselle talks of witnesses." De Gleeb waved his gun at her. "His Excellency and I and the Vaudraye priest discovered the Guillaume musket in Marsan's lodgings. Wrapped in one of the rogue's fine shirts, a shirt with the frill of one sleeve torn off. We know where he left that torn frill, do we not? The priest holds the evidence for us. Mademoiselle will not deny the word of a priest, surely?"

Veronique glanced at Marsan. He was alert, watching for the slightest move from the gamekeeper. Meanwhile, they could all hear Marie-Josette's voice calling, "Monsieur le Vicomte . . . quickly!"

"Thank God!" Veronique thought. At least de Gleeb would not dare to try any of his tricks under the very eyes of his employer. Moving to the center of the stable she too called her father's name, and in the distance saw his groom and then the Vicomte himself step onto the scattered straw before the estate road entrance to the stables. The Breton cook and Marie-Josette started back into the stable after him.

It was scarcely two or three seconds that Veronique had turned her back on the gamekeeper and Marsan when she heard Mathieu call out, "M'sieur, His gun!" And she heard the explosion of the musket. In the smoking air Veronique watched as Marsan leapt at the gamekeeper and the two men fell together against the wall and then onto the floor, all the while struggling for possession of the musket. Then suddenly Marsan managed to pull the weapon free and in that same motion brought the barrel across de Gleeb's cheek and jaw.

The gamekeeper wavered, clutching his face. Blood trickled between his fingers and he collapsed, groaning, before the shocked eyes of the Vicomte de Vaudraye.

6

MARSAN swung around to face the Vicomte with the musket still in his hands. The Vicomte called angrily to his groom. "Fetch my pistols—"

"No, Papa!" Veronique was frantic that her reckless father would commit murder, or worse that Marsan would attack him. "Mathieu saw it happen. Ask him."

"It's true, Monseigneur," the old man said as Veronique helped him to his feet. "The gamekeeper tried to shoot M'sieur Marsan. This de Gleeb, he did. M'sieur did not move until de Gleeb fired. It is true."

Marsan offered the gun to the Vicomte, who took it while ordering his groom to bring up two of his private guards, the half-dozen ex-soldiers who collected his feudal rents and acted as a unit to police the area. Seeing the commotion at the stable entrance they came running from two directions, while the Vicomte remarked sourly, "Well, daughter, has your seditionist friend added a second murder to his catalogue of crimes?" He used the musket's barrel to examine the writhing body of Arnauld de Gleeb at his feet. "Poor devil, a nasty piece of work. But we've got the right one this time, no mistake."

"Papa, I tell you he did not—" She got no further. Gilles Marsan's stern, quiet warning stopped her.

"Say nothing. It can only be settled by witnesses. He must listen to them," Marsan said.

"I am the magistrate here, young man. Which means I determine what must or must not be done." To the gamekeeper he promised, "You'll have your revenge, my friend. Meanwhile, we had better get you inside where a poultice can be applied to that mouth of yours."

As he tried to conceal his torn mouth with a clenched fist, de Gleeb's eyes showed his fury. "He attacked me . . . I shot . . . self-defence . . ."

Mathieu protested at this but Veronique, after another look at Gilles Marsan, silenced the old man. Marsan believed Mathieu's own safety was at stake—if he drew the Vicomte's ire too stronly, he himself could be sent away, perhaps to an almshouse, assuming he would be taken in.

The guards now stood near de Gleeb, looking rather menacing to Veronique. They had been returning from the fields and did not even wear the Vicomte's livery, but the one who carried a pistol slung from an improvised baldric over one shoulder got the weapon out and pointed it at the gamekeeper still on the ground.

"No, damn you, no!" the Vicomte said, annoyed at this misunderstanding of the situation. "*That* one!"

Confused, the two guards exchanged glances.

"You wish to arrest the—ah—gentleman, Monseigneur?"

"He is not a gentleman! Now, get him along to the château. Lock him in the wine cellar. He tried to assassinate the Vicomtesse last night."

The guard with the pistol nodded and motioned Marsan to go in front of him and followed close after with his weapon poised. The second guard gathered up the lank body of the groaning de Gleeb and carried him into the château through the south portico. Veronique, knowing that passions were still dangerously inflamed, spoke to the watchful Breton cook.

"Tregastel, go with them. Be cautious but see that the guard does not accidently discharge his weapon." Her voice carried to Marsan and his guard.

For the first time the hard-faced Breton seemed to look at her with approval. "Understood, mademoiselle."

Marsan, smiling at his guard's startled expression, saluted Veronique and went on.

The Vicomte crossed the lawn and waited for his daughter to join him on the south portico. When she'd seen Mathieu off in Marie-Josette's care, Veronique hurried after her father, who demanded, "What do you mean by sending my cook to oblige that murderer? Am I now to wait my dinner while Tregastel prepares a fine ragout for the man who shot at your mother?"

She took his arm, which he yielded stiffly, and as if by accident. "Papa, I wouldn't defend anyone who tried to hurt mother. Surely you know that?"

"The good Lord only knows what goes on in your mind. I thought you were more sensible than to be led astray by some troublemaker with a glib tongue."

She said nothing. She was remembering Gilles Marsan's betrothed, the golden-haired Yolande Berthelot. Sensual and seductive . . . something Veronique believed she was not.

Self-consciously Veronique thought about how she must look to someone else—taller than was considered ideal, and certainly not as round as she would have liked to be. . . .

"I begin to think your mother is right. The sooner you learn submission and make you vows, the better it will be for all. Had you been permitted to marry some dandy with a beauty patch, like your Rouen school friends, you would at least have been true to your . . . your class."

"But, Papa, surely showing compassion is not a betrayal of my class?"

"Compassion! De Gleeb will be marked for life."

"I'll go see to him now, but really, Papa, it was entirely his own doing. Monsieur Marsan did not strike him until he had fired. I saw that myself."

"Ridiculous! It's just this kind of foolish talk from you that determines me. The Convent of Ste.-Veronique is where a lady like you belongs. God knows I will miss you, that is, your mother and I will miss you." He patted her hand. "But when you have taken your vows, we will have your Cousin Alex take a house in Paris for us. As your mother and the Sister Superior of that little order are old schoolmates, there should be very pleasant times for all of us. And you will be much too busy with the affairs of our Lord to take notice of assassins like this Marseau . . ."

"Marsan. And, Papa, he is betrothed, and it is wicked of you to talk about my noticing him. As if he were a—a prospective lover, or—"

"Daughter!"

"And besides, he is not an assassin. He has at least two

witnesses, a beautiful young lady and a friend of his from Paris who can prove it."

"Frankly, I had rather meet an assassin than a Jacobin."

There seemed nothing else to be said. Since her father was on his way up to calm and comfort her mother, she left him and went to see what she could do about repairing de Gleeb's injuries. As she neared the apartment assigned to Mme. de Gleeb she brought herself severely to task. She realized that she had been thinking about herself and Gilles Marsan in the most personal of terms, which at least was foolish and perhaps even an occasion of sin. He was betrothed, and the Church recognized a betrothal with almost the solemnity of a marriage. Her presumption made her feel shame and she decided that her penance would be to care for the battered gamekeeper without showing her distaste for him.

Mme. de Gleeb met her in the little antechamber with suspicion and bitterness. Even Veronique's offer to help only provoked a melancholy recital of her husband's injuries.

"And he has borne them with a saintly patience, mademoiselle. Fortunately, the cheekbone was not shattered, but he has lost two teeth and I believe his jaw is broken—" Mme. de Gleeb's voice broke. "He will be scarred, I know it. He was such a handsome man . . . how often I've remarked my good fortune in having been his choice in life—"

"I'm so sorry, madame." She caught a glint of malice through the tears and added hastily, "So sorry he was injured, I mean to say. I have had some experience at tending wounds, and so perhaps I might be of some help."

"My dear mademoiselle, I very much fear your presence now would—pardon me—set back his recovery."

"Then please call for anything, anyone, to help you."

"Naturally, mademoiselle. The Vicomtesse has been good enough to give me carte blanche." The door was closed in Veronique's face.

Undecided as to whether she was annoyed at the woman's candor or simply relieved to be free for the time of de Gleeb's presence, she stood there a moment, then turned and went down to supervise the kitchen staff that was without the direction of the Breton cook. The mid-afternoon dinner preparations had already been delayed, and she knew her father's temper would hardly be improved by further tardiness.

It was too late to carry on the planned meal, an hour's-long preparation of duck with a hint of the strong local apple brandy. But when Veronique reached the kitchen galley she saw that Tregastel had returned and his assistants were flying about under his orders. When he saw her he scowled, as if to question her need to be in his kitchen, but she got up her courage and went to him—despite his fingers, which, mixing pastry for *vol-au-vent*, somehow looked lethal as he raised them.

"How is the prisoner?"

"Well enough, mademoiselle. There is a kind of cell beyond the rear wall of the wine cellar."

"I'm familiar with it," she said. "One of the household went mad a year ago and was placed there until he could be carried away." It was ironic because it had been Tregastel's predecessor, who had threatened his mistress in a fit of rage with a meat-ax. "Is there word about when Gilles Marsan's case will be heard? Did my father send to the village for any of the townspeople? In the past he's often asked them to act as a kind of jury."

"I think not, mademoiselle. Before, the prisoners were merely criminals. It's rumored that Monsieur Marsan is only an artist who creates political sketches. But this may be a far greater crime . . . to the gentlemen who will judge him."

"Monsieur Tregastel, I have not heard that. It would be impossible for you to remain here if I had."

He nodded. "We forget at times that you are one of them, mademoiselle. I will remember."

"It has nothing whatever to do with, as you say, 'being one of them' . . . it is a reflection on my father's fairness that angers me. In any case, what is to happen next?"

Just then the scullery boy looked over at them and Tregastel struck the top of the old deal table sharply. The boy jumped and went off to the stillroom while the kitchenmaid giggled at his haste. After this display of *his* rank, Tregastel replied: "In the morning Monseigneur will hear the case. By that time the gamekeeper should be able to testify."

"But his testimony will be matched by Mathieu. The old man saw it happen this afternoon. He will prove de Gleeb is a liar."

"Old Mathieu may not testify, mademoiselle. He has been given laudanum to help him rest."

"Well, there is still my own testimony about the spent musket ball. That should make my father see the truth of the attack last night."

He looked at her, his voice edged. "The curé saw the musket wrapped in his shirt. The curé, mademoiselle! Was it not remarkable that Mother Church should be witness?"

She knew it was not a question she could answer. She left by the stillroom and went along the path beside the copse until she reached the stone steps that led down to stored vegetables, salt-preserved meats and the modest little corner the Vicomte dignified by the title "Wine Cellar."

One of the Vaudraye guards squatted on a three-cornered stool, drinking from a jug of apple brandy. A storm lantern swung from a hook over her head as Veronique started down the stone steps which were moist and in many places covered with green fungus. The situation had not improved since the floods of the past winter. She could feel the floor of the cellar through her thin-soled shoes. Some of the paving stones were missing, leaving only mud and hard-tamped earth in their place. She walked quickly up to the guard, trying to present a bold appearance, as though she had a right to be there. The guard, however, was too busy hiding the jug in his coat as he stood up to pay much attention to her manner.

"Ah, Jacques, what a wretched way to spend this sunny afternoon. My father wishes to know if all is well here."

"Excellently well, mademoiselle. Chilling, as you see, but then I am to be relieved within the hour."

"My poor friend, your stomach must be in need of a little more heat." The guard grinned sheepishly as he dropped himself onto the stool, pulled out the jug and tipped it to his lips.

"My father has asked me to question the prisoner . . . merely because I knew him in the village . . ."

He waved the jug. "Take care. S'time tomorrow he may hang. . . . Must hang. Sure to. De Gleeb will order—"

She shivered. "How cold it is down here!" She moved behind the guard to the door beside the wine corner. The door had a small window with wooden bars. She stood on her toes and looked in, then started back in surprise. Gilles Marsan had been watching her performance with interest, and their faces were barely separated by the thickness of the bars.

"He will have a large head tomorrow," he said, referring to the guard.

"This is dreadful. Let me get you a bottle to warm you." She found a dusty jug of brandy but as she could not wedge it between the bars, she offered him a bottle of a local country wine. Marsan whispered his thanks and set it on the dirt floor of the cell. The cell itself was a horror to Veronique. Scarcely any light filtered in and the air seemed damp and cold.

"Is there a cot, a matress, anything at all?" she asked, remembering with some embarrassment that this very room at one time was used by her as one of her hiding places. A place for a child's sense of adventure was now transformed into something adult and ugly.

"No, everything seems to have been removed. Frankly I prefer that to the remnants of straw the last inhabitant slept on. I assume he, or she, departed some time ago. Happily, I hope."

"No, I'm afraid not. Monsieur, your witnesses must be here at the château tomorrow morning. My father is in a great hurry to deal with your case."

He rubbed his neck thoughtfully. "In that event, I suspect you were right. This whole business is looking more like entrapment than some misunderstanding."

"Where do the Berthelots stay in the village?" She had decided what must be done.

"At the local inn. On the left as you leave the church." He added gently, "Mademoiselle, no one on the Vaudraye lands can possibly make such a trip. Your father would dismiss them immediately. Your cook told me earlier how the Vicomte regards liberal deputies to the States-General, and Raymond is a deputy. And, besides, Raymond and I quarreled last night . . . about you."

"About me?"

"I told him about how much I admired your work with the poor and sick in the village and he was less than kind about . . . about *your* kindness."

She was thrilled that he had noticed.

"Yes . . . but then . . . surely a messenger must reach your betrothed, Mademoiselle Yolande Berthelot, to tell her what has happened?"

"My what? Yolande Berthelot? Look here . . . it is true her father was very good to me, and Yolande was fond of my aunt, but we are not betrothed."

She forced herself to turn away before he might see the pleasure in her face. "Well, then, I must leave now. There's very little time."

"No. Wait!" He began to understand. "You cannot go. I absolutely forbid it." He reached between the wooden bars. "Please promise me you will not leave the château."

"Very well," she lied, "but you have friends here. Remember that."

"I remember that I have a good angel." His fingers reached out for her. They nearly touched her hair and for a fraction of time she imagined what it would be like to be caressed by him but managed, with effort, to avoid his hand.

The awful thought occurred to her as she went up the steps that if her father failed to believe the Berthelots, she might not see him alive, by noon tomorrow. And thinking it, quickly banished it from her mind.

He said after her, "Goodbye, my good angel."

She called back cheerfully, "What nonsense! Good night . . . until tomorrow."

Marie-Josette was in Veronique's room waiting to dress her for dinner, but Veronique waved aside the pattern book impatiently.

"You and I are going to the village. Hurry—"

"But your papa would never permit it. At this hour . . ."

"Papa is not to know."

The girl was not as shocked as she might have been. She knew her mistress much too well. In a very few minutes the two young women, their faces hidden in their hooded cloaks, had left the château after sending a message to the Vicomte:

> Forgive me, dear Papa, but I cannot be present at dinner, nor yet at supper, I think. There are several crises at the pesthouse of the Hôtel-Dieu in the village. My maid is with me, as you would wish, and we shall sleep the night at some respectable place.
>
> Your loving daughter,
> Veronique

Marie-Josette, who had learned to read with Veronique, scanned the note, then stared at her mistress. "And you are to be a Holy Sister!"

7

THERE were times when Veronique considered it a handicap to have been born a woman. A man would have taken one of her father's horses, perhaps Cousin Alex's stallion, and made the journey in excellent time. In the circumstances she did the next best thing, secretly harnessing her pony to the cart and starting out with as little attention drawn to her departure as possible.

While Marie-Josette sat clutching the car seat and hoping for the best, Veronique made good time over the rich green countryside and the toll-crossings, and ignoring Marie-Josette's constantly expressed fears that every worker seen in the fields was actually a dangerous ruffian waiting to prey on hapless travelers. "That man in the pasture there," she said once about halfway on their journey, "he saw me. He shook a tree limb at me. A highwayman!"

"I don't doubt that he resents our traveling in a cart while he must walk," Veronique assured her, "but he is no highwayman."

The two girls arrived on the hill above the village shortly after sunset. The stream below still glowed and winked in the light as it carried its memories, and the sewage of Paris, toward the gray English Channel far beyond. From here Veronique moved a trifle less confidently into the village.

88

She and Marie-Josette drove through the narrow high road
between half-timbered buildings that cut the light to dusk
in the center of the village. Then, without warning, she drew
rein to avoid running down two women who darted out into
the cobbled road, shrieking with delight. Veronique noted that
they wore feathered bonnets and too much jewelry for peasant
villagers. They were apparently passengers from the Calais-
bound diligence which had pulled up at the local inn to
change the team and offer refreshment for the passengers.

"Oh, mam'selle, those women had been drinking!"

"Very likely."

Two royal troopers quickly followed them with enthusiasm.
Veronique wondered what life might hold for her if she had
decided that love and marriage were more worthwhile than
her own planned future as a Sister of Ste. Veronique, and
even what it would be like to be so confident of one's own
beauty and charm as to charge a fee for one's company.
Shocked at her own thoughts, Veronique jerked the reins,
startling the pony. The creaking little cart, like the frightened
pony, followed the path of least resistance, turning sharply
into the alley behind the inn.

Marie-Josette grasped her mistress's arm.

"This is a bad quarter today. And the faces from the
Calais diligence! Cutpurses and rebels and radicals preaching
sedition. . . . Look there!"

The backs of buildings huddled together like gossiping old
crones, and in their shadow a group of townspeople gathered
around a speaker lecturing them about the panic that gripped
the nation.

"Bankrupt because only the Third Estate, the Bourgeoisie,
pays any taxes! You, my friends. You alone pay . . ."

The mutter of agreement that moved through the attentive
crowd reminded Veronique of the growl of warning from a
watchdog before it leaps. The impassioned young speaker
went on.

"Bankrupt so that a cardinal's diamonds—worth two million livres, mind you!—can deck the body of the Austrian
Bitch!"

Marie-Josette and Veronique exchanged glances. "I never
thought to hear that word spoken in your presence, mam'-
selle—"

"Hush!" Veronique hoped the girl would understand the
danger of calling attention to themselves. This was no place
for the daughter of an aristocrat who held to feudal privilege,

nor for a personal maid who was better dressed than most of the audience that paid the country's bills.

Veronique decided it would be more sensible to keep on this route than to panic, try to turn, and risk attracting atten-toin. Having passed the angry group in the square, the mare picked her way carefully between a laundress's cart waiting for its fresh load and a fishmonger offering his day's catch. On the cobbled street nearest the church a one-legged man stumped along peddling bundles of dried herbs from the country. By the cap he wore Veronique assumed he was formerly a seaman.

Marie-Josette's teeth chattered. "In a Breton village last week a mob hanged the tax collector."

Even in this moment when the two girls shared a common danger Veronique marveled that such news had already reached the Vaudraye servants from an obscure village in another province. Were such stories being spread by paid *agents-provocateurs,* or had sedition actually begun to eat away at the fabric of loyalty between classes? How dreadful, she thought, to be suspicious even for a moment of this trembling young girl beside her, a girl she had known all her life. . . .

"We are not tax collectors," Veronique reminded her firmly. But the girl looked unconvinced.

Before going to the inn to see the Berthelots, and especially Yolande, Veronique studied her gloved fingers and the cloak that covered a gown of soft tabby silk without hoops or padding. The color was called "blush"—a deep unobtrusive pink that flattered her dark hair and her healthy complexion. But she wore no jewels and scarcely looked like a daughter of Normandy's ancient nobility.

She dropped lightly down from the cart, forgetting that Marie-Josette was not in the least agile. A new stableboy who did not know her appeared out of the shadows and assisted the maid down, calling her "mademoiselle," ignoring the more plainly dressed Veronique. It was not the first time Veronique had been mistaken for a ladies' maid, an idea that had always amused her until now. She would not like to be taken by Yolande Berthelot for her own maid. She asked the groom, "Would you please discover if Mademoiselle Berthelot is at home?"

Dismissing Veronique's request for the attention of pretty Marie-Josette, the boy prepared to lead the pony and cart away, "You must ask the landlord. He will speak to mademoiselle's personal maid. That's the proper way of it."

Marie-Josette drew herself up. "I've never met such a booby. That lady happens to be——" Behind the stableboy's back Veronique gestured to Josette not to make an issue of it. Deflated, she ended on a plaintive note . . . "that is to say—won't you please help us?"

Properly appealed to, the young stableboy dropped the reins which Veronique picked up just as a young woman, probably Mlle. Berthelot's maid, peeked out through the rear door below the heavy, half-timbered upper part of the house.

"Mlle. Berthelot is not at home to visitors."

This flat, unequivocal announcement angered Veronique, who wanted to waste no more time, particularly in the fripperies and fine manners of her ancestors. She also forgot her own cautious desire not to have her identity known.

"I wish to see mademoiselle. Instantly!"

Her voice came so harsh and sharp, she startled them all. It was the maid who quickly recovered and led them through the old inn and up the staircase to the private parlor occupied by Mlle. Berthelot.

Veronique had become impatient and worried, feeling too much time had been wasted. Up on the first floor she and Marie-Josette were led into a parlor that Veronique thought was rather oddly shaped, rectangular, in fact. And she also noted that the hearth was not centered along one of the walls but was placed near the windowed end of the room. This, she knew, would mean that much of the heat in the winter would be lost. She could only assume that the room had been converted at one time to account for this strange arrangement. It was a long room but not really large and the pieces of furniture were uniformly dark and heavy appearing, not her idea of an attractive parlor. Not, she suspected, that these temporary accommodations represented mademoiselle's taste; on the contrary, its decor revealed a man's hand. But this room did prompt Veronique to speculate as to the kind of other tastes a man such as Marsan might prefer, particularly in a woman. Her father, the only man she knew well, required constant sympathy, along with a reassuring general praise, for virtually everything he said or did, from his wife. Fortunately for him, her mother's singular virtue was the wish only to please her husband. She wondered what kind of relationship existed between Yolande Berthelot and Gilles Marsan despite his denial. Did he too prefer a wife who depended upon him in every respect, who would find him the sun and moon of her world? . . . She wasn't sure what her feelings would be if she were that wife. . . . The question intrigued her, even though she was certain she would never have its answer.

"How very cozy it is," Marie-Josette said as she rustled toward the crackling fire in the hearth, then remembered herself and turned apologetically. "Shall I take your cloak, mam'selle? I know you are not comfortable in such warm, tight rooms."

"No, go to the fire. You're still trembling. I'm sorry to have put you through all this trouble. I had no notion. The village seems possessed." She turned back her hood, became conscious that her hair hung lank and disheveled and gave it a quick, nervous brushing with her palm. She caught a glimpse of herself in the small, half-silvered mirror set in the armoire. Though her recent street adventures had given her a glow of excitement that flattered her features, she still felt self-conscious facing the beautiful Mlle. Berthelot. She removed her riding gloves and began to massage her cramped fingers.

Marie-Josette had been warming her hands at the fire and biting her lips to restore their color when she suddenly sank to her knees in a billow of skirts.

Startled, Veronique reached out to steady her, then realized that Marie-Josette was curtsying to the golden-haired Yolande, who had entered the room behind her, accompanied by her maid. She moved gracefully across the threadbare carpet, dipped into a slight curtsy in Veronique's direction, then took the hand Veronique belatedly extended. Veronique thought her stunning. She also, never mind Gilles Marsan's denial of betrothal, felt jealousy such as she'd never known or imagined.

"How nice to meet you again, mademoiselle!" Yolande greeted her warmly. Her fine features were made all the more so by the remarkable way in which the blue of her eyes was set off by her rich, flowered taffetas and dainty silk shoes. Confronted by her obvious elegance, Veronique felt like a chimneysweep.

"I would not have intruded at this awkward hour, mademoiselle, but for Monsieur Marsan's serious danger. If you will forgive me, I need your help—"

"Yes, certainly. But please, you must be very tired. Do sit down. Here, on this sofa beside me. Leonie, will you see to mademoiselle's companion? Some ratafia, perhaps? Or—some of my brother's brandy? A local product, and very strong, I'm afraid. But we'll have a sip. In the circumstances, I think it might make things easier for us all, and you and your maid do look spent."

The maid Leonie returned quickly with the brandy. On the badly worn and bristly brocaded sofa Yolande Berthelot gazed at Veronique over the gold lip of a miniature ruby cordial glass. She appeared sensible and calm, two qualities which tended to disarm Veronique, except for her jealousy.

"Now then," she said, "you must tell me how I am to help you. You know, of course, that Gilles's aunt died yesterday."

"My father and I were very sorry. It was a dreadful thing. But this afternoon my father witnessed what he believed to be an attack on our gamekeeper. And it came fresh on what my father also believes was an attempt by Monsieur Marsan to assassinate my mother late yesterday afternoon—"

Yolande Berthelot caught her breath.

"The man must be mad . . . I beg your pardon, mademoiselle. It was inexcusably rude to insult the Vicomte, but such an accusation!"

"Gilles Marsan was here in the village at sunset yesterday, was he not?"

Yolande sipped from her cordial glass. "Yes, indeed!" She punctuated by waving her glass. "He returned from Vaudraye House in mid-afternoon. Then he and my brother had a long discussion. Their political society, you know. The meeting lasted well into the evening."

Veronique felt relieved.

"But your word, your appearance, would satisfy my father. And you would be far more convincing than a dozen members of the Jacobin Club. My father detests them—"

Yolande Berthelot appeared somewhat affronted by that but seemed equally aware that her presence at Vaudraye was needed. "Naturally I couldn't make such a decision alone. I will discuss it with my brother. He should be here shortly. He is very devoted to Gilles politically, or at all events he was. I believe they had a few words last night. As you may know, they once attended the Lycée in Paris together. Gilles paid his way with some clever political sketches. My brother was very methodical. Gilles was the original of the two, a romantic, I'd say. I am afraid some of the masters didn't approve."

"Nor does my father."

They heard footsteps at the double doors behind them and

Yolande said happily, "That will be Raymond, my brother."

Veronique looked up and saw the gaunt young man who had shown his dislike of her at their previous meeting. To judge by his gloomy, stern expression this second encounter with him was going to fare no better than the first.

"Mademoiselle de Vaudraye, I believe you know my brother Raymond?"

He barely inclined his head.

"Raymond, are you aware of this young lady's identity?" Yolande was miffed at his seeming casualness toward Veronique.

"I am indeed. But are you really, my dear sister? In addition to being the daughter of the Vicomte de Vaudraye, I believe she may soon become the betrothed of our friend Gilles Marsan."

Yolande turned to face Veronique. "But . . . but how delightful." And then dropped the cordial glass she was holding.

In the moment's confusion of getting the maid in to clear away the broken glass everyone seemed to take the opportunity to collect themselves. As Veronique was about to break the silence Yolande smiled at her . . . warmly.

"I had not wished you well in your marriage, mademoiselle. I had no notion you and Gilles were so well acquainted—"

Veronique shook her head. "Nothing could be further from the truth. I have really only just met M'sieur Marsan. And besides, the idea of marriage is simply out of the question—"

Yolande said softly, "You must not think you owe me an explanation." Her voice was soft but something in her gaze suggested to Veronique that she was carefully taking the measure of her.

"But mademoiselle," Raymond broke in, "on the contrary, Gilles told me he had been observing you for years whenever you came into the village, admiring you from a proper distance, I believe was the way he put it."

"I don't see, m'sieur, how that could be possible. In any event Gilles Marsan's sole interest in me was . . . is . . . political. He only wanted to convert me to his egalitarian ideas—"

Raymond said stiffly, "Believe me, I was quite aware last night what kind of impression you had made upon this man I introduced into my house as a good and loyal friend of the people. He could talk of nothing but you, an aristocrat. One would think he was considering an exchange of his so-called convictions for your affections."

"Raymond, you forget," Yolande quickly put in, "mademoiselle is our guest. Besides, she has just been telling me that Marsan is in serious trouble. It seems the Vicomte believes Gilles attempted to assassinate the Vicomtesse yesterday and is holding him right now—"

Raymond reacted in surprise. "Why would anybody imagine Gilles would want to do such a thing?"

"But he did *not*." Veronique's voice nearly broke, and Raymond looked at her as if to say he now knew something about her true feelings that she may not have wanted to reveal. "It is all a terrible mistake, but the only witness my father will listen to at his trial tomorrow morning is the man I believe may have committed the crime. Now do you see how very important it is that you tell my father where Gilles Marsan was late yesterday afternoon?"

Raymond paused for a moment and looked away. "Yes, I see how important it is, mademoiselle, for you and for Gilles. But how important is it to *us*? Your father would not believe me for a moment. In fact, my appearance there might only aggravate the situation for Gilles. And it is always possible the Vicomte may find some imagined offense I have committed and hang me as well."

When Veronique heard him say "hang" she felt as if she had been struck, and it both frightened and angered her. Did Raymond really misunderstand what was at stake?

"Isn't it possible for you to persuade your father that Gilles is innocent? Surely he would believe you, his daughter, before this other man," Yolande said.

"No, I'm afraid not. My father is an honest man, and he is just. But, perhaps like M'sieur Berthelot here, he tends to believe not only what he sees but what he thinks he has seen. In Gilles Marsan my father sees a wildly criminal Jacobin who has first threatened his family by implications and then actually attempted murder. In my father's frame of mind my opinion now means little. Only the most bonafide testimony that Gilles Marsan could not possibly have been at the house when the crime took place will dissuade him."

"Bravo, mademoiselle." Raymond applauded. "Such impassioned eloquence will surely rescue Marsan, even from the likes of your father."

"Raymond, please. This is a grave matter and your sarcasm is not welcome." Yolande seemed genuinely angry. "Mademoiselle, we will do whatever we can to help you."

Raymond looked directly at Veronique. "Gilles Marsan's role in the revolution as a martyr in the provinces may ironically serve his sense of theater, but it would be a foolish waste of his talent as a propagandist. And so, to avoid being foolish and impractical we cannot expose M'sieur Marsan to a fate he apparently so craves."

Veronique still felt ambivalent about Raymond's support. She had never heard anyone speak with such cynicism before. But she was confident of Mademoiselle Yolande's sincerity, and this somewhat comforted her. And the fact that her father always enjoyed the attentions of pretty ladies caused her to hope that he would at least listen to Yolande.

8

"BUT, mam'selle, it is so far back to Vaudraye. And so very dark!" Marie-Josette protested anxiously as Veronique climbed back into the cart.

"Yes, Marie, it is always dark at night and it is always the same distance back to the house."

They made their way through the village. Few people were abroad. As it was a moonlight night there were no lanterns lighted before the houses, although such a frugal system was being replaced in Paris by the requirement that there should be some illumination, no matter what the state of the moon. But then, thought Veronique, Paris streets were notoriously unsafe at night.

Since her companion kept peering at the dark landscape and pointing out sinister shadows, Veronique tried to turn her thoughts to a potentially more realistic danger. She wondered if perhaps she'd been too charitable toward Raymond Berthelot in thinking that, despite his cynicism, his intentions were decent. It was conceivable he only wished to humor her and that he genuinely believed his new world at the moment needed a martyr more than justice.

". . . Oh, how awful if that were true . . . "

Her voice startled Marie-Josette, who already was a frayed bundles of nerves.

"Mam'selle?"

After reassuring her that nothing was wrong, Veronique continued to speculate about how her father would view any witnesses at all. If Raymond did come out tomorrow the Vicomte could say he was lying just to protect his revolutionary friend. And Yolande might be dismissed because her father truly believed that no woman could possibly offer reliable testimony when under the influence of a determined man. And Raymond Berthelot, her brother, was certain that . . .

"Josette, did you hear everything Raymond Bertholet said tonight?"

"Oh, no, mam'selle. . . . I wouldn't dream of eavesdropping—"

"I'm not accusing you of eavesdropping, but you cannot have missed his conversation about—well—about what Monsieur Marsan talked of last night."

"Of you."

"Very well. Now think, Josette. If Berthelot talked with him last evening, it proves Monsieur Marsan was in the village at the hour when he is accused of shooting at my mother."

"Unless," the girl suggested, "unless he shot madame and then rode to the village—"

"Josette!"

"I mean to say—but we do not know for a certainty what time he—arrived in the village . . ."

"Mother of God, give me patience. This Berthelot said Monsieur Marsan came at sunset. That would be late afternoon." Had he actually said Gilles arrived before sunset? Fortunately, this might not occur to Josette. "Then he and Berthelot had a long meeting. Isn't it so? *Isn't it?*

"Yes, mam'selle. Indeed, yes. Whatever you say."

"Very well, then. *Remember* that."

Watching the girl, Veronique found herself softening. She put out her free hand and patted the girl's shoulder. "Don't cry, for heaven's sake! You have been very brave and helpful and I'm grateful to you." She added without the least compunction at her lie, "I am persuaded no one in the household could have helped me as you have today."

This seemed to restore Marie-Josette's pride. It also restored her to a sense of her grievances and she sat in a silent huff while Veronique maneuvered the way out onto the high road.

Veronique, who was not naturally silent, made several remarks about the road, the time it would take to reach home, and whether it would be possible to enter the château without being discovered. But to all of Veronique's talk now her companion sat only regarding the dark, tree-shaded road.

For the first time Veronique thought about why she was out here on this road after sunset with only her maid in an attempt to help someone she'd known for only two days. Everything had developed so quickly that she found herself in the situation without giving it the kind of thought she normally would have. But then there was nothing very normal about this entire affair. As usual, someone was in trouble and needed her help, but on this occasion he happened to be a young man, charming and handsome; and to her delight she learned that he'd been thinking of her for years without her even being aware of it. It would have been wonderfully romantic to think about a pair of lovers meeting this way if only his life were not in such jeopardy and her own father threatening to end it. It was almost absurd to her that this whole matter had grown completely out of hand before anyone, certainly herself, could see its consequences. Young men were not supposed to appear in her life the way Gilles Marsan had and then in only a matter of a day be drawn, as if lured, into a deadly cul-de-sac.

They were well beyond the environs of the village when Marie-Josette, staring out at a heavily wooded pasture, fancied she saw something moving.

"Cows," said Veronique, giving the pasture a brief glance. She signaled over the lines to the patient pony.

"Then why are we hurrying?"

"Because I want to reach home. Aren't you hungry?"

Marie-Josette studied the moving shadows. "I was. But I am not now. Mam'selle, I think those are men. I heard Tregastel say many are starving because of the bad crops and the hard times. They wander the fields and forage like wolves. They attack people on the roads too. They are very dangerous."

Since this was all too true and had been the first thought that occurred to Veronique, she flicked the reins and the tired pony broke into a brisk trot.

Marie-Josette murmured, "Nothing is the way it was. People are so different. So little respect. That horrid M'sieur Berthelot . . . the way he spoke of the Vicomte, what is the world coming to—"

"I often wonder. You had best sit straight. You don't want

them to notice you." Marie-Josette quickly took her advice.

After a few moments Marie-Josette said, "Those cows you spoke of, mam'selle, they seem to be moving toward the road in a group."

Veronique detested admitting to physical fear. Very early in her life the Vicomte had sternly taught her to face any adversary. In those days it meant exchanging mudballs in wars with the peasant children or, on one noteworthy occasion, coming to blows and hairpulling with a village girl twice her size. But she could not conceal a tremor now at the idea of falling into the hands of hungry, angry men with every reason for hating her class.

The pony and cart clattered across a small bridge over a swollen stream and soon passed an orchard still standing in mud whose fruit, if it bore fruit at all, would come too late to be of any use to anyone. At the same time every tree cast a shadow in which an assassin might wait.

In spite of Veronique's order, her maid peered into the moonlit road behind. "A man is in the road now. No. Two more have come out of that pasture. They are pointing at us. One of them is waving a stick."

"Well, they can't catch us while we're riding and they must walk—"

"Are we—oh, please, Mother of God, are we nearly there?"

The girl might be praying, but Veronique saw that she was the only one who probably could answer the girl's prayer now. "Almost," she said, hoping she sounded calmer than she felt.

. . . Why in heaven's name didn't I borrow a pistol? . . . not that I would have used it but the sight of a pistol can be more persuasive than prayer at times like these. . . .

She felt particularly guilty about having involved Marie-Josette in this dangerous journey. Her gloved fingers curled about the reins as though she already had an enemy in her grip. Ahead the road narrowed as it curved around the foremost in a line of populars, and she was obliged to slow the pony just as the animal galloped along at a fine pace, with the cart rattling and bumping behind it.

As the pony proceeded around the tall lean poplar, a man suddenly leaped onto the seat, falling across Veronique's knees, groping for a handhold by clutching at Marie-Josette beyond her. Both girls screamed, and Veronique was knocked breathless. The man struggled to his feet and while Veronique was recovering her breath the cart came to a halt. Veronique

kicked him across his stockinged shinbone and at the same
time threw all her weight into a hard push at the small of his
back. He tottered and fell against Marie-Josette's feet.

"Push him over. Over!" Veronique shouted. The girl shrank
away, shuddering, hysterical. He then caught at the side of
the cart and lunged back at Veronique, who meanwhile had
tried to grasp the drifting reins. His huge fingers caught her
wrist in a crushing grip. Through her pain she saw a bearded
face loom over hers. His speech showered her with fumes of
sour wine.

"The pretty aristo has courage. *Brava!* Now, let's see. How
much gold do you carry, *ma belle?*"

He thrust his bent knee against her body, pinning her
down, and tore at her skirts. "The pocket with the gold louis.
Where is it? You fine aristocratic women always carry for-
tunes in those pockets—"

The pain began to subside but she could not move.

"In the étui case . . . my waist."

He found the velvet case and tore it off the ribbon that
held it to slender sash at her waistline. Summoning up all her
remaining strength she thrust at him again as one of his
hands released her briefly while he tried to examine the contents of the velvet case. At the same time Marie-Josette
started to scream. . . .

Jeannot Dumas was a young man who dreamed of his
future but without the conviction that it was anything more
than that . . . a dream. His mother ran a *mercerie* in the
village but it provided only a meager living, and so he had
to find work as a dray man or a field hand. His one ambition,
that he shared with no one, was to have a restaurant of his
own and not in the village of Vaudraye or in a nearby town,
but in Paris itself, a place he had never even seen. His politics
were no more complicated than the belief that a man had his
duties and responsibilities and was required by life to discharge
them honestly as best he could. This did not mean that he
found all of these political young men, Jacobins as they
called themselves, unlikable. On the contrary, over the years
he'd seen Gilles Marsan come back to visit his aunt and
uncle and thought him to be sensible and decent. But the
person he held in the highest regard was a member of the
aristocracy—a young girl he'd come especially to respect and
admire for her work at the Hôtel-Dieu. And he was not alone.

Most of the people of the village of Vaudraye saw her as their "good angel." . . .

This evening he and five others were returning from a neighboring town where they'd gone in search of work. Suddenly he thought he heard a commotion somewhere up ahead. Pausing for a moment, he heard a woman's scream and with the others began to run in its direction. . . .

Struggling, Veronique did not understand what was happening around the cart until her assailant, surprisingly, yielded and seemed to tumble backward out of the cart. When she recovered herself she found a half-dozen faces staring into the cart. They were brutish-looking in the moonlight and badly mudstained. But the toothy grin of one of them was familiar. Marie-Josette clapped her hands and called out joyfully as Veronique attempted to regain her composure.

"They are from the village, mam'selle. You remember Jeannot, whose mother has the mercer's shop? And Joseph Faure, who worked in the hospital last winter."

Still shaken, Veronique was only partially aware that Josette was actually introducing these mud-covered faces to her. As she collected her wits, she realized that she owed her thanks, perhaps her life, to these men.

"I saw you this afternoon, mam'selle," Jeannot said. "I waved but you didn't see me. We assumed you wouldn't be returning until tomorrow. We decided to ask you if you would speak to His Excellency and see if we could have a little work. There was none to be found in Rouen. But we will do anything. It's only until the harvests . . ."

"I promise you, Jeannot, I will see that there is work for all of you. But meanwhile—" She leaned forward, looked at the hulking body of the bandit on the ground behind her rescuers, apparently knocked unconscious by his fall when Jeannot and Joseph dragged him out of the cart—"he has my purse. Will you divide its contents among you, with my deep gratitude?"

They began to thank her while forcing the case out of the bandit's fingers. "And tomorrow afternoon, come to our home. We will see that you have work—all of you."

They had the case open now and were dividing its contents with great attention to equal shares. There were four of them, faces she vaguely knew as decent, hard-working peasants of the region, men who deserved better than their long, fruitless trek to Rouen merely in the hope of finding eighteen hours' work a day.

She pointed to the unconscious man. "What will be done with that fellow?"

"We best leave him, mam'selle. He seems to be dead." At her sharp breath, he assured her, "They have his description posted in Rouen. He attacked an English Milord and his bride two nights ago. The young lady was"—he avoided her eyes—"was murdered."

Marie-Josette covered her mouth.

"Scream if you like, Josette," Veronique said. "Your screams probably saved our lives." She considered the carriage seat, studied the tired, grubby faces of the men. "Is it possible one of you would be good enough to accompany us, messieurs? We would be most grateful for an escort."

The tired faces brightened. The men looked at each other. "Who is to ride?" It was easy to see how much each wanted to be chosen, and to reach home without that long, all-night march the others must make. Joseph Faure had the only fair solution. "We shall draw lots for it."

One of the men tore off several twigs from a nearby tree. "Mam'selle will hold them?"

She did, wishing profoundly that the little cart had been large enough to take them all. Each man carefully rubbed the palm of his hand on his breeches before drawing the rough, prickly wood from her hand. Jeannot won. He tried not to show his pleasure at his good luck, promising to carry messages from the others to their families in the village at Vaudraye.

Veronique called to them, "Tomorrow afternoon at Vaudraye . . . and again, my thanks, messieurs."

The cart rolled away toward Vaudraye, with Jeannot taking the reins, while Veronique and Marie-Josette crowded together to give him as much room as possible. While Marie-Josette, who clearly found him attractive, told Jeannot about the next day's trial of Gilles Marsan and the Vicomte's accusations, Veronique thought of those three tired men left in the road behind them, obliged to continue to walk the remainder of the way home. It struck her as ironic that she now was in their debt for much the same reason her father was indebted to Arnauld de Gleeb. Her father's remarks about loyalty that previous evening now carried a special weight.

"Mademoiselle?" Jeannot spoke, breaking into Veronique's thoughts. "I only wish that I could be of some help to you

and M'sieur Marsan. It seems a terrible thing that's about
to happen."

"Jeannot, you've already done quite enough. But yes,
M'sieur Marsan is in a terrible situation and I don't quite
know what else can be done to help him."

"I don't wish to seem impertinent, but the gamekeeper is
a much disliked man, and it is known in the village that the
Vicomte strangely trusts this man, who most of us feel
doesn't deserve it. If he accepts his word tomorrow, M'sieur
Marsan has no hope whatever."

Marie-Josette nudged Jeannot and gave him a look to
silence him, and for a moment all that was heard was the
creaking lurch of the pony cart. Finally, Jeannot said, "I
think that someone should at least be there tomorrow to say
that de Gleeb's word is not believed by many, that he's a
man who can be trusted only to plot against others. He's
cunning like a weasel who leaves more than one trail to
follow."

"That's all well and good, Jeannot, but you must be careful. My father is not partial to those who speak against his
gamekeeper, including myself."

"I understand, mademoiselle, but your father is known
as a decent man. Maybe he knows that in times of trouble,
as the proverb goes, a man should keep his friends close . . .
and his enemies closer. Perhaps he knows de Gleeb as we
do, but doesn't say so."

Sounding weary and not convinced, Veronique said, "Perhaps, but my father also believes that Gilles Marsan is his
enemy."

9

BY the time Veronique reached her bedchamber at the château that night her naturally sanquine temperament had nearly conquered her fears about Gilles Marsan's trial, which would take place the next morning.

Marie-Josette's thoughts were elsewhere too as she helped Veronique wash away the stains of travel in the portable bath. "Jeannot said it makes no mind how many shirts were found with guns wrapped in them," she said. "He can't believe that anyone should believe M'sieur Marsan shot the Vicomtesse. Anyway, he said his mother sells shirts much like the one found in Marsan's quarters to many gentlemen who do not have theirs made by their ladies. The shirt could belong to anyone who wanted it there, Jeannot said."

"All this may be true but it doesn't help Marsan one measure if it fails to persuade the Vicomte of his innocence."

When the girl had gone Veronique snuffed her bed candle and lay there in the dark, thinking of the man in that ghastly cellar far below her room, wondering how he would sleep, or if he would sleep at all.

By the time she got to sleep she had decided what could be her only strategy at the trial. Along with Mathieu's testimony about the so-called attack on de Gleeb, she could tell her father what had happened in the village—whether he would believe her was another matter. He might well dismiss what she had to say as mere "feminine chatter." And of course Josette's testimony would not be seriously considered. No, she would simply *force* him to believe her. . . .

Finally she slept, her dreams filled with Gilles Marsan. When she awoke on the April morning that was overcast and threatening more rain, she asked herself for the first time in her life what the future would hold for her if she refused to take her vows. . . . Her mother's life would be shattered and for that her father would never forgive her. But must she give her entire life to oblige her mother? . . .

By the time she'd quickly breakfasted and was being dressed for the trial, she was able to confess more of the truth to herself. It was not entirely her mother's dream that she live the rest of her life at Sœur Veronique du Calvaire. Veronique knew it was the only possible way she could continue to work in the hospitals, countering in a small measure the drunken incompetence of the female help who were not nursing sisters. Even the local Hôtel-Dieu only permitted her to work there because it was known that very soon she would be delivered to the Convent of Ste. Veronique of the Holy Cloth as a novitiate.

As for the Berthelots' assumptions, her common sense told her that they were unfounded. Men like Gilles Marsan did not fall in love with girls they referred to as their "good angels." Gratitude had very little to do with physical love. Marsan's original praise of her at the Berthelots' house could be no more than his expression of his admiration for her work at the hospital and her chosen future.

Nevertheless, this was of no importance considered along with his immediate fate. Marie-Josette had not made her usual appearance in Veronique's room the next morning, which seemed ominous. By the time Veronique was called to her father's presence in the ante-chamber of her mother's suite, she found herself so cold with apprehension that she had to force herself to smile and greet him respectfully.

As for the Vicomte, he gruffly stopped her in the middle of her curtsy. "I know about your little journey yesterday, and the reason you were not present to take dinner with me or supper with your poor mama."

"Monseigneur, justice and a fair trial have always been as important to you as to—"

"What is this about a fair trial? What I am referring to

is your behavior, which brought discredit to your good name and your reputation."

"But, Father, I was very proper. I took my maid and—"

"You call that half-witted girl a proper chaperone? The girl cringes at everything. When I merely asked her a few questions this morning she nearly fainted."

How very inventive of her! thought Veronique. "I am not surprised, father, if you shouted at her as you are shouting at me. Take care, you may have a second fainting on your hands."

That seemed to put him in a better humor. "What? You? Not likely. You have more courage than some men I know. But damn it! You might have been raped and murdered last night. Do you realize that?"

The Vicomtesse's maid, Edwige, overhearing this, made a choking sound and her father swore, waving a fist before her startled eyes, and said, "Woman, if you utter a word of this to your mistress I'll have your head—"

The poor woman bobbed with several curtsies and finally got out the message, "Her ladyship wished me to say she will see you now, Monseigneur. And mademoiselle, if no voices are raised. Her ladyship is just recovering from a migraine."

Veronique generally viewed her mother's swoons as little more than a melodramatic appeal for attention, but was pleased at the Vicomtesse's apparent good spirits. Soon, though, her thoughts moved to Gilles Marsan, and she wondered just how his spirits fared this morning. It distressed her to think of him waiting down in that prison cell while she and her parents made small talk in this pristine white bed-room-salon.

"Dear child"—the Vicomtesse delicately brushed her cheek against her daughter's—"my good de Gleeb tells me we shall soon have this dreadful business settled and the fanatic put out of his misery. Then I at least may see more of my naughty girl. You have been neglecting me lately, you were missed last night. De Gleeb was torn between her poor husband's injuries and my own. But bless her, she knew where her duty lay. Upon summons, she came directly to me . . ."

"Mother," Veronique began, unable to endure these misconceptions any longer, "that awful man was injured because he tried to shoot down an unarmed—"

Her father shook his finger at her, but this proved unnecessary at the Vicomtesse broke in.

"I know, dear, I know. Lise de Gleeb has explained it to me most carefully. The creature belongs to some horrid political club with a religious name. Sacrilegious, I call it. And they go about the country trying to kill people. Though why they should choose me for their victim, I really cannot think. Dear Claude!" She raised her injured arm. "I do feel that this is not too severe a price to pay, if at least the madman has been taken—"

"Well, well, my love, he shall pay," the Vicomte assured her. "Have no fear of that. And now, I have work that requires my presence." He kissed her on the brow. "Veronique, I trust you will stay and bear your mother company."

Knowing perfectly well that Madame de Gleeb would be present at the trial and that she was the last person her father wanted to see there, Veronique suggested with deliberate malice, "Madame de Gleeb is always happy to bear mama company in my place."

Annoyed that she had seen through his attempt to keep her away from the trial, the Vicomte spoke sharply. "She will be required elsewhere," and left the room.

Veronique decided she must get Mathieu at once or Marsan would have no defense at all. But first she had to soothe her mother's nerves, which began to flutter when the Vicomte left. When Veronique suggested that Edwige should read her to sleep, the Vicomtesse murmured, "But Edwige's voice is so tiresome. However"—she touched Veronique's flexing fingers lightly—"I must learn to go on without my little girl. Sister Marie-Jacques of the Hôtel-Dieu in the village was here for a pleasant chat yesterday afternoon. Sister Thérèse—her brother is that dashing Abbé de St.-Helier—has been in Brittany organizing the Hôpital du Calvaire, and when she returns to Paris in August she tells Sister Marie-Jacques she will need my little girl—"

"Yes, Mama. I must go now." She started to say she would be back soon, but didn't. The notion of her mother lying there in her bed as if she might never want to get up and talking about the vicarious life that was to be lived through her daughter threatened to suffocate Veronique. She left the suite with decorum, but when she reached the hall and staircase, rushed down to the gallery. Hearing footsteps on the ground floor, she stopped and watched from the balustrade above.

Two of the Vicomte's guards, crowded into their seldom-used livery, were escorting their prisoner to the ballroom at the far end of the château. Because the empty ballroom could accommodate many of the village citizens on benches, it was always used for the local trials. Veronique leaned over the balustrade and saw that Gilles Marsan's wrists were manacled behind him. His dark hair was clubbed somewhat carelessly at the nape of his neck as if it had been done in a hurry. The sight of him made her sick with worry.

One of the guards made a remark and he smiled grimly. Peering farther over, she studied him until he was gone from her sight. He'd managed to clean the mud off his boots but there were dried mudstains on his breeches and coat, and his white cravat was missing. . . . Strange—wonderful—the more imperfections she could find about his appearance, the more tenderly she felt toward him.

And yet he was a stranger. Without knowing—intending?— he'd come between her and the vows she must take. She wondered if what she felt for him now could ever be matched by the life that had been planned for her.

As she went down the stairs and off to the kitchen quarters to find Mathieu she tried to remind herself that her personal feelings were irrelevant. There she found a sullen, silent group of men who carefully watched her as she walked up to Tregastel. The cook was as usual busy with the dinner preparations. His heavy brows raised slightly at sight of her. While she spoke to him she noted that the silent group was made up of peasants from the fields. The household servants did not seem to be involved.

"Maître," she said to Tregastel, "I must see Mathieu at once. They are beginning the trial."

Someone in the group at the other end of the kitchen started to speak, sounding indignant. She looked around.

"Is he ill?—he is not *dead?*"

Tregastel slapped the great carp on his deal table. "Not so, mademoiselle. But it would seem he is too ill to make any use of his knowledge. Not in the judicial chambers of a grand seigneur, at all events."

"I am here to see that he does appear in our judicial chambers—in this case, the ballroom. Where may I find him?"

He continued boning the huge fish before him with a skill she might have admired at another time. Having finished, he waved the knife to his right. "He was placed in the little room behind the hearth."

She thanked him and went out of the kitchen, keenly aware

that once she had gone the Vaudraye family would again be discussed and perhaps condemned by those men, some of whom she was sure had never worked for the Vaudrayes.

She rapped lightly on the door beyond the kitchen. It was a minute or two before the door opened. One of the kitchen maids peered out at her.

"Oh . . . mam'selle . . . I thought you were that woman . . ." She stepped aside and Veronique made her way into the tiny room. The old man lay on a cot against the wall, which apparently backed on the kitchen hearth. He groaned and muttered but was clearly asleep.

"Is he all right?" Veronique asked anxiously, clearing her throat to awaken the old man. He didn't stir. She asked the girl, "His wound? Is it healing?"

"The wound does very well. It is the medicine."

"What medicine?"

"Madame de Gleeb gave him spoonfuls of laudanum. Last night and this morning. For him to recover while he slept, she said."

That woman, indeed! "Yes, It *would* be the charitable madame who thought of Mathieu's suffering." She shook the wounded man slightly, but any pressure caused him to groan even in his drug-induced sleep, and she finally gave up. "Is he likely to regain consciousness within the hour or a little longer?"

"He did not last night, mam'selle. I don't think so this time either."

Wondering what further disaster could happen to Marsan's cause, Veronique asked, "What about Tregastel?"

"He promised M'sieur Marsan he would send to the village for witnesses who saw M'sieur Marsan at sunset yesterday. They were to come and speak for M'sieur Marsan."

"Well?"

"But he lied."

"What?"

"Tregastel lied to M'sieur. He doesn't want the gentleman freed. He wants him hanged."

"You are mad!" Veronique got out the words more in amazement than shock. The girl must certainly have mis-understood the Breton cook.

"No, mam'selle. It's because when they hang an innocent man like M'sieur Marsan, it will mean an uprising in Normandy. That is what M'sier Berthelot told Tregastel, or at least so we heard. Just like the uprisings in Brittany. It's a great help to them when an innocent man is condemned and dies—"

"Mother of heaven!" She closed her eyes as nausea nearly overcame her. She suspected it was this same reason that kept Raymond Berthelot from testifying to Marsan's inocence, despite his denial. She bent over the wounded man and shook him again, in spite of the girl's . . . "take care, mam'selle, he's wounded . . ."

Because he was now her last hope, she called to him sharply, but it was clear that Lise de Gleeb had done her work efficiently.

She left the small room and went the length of the hall to white door with gold moulding that opened on one side of the ballroom. Because he was constantly in her thoughts, she saw Gilles Marsan first at the far end of the long empty salon. He stood between his two guards on one side of her father's wide mahogany desk that had been removed to this salon from the Vicomte's bookroom. The Vicomte presided at the desk on a raised platform whose normal occupants —a harpsichord, violin and tambour—had been pushed into a far corner.

It was all very unlike the crowded room full of witnesses invited to attend the usual examination. Today, present as witnesses, were only the frail young curé of the Vaudraye Church, Father Nathan, looking troubled as if he wished himself far away from these doings, and Marie-Josette, sitting straight up, clearly frightened to death, and Arnauld de Gleeb, huddled in blankets, his cheek puffed and red, and his lips parted to reveal a rim of blood and two missing teeth. Madame de Gleeb sat at his side, busy fussing over him. They all shared the long bench, while on the bench behind them sat three of the older and more irascible members of the village council on local well-being and antisedition. These must have been invited to give the Vicomte's verdict an endorsement by the village. Two of these men, the apothecary and an ex-guard of the Vaudraye lands, were pensioners of the Vicomte.

The room was poorly lighted, depressing and gray at the moment, due to the overcast day, although the portieres of the windows behind the Vicomte's desk were open, revealing the northwestern end of the Vaudraye woods. Only her father faced Veronique and he was too far across the room and too intent upon the evidence piled on the desk in front of him.

There'd been some controversy before she came into the ballroom and she heard the end of it.

"—what you will, you cannot deny that this was the weapon belonging to your uncle, the man Guillaume."

"Certainly not, Monseigneur," Marsan agreed with ironic politeness. "I merely claim that such a musket could never have fired a shot into that high window from the copse." He glanced out the nearest window, and Veronique wondered if he expected those village witnesses that both she and Tregastel had promised to bring to his aid.

"Your comments are not of any weight, but your admission is at least something," the Vicomte went on. "Now let us proceed further. Do you have any reason to doubt the honesty of our local curé, Father Nathan d'Essart?" The Vicomte appeared to regard this as a rhetorical question. While the priest attempted to avoid Marsan's gaze, the Vicomte went on. "Now, Father Nathan, Arnauld de Gleeb and myself found this musket in your lodgings at the village inn, wrapped in this shirt and concealed behind your bed. Or would you deny the evidence of my own eyes?"

"I have not denied any of this so-called evidence, messieurs. But may I point out that every gentleman in Vaudraye— perhaps in the entire province—wears white frilled shirts like that one. It might have belonged to anyone."

"Gentleman," Madame de Gleeb repeated to her husband, but the Vicomte's look silenced her. He pursued Marsan's remark.

"But it belongs to you."

"Possibly." Marsan took a step forward but was forcibly restrained by one of the guards.

At this point Veronique stepped forward and walking quickly moved the length of the room, the taffetas of her overskirts rustling loudly. All of the witnesses looked around at her. Her father dropped his hand flat on the desk.

As Veronique approached Marsan she said, "I could not make them come, monsieur, but I heard them state you were in the village when mother was attacked." She spoke loud enough so that her father and the others might also hear.

This close to him, she could see that recent wounds had left their mark on him. His face looked strained, but his eyes were angry.

"You promised me you would not go, mademoiselle. You are not very obedient." Then he smiled, with some effort. "All the same, I wish I might thank my good angel properly."

For a mad second or two she hoped he would kiss her there and then—

"Veronique! You will come here." There was no mistaking the authority in her father's voice. "Since you insist on taking part in this painful affair, you may sit with the witnesses. As for you, Marsan, I think we have disposed of your case with the final link between the musket found in your lodgings, wrapped in an object of your clothing, and the musket ball which clearly came from that musket." He felt around on his desk, took the crushed and marked ball in his palm and held it up to the light which filtered in gloomily behind him. "You, Marie-Josette. Is this the musket ball you found after the shooting, and which my daughter took from you?"

The girl glanced uneasily at Veronique, who became white with anger. "Y—yes, Monseigneur. It is as you say . . ."

In a loud and distinct voice Veronique said, "*Josette* . . ." Veronique understood why she'd lied—fear of displeasing the Vicomte, or even of some possible reprisal from de Gleeb himself. Nonetheless, she was furious, which the Vicomte chose to ignore and turned to de Gleeb. . . . "Is this the ball?"

The gamekeeper moved his mouth painfully. "As you see, Monseigneur. The marking is the same . . . the musket barrel makes these markings. So." He raised one arm from the blanket which almost engulfed him, and pointed.

Veronique saw Marsan glance out the window again. It seemed clear to her that he still hoped Tregastel would bring witnesses from the village, because it was becoming apparent that the Vicomte truly believed him guilty and would accept almost no testimony from him to the contrary, knowing that as he might play for time it was all to no purpose. Impulsively she reached for the musket ball but her father reached out and took hold of her hand. Someone laughed. She ignored that.

"I saw the musket ball, father. I took it in my hands. I wrapped it in a handkerchief."

"This one," her father said.

"No: But I swear to you—to you all, as I hope for salvation, that what you have there is not the spent ball I found. This one was substituted so that you would believe Guillaume's old musket was used."

The apothecary, seated behind the witnesses, interrupted hesitantly. "Excuse me, Monseigneur. I do not understand about the musket ball."

Veronique turned in the direction of the question. "Because the musket Monsieur Marsan is accused of firing could not have traveled so far. Monsieur Marsan explained that. Don't you see, all of you, that another and much better weapon was used?"

"Daughter!" the Vicomte began, but the apothecary went on plaintively.

"I don't understand at all. Is it suggested that Monsieur Marsan used a better weapon?"

"Dear God! No! I mean another weapon was fired by another person other than M'sieur Marsan——"

Her father broke in: "That will do. I am satisfied that this spent ball with its barrel marking came from the musket found in the prisoner's room."

Veronique gave up for the moment the matter of Guillaume's musket, but she then ventured in a quiet voice that she hoped would appease her father. "I visited the village with my maid last evening. I was told by Monsieur Raymond Berthelot, a gentleman from Paris, that Gilles Marsan was his guest the previous afternoon before nightfall. His sister was present also. The gentlemen held a . . . a meeting."

"A Jacobin meeting," the Vicomte put in.

Madame de Gleeb spoke up. "And we are to believe such people?"

The Vicomte looked at her. "Do you call my daughter a liar?"

"No, no! Dear no!"

"My daughter is kind-hearted, as we all know. And strangers may impose upon her credulity. She genuinely believed these Berthelots. However," he went on more judicially, "the evidence is clear. We have the testimony of Father Nathan, of the girl Marie-Josette, and of my game-keeper, Arnauld de Gleeb, none of whom has any personal reason to lie. I believe we are dealing with a notorious seditionist, a Jacobin who believes in a constitutional monarchy. He would tear down all that we have built to protect this land for eight hundred years—and his methods apparently do no fall short of attempted murder."

A silence followed. Everyone realized that sentence had been passed on Gilles Marsan. It was he who cut in suddenly, his voice bitter, "I see you are determined to silence me, Monseigneur. I credit you with the intelligence to know I am not guilty. So I am to be executed merely because I belong to a political club of which you disapprove."

The Vicomte, livid, half rose in his chair. "How dare you. . . . You tried to murder my wife because you knew that way you would do me the greatest injury. You are an unmanly coward and you deserve precisely what is about to happen to you."

The blazing fury between them seemed to burn Veronique as well. She was stunned into silence.

The Vicomte was signaling the guards to remove their prisoner when the doors at the far end of the room opened and a liveried footman entered tentatively.

"Who is it? What do you want? How do you dare interrupt—"

"If you please, Monseigneur, a visitor asks to see you."

. . . Let it be the Berthelots, Veronique prayed.

But it was not. Even while the Vicomte was refusing to see anyone, a young peasant pushed his way in with a stout elderly woman behind him. It was Marie-Josette who called out, "M'sieur Jeannot!" then looked around, abashed at her own voice.

None of the principals—the Vicomte, or Gilles Marsan, or Veronique knew whether Jeannot's arrival would harm or help them. . . .

10

THE VICOMTE recovered his voice first.

"Who the devil is Jeannot? If you have business with me, let it be later."

"Monseigneur, I must speak to you . . . my mother, that is to say—"

"Later."

"But it of importance—"

"Who are they?" Marsan asked Veronique. There had been a minute when he looked almost relieved. Now he remained apprehensive but curious at this interruption in the proceedings.

"It is the *mercière* in the village, and her son. Monsieur, I am persuaded your . . . Mademoiselle Berthelot wanted to come and testify to papa, but her brother is a difficult man . . ."

"I'm afraid you're right. We used to argue at the Lycée. His notion of paradise was to destroy everyone who disagreed with him. Not very practical. At all events, any delay this morning will serve me, including this Jeannot, whatever his cause."

She knew she should tell him now that the witnesses he counted on would not be summoned by the cook. Perhaps, like Berthelot, Tregastel presumably preferred a dead martyr for the cause. But she lost her courage, took a breath and said, "Mademoiselle is a great beauty."

"Yes, from childhood . . . she certainly does not resemble her brother."

"She will eventually come and testify. I know she will. She was so lovely."

He looked at her. "Loveliness may be many things . . . your great charm, for instance . . ."

She felt warm with pleasure but had little time to enjoy his praise. The Vicomte cut into their low-voiced exchange. "I have promised to hear this fellow out. Daughter, go and sit with the others, and kindly remember who you are."

She obeyed and forced herself not to look back until she reached the bench beside Marie-Josette. When she did glance his way again, she could see that he still watched her. Though he could scarcely be happy in the circumstances, his expression seemed gentle . . . amused? . . .

Meanwhile there was this mysterious business of Jeannot and his mother who owned the mercerie. The most mysterious part of it was the uneasiness of Monsieur and Madame de Gleeb. The two of them were consulting *sotto voce* . . . it seemed clear they were upset by the presence of Jeannot . . . or was it his mother? Veronique became very interested in her recent rescuer and his mother.

"Jeannot and three of his companions saved Josette and myself yesterday, Papa," she told the Vicomte. "I owe him a great deal for that."

"So do we all," the Vicomte said, but he was impatient to get on. "You say you've something to offer at this examination. Something pertinent?"

"My mother, Monseigneur, is shy. She asks you to forgive that. The young ladies were good enough to explain to me last night M'sieur Marsan's problem—the evidence against him . . ."

The Vicomte began to drum his fingers on his desk. "I trust this is pertinent. We're not concerned here with mere sympathies. . . ."

The stout little woman shuffled out from behind her son. She curtsied repeatedly, further irritating the Vicomte, but Veronique saw that Gilles Marsan had taken a step forward. Obviously, his curiosity if not his hopes were roused again.

"What do you have to offer?" the Vicomte asked.

"Monseigneur. I believe I sold the shirt in which the gun was wrapped."

"How can you be certain? The evidence has not been out of Father Nathan's possession since we found it."

The woman wrung her hands nervously. Tense and excited, Veronique sat up, watching her.

"When my Jeannot told me of the evidence, I wondered, because it was the first time the—the gentleman had ever purchased any linen made by my hand, and it seemed strange at the time. It was only minutes later, as my seamstress was delivering a set of my best new cravats to the apothecary here that she saw the gentleman entering the inn through the back door—"

The Vicomte broke in. "You thought it strange that Gilles Marsan took the packet into his own lodgings?"

The woman's hand fluttered. "Not M'sieur Marsan. It was that one who bought the shirt." Unsteadily she pointed at Arnauld de Gleeb.

"She's lying . . . I was never in her shop." De Gleeb looked shaken. "She's one of them, one of the enemy, the seditionists—"

This aroused Father Nathan, who felt obliged to say, "Not that good woman, my son . . . she is a faithful daughter of the Church."

The Vicomte said, "How can we believe your seamstress? You may be honest, Father Nathan vouches for you, but this other—"

Jeannot put in eagerly, "She's waiting in the corridor, Monseigneur. She was too frightened to come into your excellency's presence unbidden but she's a truthful girl . . . a mere child but she will swear to the truth."

The gamekeeper came up out of his blanket to his full height and reminded the Vicomte: "They know quite well they could never prove such a claim. My wife makes my shirts. And one shirt is very like another."

"With permission, monsieur," Jeannot's mother corrected him, getting up her courage, "this shirt was not like any other. One night when I worked on it I misplaced my spectacles the Hôtel-Dieu had been good enough to provide me, thanks to the charity of your gracious daughter . . ."

The Vicomte's fingers stopped drumming. "Yes, and then?"

"I took up a spindle of thread that was cream-colored, not white. When I sewed the frill on the cuff of the left sleeve— on the under side—you will see that the thread is not true white."

The Vicomte pulled the shirt toward him. The ballroom

became so silent Veronique could hear the heavy breathing of the gamekeeper, from whom she was separated by three persons.

The Vicomte took up each sleeve. No one thought it strange that Marsan should move toward the desk as if to examine the shirt himself. Veronique watched him flex his fingers nervously, though she thought that his manacled hands must still give him some pain.

The Vicomte turned the cuff and frill inside out. "I see no indications of this thread you describe."

"Forgive me, Monseigneur . . . the left sleeve."

Watching him, Veronique thought it was as though her father didn't want to find the evidence that might clear Gilles Marsan. Madame de Gleeb had risen also and leaned forward as the Vicomte found the left sleeve, pulled the cuff-frill inside out and held it up to the light. Veronique could not make out the thread, but Marsan saw it, closed his eyes briefly, then looked at Veronique and nodded slightly.

Jeannot offered, "If Monseigneur wishes to question the seamstress, I will fetch her in."

Madame de Gleeb burst out, in her panic. "None of these people can be trusted. The priest is his friend. They are all his friends—"

"Be silent!" Her husband had stretched the sore muscles of his face with that order and held his cheek now as he tried to repair the damage. "Monseigneur," de Gleeb went on painfully, "you yourself have often said that the villagers might be persuaded to any belief, any crime. You know what the prisoner represents, everything despised by decent men such as yourself. How easy to persuade them all that they must lie so that this assassin may go free, the next time to succeed in murdering the Vicomtesse!"

He knew his man. The Vicomte dropped the shirt as if it had scorched his fingers. Veronique was shocked by her father's reaction, but Gilles Marsan, whose life depended on the outcome of this examination, tried to keep to the matter at hand.

"Monseigneur, your gamekeeper always maintained that I took my uncle's musket and shot at your wife."

The Vicomte swung around in anger. "I will not have her ladyship's name on your lips."

Veronique started to add her voice to Marsan's but realized that his calm at this moment was his best defense.

"Well, then, Monsieur le Vicomte, may I suggest once more

that there is a very quick and simple way to prove my guilt or innocence?"

The gamekeeper apparently anticipated him. "Not so . . . don't let him test any musket . . . free him for a test and he will have his chance to kill us all—"

The Vicomte clearly disliked this talk, and Marsan quickly tried to take advantage of it. "Then I suggest you make the test, Monsieur de Gleeb. Take the musket you say I used. Load and fire it yourself from wherever you claim I stood. Fire as many times as you wish. I looked at that area yesterday. I'm satisfied that a test will prove me innocent."

He then turned to the Vicomte: "Then ask yourself, Monseigneur, why one man has worked so hard to create evidence against me. Perhaps you will remember this man's quarrel with me in the village two days ago. When he promises revenge, he has a way of taking that revenge."

"Assassin!" The gamekeeper was still holding his mouth as he shouted this, but the Vicomte had already risen with the musket in hand.

"De Gleeb, you have ammunition for this weapon?"

The gamekeeper reached for the musket.

"You will go ahead of me," the Vicomte told him, which remark told Veronique that her father's belief in the gamekeeper's innocence—or at least in Marsan's guilt—had finally begun to erode. He didn't mention the prisoner or look his way.

Marie-Josette whispered to Veronique as they hurried after the guards and their prisoner, "Isn't he truly wonderful?"

"He is indeed wonderful. I hope we may thank Monsieur Jeannot properly when this thing is settled. He deserves well of us. And his good mother has also been very courageous."

"And think of it, he has no wife—"

Veronique laughed, but to herself envied the girl's right to dream such dreams without feeling guilty.

Outside the east front of the château they all gathered between the copse and the building. One of the peasants employed in the fields brought a shot-bag to Arnauld de Gleeb, who stationed himself with legs apart and gave every indication of shooting from a covert only a few steps from the narrow terrace outside the dining salon.

Veronique protested. "Papa, the man who shot at mother's window that night was farther away. In the copse. You and I came out this far, don't you remember?"

Marsan turned to her. "It doesn't matter. Even close in

it's too high a shot for that gun, the angle is too great."

Paying attention to his daughter rather than Marsan, the Vicomte told the gamekeeper, "Arnauld, your memory seems at fault. You brought me to the place where you said the assassin stood. Well within that copse."

De Gleeb retreated, stopped at the extreme outer edge of the clump of woods next to the orchard, snapped orders for ramrod, the funnel of paper with powder and ball, pushed everything down with the ramrod and fired before anyone expected it. The musket misfired. "It was the flint," he said quickly, and started again.

As de Gleeb continued to fail, the Vicomte decided to make an end of it.

"Let me see that musket again." His hand trembling slightly, the gamekeeper offered him the weapon. The Vicomte examined it. "The barrel is slightly irregular. It could never fire that far. But no matter. One musket did fire up to my wife's window. A very good musket." He turned to the nearest guard. "Fetch me that prize weapon my gamekeeper uses."

It was only minutes before the gamekeeper's gun, obviously superior, cut a section off the cornice below the roof. The matter seemed settled.

The Vicomte, without a word, turned to Veronique and lightly but firmly held her arm until the crowd slowly dispersed and the guards had disappeared with Marsan, apparently determined that although the latter may have been shown innocent he was not to be rewarded with further meetings with his daughter.

De Gleeb, the last to be marched away, began calling out to the Vicomte, "I thought to hear you thank me . . ." and was cut off as the Vicomte waved the guards on with their prisoner while he turned to Veronique. "You say, and I must believe you, that you found a spent bullet, a musket ball, neither marked nor flattened shapeless like these, in your mother's room . . ." Veronique nodded. And yet, he thought to himself, even if Arnauld's intent was as it finally appeared, how could he have so endangered his own wife . . . ? He would need some further answers, in private. Sending Veronique to care for her mother, he went off to find them.

Arnauld de Gleeb stood now before the Vicomte in his study, having been diverted there by sudden and unexpected orders to his guards from the Vicomte.

"And so you really expected me to thank you," the Vicomte was saying to him. "For nearly killing my beloved wife, betraying your trust—"

"But, sir, you don't understand. It was arranged with Lise that she was to have the Vicomtesse out of the room . . . safe . . . but at the last moment, unexpectedly, the Vicomtesse went to the window, perhaps to admire the evening or see to something that may have caught her attention outside . . . my wife was helpless, there was no time to signal me what had happened. I grant you, sir, it may have been a foolhardy scheme in retrospect, but it seemed quite safe, and so uncomplicated, at the time, and if it meant the dispatch of this Jacobin whom I detest as I know you do—"

"Arnauld, it is only my debt to you for saving my life, and your past loyalty, that stops me from having your neck stretched. As for the political sympathies that you presume to share, they are entirely beside the point, I assure you, when it comes to endangering my family." The Vicomte turned and gazed out of the window, then turned back. "A *final* chance, de Gleeb—note my emphasis is on 'final.' Your service here as gamekeeper is clearly at an end. And if it were not for an urgent mission I hope you can excute without bungling—it will be your last mistake, I promise you, if you do—I would see that you at least will pay in the Bastille for the conquences of your outrageous plan. Now, damn you, listen *carefully* . . ."

And Arnauld de Gleeb did as he was told, feeling that his life depended on catching and following out every word. He was right.

Having watched Marsan being led away and knowing her father would never allow her to see him before he left the château, Veronique believed she'd lost her last opportunity to put herself, somehow, even casually in his way for at least one more meeting.

Crossing the lawn toward the house, she had to fight against the temptation to indulge herself and visualize such a longed-for encounter. Why torture herself? She knew it was fantasy to assume or even hope that her parents would ever permit a friendship with Marsan . . . friendship . . . what a pretty word, and how inadequate, to describe what he had already indicated he felt for her, and the haunting and yet very real images of his presence that flooded to her now . . . his touch, his love . . .

His love. Yes, his love and her response to it. She would

not quibble with herself. She knew far too much about the human body to pretend or deny that love also included physical attraction and satisfaction between a man and a woman—and she and Marsan undeniably felt those sensations. She also knew that such attraction could lead to disaster . . . she'd tended girls barely out of childhood themselves, suffering through a childbirth whose origin they didn't even comprehend. She'd sat night after night beside poor drabs who'd sold their ill-used bodies for ten sous. For all her short life she'd been trained to remain above fleshly temptations, instructed that only thereby could she be of service to God and His children, and perhaps even serve a minute part of his divine purpose. But no training, no dedication could stop her from feeling as she did for this man Gilles Marsan. Was there not, she asked herself, also some divinity in sexual love, as in her love of Mother Church . . . ?

Precipitous as usual, she burst into the house by the small door behind the grand staircase, running directly, impossibly, into Gilles Marsan's arms.

11

MARSAN caught her, restored her balance in firm hands that still showed bloody traces of the manacles. He drew her into the large recess behind the staircase. She didn't look at his hands again, afraid he would let her go if she reminded him in any way. He went on quickly, trying to make light of the moment.

"Thank God, I thought I would have to talk to you out there on the grounds, in front of all of Vaudraye."

"Especially my father."

His mouth tightened. "If we speak of him, I can never tell you what I want you to know. And there is no time, no time at all. I'm expected in Paris before the opening of the States-General and am already late by two days. I was only able to manage this moment with you because my former guards agreed an innocent man was entitled to at least this minimum indulgence. I must not, however, take advantage of their generosity—they do, after all, serve your father."

"You are going to Paris?"

His eyes searched her face. "They told me you were to be a postulant at some convent there for nursing sisters. I tried to think of you like that, my good angel . . . is it true?"

Afraid of his reaction, her voice was a whisper. "Is it what you would wish me to be?"

He continued to study her as if to fix her face in his memory. "I want you to be as I see you. Alive, enchanting, with everything possible for you . . ."

Recovering a little of her self-possession she told him, teased him, "I am not your good angel, monsieur. I am very much of this earth—"

"Don't play at passion, Veronique!" he said abruptly, and pulled her against him. In the dizzying moment before he kissed her, she was aware of the pain of his hard grip. She tried to protest, found herself more closely enmeshed. But in that first feather touch of his lips all her very earthy imaginings about him took hold of her. The woman who existed in her body responded to him now, and for a breathless few seconds she had not sensation that was not involved with him. When he finally let her go, she was so lightheaded she could only say what she honestly felt . . . "If this is gratitude, monsieur, I am grateful for it. . . ."

For a long uncomfortable minute she thought he was still angry with her—perhaps for her too facile turn of phrase? . . . His eyes seemed darker as he watched her, but then, after she had almost given up, he smiled.

"You are very young, Veronique, not to mention being the daughter of a grand seigneur who happens to believe heaven and doubtless hell would be best served by my instant demise. My innocence today was sufficiently demonstrated to invoke even his sense of justice. . . . I'm sorry, but this is a time for speaking as we feel . . . and I doubt that he will forget this day or leave us to chance. And what, exactly, do I have to sustain us against him and the normal adversities of these not so normal times? About ten sous to jingle in my breeches, if that . . ."

Veronique had been controlling herself with difficulty through his speech, which she felt entirely too long for the occasion and the few moments allowed to them. Nonetheless, she was astonished to hear herself saying, "Oh, my dear Gilles, it is what you have of mine that is important. My love must have value . . ."

Astonished as she by her forthrightness, Gilles at first looked at her quietly, seriously, then smiled and said, "And a fine speech, darling, which I thank you greatly for. But have you considered what would happen if we could never marry? Would you be willing to come to Paris with me as my mistress and do you suppose we'd then live happily ever after, as they do in the fairy tales?"

She hoped his eyes did not read the flush that burned her face, but she said with this new boldness that continued to amaze her, "If that were the only way we might be together . . ."

He took her face and framed it between his hands.

"Veronique, what an extraordinary discovery you are for me. I was so confident about my life that I knew very far in advance what was waiting for me. My world of politics seemed to have closed off all possibility of my knowing and loving someone like you. And now that you are here in my arms giving lie to my silly notions about what I was capable of loving, I can only think of how difficult it will be."

He took her hand and examined her fingers as though he found them rare and special. "I may imagine that the Duc d'Orléans will buy a new series of my political sketches, but I can't imagine the Vicomte de Vaudraye's only child in garret lodgings, dependent for her bread upon the sales of antigovernment political sketches."

Looking down at her hand, she said, "And do you find those the fingers of a pampered aristocrat, a member of the Privileged Class?"

He turned it over. She was profoundly aware of his touch, the warmth of his hand, and its strength. "They are small and they are slender, and they most assuredly have proved to be very useful as well . . . certainly too useful to be wasted in a garret—" She tried to withdraw her hand but he held it firmly. "When I return for you, will I find you a holy sister? Or perhaps a comtesse, as befits a vicomte's daughter?"

She would not dignify this by arguing and was totally unprepared when he kissed her again on the lips, this time softly.

"I *am* coming back for you, you must know that, despite all my fine and sensible arguments against the wisdom of it. By July the States-General *cahier* of grievances must surely be in the King's hands. Immediately thereafter I will come back—they'll hardly be expecting it—and will send messages to the village here by the Rouen Couriers of our club. Ask at the inn. Promise me?"

While he'd been talking she'd been involuntarily backing slowly up the great staircase, mindful of the constant danger of being discovered as well as of her delay in going to her mother, as her father had asked. Now she stopped in the sudden realization that she might never see him again. His words were meant to be assuring, but they hardly fitted with

the terrible things happening—that had already happened—
these days. He could die . . . he could forget her. . . .

"Veronique," he said, looking up at her over the balustrade
and as though guessing her fears, "please take this and remember and believe when you look at it that I will do as I
say. That I will be back for you."

She came back down two steps, reached over the balustrade
and closed her fingers around a small crucifix carved out of
what appeared to be light pumice. "It is lava rock," he told
her. "In my family since the sixteenth century. Token of my
guarantee that I will return here for you. Take care of it,
darling. It is for our first son."

First son . . . the thought of him possessing her body
brought no embarrassment, as such a thought almost surely
would have done before. . . . But not now, not with this man
with whom she felt so suddenly and so satisfyingly a woman.
. . . She floundered only for words to delay him, knowing
that no delay was possible or even desirable. "I know you
must go," she told him, "and I believe you. . . ." And all the
time wishing to herself that there were more time to go beyond the confident words neither of them could completely
believe, to let him know her and the not-so-perfect sides of
her character that would test his love . . . her impatience, her
pettishness on occasion . . . and she to know him, oh yes, to
know him in all his ways and manners, how much she would
have loved to be tested by them. . . . And what of the time she
needed to tell him she would want to work at the hospitals
in Paris, whose conditions were said to be even worse than
the monstrous ones in the provinces? She might give up her
mother's dream for her of being Sœur Veronique of the
Convent of Ste. Veronique, but she must still continue her
work and would he understand that? Could she convince
him that even though she'd never known anyone who could
spend long hours in such as the Hôtel-Dieu and also rear a
family and care for a beloved husband, she was strong and
determined and for her, for *them*, all things were possible
. . . especially with a man such as himself who put ideals and
humanity above personal career? . . .

He was watching her, as if he suspected her misgivings.
"Veronique, promise me you'll ask at the inn for my messages
and that you'll answer them. And if you change your mind—"

"I'll never do that."

"You are very young for a word like 'never.' You can't be
sure—"

But she was very sure. Still solding tight to the crucifix, she leaned down and kissed him, then quickly went on to the top of the stairs. When finally she looked before stepping into the gallery, she saw he was still watching her. She smiled, turned and went to her mother's suite without again looking back, preferring to hold and remember the way he had looked up at her, hopeful and tender, and not a little doubtful, as though worrying that at her young age she might change her mind and fall out of love with him. . . .

What terrible nonsense. Seventeen or seventy . . . as if by instinct she was certain that what she felt inside had no respect for chronology. . . .

By the time she reached the antechamber of the Vicomtesse's bedroom, Veronique could hear her mother's voice rising in an hysteria that fed itself when unattended.

"You did pull my hair. Don't deny it, only Lise knows how to stroke my hair when I have my palpitations. Lise! What have they done to her?"

Before entering, Veronique tried to reduce her own tension, hoping to find a calm air that would be contagious as she walked into the room.

Edwige, with brush in hand, was sobbing and the Vicomtesse, flushed and disheveled, sat on the edge of her bed.

"Dear child," she said to her daughter, "they've taken de Gleeb off in chains, I saw it from that window, Lise is with them, and all that horrid shooting that went on forever. . . . I managed to get as far as the window but I had such a dreadful time getting back to bed and no one would come and then Edwige . . . there, there, I shouldn't have jerked away. But I was so unnerved . . . please don't cry, Edda, dear. . . ."

The Vicomtesse held out her frail arms, embraced the maid and all seemed well as Edwige and Veronique got her tucked into her high regal bed, with the crisp curtains pushed back so that she might see what everyone in the room was up to. Soothed, the Vicomtesse went on discussing her problems, and Veronique marveled how quickly her mother could recover from her nervous hysteria when properly soothed and cosseted.

The weakness of the Vicomtesse was genuine . . . her heart often lapsed into strange palpitations that were as terrifying to her family as to herself. Still, it was Veronique's opinion that if her mother exerted herself just a trifle, walked about the room, perhaps appeared more often at dinner, she might strengthen those frail muscles. Veronique had seen it happen among the convalescing men and women at the Hôtel-Dieu who were forced to rise early from the straw pallets in the long crowded hall to go out into the fields again. And they became healthy, particularly when there was bread to eat and wine to drink.

"Madame is asleep," Edwige whispered. "It's very warm, which gives her headaches, I do believe."

Veronique nodded and set the brush down. The room was stifling close as usual. "We'd best open the south windows at least a little."

Edwige helped her to force open the windows as noise-lessly as possible, and whispered, "Oh, mam'selle, look—"

Wondering what new catastrophe had befallen Vaudraye, Veronique looked in the direction she pointed and saw a young woman being lifted down from a closed carriage by her coachman. She walked to the foot of the partico steps, where the Vicomte made a bow and raised her gloved hand to his lips. The horse that drew her carriage was an ancient nag, the carriage a generation out of the mode, but the young lady with a tilted hat that revealed a mass of glorious golden hair was a breathtaking portrait in sky-blue taffetas and a darker blue spencer.

At the sight of Yolande Berthelot, Veronique realized that at the back of her mind since her journey to Rouen she'd dwelt on the prospect of having helped Marsan more than the girl once referred to as his "betrothed." At one time she'd have liked to have hated Mademoiselle Berthelot, except she'd behaved so properly and politely on her visit to the village the day before that Veronique now felt obliged to return her politeness.

In spite of Gilles's assurances that he loved her, Veronique was unable to free herself of jealous thoughts toward this true beauty. She hoped Marsan at least had left the château by this time. She started across the room. Her mother turned in bed, her coppery hair flowing around her fragile face on the satin pillow. She murmured sleepily, "You are not leaving me, dear?"

"Only for a little while. A young lady is visiting us and I must see that she is properly cared for. Papa will be with you in just a few minutes."

"Young lady?" her mother echoed, rising with an effort on one elbow. "Will someone please tell me what's happening in my own household?"

Leaving the maid to describe, no doubt, the beauty of Mademoiselle Berthelot on the portico steps below, Veronique went quickly down to the visitors' Blue Salon. Her father seemed captivated by this lovely visitor, which wasn't unusual—he had a gentleman's admiration for attractive females, and Yolande was surely far above average.

Smoothing her ruffled hair and gown, Veronique went into the Blue Salon.

"Ah, Gilles's good angel," Yolande Berthelot said, and without a trace of sarcasm. As Veronique came toward her, responding in spite of herself to this friendliness, Yolande rose and curtsied. This sort of thing had always seemed absurd to Veronique. It at once set a barrier between herself and those who might otherwise have been her friends. She often found herself much more at home with the nuns and the peasant women in the hospital, where everyone was too busy to bob curtsies.

"Mademoiselle, you were very kind to come. But I know papa must have assured you about Monsieur Marsan. He was released and left here an hour ago—"

"Oh, yes, I understand he has indeed. I was very worried —I was twice delayed on my journey here. First the carriage broke down—you no doubt have seen its sad condition—and then the horse threw a shoe. My brother Raymond would have come as well but decided at the last minute his presence might be disruptive. . . ."

It was perhaps better, she said, not to explain further about Raymond, who she doubted had any intention of coming at all and would, she suspected, have stopped her if he hadn't worried that it might be too crude a stroke against a man supposedly his personal friend and political accomplice. . . . "And so, mademoiselle, I arrived very concerned until your gracious father laid to rest my worst fears by saying he'd disposed of the entire matter and released Gilles."

Her father tapped his fingers on the mantelpiece before stepping forward to dismiss the matter of the recent prisoner. "Yes, yes, it seems he was innocent of that business, but he is hardly a desirable citizen in spite of—" The Vicomte broke off and everyone followed his glance to the doors of the hall. The Vicomtesse de Vaudraye stood there, in layer upon layer of white with an underdress heavily embroidered in miniature roses that caught the copper-gold of her high-piled, unpowdered hair. She leaned slightly on Edwige's shoulder, but had obviously made the journey from her bedroom on her own small satin-clad feet. It was hard to guess what her mood might be—she looked surprised at her own astonishing achievement in making this journey.

"We have guests, Claude? I wish I might have been here to greet this young . . . person."

Yolande descended in one of her deep curtsies. As she rose under the fixed and gentle smile of the Vicomtesse, she said, "I had heard it said that the Vicomtesse greatly resembled Her Majesty, but I see now that Her Ladyship has the advantage of youth."

The Vicomtesse avoided a pink tapestry sofa whose shade would have been disastrous as a frame for her lovely hair and allowed herself to be assisted onto a modified silver chaise, where she soon encouraged Yolande to join her. Within no time the Vicomtesse had adopted the winning Yolande as her confidante, and Veronique noted that her father was in his element as both women appealed to him to settle nearly every question. Actually, for her own special reasons, she was delighted at the visitor's popularity—the longer Yolande Berthelot remained, the less likelihood of her meeting Gilles Marsan at the Berthelot house.

Later in the afternoon Marie-Josette came to inform Veronique that their rescuers of the High Road had arrived to take up their promised work. Veronique couldn't drag away her reluctant father to thank her rescuers, so she went herself and offered the men more than the Vicomte might have paid them, putting one to work as footman, her friend Joseph Faure as a temporary gamekeeper in place of the departed and unlamented de Gleeb, and the others where they seemed best-suited.

This occupied more than half an hour and when she returned to the salon Yolande Berthelot was preparing to leave. The Vicomtesse, looking strained and tired after her exertions and the excitement of so much gossip, was still able to wish her new-found friend a safe journey.

"His Excellency will send you with two of our men. Your coachman can follow . . . our own Veronique was rescued only last night on that road."

"I will be grateful for your guards," Yolande said. "Had I known how dangerous the High Road has become I'd have insisted that my brother accompany me—"

The Vicomtesse, apparently feeling this might somehow be a reflection on her care of her own daughter, said quickly, "I thank the good God it cannot happen again to our Veronique. Sister Thérèse du Calvaire is expected at the château tomorrow. She's been with the Mother Superior in Brittany, but as we are old friends. . . . At all events, she is to escort our child to her cousins in Paris. Claude, we must be quite certain that an escort is sent with them—"

Veronique looked quickly to her father, who avoided her eyes. She had no doubt whatever that her obvious interest in Gilles Marsan today had prompted this haste.

"I am to go to Paris? At once?"

"To our dear Alex and Sylvie," her mother put in, as one who brings glad tidings. "But you've known this for months, child. It cannot come as a surprise. Don't you wish to have a little visit with Sylvie before your novitiate?"

Yolande Berthelot brightened. "What a splendid future, my dear mademoiselle! I envy you!" And she went out, escorted by the Vicomte.

Was she to be sorry or pleased at this tightening of the lines of her future, Veronique wondered. Marsan would be in Paris. . . . She didn't fully understand her father's motives. By rushing her off to Paris didn't he realize that it increased her chances of seeing Gilles again? He usually didn't allow this kind of oversight . . . if indeed it was. . . . Her hand found the pumice crucifix in her skirt pocket and she held tight to it, remembering Gilles's earlier skepticism that her father would leave their relationship to chance. . . .

12

SHORTLY after Veronique returned from the village hospital on the following afternoon she saw Sister Thérèse's carriage approaching the château on the estate road under the long shadows of the poplar grove. Marie-Josette came hurrying out to remind Veronique that she must change from her riding habit into something more suitable.

"Sister Thérèse must be a great lady. Have you seen her carriage? Quite like a barouche, I believe. And two splendid animals. Two, mind! No mere pony cart for travelers of the cloth . . . the *réligeuses* are very grand."

"Grander than they were in Christ's day," Veronique remarked drily. "Well, let us be on our way to shifts, petticoats, underdresses, overskirts, and all my very finest diamonds—"

Josette giggled. "But you are not Her Majesty. And Sister Thérèse is not the naughty Cardinal Rohan that Her Majesty has so grossly deceived in the matter of the diamond necklace."

"We don't know that Her Majesty deceived anyone. I have no doubt the propagandists were at work on the matter."

Propadandists . . . was Gilles Marsan one of them? It was a contemptible thing to distort the truth and she could not think of him doing anything contemptible. . . .

"All the same," Josette went on, "I'm afraid your modest diamonds wouldn't impress a lady whose convent is so close to Versailles." As she followed after her mistress she asked between breaths, "Why not send for M'sieur Marsan? Any of the men you found work for yesterday will carry a message. You said he would write to you. What will happen to those letters?"

"Be silent. I must think."

"Pardon, mam'selle, but you have thought since yesterday, and nothing comes of that. I would not let that fine fellow Jeannot go from me so easily——"

"Nor would I. I went to the Guillaume lodging house this morning, but too late. Monsieur Marsan was on his way to Paris." She did not add that this visit had been in response to a sudden onslaught of self-doubt about her lasting appeal for Gilles Marsan. It would never have occurred to Marie-Josette that her in most ways confident mistress, whose authority was a byword at the terrible provincial hospitals, might be afraid of rejection by a young radical bourgeois. Nor, Veronique decided, was it wise to confess to Marie-Josette that she'd wondered for hours whether Gilles Marsan might have met Yolande Berthelot on the road as she returned to the village.

And, of course, there were dozens, perhaps hundreds of women in Paris that he might have for the asking. He need only stroll through the Palais-Royal, whose owner the Duc d'Orléans had turned it into a gigantic gardenparcade of expensive restaurants and brothels . . . why should he settle his affections upon a provincial girl like herself? . . .

As she bathed and dressed she thought of prayer—the selfish child's request that she get what she wanted—and quickly banished that notion. Long ago she'd made a pact with herself never to pray for a personal gift. It was permissable to pray for the skill and understanding that might save a life, or reduce pain. One might pray for strength to bear an ordeal, strength to face disappointment or loss. But she could not pray for anything as petty in God's plan as the love life of Veronique de Vaudraye.

Her gown was already chosen for the occasion by her mother, who'd taken to her bed after the exertion of entertaining Yolande Berthelot the day before. But with a little extra effort she felt she was managing to keep her daughter's life on the path chosen by her. The gown was of silver gauze, tight across the bodice and pulled into great puffs over the hips to reveal an elaborately embroidered mauve underdress.

She was laced into the gown by Josette and an unskilled chambermaid who took Mme. de Gleeb's place, the latter having departed with her husband under guard, Veronique presumed, to the coast from where she thought she heard her father say it was expected they would be shipped to the French colonies in the Caribbean.

Josette flattered Veronique about her narrow waist—even Josette's partisan eyes could scarcely praise her mistress's slight bosom. Eager to take part in such pleasantries, the maid chattered on . . . "and such pretty shoulders, mam'selle, a nice slim throat with attractive—"

Josette hushed her patronizing. "Mademoiselle is not interested in such matters. Mademoiselle will soon be entering the Convent of Ste. Veronique in Paris. What does she care about silks and shoulders and slim throats? Most improper . . ." Veronique suspected this was Josette's not so subtle way of reminding her mistress that she might still take action to save herself from such an austere future.

After some effort they managed to get her hair up, one dark curl brought forward over her shoulder, and promised to have it perfectly powdered later, after the approaching dinner. Veronique wrinkled her nose at that, gave herself a quick look in the mirror and wished that Gilles Marsan could at least see her now. . . .

It was just as well the girls had worked on her appearance so carefully. Not only was Sister Thérèse a woman of statuesque beauty in the robes of her order, but she was accompanied by her brother, a most handsome and fashionable abbé. The presentation took place in the elegance of the Vaudraye Gold Salon, a long chamber that was at the opposite end of the building from the ballroom. The gold had long since begun to crack and peel off mouldings, rococco cherubs on the ceiling and the two exquisitely unreal Fragonard copies which were treated by the Vicomte as originals, though he never stated so. Guests sometimes acquired coughs after enjoying the hospitality of the Gold Salon, but they were invariably flattered to find themselves amid such provincial richness where gold dust fairly dripped down upon them.

Before the arrival of the church guests, the Vicomtesse had allowed herself to be assisted down by her husband and placed on a white-and-gold chaise longue, from which she played hostess. When Veronique entered and curtsied, she found herself rising under the rather cynical but admiring gray eyes of the Abbé François de St.-Hélier. Her mother presented her.

"But she is charming. Completely charming. And what beautiful eyes." He kept looking at her so that she found herself ill at ease but unable to avoid him. A tall, elegant man, possibly forty, he appeared even taller and more elegant in a soutane she thought astonishing in its richness. Of a shade between violet and gray watered silk, it suggested church royalty and wealth, as did the stunning amethyst and diamond ring on his forefinger and—was it possible?—his shoes with violet heels.

Flattered by the Abbé's compliments of her daughter, the Vicomtesse made the Abbé promise that "my child will be enabled to visit the court at Versailles."

"But of course, Madame la Vicomtesse. The good sisters do not immure their charges, you know. These are modern times."

Sister Thérèse explained that the nursing work of the nuns at the huge Hôtel-Dieu of Paris occasionally brought them to the attention of the Court. "And Colonel Alexandre de Vaudraye is known to Their Majesties."

"Cousin Alex performed valiantly in the American War of Independence," the Vicomtesse said to Veronique, only to have her husband say, "Valiantly! Those medals had better been awarded to his mount. The poor devil of a horse bore double proper weight when it carried Alex to Yorktown."

While they discussed cousin Alex and his unpredictable wife Sylvie, Veronique was preoccupied by her own thoughts. She had only a mild curiosity about King Louis, and shared more Frenchmen's dislike of what was considered his extravagant, self-centered queen, Marie Antoinette. Her chief concern was at least to meet Gilles Marsan "by accident" before being taken to the convent—she knew if she did enter the convent, even as a postulate, she could never permit herself to see him again. The decision about her future life would have been made for her by a greater power than her family or herself.

At the moment she did not have Gilles's crucifix with her, having left it in her room. Its rough touch in her pocket, the knowledge that it was near her own flesh and had once rested near his helped give her the sense that *he* was near, that through it they were somehow linked together. . . . It was a cross, and yet the overpowering sensation of him that it brought her had very little, she realized, to do with matters spiritual. . . . She thought again of her impending religious vows and how, once taken, they would bind her from her novitiate to her grave. . . .

At dinner, served nearly at dusk to conform to Paris hours, Veronique had a good look at the Abbé de St.-Hélier across the table, and became convinced first that the black mark high on his cheek was a beauty patch and second that the vivid color of his lips was not natural. She knew that many Versailles *gallants* prided themselves upon such decorations but had not until now realized this spreading to the Church. What was the world coming to?

The two full dinner courses were elaborate and complete. One would never have suspected half the country was on an enforced diet of black bread and sour wine, or that others lacked even bread. Much of the roast ducklings, the ragout of lamb, the grilled trout and the stewed eels would be eaten by the servants the next day, but there was always a surplus, along with the sauced cauliflowers and broiled mushrooms, which would be delivered to the hospital and the lodgings of the poor in the village.

The guests talked with surprising personal knowledge of Versailles, a subject which greatly entertained the Vicomtesse and therefore pleased her husband. Veronique, however, found it a long evening. When the Abbé de St.-Hélier noted her yawning, an hour after she would have liked to have been in bed and asleep, he moved gracefully across the corner of the Gold Salon to share her seat on the worn brocade sofa. She noted his elegance but felt a curious revulsion at these very qualities which for others made him so much admired.

"My child," he began, patting the hand which she had hastily pulled down from her mouth after covering her yawn, "you must not permit the frivolity of your life as a grand seigneur's daughter to tire you in this fashion. Besides, these are provincial joys. When you find your proper place in Paris and at Versailles, your pursuits will likely keep you from your couch until dawn."

Trying not to resent this, Veronique said politely, "Thank you, monseigneur, I will remember." She wondered if it would do any good to tell him how she spent her day of "frivolity" before his arrival.

The Abbé sipped his host's powerful apple brandy, and continued to regard her. She was annoyed with herself, in spite of herself, for finding him not wholly unattractive. She dared to wonder what happened to novices—even nuns?—not protected, as she was, by a love for another man.

"My dear child, you are shocked. Confess, you did not expect to find the Church so knowledgeable about the world's affairs."

She got up the courage to remind him. "I have met curés, monseigneur. They do not seem to me like the higher—some of the higher—clergy. They have even been elected to the Third Estate instead of to the Nobles or Clergy. Their sympathies seem to lie elsewhere. In some cases, may I say, with reason." She felt nervous to have hinted so boldly at his own behavior but couldn't stop herself. The truth often had that effect on her. . . . "I believe a return to the principles of the early church might bring back the people—"

"You are naïve. I find this charming, but alas, Paris will soon bring you to a different view." He tilted his glass in salute to her. She thought his gray eyes held something she'd not seen before, a note of wry sadness. "Prove me wrong, mademoiselle. I challenge you. In fact, I entreat you. . . ."

"I accept the challenge, monseigneur."

The Abbé smiled. To the others in the salon he remarked, "I daresay, for all this child's enthusiasm, we will meet at the end as companions in Charon's boat."

His sister, who apparently understood his allusion, chided him coolly. "François, your jokes are not becoming to your cloth. And it is highly unlikely that a devout young lady like Veronique will ever find herself, in your company, facing Charon."

The Vicomte muttered in a loud aside, "Who the devil is Charon?" The Vicomtesse, who also did not know, smiled uneasily behind her fan at their shared ignorance, but the Abbé, disturbed by his sister's remark, said unsmilingly: "Death."

The single syllable set a pall upon the social evening.

Sister Thérèse flashed a beautiful smile at Veronique across the room, assuring her, "My brother says many foolish things. Forgive me, François, if I have contradicted your view of mademoiselle's nights in Paris. Our sisters often spend twenty-four hours at a time attending the wards of the Hôtel-Dieu and other hospitals. And not, I'm afraid, in the *pétits* salons of Versailles."

Veronique was grateful for her honesty, and didn't even find herself depressed when the Abbé, resuming his former easy manner, spoke of the great balls and delightful soirées in store for Versailles, the château and the town, during the forthcoming meetings of the States-General. "All this before your charming daughter is shut away in the convent. It is only fair that she discover the frailties of the world before she abjures them."

Although the Abbé surely was not aware of it, Veronique thought his description might suggest a way for her to meet Gilles Marsan during the meetings of the States-General. As a political artist he must almost certainly be in Versailles for this all-important event. If he had changed his mind about the "good angel" he had met so briefly in Normandy, she would know it after their first encounter. If she found his manner cool or embarrassed she would know that her choice for that other life, as Sœur Veronique, would at least be made easier.

While she was being undressed that night she said to Marie-Josette, "Everyone will go to hear the States-General conduct its sessions. *Everyone*, Josette! Especially the artists who make political sketches. . . ."

She held tight to this hope throughout the night and the next morning while her portmanteau, endless trunks and band-boxes were being lashed to the carriage and she said good-bye to her parents. Her mother was tearful but proud, embracing her and promising, "We will visit Paris very soon, when I am feeling a trifle more the thing."

Her father made an elaborate pretense that farewells were stuff and nonsense, but Veronique understood him very well, and sprinkled his fierce hug with a few tears that she did not try to brush away.

Minutes later the carriage rumbled off beneath the line of poplars, with Marie-Josette and the Abbé's valet seated facing the two women and the Abbé. Depressed now over her growing conviction that something would happen and she might not meet Gilles after all in crowded, tempestuous Versailles or Paris, Veronique did not immediately respond to the efforts of her companions to make conversation. Instead she held Gilles crucifix between her fingers and tried to convince herself that here was the assurance of his fidelity. . . .

At one of the large windows inside the château the Vicomtesse and Vicomte stood watching the retreating carriage.

"Claude, I am so pleased the Abbé will be accompanying Veronique to Versailles and on to Paris. I feel she is in the most . . . capable of hands."

"Yes, I suppose. . . ."

"You don't sound very convinced, dear."

"Well, Paris is a motley place, with all kinds of ruffians and low types roaming the streets—"

"But our Veronique won't be exposed to that street life—"

"No, but there are people there with dangerous ideas I would just as well not have our Veronique exposed to any more than she already may have been. In the case of one individual I have taken special precautions to prevent any such contamination. . . .'

"I don't understand, Cluade."

"It's not necessary for you to be bothered. I have merely acted as a father should in such matters to protect the welfare of his only daughter. Paris and Versailles may be a distance away, but nonetheless I shall have a special set of watchful eyes . . . well, no need, my dear, to discuss it further."

And that, for the moment was that. . . .

The Abbé tried to divert Veronique by repeating one of the scandalous anecdotes about the Queen that was presently spreading across the country, but Sister Thérèse cut in quietly with what she doubtless considered a more appropriate description of a nursing nun's life in the great Paris Hôtel-Dieu, and this so diverted Veronique that when they reached the High Road she neglected to look back along the row of poplars to the château in which she had been born.

It did not occur to her that she would never again enjoy the beautiful symmetry or the rose-gray stones of Vaudraye House as they looked that last April day of 1789.

Book Two

May 3—July 14, 1789

Lightning Overhead

1

AFTER three days of bumping over the badly rutted High
Roads, they entered the Abbé's "center of the universe." The
nights on their journey had been spent at the best inns available among what the Abbé dismissed as "a bad lot."

And very soon now Veronique knew she must face her own
future. Perhaps there would be no opportunity for ambiva-
lence. Perhaps God alone would want her—accept her—but
during the last three days' journey she had gotten a very
strange notion of God's emissaries, if one judged by François
de St.-Hélier. Nevertheless, the glories of Versailles and its
environs lay before her and Veronique leaned forward in the
coach, determined to see everything—every house, statue and
fountain, every distinguished citizen and member of the
sparkling court. . . .

So this was what the center of the world looked like, this
crowded, glittering little town of Versailles, almost within sight
of the customs gates of Paris! And perhaps at no other time
in France's history would a wide-eyed visitor like Veronique
arrive at her cousin's rented townhouse near the great Château without having at least desired to see Paris first.

Sister Thérèse suggested that on the way to the temporary
Vaudraye residence in Versailles Veronique might like to
glimpse the mother house of the Order of Ste. Veronique,

which was buried deep in the overcrowded Marais quarter of Paris. But the Abbé objected in his ironic amused voice, "My dear Thérèse, do not seal up the child until she has a taste of life. Today, all of life that is worth living is at Versailles."

"Yes," Veronique put in quickly, hoping her eagerness did not show what lay behind it, "with the States-General about to meet, it should be just about the most important place in the world." Sister Thérèse need not know why that meeting was so important to *her*. She caught Marie-Josette's quick look and wondered if anyone else suspected.

The Abbé stifled a yawn, his amethyst and diamond ring bright as a winking eye.

"Child, child, when one speaks of Versailles, one talks of the Château. Not this absurd little town, which is a mere adjunct to the royal residence. Wait until you have met the Austrian Woman. I suspect you will abandon Holy Church and bankrupt your papa in order to look like her."

"Is Her Majesty so beautiful then?" asked Marie-Josette.

"To some eyes. I find that Habsburg lip too arrogant by half. I'll wager her kisses would produce an Alpine frost."

The maid looked shocked. Sister Thérèse, who had obviously spent a lifetime coping with her brother's indiscreet remarks, told him, "You are not asked to kiss Her Majesty."

"If so, I am the only gentleman at Versailles who is not."

Conversation like this appeared to be a commonplace at court but it made Veronique and her maid uncomfortable. It was also disappointing. This was not the type of church prelate Veronique had been taught to regard as without sin. She was pragmatic about the sins and shortcomings of ordinary people, but surely those who had taken vows to God ought to be superior in some respects. Otherwise they served no purpose in this world of great wealth and great misery. It was a world separated only by a restless bourgeoisie, growing daily more radical and feeding its radicalism on just such indiscretions as those of the Abbé St.-Hélier.

Veronique watched the busy scene around their coach, which rattled and jingled its way through the crowds of walkers, most of them surprisingly well dressed in their neat white neckcloths and dark suits, some elegant in satin and high heels. And churchmen. She had never seen so many churchmen of the noble class, gorgeous in their robes and jewels. If these were elected members of the three estates, the Nobles, the Clergy and the People, this first convocation of such an assembly in two hundred years would put everything to rights.

These were the greatest intellects in France, and therefore, as every Frenchman knew, the greatest in the world.

Somehow Veronique felt better on seeing them, just as she felt on noting the charming little streets with their narrow buildings side by side and only the normal animal and human excrement running in the gutters. The scene was nothing like the terrifying descriptions of Paris she'd read about. Versailles was very near the great capital and yet it looked as if it really belonged in another world.

It had rained for several days previously and the elegant nobles and clergy seemed to go out of their way to splash the soberly dressed lawyer-delegates of the Third Estate as their carriages passed. But perhaps it was a coincidence noted by Veronique because of things she'd recently heard said by Gilles Marsan and others.

Then, suddenly, the first unpleasant incident occurred. Just as the sun cast its diluted rays out through the overcast the St.-Hélier coachwheels spun through a sinkhole of mud, showering several pedestrians walking along the narrow, shop-lined street. Among them were two men walking together, neat and a trifle forbidding. They both wore spectacles, not a common sight. The shorter man, in his bottle-green suit and precise, almost mincing walk, turned as he was splashed and removed his spectacles to wipe them clean. His every move was unhurried, thoughtful. He looked up at the occupants of the coach and then directly into Veronique's eyes. She had the peculiar sensation that he was fixing her face in his memory, but there was no emotion in that gaze, neither hate nor admiration, nor any other discernible human feeling.

His companion, on the contrary, was a tall, gaunt man who looked familiar. It was Raymond Berthelot. He angrily shook his walking-stick at them, and in the circumstances Veronique could hardly blame him.

"Parasites," Berthelot shouted out, "lapdogs of the Church. . . ."

He'd seen Sister Thérèse's habit and her brother's mauve silk surcoat. Raymond Berthelot was clearly a delegate, and it was also obvious that he represented the Third Estate made up of the bourgeois and the working classes.

"Canaille," said the Abbé coolly.

As the coach rolled on, Veronique saw Berthelot turn to his friend, the little man in the bottle-green coat, and finish his complaint, still punctuating his words with his stick. Veronique settled herself again, but now she had something new to worry about. Had Yolande Berthelot come to Versailles with her brother? And was she here to see Gilles? *Would* she see Gilles?

"Curious creature," murmured the Abbé. His thoughtful manner was new. Up to now Veronique had not noticed that anything disturbed him except physical discomfort, or boredom.

Marie-Josette started to mention Berthelot to Veronique, who said, "Do you mean the man who shouted at us? I can tell you that he is a member of the Jacobin Society and a delegate of the Third Estate—"

"No," the Abbé said, and buffed his fingernails on his sleeve. "I refer to the other fellow, the little one who said nothing. I doubt I have ever seen such cold eyes."

Sister Thérèse sat forward, showing her first signs of real animation. "Come, no more politics. We are passing the Château."

Veronique and Marie-Josette pressed excitedly against the windows to see the palace, where their majesties lived.

Marie-Josette was awed, but Veronique's first reaction was disappointment. The coach was passing the enormous square called the Place d'Armes, and Veronique found the throngs of sightseers, the citizens, visitors and delegates more interesting than the great drab gray front of the fabled palace beyond the square.

"The buildings might as well be a prison," she murmured, shocking her maid and surprising Sister Thérèse. The Abbé laughed.

Millions upon millions of francs spent to create it; three kings have lived there; the greatest roster of guests in history . . . and our young postulant sees that collection of monuments to the Great Louis as a prison." He looked out briefly, with his now nearly familiar wry detachment: "Well, then, perhaps it is. Who knows?"

Veronique wondered if anything would ever overturn that cynical amusement of his. All the same, her opinion of the series of heavy gray buildings forming the Palace of Versailles had not changed, and was only reinforced by the swarms of satin courtiers, and the uniformed officers coming and going through every conceivable opening in the enormous enclave.

There was so much traffic through and around the great Place d'Armes that the St.-Hélier coach was forced to draw up and wait while troops of foreign-looking cavalry crossed their path in both directions.

"Swiss, mademoiselle," said the Abbé's valet, speaking for the first time that day. "His French majesty is protected at all times by foreigners. He would not place his life in a Frenchman's hands—"

Veronique was so startled at his tone that she turned to the Abbé, who made a sweeping gesture in his manservant's direction. "Pettré is a democrat, *chérie*. But we deal very well together, he and I. He considers me worthless, I consider him canaille—so we can despise each other but never ourselves."

Her sense of irony did not stretch this far and she was relieved when the coach started up again, turning off into a narrow crowded street of seventeenth-century houses pushed in against each other, with an occasional shop set into a ground floor. The neighborhood looked intriguing to Veronique but she was surprised to find Cousin Alex living here. And as for Cousin Sylvie, her desire to be present at all the royal activities must be excessive. Cousin Sylvie gravitated between miserliness and extravagance, depending on her mood, but she never forgot that her great grandfather had been in the ministry of the Sun King when the great Château of Versailles was being created.

Two of Cousin Alex's liveried grooms strolled up and down in the street outside the door of the fourth house from the corner, obviously waiting for Veronique and her escorts, who would stay long enough to greet the gregarious Sylvie. Veronique wondered how many hours the grooms had been waiting. Not that it would matter to Alex and Sylvie. They were hopelessly improvident and lived their lives on her father's benevolence and the credit gained as his heirs. Nonetheless, Veronique tended to share her mother's liking for the jolly pair.

"That's the house," she exclaimed, and tried to open the carriage door. "It must be. No one else would waste servants' time like that. Would you open the coach door and let down the steps?"

The team had halted with a jolt that made the carriage jerk back, then forward, and while Sister Thérèse was saying, "Be easy, my dear," Veronique had already started down the steps, her heavy skirts swinging around her hips and displaying trim ankles, to the delighted shock of the Vaudraye grooms and the enjoyment of the Abbé. It was the latter who lifted her down to the cobbles, but she managed to slip through his hands and run to the newly gilded iron gate that opened on a dark staircase to the right and a miniature garden straight ahead. Veronique peered in through the bars, saw that many rooms of the surrounding three-story buildings opened on this theatrical-looking little pocket of greenery. How ingenious they were, these people who were forced to live in cities . . . they brought the green countryside with them even if it was only a dream, no bigger than a patch pocket, with one tiny tree, some grass, a stone bench, and a flowery bush or two.

She decided that if she should marry Gilles Marsan and they were very poor, they too would have a garden like this, no bigger than a handkerchief.

By this time a tall, liveried fellow with a huge moustache had appeared behind the gilded bars and opened the gate, with a low bow that made Veronique suspect he'd acquired his manners either in a palace or a bordello. While this obsequious air did not suit her, it was eminently correct for the distinguished Abbé François de St.-Hélier and Sister Thérèse, whose beauty was only exceeded by her calm, elegant presence.

"Two grooms with nothing to do but wait for us day after day until we arrived! How grand they do live, your cousins!" whispered Marie-Josette, close enough so that she tickled Veronique's ear and set her hat brim even more crookedly than the current style permitted.

The Abbé and Sister Thérèse followed the magnificent major-domo at a decent pace up to the living quarters of the building while Veronique ran on ahead. Knowing she could count on the exuberance of her cousin's wife, she called out as she reached the exquisitely furnished little foyer. "Sylvie, we are here!"

A footman appeared from nowhere to open the narrow but elegant doors on a salon that ran the length of the building and was so excessively mirrored that Veronique saw herself reproduced everywhere: her muff half off one wrist, her hat and hair disheveled, one of her skirts caught on a side puff over her overdress, her cloak hanging from its cloakstrings, threatening to strangle her. The long, gold room was lighted at midday by crystal lustres of superb brilliance, but no more brilliant than Sylvie de Vaudraye herself, a woman of middle age and comfortable figure even when heavily laced.

Her short neck and substantial throat seemed by custom the perfect repository for the collar of diamonds she habitually paraded at evening functions, though today she wore only the matched diamond hair crescent and heavy earbobs. Her white gauze gown was in a new style, with tight, long sleeves, a higher waistline, and the skirts falling in full natural folds.

But the face that rose out of the short neck was the object of Veronique's great interest. Born with thick lips, narrow eyes and a powerful Roman nose, Sylvie-Marguerite du Plessis de Vaudraye had learned as an infant how to captivate her audience with her manner if not her face. She showed fully as much enthusiasm as Veronique, hurrying now to greet and embrace her.

"Veronique, my love, what a blessing to see you! You're a breath of pure country air, we've been so bored! You can have no notion how dull it's been since the little dauphin's illness. . . ."

Before Veronique could offer sympathy for the Queen who, heaven knew, was in enough trouble without having family worries, Cousin Sylvie bubbled on. "Court ceremony cut to a minimum—less than two hours for the King's *levée* yesterday, Alex tells me. Because the King wanted to go and sit by his son's bedside. And—"

"Darling Sylvie, two hours are quite long enough even for a king to rise on a busy morning—"

"Hush! Always so sensible. My love, I cannot wait to have you properly gowned and your hair . . . is it always that straight? Well, no matter. Oh!" she exclaimed renewed pleasure over Veronique's shoulder. "My dear St.-Hélier, how good to have you back among the living . . . now the court may proceed with its soirées for those tiresome delegates. Life has been intolerable in your absence. And then to have every decent townhouse taken to hold the rabble. What's France coming to?"

To the Abbé's sister, Thérèse, she was a trifle less informal, but by this time maids were fluttering around and the Abbé had asked for a cordial of some exotic essence known only to Sylvie.

Veronique thought the household would be quite easy to fit into—or out of. And ideal for her purposes. No one would miss her when she was gone. Everyone would be sure to say how captivated they were when she returned. . . . Had Sylvie du Plessis married Louis XVI, she would have conducted affairs at the palace of Versailles in much the same haphazard fashion.

Veronique was anxious to go to the vicinity of the hall where the States-General would meet in two days, but unfortunately her hopes of catching an early glimpse of Marsan—didn't artists go to the scene of their future work and study it beforehand?—were quickly dampened by the prospect of the many activities planned by Sylvie and Alex.

"Tomorrow is the formal procession of the court and the delegates of the three estates," Sylvie at once informed her. "They go to the Church of St. Louis for the blessing and to sing a *Te Deum* for the success of the silly business."

"We've rented a balcony," Alex said proudly, inflating his plump cheeks. "A perfect place opposite one of the lesser buildings of the Palace. As a delegate I will, of course, take my place in the procession. I represent the nobles of the Paris-Meudon section."

"Shall we see the King and Queen?" Veronique wanted to know. She was surprised at her own eagerness.

Alex waved a stout hand. "Certainly, certainly, cousin. And there will be some excitement out of that, you may be sure. The Queen's appearances these days usually produce a show of some sort."

But first, Sylvie reminded, none of Veronique's wardrobe would be suitable for introductions to their majesties when the proper time had been arranged. It was quite useless for Veronique to remind her that within three months she would very likely be wearing a postulant's clothing together with the heavy, bloodstained pinafores or aprons used during the operations at the Hôtel-Dieu.

When Sister Thérèse and her worldly brother had departed, Sylvie told her, "Veronique, you simply do not understand court etiquette. One wears a gown only once, and hopes to look as much in the manner of her majesty as possible. She is the model by which we judge our own dress. That she is too concerned over that wretched—that unfortunate—boy to notice is quite beside the point . . . *we*, at least, follow propriety. . . ."

Veronique looked directly at her and spoke with a conviction that momentarily startled her. "Dear Sylvie . . . in the provinces where I come from, men and women—and children too—are dying in the fields. Only a few can be cared for even when we do get them to the hospital or the pesthouse. Have you any conception what starvation means?"

"Yes, my love. Naturally, I know. It's dreadful. That busybody finance minister, Monsieur Necker, is forever reminding us. It has something to do with the treasury being bankrupt. Her majesty detests him. He will be dismissed again soon, mark me." Sylvie tapped her fan against her teeth, considering this weighty problem. "It's all so absurd, really. As I said to dear Alex yesterday, or the day before, if there is no gold, we must manufacture more silver. Or buy the gold from some country that enjoys an abundance. Those dreadful Swiss, for example. Monsieur Necker is a Swiss. Between us, I suspect this entire bankruptcy and the talk of starvation is some devious plan of his to sell us Swiss gold."

"Cousin Sylvie . . ." Veronique began, but then gave it up, defeated. Despite herself, she felt almost amused, and only the remembrance of Gilles Marsan's starving aunt and uncle kept her from giving way to the ridiculous aspects of Sylvie's economics.

However, she flatly refused to have a new wardrobe made; so Sylvie, in despair at her lack of taste, was forced to compromise on having her gowns, hats, pelisses and cloaks revised to the present fashion.

". . . for they change momentarily. Meanwhile, tonight you must be tired after your boring journey; we will take care not to excite you too much. Only a few visitors. No one of any consequence."

Once Veronique reached her elaborate white-and-silver bedchamber she hurriedly bolted the big paneled double doors leading from the entrance foyer of the suite and turned to Marie-Josette, who was examining the little salon that adjoined the bedchamber on the far side.

"Josette, I want to leave here and return without being seen. Is that possible?"

"Now, mam'selle? But you've only just arrived." Seeing this meant absolutely nothing to her mistress, she added doubtfully, "You could reach the main staircase through the little foyer beyond the salon. Some wandering servant might see us, but then—"

"He might not. You could go first, Josette, and attract his attention. Heaven knows you are pretty enough."

Josette accepted this as her due and agreed to lend her pretty face to the enterprise.

"And one more thing, Josette. I must not wear anything as noticeable as these silly skirts. Get me something simple and unobtrusive."

"Not one of those dreadful things you wear to the hospital, I hope, mam'selle." Nevertheless, she went through the clothing in the nearest chests and came up with layers of what Veronique called the "absurd fashion" of the day; yet even as Josette pushed, shrugged and pinched her into the moss-green taffeta undergown with puffed overskirt of lace open down the front, she admitted, "All the same, I'm glad I'm not

expected to wear those dreadful panniers that were so popular
when mama was young."

"You will wear them when you're invited to court functions, mam'selle."

As Josette laced the bosom of her gown with white silk,
Veronique grumbled, "What a waste of time. When Gilles and
I are married I won't be invited to the Palace . . . and if Gilles
doesn't want me—"

"Want you? Oh, mam'selle . . ."

"—then I will go into the Convent of Ste. Veronique and
will be even less likely to be seen at Versailles. So, either way,
why can't I dress simply?"

"You would make a perfect Sister of Ste. Veronique. In
those robes you look so tall and splendid. All black and white,"
Josette said as she finished the lacing, then stood aside.

Veronique looked at herself in the long glass. She felt a
queer little twinge of the heart. A regret? A conscience? A
lifetime of dreams and plans banished for the love of one
man?

But such a man! Nobody, she felt sure, had ever loved
quite as she loved Gilles Marsan. His touch, even the thought
of his long, strong fingers caressing the flesh of her body gave
her a surge of delight. She saw her healthy golden flesh turn
pink at her own lascivious thoughts. The dream of childhood
and the immaculate purity of Ste. Veronique dissolved. She
clasped Josette's shoulders. "Think of it! I may see Gilles
today, or at all events find out how to reach him—"

"Will you run away with him, mam'selle? It would be very
cruel to your mama and the Vicomte."

"Gilles himself once asked me that. . . . I hope it will not
be necessary. I am not ashamed of loving him. . . . I expect
somehow we'll manage to persuade my cousins and then even
papa . . . mama will come around to it eventually—"

Josette shook her head. "I've heard tales—dreadful things
about sealing up young girls alive in those Paris tombs where
the Cemetery of the Innocents used to be. They say they were
fed through slots in the wall and never again got out until
they died at a hundred, or some such age. And the *lettre de
cachet* that nobles can get from the king that entitles them
to put away someone who doesn't marry as he's supposed to,
or who seeks to marry as he shouldn't . . . they could do that
to Monsieur Gilles. . . ."

"We are *not* in the Middle Ages now. No one is going to
seal me up in any tomb. And as for Gilles being thrown into

prison for daring to seek my hand, I should then go to papa and swear never to speak to him again. After all, he does love me. I am his only child. He would come around. He almost always comes around after we quarrel. . . ."

Saying all this, Veronique hoped she sounded more confident than she felt. It would help if at least one of them felt certain of that future. . . .

Marie-Josette nonetheless still had her doubts, but understanding Veronique's need of reassurance, made no more protests. The two girls started through the little hall to the entrance foyer at the head of the great circular staircase. No one stopped them. A door closed somewhere above the stairs and Marie-Josette fancied she heard a footstep, but was soon reassured by Veronique's calm. Somehow it seems almost too easy, Veronique thought, and then reminded herself that it was not as if they were committing a criminal act. Why should anyone be so concerned with their actions as to spy on them? Nevertheless, when they stepped out upon the street it seemed a *trifle* odd that not a single servant from her cousin's house was on or near the street to observe their departure.

2

VERONIQUE asked a gentleman in an exquisite barred silk coat and clocked hose where they might find the hall where the States-General was to meet. Much to the surprise of curious passersby, she then walked the distance to the *Salle des Menus Plaisirs*, with Josette taking small hurried steps beside her. The streets seemed perfectly safe on this spring afternoon. Versailles was temporarily drying off between rains. But Josette kept reminding her that ladies, especially ladies of good families, did not walk about the streets without male escorts.

This seemed rapidly disproved at the hall, Veronique's goal, when she had to push her way through crowds discussing the utopia ahead when the three Estates of Clergy, Nobles and Commoners would begin to work together for the good of France. . . .

"*If* they ever do," Veronique said to Josette, "and a very large *if* it is, too."

She credited them with sincerity, which was not enough. She'd often observed her father's friends, or the nuns and local ladies at the Hôtel-Dieu in Vaudraye as they talked endlessly of proposed improvements. But nothing was done until someone among them took command, assigned tasks and put the proposed improvements into action.

As she tried to make her way through the crowded area between the open doors, she wondered whose voice and whose command would save France now. Certainly not the haughty doorman in the royal livery who was forbidding her entrance, though his self-importance seemed boundless.

"Visitors with credentials will be permitted into the galleries in two days, mademoiselle, upon the opening ceremonies of the States-General. The procession is tomorrow."

She knew all of this and while seeming to agree meekly tried to slip behind him as he majestically addressed another intruder. Here she found herself elbowed aside by a nobleman's lackey but managed to get herself pushed into a corner within the forecourt of the great pillared meeting hall. Had she visited Paris, or even the palace at Versailles before coming here she might not have been so impressed. As it was, she caught her breath and then made her way between groups of men discussing the weighty problem of the moment, which seemed to be the seating arrangements. Josette frantically clutched the hem of her mistress's lace pelisse.

"We should not be here, mam'selle. Truly, we should not!" All of which Veronique ignored.

She was, however, shaken when a voice called her name and she was greeted by Yolande Berthelot, somehow in the midst of all this confusion managing to look like a dainty jonquil.

"Mademoiselle! What a surprise . . . you have come to discover the hall where France will be forever changed—"

"More or less," Veronique said, trying not to join Marie-Josette in examining every seam of Mademoiselle Berthelot's yellow gown and spencer.

"If you will accompany me, I can show you an excellent vantage point where the delegates may be heard testing their voices for resonance and possible echoes—"

"Thank you. You are too kind, but I thought I would merely walk around behind these pillars and—"

"It's forbidden to remain on this floor today unless one is a representative of the States-General. There are excellent places in the gallery arcade above us where, by the way, you may hear my brother being tutored in his maiden speech by our old friend Monsieur Marsan."

Veronique somehow managed to retain her outward poise. "That sounds very instructive. I'd no idea Monsieur Marsan possessed such talents."

"Yes. He's a man of many talents, as those of us who know

him well have so often seen him demonstrate."

Veronique ignored that. They ascended the great stairs at the end of the arcade and passed on to a gallery with several levels and a view of the floor below impeded only by the magnificence of the pillars that lined the hall. After glancing at Veronique, Mademoiselle Berthelot looked away and said, "I trust you will stop by to see Gilles afterward. He's talked endlessly to my brother, and others, about you . . . claims, in fact, that you're a better democrat than any of us—"

Marie-Josette cut in with her artless enthusiasm. "Oh, I believe mam'selle will be ever so pleased to see monsieur—"

To cover the awkwardness of this disclosure was impossible, Veronique saw, and so she said quietly that, yes, it would be nice to see Gilles Marsan again.

Yolande, nodding, made a sweeping gesture toward the floor below. At the end of the long hall was the baldachin with curtains draped aside, revealing the place beneath where the King's throne would be set, with Marie Antoinette beside him at a lower level. On this raised dais the favored members of the court would sit while the members of the three estates would be below the steps, on the floor of the hall.

It was here at the break of the steps and directly in front of the throne's position that Veronique, following now Yolande's more pointed gesture, made out Raymond Berthelot, tall, gaunt, seeming perhaps too reserved to be an effective orator, taking instructions from Gilles Marsan, who stood on the floor below him, lithe and agile in breeches and boots and rolled shirtsleeves.

"No, no, good God, no!" Marsan was shouting. "Have you no imagination? Do you *know* what it is to be hungry? Get it into your voice!"

"I am, damn you! But I'm not a playactor, and when you attack the Church you make unnecessary enemies—"

Gilles swung around, walked away to calm himself and then came back. "All right. I know only one person who genuinely believes in the business of the Church—"

"I know! And I am growing sick of your precious angel!"

"And I with your cold-bloodedness. Now, shall we try it again?"

Berthelot took a deep breath. "Monseigneurs . . . messieurs . . . this is the food of the people of France! Eat it. Let me see you chew this moulding straw if you dare. . . ." It was absurdly melodramatic for a man of Berthelot's tight, monotonous voice.

"Throw the pieces of bread."

"Throw—oh, yes, damn . . ." Veronique had never thought she would pity Monsieur Berthelot, but it was obvious he was pitifully inept at rousing multitudes. He made stiff gestures meant to indicate the throwing of bread among the delegates but which looked more like salutes to a commander-in-chief.

Marsan went up the steps to the dais. "Good God, Raymond! You say you believe in overthrowing this medieval tyranny of the Church and the throne, but when you mention something as practical as rotting bread, you sound flat and cold. Indifferent. I repeat, you don't seem to know what it is to feel your vitals burn and twist with such hunger that you'd kill for that rotting garbage—"

Berthelot answered impatiently, "I do not have to starve in order to understand suffering, and I repeat that it is dangerous to fight the Church. They have more power than Louis and Antoinette and the entire court. Indeed, half Paris is Church property."

"All the more reason they should pay their share of the tithes and taxes. It is you delegates who must pass those laws. And if your speeches sound like this, you'll never persuade anyone to vote your way. . . ."

Suddenly Marsan raised his arm and seemed to point directly at the three women in the gallery. "There stands a follower of Christ. A man of poverty and humility. A man who would give the hair-shirt on his back to the poor and hungry. Look at him!"

Berthelot shaded his eyes and looked up. Veronique, who was behind a pillar, looked for the other witness farther along the gallery, and found herself staring into the amused gray eyes of the Abbé St.-Hélier. He nodded to her, then leaned over the low carved stone balustrade to answer Marsan.

"Bravo, Monsieur Marsan! I could not have expressed your admiration better myself," and he applauded delicately.

Gilles bowed his thanks but the disdain in his smile and his exaggerated bow equaled the Abbé's contempt. "Your opinion, monseigneur, will, of course, guide all our actions."

It was plain to Veronique that the Abbé was more disconcerted by this sardonic response than by the original insult. Surely, she thought, anyone would know Gilles did not really believe those terrible accusations against the Holy Church. All were not like the Abbé with his jeweled fingers and buckled shoes. Gilles said those things because his aunt and uncle had died in poverty. . . . But he could not mean all of it . . . not the fair-minded man she loved. She knew that once Gilles came to know her well and to understand the glory as well as the great usefulness of the Church he would atone and return to the faith he'd been born to. . . .

"He cannot see you behind that pillar," Yolande said. "Shall I tell him you are up here in the gallery? Or will you go to meet him?"

"We will surprise him."

They started toward the stairs, where they were overtaken by the Abbé and his ubiquitous valet.

"Do let me escort you home, mademoiselle. I hardly think you will be further entertained here today."

The Abbé's manners were usually flawless. It was not like him to ignore the beautiful Yolande. But then, it seemed clear that Marsan's remarks had ruffled him. Veronique excused herself to her companions and walked over to him.

"Monseigneur—"

"After all those hours of travelers' intimacy, am I not François?"

"Monseigneur, pardon me, but do you wish to join in bringing down our Mother Church, which I should think you would agree is our most sacred possession?"

He was about to say something flippant, then quite obviously changed his mind. "And how do I bring down this sacred possession?"

"Look at yourself. In your manner of dress, in your jewels, your indifference to the suffering around you."

"Around *me*?"

"Ask yourself this, monseigneur. If Christ were to return today to seek out his followers, would he recognize you as one?"

"Or you, mademoiselle?"

"Very true. Thank you for the reminder." She turned and went to join the two curious young women at the foot of the steps.

Josette peeked around. "He isn't smiling," she observed between shock and satisfaction. "What on earth did you say to him, mam'selle?"

But by that time they'd reached the floor of the hall and Veronique did not hear her. She was too interested in observing Gilles's attitude toward the lovely blond Yolande. The latter came to the edge of the low barrier in front of the pillars, where she was now visible to the men on the dais.

She called out, "Raymond, how are you coming with your

speech? Do you think you can make them vote to tax the Church properties—"

"God knows," he said, then added in a melancholy voice, "or are we about to abolish God?"

Yolande was amused and Gilles said, "Congratulations. Your first joke, Raymond, though I doubt you meant it as such. In any case, I feel rewarded for my efforts. I'm going to dinner."

"Before you leave," Yolande added, "I have a surprise for you, Gilles."

He reached the barrier, gave Yolande a careless wave and was about to leap over the barrier when he finally spotted Veronique and looked so astonished she had to laugh.

"No, monsieur, I am not in Vaudraye, as you can see."

"I see, but I can't believe. My darling—" He saw a dozen interested bystanders and amended—"my darling mademoiselle, I must see you . . . that is, to discuss . . . everything. . . ."

"Everything?"

She had extended her hand above the low barrier separating them, and he was bent over it. Now he looked up suddenly. "Let me show you around the hall."

"But, monsieur!" Josette said, anxious to have a part in the reunion, "We've been shown around the hall."

"In that case," Gilles said politely, "you will not care to accompany us."

"Come along," Yolande said to Josette, as if exasperated. "We will go and drink some English tea." And to Veronique she said, "Beware, mademoiselle, as you walk about the great hall. It inspires flights of oratory on almost any subject."

Marsan reached for Veronique, his hands closing around her waist. He lifted her over the barrier. In her dreams of this meeting, she had expected a slow, profoundly romantic encounter. His kiss would begin at her fingers and ultimately touch her lips, gentle and tender. Instead there was this hard, almost painful grasp and a kiss that robbed her of breath. Unexpected or not, her entire body responded to his, and with enthusiasm.

They were shaken out of this brief, delicious reunion by Berthelot's cold voice. "It would appear you have converted at least one aristo to the people's cause, Gilles."

Marsan released Veronique slowly, but kept his arm around her waist. "Be quiet, Raymond. You never understood starvation in any form."

He then led Veronique to a quiet, shadowed corner of the

hall behind the baldachin prepared for the royal throne. Here he took her hands, stood off and looked her over from her crooked bonnet to the pointed silk toes of her shoes. His dark eyes seemed lighted, his smile youthful, almost boyish, different from the fiery, almost arrogant quality he demonstrated when urging on Berthelot in his speech.

"I was nearly resigned that you'd been playing at one of those aristocrat games . . . the Jacobin courier has been to Vaudraye twice and not a single word from you." He paused and looked at her hungrily. "Do you know, you haven't changed in the least detail?"

"After less than a week?"

They laughed together. But he stopped suddenly and looked at her in the serious, tender way she remembered from Vaudraye that last time. He touched the thin silver chain at her throat. "Is it mine?"

She teased him. "How many lava stones do you imagine I wear so close to my heart?"

His fingers caressed the chain and drew it up from the warmth between her breasts. He held the ancient crucifix in his hand, then brought it to his lips. "This surely must be the first time the old pumice cross was ever so sweetly perfumed—"

She colored. "When you make speeches like that, you might almost be François."

"François? Is he a rival?" He pretended to be amused but she was delighted at the spark of anger in his eyes.

"The Abbé de St.-Hélier."

"*That* popinjay?" His relief further pleased her. He reached for the front of her gown. Much as she desired his intimate touch, she drew back slightly.

"Gilles, please . . ."

"But I am only about to return my pledge to its rightful place."

She laughed to cover her excitement. "No, indeed, monsieur," and so saying, took the crucifix from him and dropped it between her breasts.

He again took her hands between his. "I've thought of a thousand reasons why you might have changed. But you *are* the same," and he drew her to him again, her head under his chin as he reminded her, "When you belong to me I'm afraid you will lose this fine silken life of yours. . . ."

"I know."

She had not thought, even an hour ago, that she could want

him so much, and find him so endearing. Even his youthful enthusiasm had a sensual impact for her. Still imagining their future, a lifetime to enjoy what she felt now with him, she raised her head to see a motionless shadow in the gallery over their heads. And then a shadow that took on features that seemed all too familiar—small hateful eyes, a loose-jointed figure. . . .

Her stiffening body warned Gilles, and he followed her glance. "Who the devil is that? Your dashing Abbé?"

"I thought he looked more like papa's old gamekeeper, Arnauld de Gleeb."

He didn't scoff at her suspicion. After a moment's observation he moved her over behind the pillar. "Don't leave this spot until I return. That madman is obviously dangerous." He stepped out onto the dais, called to Berthelot in a low voice, "Raymond, we may have a murderer here—that damned gamekeeper from Vaudraye."

Veronique wished now she'd not called Gilles's attention to his old enemy, if that solitary, shadowed watcher actually was de Gleeb. Berthelot looked uneasy as Gilles pointed to Veronique. "Take care of her." Then he uncovered the jacket he'd hung over one of the chairs stacked at the side of the dais. Veronique heard him draw a curious whirring sound, a metallic rattle. She watched him draw a slender rapier from beneath the jacket. She hardly had any interest in de Gleeb's well-being, but she also did not want Gilles to go after him with a sword. As a commoner he could face awful penalties if de Gleeb were harmed.

She stepped out onto the dais and would have followed him, but Berthelot stood in her way. "No, mademoiselle!" he said icily. "You have caused enough harm—"

She was about to answer when Yolande Berthelot and Marie-Josette came hurrying across the empty hall, where lackeys at the far end were placing temporary benches for the meetings to come. And soon, to her relief, Marsan appeared in the gallery where she'd seen what she thought was de Gleeb.

Marsan looked down at the anxious group below him. "One of the guards says someone of de Gleeb's description left by the far door. In any case, he seems to have vanished into the street crowd."

As Marsan left the gallery and started down to join the others on the main floor, Veronique said anxiously, "I didn't think Monsieur Marsan wore a sword. Isn't that considered a dangerous challenge to the Nobles?"

Berthelot ignored her but his sister explained. "It would be dangerous for Gilles not to have a weapon. They say one of the first acts of the Assembly will be to put the delegates beyond arrest. This may protect Raymond and other delegates, but Gilles has no such protection. Lately some of the nobles who will thereby be safe from arrest have hired cutthroats to eliminate people like Gilles who oppose them. They fear particularly the power of Gilles's satirical sketches."

"Marsan is a fool," Berthelot said. "He should have gotten himself nominated to the States-General—"

"What? And be bored to death by your speeches every day?" Marsan had come down the last steps and over to the dais. "Besides, my real weapon is the pen and brush."

"So long as it isn't that sword," Yolande remarked, but he merely shrugged as he sheathed it and, having put on his coat, casually hung the sword belt over his shoulder. He obviously intended to escort Veronique and Josette back to her cousins' house, even though Veronique worried that de Gleeb or someone else on his mission might be waiting to attack Gilles near the Vaudraye house. Arguing him out of this, however, was like quarreling with the wind. When they reached the house Veronique turned to him. "Please take care when you return, watch for ambush, a quarrel, anything . . . promise me."

"Of course, I've no intention of getting myself killed now." He took her into his arms, ignoring her reminder that they needed to be cautious, and kissed her, which, delightfully, made further protest impossible. It was Marie-Josette who tapped Marsan on the shoulder.

"Monsieur, take care. I believe there is someone in the house watching at that window on the second story."

Veronique broke from him quickly but could not help smiling as he said, "Then perhaps I should go up now and ask permission for the banns to be posted."

"And thoroughly shock them?" Veronique said. "Remember, they think I'm to enter Ste. Veronique as a postulant. If I remain in secular life they will lose father's estate—since it will then fall to me."

"Your father's estate?" And then, with that gentleness which already surprised and moved her, he said, "One of the laws to benefit France must take away those medieval tithes and taxes. It may leave your father much poorer. In the end

I suspect you will have to choose between your father's world and mine. And however his may be diminished, mine is sure to be even poorer."

"I haven't spent all my days in Vaudraye House. I know how the poor live."

He held her hands tightly in his. "This is a devil of a place to talk," and when Marie-Josette nudged him and whispered, "Hurry!" he told Veronique he'd contact her through her maid. . . . "And I think you'd better see something of my world before you give up your father's."

She didn't remind him that life in the cloister would have been poorer in physical comforts than any he might offer. Instead she leaned over their joined hands and kissed his cheek. "I believe you're challenging me—and a lady always accepts a challenge." Which was the light note on which they parted.

After he'd gone, Josette looked around her. "Did you see anyone along the way who looked like de Gleeb, mam'selle?"

"Certainly not . . . I've a suspicion I imagined the whole of it. I only wish I hadn't mentioned it to Gilles. . . ." But Veronique was not really so convinced that it was only the product of her imagination. It occurred to her that conceivably her father had not sent de Gleeb to the colonies but rather here and to Paris to "serve his sentence." He might well have reprieved him for the mission. . . . It was probably foolish of her not to have assumed all along that her father's dislike of Gilles, together with her apparent affection for him would have led him to do *something* to keep them apart. . . .

They were ushered now into her cousins' house by a lackey whose poorly concealed half-smile indicated he'd witnessed the tender moments in the street between Veronique and Marsan. When Veronique reached her bedchamber she directed Josette, "Please find out, if you can, who saw us from that window a few minutes ago besides the lackey. And also whether they've told anyone."

A few minutes later Sylvie came to inquire if her cousin had everything she desired. She seemed sincere and made no mention of Veronique's absence from the house. When Veronique casually asked how she'd spent the day, Sylvie dismissed it with a wave of her bejeweled hand.

"In bed, my love. Otherwise, how should I be able to glitter and charm all night? I see that you do the same. Believe me, a lady is always safe in bed." At Veronique's smile she added, "Providing, of course, she takes care what company she admits there."

Watching Marie-Josette come into the room now behind Sylvie, Veronique said after a slight pause, "Madame de Gleeb also used to say that. But I suppose she had a different problem with her husband. . . ."

Josette started nervously, but Cousin Sylvie yawned with apparent boredom. "I daresay. However, those Norman friends of yours are hardly suited to Versailles conversation." She patted the bed. "Beauty sleep, my love. Don't let me disturb you. Fortunately, tonight's soirée will be a small one. Nothing to concern you."

When she'd gone Josette closed the double doors carefully behind her and came back to her mistress. "Mam'selle, they were very strange to me, the servants in this house. They stop speaking among themselves when I come into a room. They are also shocking flirts, Jeannot would not approve at all . . . the first footman is so handsome you would not credit it. Truly, mam'selle, he asked me to attend what he called a petit salon for the upper servants. . . . May I?"

"Yes, certainly." It was clear nothing more of consequence was to be learned from her.

Cousin Sylvie's soirée that evening proved to be one of those rare occasions when Sylvie was guilty of understatement. The crimson salon, the fragile intimate salons on the floor above were all filled with the nobility and not a few of the upper clergy, to all of whom Veronique was presented in turn. She'd always supposed most of the nobility were like her father. Those she met this night seemed much more like pale and less interesting versions of the Abbé de St.-Hélier.

Late in the evening, during a "small supper" that would have seemed a banquet to Veronique's hospital friends at Vaudraye, one of the guests, a marquis and intimate of the king's youngest brother, the Comte d'Artois, brought out a placard that one of his lackeys had torn off a Paris wall. It was some sort of propaganda. Probably the Duc d'Orléans, the king's cousin, was responsible. Everyone knew how bitterly he hated his royal cousins.

"He only hires the best," someone remarked as they all gathered around the marquis. To Veronique's surprise and disgust these same courtiers who spent most of their nights fawning on Marie Antoinette and her circle now seemed bent on collecting and encouraging the libels being printed about the queen. She turned to her Cousin Alex, who looked as though he'd been stuffed into his tight satins, and said, "One would think they might sympathize with Her Majesty at a time like this. The dauphin ill, the country in a turmoil, so much hate directed toward her . . . and yet they dwell on that propaganda. Why, they don't even give her time to grieve. She is a mother, after all is said."

Alex was trying to balance a plate of salmon and goose liver pâtés while he raised his champagne glass to Veronique's lips.

"Drink, cousin. It will make you see the world as it is, not as an anteroom to a convent. You will do well to be out of it and safe in Ste. Veronique's before long." She turned her head away impatiently, but was shocked to hear him add, "Besides, it may be for the best if the poor brat of a dauphin dies. Who believes anymore that the King was his father?"

"What an infamous thing to say!"

He seemed hurt by her reaction. "But see here, cousin, I only repeat what is said everywhere. Orléans has been spreading it for years. And he ought to know."

"Orléans wants the throne!"

Sylvie, at her best as she moved from group to group, glittering like a crystal lustre, called to her husband. "Alex, you must see this. Quite extraordinary. And you, cousin."

Veronique would not allow herself to be dragged into that eager, scandal-loving crowd to admire one more piece of scurrilous propaganda, and so she let Alex join his wife and others while she stood apart, feeling utterly estranged from these people of her own class. Am I too priggish, she thought . . . too naïve and pompous? Too angry was perhaps closer to it. Her father and mother had taught her respect for the royal family, and it was not an easy thing to turn on them now, whatever their failures and stupidities.

As Alex studied the propaganda sheet Veronique wondered why those closest to the royal family enjoyed spreading scandal and the most brazen lies about them. After all, the destruction of the Queen might also bring down those around her. . . .

Suddenly Veronique became aware that the group with Cousin Alex had turned to stare in her direction. All the satin of their sleeves, the lace at throat and wrist seemed to reflect the candlelight everywhere. She felt blinded and confused. Why were they all staring at her?

Sylvie called, "Come, Veronique, see this astonishing thing."

Led as much by their odd stare as by her cousin's beckoning hand, Veronique moved to join them. No one said anything but she knew their attention had been fixed by the paper sketch torn off a wall on a street in Paris. She looked down at the sketch.

In its upper left corner a necklace, probably of diamonds, hung from the sill of a tall window. There could be no doubt that the window represented a church. A crucifix decorated one of its panes. In the lower right corner a girl's high-boned face looked up in anguish, her two thin hands holding out an empty bowl. The juxtaposition of the starving girl and the fabulous necklace was crude but enormously effective.

"Don't you see, cousin?" Sylvie prodded her, and then, as Veronique continued to study it, she led the general burst of laughter. "It's the very image of you."

The beautiful young Duchesse de St.-Aubans raised her voice which was thin, almost childlike, somehow at odds with the fabulous emeralds at her throat and her high-piled hair. She was one of the Queen's Ladies of the Bedchamber, but this didn't hinder her reveling in gossip about her mistress. "According to the artist, it would appear, this poor sweet starving wench asks for bread and receives no more than a glimpse of the necklace the Austrian swore she never ordered, and for solace hears the Queen's 'Let them eat cake.' God knows how, but our artist has made his starving wench look exactly like mademoiselle here."

The sketch was done with charcoal and brush. The only color appeared in the face of the girl, in the cheeks and eyes, the lips and the long, uncompromisingly straight black hair. She recognized it as the work of Gilles Marsan.

To everyone's amazement Veronique flushed with anger and said, "But think how the Queen must feel when she hears of this kind of slander."

"My, my, such anger from one so young and attractive." It was the Marquis who spoke. "Are you really so well informed as to be able to distinguish falsehood from truth? If so, I must say, mademoiselle, you are quite unique."

It was Alex who quickly came to Veronique's support. "But my good friend, I suspect my young cousin protests more the hurt of the thing than the truth of its inspiration. She is compassionate, and, of course, very young. . . ."

The Marquis smiled. "Oh, but you now introduce seriousness to this matter, which always dampens my interest in nearly everything but one."

The ladies all giggled appreciatively and fanned themselves.

"But isn't it interesting, my dear Marquis, that that one exception is primarily responsible for the whole 'affair of the diamond necklace?'" Alex now turned more to Veronique, as if to suggest that everyone else in the room already knew most of the story and from here on his recital was primarily for her benefit. "The necklace in question was ordered by Louis XV for his mistress Madame du Barry, and it was said it contained some five hundred diamonds. But the necklace wasn't finished in the King's lifetime and after his death du Barry retired from court. At this point another figure in the drama appears—Cardinal de Rohan. He'd fallen into disfavor with Marie Antoinette and so was anxious to repair his position with her. Well, the good cardinal was led to believe by a so-called Countess Jeanne de La Motte that the Queen was infatuated with him and furthermore that she was anxious to buy the diamond necklace and wished him to act as security for the price.

"The willing Cardinal Rohan agreed but the necklace was never delivered to the queen. It seems that Countess de La Motte's husband had disappeared from Paris and was selling some diamonds individually in London. None might have been the wiser, since all such affairs usually can be silenced at court, but when the jewelers went to court complaining that they had not been paid for their work the plot was exposed. The cardinal and the others were all imprisoned, as they should have been. But now politics enters the plot. Certain opponents of the Queen had the cardinal released, to humiliate her. You see the popular dislike of the Queen had been intensified by the affair in the first place, and this merely fueled it. By the way, the Countess de La Motte was sentenced to life in prison but she later escaped and no one knows how, with whose help, or to where."

Veronique, trying to absorb this complicated lesson in the cynical intrigues of the Court, was tempted to say her sympathies now lay even more with the Queen, but decided, uncharacteristically, that at least in this instance she would fall back on the discretion of silence.

3

VERONIQUE awoke frequently that night to painful thoughts. First was the possible threatening presence of Arnauld de Gleeb. Then came the memory of Gilles's disrespectful use of the Church to make his political point—and using *her* as his model.

Next morning Sylvie surprised her by rushing her out of the townhouse into the Vaudraye barouche and taking her on a far too comprehensive tour of the countryside, although she knew quite well that the great procession which opened the meetings of the States-General would take place almost before the ladies had time to change for the occasion. It seemed odd to Veronique and strangely impromptu, but it mattered little since her thoughts were almost entirely centered on Gilles Marsan and her own sense of disillusionment about him. She'd told herself she could not live without his love, but such an attack on the Church was an attack on her deepest being—on her, personally, she couldn't help feeling. . . .

As she noted the condition of the balcony rented by Alex for the view of the procession, Veronique had another surprise. She supposed she should have known that a simple balcony could never satisfy her cousins. The entire floor of the building on the main avenue had been leased for the day, and while Sylvie's party gathered around the court circular to read all the news of the Court and its Paris adjuncts, Veronique made her way across the floor to the balcony.

"Cousin, they mention you as arriving here yesterday," Sylvie called in triumph.

Veronique reflected on the strange values of these courtiers who found religion, the Church and even God obsolete, and yet prayed to be mentioned in a court circular issued in the name of a monarch they discredited. She smiled, pretended to be pleased at her cousin's boast and made her way past an exquisite console commode with a Chinese motif in black and bronze. There were already trays of food, hors d'oeuvres and pâtés for the most part, strategically placed on the various tables and low tabarets. Sylvie's chef had his own magnificent display, armed as he was with carving knife and haunches of venison and beef, along with trout and eels in sauce. But all were quite overshadowed by a boar's head stuffed with some exotic yellow fruit, surely no common Normandy apple. Vaudraye footmen stood by to pour champagne into goblets being passed about at a great rate.

Two of the glass doors to the balcony were open, and Veronique saw that no one need stand while watching the procession. A line of very low-seated chairs with green tapestry cushions had been provided. Marie-Josette and several other personal servants were not forgotten. They had their own chairs, less ornate, positioned behind the family.

"How splendid we are," Marie-Josette whispered as she followed her mistress out into the thick, muggy air of the balcony. "I'll wager your papa would be shocked at what is spent by these Parisians."

"That's a wager I couldn't afford to challenge," Veronique whispered back to her. They exchanged knowing glances and then turned their attention to the view in front of them. This rainiest of springs had brought another shower the night before and the sky was still gray and threatening. The air itself seemed heavy. For an instant it was difficult to make out distinctly beyond the street and the distant Place d'Armes the great mass of buildings that was the Palace of Versailles.

"That odd old building across the way," Josette pointed out excitedly, "they say is part of the royal stables."

"That grand edifice was a stable?"

Josette sighed but enjoyed the drama of her next disclosure. "They tell me the little dauphin is there, very sick, waiting to catch a glimpse of his mother. He's dying, you know."

Veronique tried in vain to make out the individuals but

could only imagine the anguish of the royal mother, forced to display herself in a public procession while her son lay dying within sight of her.

The streets were so tight-packed half an hour before the Vaudraye party arrived that it seemed not one more person could squeeze his way through the throng, but now, miraculously, a wide path had been forced along the center of the street. The mob of visitors and sightseers from Paris were herded into the gutters or pressed back against the buildings lining the way. Hanging from the balcony rented by Cousin Alex was a huge tapestry proudly bearing the coat of arms of the Vaudraye family, a white stag on a green field. In a long line beyond the building were houses whose windows or balconies were similarly decorated. In spite of the previous night's rain the decorations were festive and the people euphoric, as if the mere gathering of this gorgeous assemblage guaranteed better times ahead. It was, after all, the first meeting of the States-General in two hundred years!

To take her mind off the unfortunate dauphin across the way, Veronique tried to guess where the different figures in the crowd had come from, whether they were Parisians or provincials or foreigners. By this time Alex had gone to join the procession as a delegate representing the nobility, and Sylvie said, "I cannot remember when we've had such dreadful weather. No hunting, the races at Vincennes constantly delayed. . . ." To Veronique she explained, "His Majesty's brother, d'Artois, challenged Orléans last week and not a horse could stir. A wretched season."

Veronique, who knew neither the Comte d'Artois nor the Duc d'Orléans except to dislike the latter, spent her time studying the faces in the crowd lining the wide street two stories below. Marie-Josette whispered, "Do you see him, mam'selle?"

"See who?"

"But M'sieur Marsan, of course."

Veronique looked straight ahead, trying not to show her true emotions. "No, I was wondering more if de Gleeb might be out there. . . ." And to herself thought again of Gilles, her love for him, and the conflict he caused her by the outrageous sketches he made for the Duc d'Orléans, and for which he presumably was paid as well.

Marie-Josette studied her mistress. The change in Veronique since her first meeting with Gilles Marsan had been astonishing, and very much to her advantage. She was prettier, her color brighter, her manner more feminine, all the qualities thought more suitable to a young woman than that formidable air she wore when running the hospital.

They were both shaken by the shrill, stirring blast of trumpets.

"The procession!" Cousin Sylvie announced and drained her champagne glass, passing it to a footman behind her without looking back. The men in the party leaned over the women's elaborately coiffed heads, replete with feathers and piles of false hair, and peered into the murky distance.

Someone on Sylvie's other side asked, "What under heaven do they hope to accomplish, all those sober fellows with their high hopes?"

Sylvie grinned. "They intend to save France."

Veronique heard the amusement of the others at her cousin's easy cynicism. Her own common sense told her that these passionate, hopeful men about to march past them would make speeches, they would shake their fists at the preposterous expenditures of the court and government, then, in the end, they probably would borrow more money, pay the bills, and life would go on as it had, at least for the next few years.

She thought of cold-blooded, doctrinaire Raymond Berthelot, of Gilles's uncle, and Joseph Faure and Jeannot, who'd saved her. And Gilles . . . Whatever else he might be, his beliefs, she reminded herself, were sincere, even if she disapproved his methods . . . what was he doing at this moment . . . could he possibly be nearby . . . ?

Leaning over the balcony to see if he indeed might be somewhere in the crowd, she saw the approach of the great procession and was frankly stirred by the excitement of it. The trumpets' blast nearly deafened the mob along the way, but the cheering had already begun as the Third Estate, the lowest sector of the States-General, marched into sight, each man bearing a lighted taper whose flame, fed by the misty breeze, slanted eastward toward Paris, the heart of the country's turmoil.

The center of the wide avenue became a pattern of black and white as the Third Estate delegates walked past in their black suits, snowy white cravats, white hose and neatly buckled shoes. Lawyers, for the most part—less than a dozen of them were members of the laboring class—they represented new hope for the nation. Perhaps its last hope. And they were incessantly cheered by the bystanders on the street.

Veronique, despite herself, kept fancying she saw Gilles Marsan in the crowd, but these shadowy figures never got close enough for her to be at all certain, thanks to the Royal Swiss and the other guards who kept the people at a safe distance from the windows of the aristocrats to prevent possible riots. It was maddening to imagine she saw him and then find he'd disappeared in the crowd. She finally concluded, as her logic had told her all along, that these many Marsans were an illusion. Perhaps Gilles was not even in Versailles today. . . .

Sylvie exclaimed, "How dismal they look—all alike in their black and white, all in tricornes. How very many of them there are!"

One of her friends said, loudly enough to be heard by the marchers below, "It's fortunate the master of ceremonies required them to dress precisely the same. Otherwise I daresay they would have arrived in paint, powder and satin to ape their betters."

Studying the faces below as they passed her, flanked by the royal standard and the flickering candles, Veronique did make out, ironically, the gaunt face of Raymond Berthelot and just in front of him, mincing carefully on his high heels, the little man who'd stared at her in the Abbé's carriage yesterday. He looked the very proper bourgeois lawyer that he was. A sensible man. And God knew there would be need of them. Again he seemed to lack expression, until a delegate on the right whispered to him, pointing at the gorgeously dressed audience on the Vaudraye balcony. Then he looked up with a tight, thin-lipped smile that did not reach his eyes, though he was not wearing his spectacles today.

Everyone on the balcony saw him. Sylvie's friend, the indiscreet and loud-voiced marquis, called out, "There, you see? That little fellow is quite an orator in the Jacobin Society. A lawyer from Arras who I believe calls himself Maximilien de Robespierre—"

"Heavens," Sylvie said, and added to Veronique behind her fan, "he just smiled at me. The most tigerish smile . . ."

Veronique laughed, teasing her. "Have you ever seen a tiger smile?"

All the same, she thought, the comparison was very apt.

Forgetting Monsieur de Robespierre and his bourgeois friends, Sylvie nudged Veronique. "There's Alex among the nobles. Really, one would never think he was so stout. How splendid he looks!"

He walked with the contingent of nobles who left a noticeable distance between themselves and the contamination of the Third Estate. One man, however, elegant, supercilious and, to Veronique's observation, a born actor, strode along in that otherwise empty space between commoners and nobles. He made it clear that he preferred not to be counted among his own noble class although, from his dress, he certainly belonged to it. Whoever he was, the crowd adored him and he played to them assiduously with every elegant step, every benevolent smile. Occasionally he spread his hands as if he were conferring a blessing upon his admirers.

"Who is that—that playactor?" Veronique asked as he passed.

Sylvie was shocked at her ignorance. "But my love, *that* is the Duc d'Orléans, the King's cousin. Of course he detests the royal family. He prides himself on being a man of the people—"

The cries were everywhere: *"Vive le duc! Vive Orléans!* The people's champion!"

So this was the man at the back of those lies about the Queen! The man who paid for the scurrilous writings, the drawings, the unspeakable slander spread against his King and Queen. This, unfortunately, was Gilles's employer.

She remarked sardonically, "He manages to wear those jewels. And those royal orders on his chest haven't yet been pawned for the relief of the poor."

Nevertheless, everyone on the balcony seemed to find him fascinating until Sylvie again called their attention to Colonel Alexandre de Vaudraye, looking immense but not unimpressive in full white dress uniform and adorned as he was with his decorations earned in the North American campaign. To those of his friends and his relations on the balcony he was the center of interest. The other nobles, for all their glitter and grandeur, seemed to Veronique no more than copies of these men and women she'd met the night before. She began to be anxious for the climax of this procession—her first sight of their majesties.

The high clergy, like the nobles, were in gorgeous array, the more noticeable in their richness because they preceded the local curés, peasant priests of the laboring class who, like the Third Estate, were a mass of somber black with their only brightness the tapers each carried. Veronique wondered what would happen if those curés decided to vote with their fellow commoners of the Third Estate. An alarming thought? She doubted Gilles and Berthelot and that little lawyer from Arras would think it so. . . .

From the distance the cheers could be heard again. The court, in all its splendor, had begun to pass the onlookers far down the avenue. As the King appeared, it was with satisfaction—relief, even—that Veronique heard the cheers of the crowd:

"Vive le roi! God save the Good Louis!" And other remarks sympathetic but far from laudatory: "Poor fellow . . . he looks like any good man from the country. . . ." And worst of all, half hidden under the warm friendliness the King produced in his subjects, was the undercurrent of "Poor cuckold, with the Austrian Bitch for a wife. . . ."

In spite of all that she'd heard, the sight of Louis XVI was a shock to Veronique. A stout man, he had none of his brothers' courtly grace. In fact, he shuffled along under his fantastic gold cloth cape with one of the world's great diamonds glistening from his headpiece. Beneath all this grandeur his massive shoulders sagged. Veronique thought that from his manner he might have been bearing the weight of the universe. Perhaps he felt that he was. His thick lips moved, trembled, as he gave a little side glance toward the building where his son lay. Afterward he stared glumly ahead. Now and then he inclined his head in a vague response to the burst of cheers from his subjects.

Unlike the King, Marie Antoinette was all that Veronique had long pictured, so dazzling in flecks of gold and silver, her head erect and imperious under its weight of white plumes that one might imagine her beauty was flawless. But the arrogant chin, the Habsburg lip, a shade too haughty, were all faults that were accentuated by the ominous silence of the crowd as she approached; for she must be keenly aware of the insult the silence implied. A pity. Because one heard that her smile could be enchanting.

The Vaudraye guests on the balcony buzzed away, everyone with a different tidbit of gossip about the Queen. Veronique heard only snatches of their talk. She found herself much too involved in the Queen's emotions at this time to note anything else. The Queen was about to pass the balcony where her son lay. She stopped. The haughty façade crumpled briefly. She looked up toward the unseen dauphin. Could the child see her? Or was he too ill even for that? For two or three seconds the world seemed to be completely silent.

Abruptly, the stillness was shattered by a voice deep in the crowd: *"Vive le roi Orléans!"*

The great white plumes that her head carried with such flawless grace began to sway under that taunt. For a horrifying minute it appeared that she would collapse. Her ladies rustled forward but once more the plumes were raised. The Queen's proud glance swept over the crowd, and she moved onward.

For Veronique and Marie-Josette the day was over. Nothing could equal the emotion and excitement of the Queen's passing. Josette leaned forward and whispered in Veronique's ear, "Poor thing!" The comment summed up the awful irony of the day.

Veronique tried to analyze her own reaction, telling herself that she'd been swayed by emotion, but even in her dreams she could not forget the one brief glimpse they had all received of the woman and mother who also happened to be the Queen of France. The Queen's glamor had momentarily blinded Veronique to the humanity beneath all those white plumes, a humanity cruelly attacked by that playactor, the Duc d'Orléans. And could she continue to love his hireling, Gilles Marsan . . . ?

But in the night, remembering the man she'd learned so quickly to love, trying to reconstruct his face from her tangled memories of him, Veronique found herself making explanations for the sketch used against the Queen. Gilles was, after all, poor. How else could he earn money but with his artist's talent? She decided she'd reacted too strongly on seeing his sketch.

Days later she was still waiting. In the hope that she might meet Gilles or at least his friends, she tried, without success, to get away from the townhouse long enough to walk past the *Salle des Menus Plaisirs*, where the States-General met only to quarrel over voting methods and the plan of finance minister Necker to tax the nobility and clergy as well as citizens represented by the Third Estate. It seemed to Veronique, hearing her Cousin Alex talk of these "preposterous demands," that no one was more hated by the court party, of whom the Queen was the head, than its own finance minister. Unless it was General Lafayette, who seemed to have brought the taint of revolution home from the Americas. His French troops, intended to guard the King as well as the city of Paris, had begun to desert at an alarming rate. There were even whispers of a Paris militia being organized by General Lafayette to protect the people of the city. But protect them from whom, if not the King's mercenary troops?

When Veronique failed to evade the constant chaperonage of Sylvie, or one of her boring friends, or, more charmingly, the Abbé de St.-Hélier, she became a very irritable house-guest, irritable particularly to Marie-Josette, who continued to assert blandly that no messages had come from Gilles Marsan. But then, Josette was so busy being shown the wonders of Versailles by her handsome new suitor, the number one footman, that she was inclined to forget her own name.

When Veronique drove past the great hall of the States-General Assembly for the third time with Josette and Sylvie, all of them looking much too elegant and noticeable for Veronique's purpose, she finally detected Raymond Berthelot coming out of the building. Startling Sylvie by her exuberance, Veronique called to him, exerting herself to be her most charming, but it was evident he hadn't much thawed in his feelings toward her. He removed his tricorne hat but immediately clapped it back on his head again while she was presenting him to her cousin. Veronique ignored his bad manners, politely expressing pleasure at seeing him and trusting he and his fellow delegates were finding the proceedings to be progressing satisfactorily.

He replied in his chilly fashion, "You must ask your friends of the privileged class, mademoiselle. If this deadlock continues, the Third Estate intends to constitute itself an assembly of the nation. Perhaps you would do well to tell this to that staunch member of privilege, madame's husband, Colonel de Vaudraye."

Annoyed at having fallen into the trap of a political argument, Veronique got down to the real purpose of her visit. "I fear my cousin would scarcely listen to my political opinions. But I do wish you good luck, all of you. . . . I trust Monsieur Marsan has not gotten into difficulties over his sketches for the Duc d'Orléans, he must be getting whole books of sketches out of your meetings. . . ."

She was surprised to note a reaction by Sylvie to the mention of Gilles's name. Did Sylvie know, after all, of her relations with Marsan? Had she known all along? . . .

Berthelot said, "No doubt he prefers to sketch his friends among the Cordeliers. That's a political club in Paris which still likes to dream of a constitutional monarchy. An idle dream, to say the least. Good day, mademoiselle . . . madame."

As soon as Veronique reached her bedchamber in the Vaudraye house she called for paper and the standish of ink and scrawled a brief note to Gilles, asking him why he had not tried to send her a message since their meeting. Her pride prevented her from openly expressing her concern, but he could hardly mistake it. She sealed the paper and directed it to Marsan in care of the *Salle des Menus Plaisirs*, but felt unable to trust anyone of Alex's household. When she failed to free herself from the ubiquitous company of Sylvie or the Abbé, she had to rely on Marie-Josette, who promised to make the journey while the houeshold's attention was fixed on Veronique.

Josette returned to report that as soon as Monsieur Marsan made another visit to the Hall he would receive the letter. No one, however, knew precisely where he was at the moment. Somewhere in Paris, working for the Duc d'Orléans, they thought.

Veronique closed her eyes, wondering how she could possibly love a man who had no greater moral sense than to serve such a master, and at the same time suspecting her feelings were beyond such noble considerations. . . .

4

DURING the next few days Veronique nearly convinced herself that her love for Gilles Marsan had ended under the bombardment of reason. Her emotions, however, did not change in the least, and so at one point she concluded it was a physical passion only, something she presumably might feel with a man of similar attractions. There were, in fact, many other equally attractive men, and she was constantly thrown into the company of the most exciting of these, the Abbé de St.-Hélier. Indeed, there could be no harm, she decided, in a mild flirtation, especially with a man who by every moral code was totally ineligible to be her lover. She thought of him as safe. It was one of her misreadings of character which she was not to forget.

Meanwhile, she let herself be paraded about the countryside to numerous townhouses and châteaux; no one seemed to have any knowledge of an artist named Gilles Marsan, or a one-time gamekeeper named de Gleeb. But all of them were familiar with the terrifying power of the political cartoons which the Duc d'Orléans had distributed throughout Paris. Veronique did not mention Gilles's name in connection with them and was relieved that though his work was celebrated, at least his name was not yet anathema. As for the

Cordeliers, the name simply signified still another political club.

Sylvie encouraged the Abbé de St.-Hélier's frequent visits and even advised him in his efforts to win Veronique's friendship. At least, Veronique hoped that what he sought of her was no more than the flirtation she intended. He puzzled her a good deal. After her first reluctant visits with him, including a ballet performance at the Petit Trianon during which she had hoped to be presented to Her Majesty, she found herself involved in a more uneasy relationship with the dashing Abbé.

No one except Veronique seemed to find it odd that a man of the Church should occupy his time in trivial social engagements. He was said to be the confessor of several of the Queen's Ladies of the Bedchamber, but fortunately he was not Veronique's confessor. She had not even told her own confessor about Gilles Marsan and managed to reason herself out of this moral and religious dilemma by promising God that when—or if—she and Gilles were ever married, her confessor, a nice, weary old gentleman of Versailles, would hear their vows.

Veronique did find the Abbé a witty and delightful companion during those days when she heard not a word from Gilles and could only devise excuses for his political drawings, his use of her against her Church and her Queen. But meanwhile there was François de St.-Hélier serving as a friend who carefully asked no questions about her private thoughts and opinions.

One midnight after a long, tedious evening of poetry reading by a protégé of the Queen's great friends, the Polignacs, the Abbé insisted on escorting Veronique home through the still-decorated streets of Versailles. It was an hour close to dawn, but a late evening session of the States-General Assembly had just broken up and there were crowds everywhere. Earnest members of the Third Estate continued to harangue bored noblemen while linkboys swung their lanterns ahead, lighting up an occasional alley whose stench was particularly pungent.

"I've seen sick and hungry patients at the hospital who were more attentive to their cleanliness. The least they might do for themselves is clean up their own filth," Veronique remarked as the Abbé looked back with his heavy-lidded gaze that made him appear so indifferent to the less pleasant aspects of life.

"My dear, perhaps *they* do not wish to . . . just as that mysterious impersonal mass you refer to as '*they*' has been less responsive than you might imagine to our fine new Assembly . . . an attitude that has allowed the Court to defeat Monsieur Necker's reforms for the past five years."

The Abbé's cynicism stood in contrast to the optimism she'd heard from Gilles. And yet she feared both the militancy of those new ideas she heard from him and the feeling that perhaps his hopes were too ambitious and unrealistic. On the few occasions he'd ever mentioned politics to her the Vicomte had emphasized that a group without a leader was only a mob, and that a proper leader should be "the father and not one of the sons." Of course he argued that those from his class were the only possible "fathers." It seemed ridiculous to her that it was so difficult for the opposing groups not to compromise, to find a less turbulent middle point instead of standing off, facing each other for weeks in the States-General doing little more than denouncing and belittling each other.

They reached the Place d'Armes and a crowd of nobles were leaving a soirée at the opposite end of the complex of buildings that formed the Palace de Versailles. Royal Swiss Guards held back the commoners, but the scene was dark and Veronique saw only a blurred silhouette of many heads. Hands were raised and waved in the direction of Veronique and others crossing the wide square.

The Abbé nudged her. "Sylvie's friend, the Chevalier de Lussac, is waving to you."

With little interest Veronique smiled and waved. She saw nothing in response, except vague movements among the crowd held back by the guards, as if someone were trying to get through to her. She didn't recall the Chevalier and had no desire to stop to chat with him; she was relieved when the Abbé took her arm and they turned to cross the street, followed at a discreet distance by Marie-Josette and the Abbé's radically minded valet Pettré, the latter trying vainly to convert the former.

Veronique overheard some of his propaganda. "Heavens! Another Jacobin is being recruited."

"Manifestly impossible," the Abbé remarked with amusement. "The girl hasn't the least understanding of his arguments. She listens because he is a male. He might be speaking in Hindustani, it would be all the same to her." He glanced at Veronique. "I wish I might say as much for myself."

"I too do not understand Hindustani." She did not smile.

He drew her nearer and with deliberation lowered his head to kiss her. Aside from a first start of surprise, she made no resistance. His kiss seemed to play on all her senses with a languorous ease so characteristic of him. He also was remarkably skilled, it seemed to her. She knew from the tightness of his embrace that he was aroused. It was, she realized with a calm that surprised her, satisfying to her vanity—no man this fascinating and worldly had ever dared, or cared, to seduce her. But all the while she was in his arms she closed her eyes and played the game that these were Gilles Marsan's arms instead. . . .

He must have guessed as much. Without a word he released her and escorted her back and into the house. In the small salon outside her bedchamber he lingered over her hand as he touched it with his lips. "Tomorrow?" he suggested, his gray eyes carefully observing her hand as she drew it away.

She laughed. "It is already tomorrow."

"And you are as fresh as last evening."

She stifled a yawn. "Nonsense!"

He was amused at her byplay and bowed gracefully. "How I envy the man whose memory inspires the special look in those large eyes!"

She blinked. "You are mistaken, Monseigneur," to which he smiled and shook his head. "We are back to titles, I see. And you are in love." He added an abrupt word of advice. "Take his love, *chérie*. These are, as they say, very uncertain times in which we live. Do not let them play their little tricks and separate you."

"François! What tricks?"

"Nothing. A joke. It is only my vanity that is crushed." His eyebrows went up in his supercilious fashion. "All the same I shall take you and the fair Josette to the races at Vincennes today."

He saw the quick disappointment in her face and recollected he'd promised the day before that he would take her this afternoon to visit a small hospital for children, supported by the Queen, whose interest in children of all races was not generally known. The hospital was said to practice such latest methods of treatment as variolation or inoculation against the pox and the isolation and fumigation of those with contagious diseases.

"Or," he added persuasively, "would you prefer the Queen's Hospital for Orphaned Children? It's a very curious place. She has ordered that there be no distinction of class, or of race. Quite unlike the reputation our frivolous Austrian has built up for herself, is it not?"

"Oh, thank you, François. I would indeed like to go there."

"And at our next Versailles theater invitation I shall present you to Her Majesty. On my word." He raised her fingers, kissed them, watching her as he did so. "But you see the irony of this hospital you've taken such a fancy to. The heir to the throne is dying of some rare bone affliction while the patients of Her Majesty's Hospital get along famously. However, she has the younger son, so at least we do not run out of dauphins. Lucky France!" Then . . . "Goodnight, my dear—my very dear Veronique."

There was certainly an excitement about his presence, his touch. Especially when she imagined it was Gilles Marsan's lips that lingered on the flesh of her wrist.

She watched the Abbé's tall figure depart as he bestowed blessings right and left on admiring servants in his path, and again marveled that a man could rise so high in the Church and remain so worldly. Was this world of his a place she'd actually wanted to enter as a nun? It was not at all the life painted by her mother or by her own imaginings. He was an amusing companion—handsome and charming, never really a threat to her love for Gilles. And still she heard nothing from the man she could not stop loving.

On the night when she was to be presented to Their Majesties during a concert of Monsieur Gluck's music at the Versailles theater, Veronique recovered her spirits at the very worldly notion of being a guest in the most magnificent palace in the world. She allowed herself to be so elaborately gowned and coiffed that she did not recognize herself when Josette and two of Sylvie's maids exhibited her before the great pier glass in the antechamber. She caught herself thinking, I wish Gilles could see me as I look tonight, I doubt he would be so indifferent. After that meeting at the Hall, surely he might have tried to see me sooner. She realized her pride was making her petulant and hoped he would soon give her a chance to understand his long absence. . . .

Now she surveyed herself in the mirror and was duly impressed. Every strand of her black hair was concealed beneath a flattering white wig that called attention to her dark eyes. Rouge was applied to her cheeks and lips, heightening the drama of her cheekbones and narrow, black-rimmed eyes. The many layers of her gown and underdress had been so skillfully constructed they didn't make walking difficult for her.

"Mam'selle, you are a pure white vision!" Marie-Josette said, clapping her hands. "One would never recognize you." A doubtful compliment, Veronique thought, but nonetheless accepted it.

One of Sylvie's maids added, "What a shame to look like mademoiselle and become a postulant. A dreadful waste of beauty."

"Oh, but mam'selle isn't going to become—" Josette began before Veronique's delicate white satin shoe came down hard on her foot.

Veronique gave her reflection one last look as she took up the mirrored fan. The rosettes on her underdress were revealed where the overskirt parted; these, too, were white and made the color of her flesh more vivid by contrast. She wore no jewels except the diamond ear-bobs given to her on her twelfth birthday by her father.

When she went out to meet the Abbé de St.-Hélier in the Mirror Salon she felt quite unlike herself and rather ashamed of her own pride in what had been made out of that plain dark Veronique de Vaudraye who always managed, willy-nilly, to look a bit disheveled. . . . The Abbé also was impressed, though apparently no more so than Alex and Sylvie. Sylvie's admiration was generous and seemed sincere, Veronique thought, but for some reason Alex did not like her finery or the impression she made as they escorted her to the Vaudraye carriage. Whatever Alex's problem, it seemed to amuse the Abbé, who glanced from him to Veronique as though he understood what had upset her cousin. The Abbé's own clerical robes tonight were resplendent white and silver.

"You are quite the loveliest thing the palace has seen since the Austrian princess arrived some nineteen years ago," he told Veronique, which she dismissed with a brisk "nonsense" to cover over her pleasure in spite of herself.

When they reached the enormous complex of the palace the Abbé skillfully separated Veronique from her family. She felt herself swept through halls and down broad staircases past the royal chapel in the midst of a hundred other courtiers and their ladies likewise invited to this private and royal performance of music by the Queen's favorite composer, the Austrian Gluck. It was interesting but not necessarily pleasant to be thrown in with so many people whom she didn't know and with whom she had absolutely nothing in common. . . .

"I feel I'm in the world's largest theater," she remarked, "and these people in their fantastic costumes—myself included—are actors."

The Abbé agreed. "Some of these guests will spend a year's rents and tithes on the costumes, coaches, horses, jewels they bring here tonight."

"When times are so bad, why must we carry everything to extremes?"

"You overlook the fact that in bad times it is our duty to provide work for our commoner brethren. Consider how many seamstresses would starve if you had not given them employment on that delicious gown of yours."

Specious reasoning, of course, but she knew it was not meant to be taken seriously. She looked about at the gilding of the theater box into which he ushered her and wondered how many of the hungry peasants in the Norman countryside could be fed a full year on the price of the decorations and furnishings in this private theater.

Marie-Josette entered behind them with the Abbé's valet. By this time the pit below had been filled by glittering silk-clad men and women, and the confusion made it difficult to study the intricate gold carving, the many facets of the screen that closed off the stage, a screen that deceptively continued the design of the theater walls and made the theater itself appear to be a cozy bandbox.

"Before your cousins appear, aren't you curious about Alex's disapproval of your gown?" the Abbé suggested as Veronique looked about her at those in the surrounding boxes. Now she looked at him. Since she felt her own guilt at being here, wasting thousands of livres for one theatrical evening, she didn't really want to know why Cousin Alex disapproved of her tonight. Was it because he thought it soiled her image as the future Nursing Sister of Ste. Veronique? She couldn't much blame him for that. But she suspected another motive.

"Well? May I warn you now, or may I not?"

"Since you are bound upon telling me. But I think my loving cousin is afraid I might attract a husband. That would seriously alter his future."

He sat there watching her. "Veronique, your cynicism sometimes exceeds even my own. Do you realize how unsuited you are to the holy life?"

"Not at all. Where possible I attempt to be realistic. I believe it is necessary to be aware of the facts of life if one is to be useful."

"A spiritual life is useful for itself."

She stared at him, astonished at such a reminder from François de St.-Hélier, of all men. Still, remarkably, she had to admit he did seem suddenly serious. To change the subject she said, "François, you're not wearing that absurd beauty mark tonight. Or the rouge. Is it possible your own life has become more spiritual?"

He ran a heavily ringed hand over his lean cheek and jaw. "Very true. Do I look much older?"

"You look more masculine."

"What a horror in a man of the cloth!"

Which made her laugh, and before she could discover further what his warning was to have been, her cousins arrived in the box with their entourage and it became impossible for Veronique and the Abbé to discuss Alex.

The beautiful gilt screen had been removed and an exquisite stage was set as a background to the concert when Veronique lost interest in her surroundings. A chamberlain appeared to announce the arrival of Their Majesties in the center box.

Sylvie confided to Veronique behind her fan, "The Queen persists in favoring foreigners. Gluck is such a bore. But she never forgets she was born in Vienna, so rather a boring Austrian than a sparkling Frenchman, I dare say."

Veronique ignored this. She was anxious to see the royal couple in happier surroundings and certainly wasn't interested in more of the sly gossip by the Queen's own court. Now the royal pair arrived to shouts and acclamations that must have cheered them. *"Vive le roi . . . vive la reine . . ."*

Veronique noted again the total lack of majesty about King Louis. Having been ceremoniously seated, he settled back, and Veronique suspected he would have liked to have gone to sleep. Marie Antoinette was in jewels, plumes and an elaborate gown of gold cloth with pink rosettes and ribbons that became her graceful figure but made her look pale, a trifle drawn.

When the crowd cheered her Veronique saw her smile for the first time. It did wonders to soften the pride and hauteur that had become familiar to those who saw her at public functions. Now she looked dazzling. With her spirits raised she addressed one of her ladies, the Princesse de Lamballe, and soon the performance onstage began. Except for Veronique, the most interesting performer remained the Queen in her box.

The small royal orchestra played selections from "Orféo"

and Sylvie began to hum the popular song, "My Lost Eurydice." No one seemed to find this disturbing. Others did the
same and the Abbé took this opportunity to leave the box.
Minutes later, between selections, Veronique saw his figure
in its silver surcoat at the back of the royal box.

When he returned he whispered to Veronique, "You are to
be presented to Her Majesty before the afterpiece. She is in
excellent spirits tonight. Those were the first cheers she has
heard in many months."

Sylvie told her proudly, "Everyone has been asking who
you were. Don't lose your heart to anyone, my love. Even a
comte tonight may be succeeded by a duc tomorrow. . . ."

Amazing advice to a niece planning to enter Ste. Veronique's as a postulant in August. Or perhaps not . . . it could
well mean that Sylvie was fully informed about Gilles, or, at
all events, about that embrace on the public street. She was
especially conscious of this when she caught François St.-
Hélier looking at her with more attention than he gave to the
performance.

The singers had made their appearance, and a voluptuous
female in a Grecian chiton made of gauze and nothing else
began to dance. She revealed so much of herself that Veronique turned scarlet and kept her gaze fixed on a point at the
peak of the proscenium arch. The Abbé seemed frankly to
enjoy it.

She glanced furtively at the Queen's box. Marie Antoinette
was not watching the stage. She listened behind her ivory fan
to another beautiful woman whose gown and jewels outshown
even the Queen's. Veronique remembered something Sylvie's
maid had said about the Duchesse de Polignac, that every
stitch on her back she owed to the Queen's favor. This did
not keep her from being called by those who knew her influence "the Queen's evil genius."

Gradually Veronique noticed a restless stirring in the
audience. The buzz of whispers grew louder, accompanied
now by giggles and bursts of laughter. The Abbé leaned forward over the box rail. Veronique's first thought was that the
nudity on stage further intrigued him, but the dancer had
retreated upstage. It was the male soloist, whose words were
badly fitted to a little-known Gluck orchestral interlude, who
stirred the audience. She began to concentrate on those
words:

"My love is lost to me
In the inferno that is the court,
Can I win my Eurydice
When the Cardinal's robes
and the necklace of diamonds
convert her to their cause?
Gone is my Eurydice,
to dine upon diamonds,
while her children dine upon dust."

There must have been more of the same bad propaganda, but so much went on in the next minute or two that no one could make out the next words. The King looked as though he'd been dozing and was rudely aroused by the Queen's hand on his satin sleeve. She snapped shut her fan, said something to the Duchesse de Polignac, who seemed to have been caught unexpectedly laughing, unlike the Princesse de Lamballe, a shy unobtrusive young woman who looked so shocked one momentarily expected her to faint.

Immediately afterward the Queen rose, her face drawn and pallid, like a death mask. The King got to his feet with difficulty, and in a flurry of noisy movement the Royal Couple retired with their entourage, leaving an empty royal box.

Veronique looked quickly at the stage. The male singer had stopped on a rather plaintive note and waved his arms, apparently for help. From the wings a lithe, tall young man appeared in a harlequin costume. He wore the horned head-piece of the demons in Hades. The half-mask concealed his eyes but not his nose or mouth. He motioned to the singer. "Come. Your performance is over for tonight."

The singer hurried past him into the wings. The "demon" stood onstage a minute while the orchestra scrambled to close and remove instruments.

"Author . . ." one of the well-dressed women in the pit called out and pointed to the man on the stage. The word was taken up by several others in the audience throughout the little theater. Veronique suspected they'd been planted there by the Duc d'Orléans. Or perhaps even the Queen's closest invited guests were turning from her now. At the same time soldiers in the Swiss Guards uniform poured into the theater and down toward the stage. The man in the demon's mask seemed to wave and bow directly toward Veronique with that grace she remembered so well . . . and then he ran offstage, the Swiss Guards clattering after him with their swords drawn.

Veronique could not control her shaking as she stared at the delicate stage overcrowded with soldiers meeting from either side and all of them trying at once to get out through the wings.

"Come, my love, it would seem that the performance is ended," Cousin Sylvie said from the door of the box, where Alex and the servants were gathered. Only the Abbé remained beside her, watching her carefully.

"Did you know that fellow?"

Veronique recovered herself with difficulty. "Know him? What a silly thing to say . . . how would I know a composer of doggerel—"

"I would hardly mistake this . . . composer . . . for Monsieur Gluck, but for a moment there I did fancy he knew and was perhaps taunting you. I wonder why?"

She had to clear her throat. "I've no notion. Please join my cousins. They are waiting."

"And you?"

She fumbled at her hairline, loosening one of the ear-bobs and dropping it. She knelt on the dusty floor of the box, her skirts billowing out around her, soiling the pure white of the silk. "I'll be with you presently, I've lost some jewelry." While she knelt, she was watching the stage, praying that she would not hear the triumphant shout of the guards in their search for the seditionist who had written that song so insulting to the Queen of France.

5

WHEN it seemed that Gilles had escaped, Veronique recovered her diamond ear-bob and prepared to leave the little jewel box of a theater in the wake of the rest of the audience, who could not wait to spread gossip far and wide about the Queen's public humiliation.

The Abbé lifted her to her feet. She was anxious and worried. When he tried to kiss her, running his practiced hands over her arms, she pulled away with a revulsion that stung him into a brief anger quite unlike himself. In spite of the feeling of panic that made her scuffle and kick at him, his fingers tightened their grip on her bare throat and breast, leaving a reddened imprint on her pale flesh. She cried out, and he abruptly let her go.

"I beg your pardon. I didn't think myself capable of such crudeness." His apology began haughtily, but he added with a rueful smile, "You have your revenge. The pointed toe of your shoe seems to have paralyzed my shinbone."

"I'm sorry, but really, François, you're a disgrace to your vows—"

His features stiffened. Was it possible she could finally have wounded his self-esteem. When he spoke it was lightly but she thought his gray eyes for once held a serious, almost somber look. "I never believed there were creatures like you left in this sordid miasma we've created in Versailles. I suppose it's too late for me to change gaits and ask for your trust. You need friends, you know . . . Alexandre is not one of them."

She didn't answer as he helped her out of the theater box, started to say something and then coughed. She wondered if he'd been about to pursue his flirtation and changed his mind. She wanted to forgive and to believe him, but all she could think of tonight was Gilles Marsan's safety and, with it, his infuriating political attacks on the Church and throne, still sacred in Veronique's eyes.

The Abbé's first words startled her. "I know your family wants to break off your relationship with your radical friend. I know because up to now I've given my aid to this enterprise. But I'm compromised by the desire to win your friendship again and so am perfectly willing to betray friend Alex's noble effort." She wanted to laugh at that winning frankness but was stopped by his next remark: "Perhaps you've noticed lately some of Alex's proprietary looks toward you. As you know any marriage of yours hardly serves his ambition to be your father's heir. And do you entirely trust your maid . . . it seems you're surrounded by intrigue—"

"Certainly, I trust Josette. I'd trust her with my life."

"And with the life of that impudent fellow Marsan?"

Did he know everything that had occurred in Versailles? That had occurred before?

"I don't know any 'fellow' named Marsan."

"Ah, I see we've further to go than I'd thought—or at least hoped." He put out his satin-clad arm. She touched it with the fingers and heel of her hand. And so, looking like two idlers, a gallant and his flirt, they made their way along the great gallery. During this long promenade to Sylvie's she was presented to the King's youngest brother, the Comte d'Artois, but she was so distracted by the Abbé's questions that she scarcely noted his elegant good looks—though she hadn't forgotten his inappropriate pleasure at the humiliation of his own sister-in-law, the Queen.

Josette now appeared, looking pink with excitement, or nervousness. "Mam'selle . . . I—what a pity the performance ended so soon. . . . I was waiting in one of the little salons with M'sieur—with Madame Sylvie's First Footman—"

"Where are my cousins? We're detaining His Excellency, who I'm sure must have many errands of mercy at this hour."

The Abbé accepted the hint, bowed and left them without

another word. Marie-Josette looked after him as he strode swiftly through other groups of departing guests, blessing one and all.

"What a very odd gentleman."

"What a very odd churchman. Come along."

Back at the Vaudraye townhouse, Sylvie and Alex were saying goodnight to her outside her bedchamber, Sylvie lightly embracing her and adding, "An unpleasant moment for the Austrian, but a triumph for you, my love. And to be seen so constantly in the company of the fascinating Abbé will surely give you importance when you enter Ste. Veronique. Sister Thérèse may appear the austere nun but she adores her brother. As who does not?"

Alex likewise attempted to embrace her, hampered somewhat by his paunch and creaking stays.

"Fine evening, not bad at all. And they're sure to capture that wretched fellow who wrote those lyrics. I've a delegate of the Third Estate . . . handy fellow . . . when old Davout died so unexpectedly in my district it was providential. Thanks to your good father I found my own choice for a delegate. Arno's a good dog on the scent, he'll find that seditionist and put us in good graces with the royal family—"

"Hush, my love," his wife said, apparently cutting off further remarks about this mysterious Arno. . . .

"How clever you are, Cousin Alex!" Veronique said. "But your friend Arno, this dog on the scent, he really can do nothing . . . there are still laws, and besides, how could he know who the seditionist was tonight?"

Alex slapped his paunch. "He may suspect, cousin. And to suspect is to act. Not publicly, of course, though even there he's protected. The States-General—no, they call themselves the National Assembly now—have passed their own law. Every member is safe from arrest for whatever crime. And now I've had Arno elected to the Assembly and he'll do as I direct him. I dare say he'll not find much time to join those eternal debates in the Assembly—I've given him better things to do with his time. I'm most grateful to your father for recommending him. . . ."

It was then that Veronique realized who "Arno" really was. She forced a smile and said, "Dear papa . . . but you're very trusting, cousin. How do you know your new friend Arno isn't a criminal? A thief, or even a murderer?"

Alex waved to his wife, summoning her to follow him. "My

dear girl, if the Vicomte sent him to me you may be certain any so-called crimes he may have committed were surely in the service of the Vaudrayes and therefore deserve medals."

"And you would do nothing if you found him a criminal?"

"Have you no faith in your father's judgment?"

She chose not to answer that. "Where is he now, this remarkable fellow papa sent you?"

"Out searching, I trust, for the damned harlequin who caused that disgraceful scene tonight. He has his suspicions as to the fellow's identity, he tells me. . . . Come, Sylvie, it's past midnight. Let the child ready herself for bed. I confess I'm tired as well, but first a tidy little supper, I think—a few pâtés, a nice capon, a fresh loaf of bread and perhaps a bottle of good Burgundy to wash it down."

After waving good night to Veronique, Sylvie went off with her husband, reminding him, "There are shortages of bread in the city, and you know what that does to Paris tempers. Perhaps we should have extra loaves baked and send them into town for distribution—"

"Rubbish! Let them earn their bread. As I do."

Veronique shivered when they'd finally gone, partly for her cousin's callousness, especially for Gilles's situation with Arnauld de Gleeb on his trail. She didn't doubt de Gleeb's ability as an assassin . . . on the contrary, she had reason to be convinced of it. Well, she'd need to remove her heavy garments, the wig and rouge before she could even begin to do anything to help the man she still loved despite tonight's performance against the Queen. Hopefully when she and Gilles were united he would be more interested in feeding the poor and less anxious to insult the government.

As she began to unlace her gown she said to Josette, "I'd best come down from the fairy-tale palace to the chimney corner."

"If you please, mam'selle, not quite yet." She sounded anxious.

"Secrets, Josette?"

"Not for long, mam'selle."

She went over to the antechamber in which a truckle bed and armoire had been placed for her. She opened the armoire and, in order, Veronique gasped, then felt an uncontrollable desire to laugh.

Arms folded, Gilles stood there in the portable closet. Somewhere in his flight, he'd slipped off the harlequin breeches and now wore his usual black breeches and boots, with his disheveled white shirt and a thin worn coat over his shoulders.

Josette explained quickly. "I told the Abbé's valet that m'sieur was my lover and showed him how to reach this room. It seems everyone in Versailles was in pursuit of him—"

"I didn't exactly intend to find myself in this position," Gilles said. "It's almost like a scene from an Italian comedy—Harlequin found in Columbine's closet. . . . Do you mind if I step out of the part?"

"What you did tonight was cruel," Veronique said. "I never thought you capable of it, but I suppose I should have known, not hearing from you once, even an answer to my own note—"

Gilles looked at Marie-Josette. "You didn't tell her?"

Josette tried to explain. "It was that awful footman, Baptiste. . . . He swore he loved me . . . he was to deliver all messages, but he lied. . . . M'sieur Marsan has tried to see you repeatedly, and that hateful Baptiste gave him false messages from you, saying you would not see him."

"That would be my Cousin Alex's doing." Veronique was so relieved at Gilles's fidelity that she nearly forgave him for the evening's performance, though she still thought it best to let him make the first move.

His dark eyes studied her face as though he were etching her in his memory. Finally he said, "Someone in your name sent a note to me suggesting I meet you when you left Versailles after the ballet that night. I stood there waiting behind those guards, as you'd asked me to. But you weren't with your servants, that paint-and-patches Abbé accompanied you . . . you waved to me casually as you might wave to a servant at Vaudraye—"

"But I did not!" She had almost forgotten that episode. "François told me to wave to someone, a chevalier, I think. I did not even *see* him . . . you."

"You were not meant to. That Abbé must have been a part of your cousin's plan to separate us." This time he drew her to him. The huge puffs of white silk and gauze on her skirts got in his way and he tugged them off angrily. Flushed and unnerved by her own feelings, Veronique let him ruin the gown within seconds before she was pulled roughly into his arms and felt his warm lips first on her throat and then at the fullest curve of her bosom. When he let her go, she almost fell. He took her forearm, held it while she caught her breath. He too was flushed but smiling as he told her, "What I really

want to say to you is come along with me right now, tonight
. . . but . . ."

She loved hearing him say it and at the same time reminded
him of the Swiss Guards, the *Gardes Françaises,* that were
looking for him.

"They are after the harlequin in the demon mask. Even the
singers in the opera don't know who I really am. Besides,
they take their orders from Orléans. I'm as free as most
of the Cordeliers. Or the Jacobins."

She delighted in his somewhat wishful confidence, but she
also knew sensible people didn't run away to live in attics in
Paris at a time like this, with poverty and hunger and half of
France looking for work that paid ten sous a day. Still, at
this minute, she was tempted. . . .

Marie-Josette, carried away by the moment, put in, "And
you will take mam'selle to the nearest priest—"

"Yes . . . when I have a hundred louis d'or in my pocket.
Then it will be Madame Veronique Marsan . . . when I can
at least give you lodgings on the first story instead of the
fifth—"

"How silly. As if I couldn't live in an attic!"

He drew her up on her toes with one hand under her arm,
and said to her very seriously, "My darling, you perhaps will
never again live as you did at Vaudraye, but at least you are
going to eat and sleep in decent comfort. You aren't, after all,
marrying a beggar. My next book of sketches is to be pub-
lished soon, and contrary to practice, my publisher will pay
me—"

Now her common sense got the better of the romantic flush
of the moment. "Your publisher! What man would risk money
publishing sketches?"

"The Duc d'Orléans."

She caught her breath. "Gilles, I think in that case I'd
rather be poor."

He laughed at that, kissed her and told her she knew
nothing about being poor.

"One hundred golden louis. I'll come for you when I have
it. It won't be long. A few weeks. Camille says I'm lucky.
He's still trying to sell his work, and his political articles are
shattering quite a few reputations among those Versailles
leeches."

"Camille?"

"Desmoulins. A member of the Cordeliers. He wants to
marry a young lady who belongs to the high bourgeoisie, and

he has my trouble—he's poor. But believe me, Veronique, he will not always be poor."

She did not want to disillusion him, or shatter these fine plans for their future, so she merely nodded.

"Tomorrow is July third. Before the month is out," he promised, "I will redeem you—"

"For a hundred louis?"

They kissed again to seal the bargain while Marie-Josette smiled delightedly.

Suddenly they heard the rattle of door latches on the great double doors opening from the antechamber into the main foyer. Veronique led him off to her bedchamber as Josette slowly went to the door.

In her own bedchamber Veronique tore off the tousled white wig and torn gown, breaking laces where she had to, until she appeared in her voluminous petticoats and shift. By the time she'd covered her petticoats with an apricot dressing sacque, Marie-Josette was at the outer door. Veronique looked back at Gilles, took a long breath, straightened her shoulders and walked out across the antechamber to find the Abbé de St.-Hélier trying to reassure a terrified Josette. They both seemed relieved at her appearance. The Abbé had been shown up the stairs and through the foyer by a stolid-looking footman who retreated to the end of the foyer and apparently made no effort to listen.

Josette stepped aside quickly. "Monseigneur wishes to have a word with you."

The Abbé raised his hands in protest. "Very brief, Veronique, and very trivial. Don't concern yourself. It's about Josette's lover—"

"But then why don't you speak to Josette? . . ." She looked back, remembering Josette's excuse for getting Gilles Marsan out of the Versailles area.

The Abbé smiled faintly. "I think you know. Sooner or later he must leave this house. And I too am expected to leave here. You see, I have arrived too late to see you; so I will turn around and depart, making it plain that the man who accompanies me is my valet. I suggest he hurry."

"But why are you doing this?"

"I confess I feel I was overpersuaded by my valet. Pettré admires all radicals, seditionists and other unsavory individuals. In short, this was all planned in detail by my valet." He was enjoying the sight she presented in the dressing sacque, and she felt the sooner this moment was ended the better. Still, she could not believe in his offer. She was about to say so when she heard Gilles Marsan's voice behind her, quiet and low-pitched. "Darling, you should place more trust in the servants of your own Church. I don't know why Monseigneur has gone to this trouble to save me from being drawn and quartered, but I do tend to believe him. . . ."

"How pleasant to deal once more with a gentleman," the Abbé remarked. "After dealing so long with these loathesome little toads at court, it's a pleasure to meet a man, monsieur . . . not that I agree with you. Please understand me, I despise your politics."

Frantically Veronique tried to get between them. "Gilles, don't listen to him. He wants to trap you. It was François who pointed you out to me as some chevalier that night. I think he sent you the note. He did that to oblige my Cousin Alex, who wants to separate us."

"Very true," the Abbé agreed. "At the time I thought your relationship with this young man an appalling *mésalliance*. However . . ."

"And I suppose you adore my cousin's hired bully, the man he calls Arno, but whose real name is de Gleeb."

"I have never seen the fellow and frankly, I adore no man, my dear. I scarcely adore the Good Lord himself!" He ignored her outrage, adding, "And now I am perhaps over-persuaded to oblige two lovers. Still, I do not think you are ideally suited for the cloister, Veronique. I disagree there with my sister. But, monsieur, will you continue to accept my word?"

"I don't believe I have any other choice, m'sieur. Indeed, though I think it wise to be cautious of an extended hand of help, I have no intention of biting it. Let's say it is your word I accept until I have reason not to."

The Abbé took his extended hand. "Really, monsieur, I do not entirely despair of liking you yet."

As Gilles fastened his coat and smoothed back his hair so it might better resemble the valet's sleek look, he answered the Abbé with a question. "Why do you make this effort on my behalf? If my politics offend you, surely the sentiment of romance can't be your sole motive, Monseigneur."

The Abbé shrugged. "Don't underestimate its appeal. Besides it's always well to have a friend in the enemy camp. When you revolutionaries overturn the world you will oblige me by rescuing my own poor person."

"That's a debt you may collect at any time."

Gilles brushed Veronique's cheek with a kiss. "One hundred louis," he reminded her, and went out through the foyer with the Abbé.

In the doorway to the foyer Veronique watched them until they were gone from her sight. Behind her, Josette said, "He must be safe, mam'selle. The Abbé will see to that."

"I wish I had your faith," Veronique answered.

In bed an hour later, she realized that of them all, she had been the skeptic . . . almost the cynic. Normally that was the role of François de St.-Hélier. It troubled her some to think of herself this way. It troubled her more, though, when she thought of the danger Gilles would be in if the Abbé had lied.

6

AS VERONIQUE might have expected, Sylvie knew all about the Abbé's late visit the previous night. She seemed to think it highly flattering that one of the most notorious rakes among the Queen's coterie was attempting to seduce her cousin. Veronique tried to ignore the woman's talk and listened to Marie-Josette's private assurances.

"The good Abbé did not lie. M'sieur must be safe, else we should have heard of his capture."

But it was not until the Abbé's valet came, presumably to call on Marie-Josette, that Veronique felt relieved of her greatest fear.

"He's safe. I visited the Café Parnasse, where the Cordeliers Club members meet. The owner's daughter Gabrielle is married to a big fellow who's the heart of the constitutional reform movement in Paris—one Georges-Jacques Danton. He and his friends, Desmoulins and Marsan, gather there daily. It would seem you have nothing to worry about."

It was at this point Veronique decided to write her parents openly about her plans, though she understood they probably suspected much of it already. She knew that for her this admission of her love for Gilles Marsan was inevitable, that Gilles was without question to be part of her life and this in at least small measure gave her the courage to face what she assumed would be their response. Knowing that this "betrayal" of their hopes for her could be more than they were capable of understanding and was certain to cause them great pain, she did hope that their faith in her would give them some comfort, and that their genuine interest in her happiness would prevent them from seriously trying to stop her once she'd made her decision known to them. . . .

Having completed the letter to the Vicomte and Vicomtesse, Veronique reread it a last time before sending it off by the Vaudraye courier.

> My dearest Madame Mother and Monsieur Papa,
> I am persuaded that my cousins have told you of my love for Gilles Marsan. His love for me did not fade during my Cousin Alex's efforts to separate us.
> But Cousin Alex is not interested in my happiness and I know that you are. I wish to marry Gilles and to know the love that my dear mama and father have known. Until I met Gilles, I thought I could live celibate. Now I feel that I desire marriage and a family and a normal life. This is what Gilles wishes, too. He wishes me to be comfortable and happy, so we are to wait until he receives certain moneys that are due him for his work.

No need to go further into the subject of Gilles's work. It would only enrage her father.

She took up her pen and dipped the point into the ink standish once more.

> We intend to live simply and without your aid, Papa, except in the matter of your love and good wishes, and those of Mama. Perhaps you can make Cousin Alex understand that we will make no claim to his inheritance. In which event he may cease to put obstacles in our path.
> Mama, I will always work for the good of Ste. Veronique's and the hospitals wherever Gilles and I live. So I implore you, dearest Mama, give us your blessing as I send you and Papa all my devoted love.
>
> > Your daughter always,
> > Anne-Veronique de Vaudraye.

She felt that it was inadequate—but what could be otherwise?—as a plea for her parents' understanding. She suspected that though her father would be the more angry of the two, he might recover more quickly than her mother. But eventually the Vicomtesse must see she could not deny her daughter what she had not denied herself, a normal marriage and family.

She'd no sooner included her letter with Alex's other correspondence to Vaudraye than Sylvie came to complain because the Abbé de St.-Hélier could not escort Veronique to a fashionable ball at a Meudon château.

"That wretch François would have to attend to his churchly duties just as we need him for your partner. He has to be with the Royal Family. He claims they need him. They! My love, he has no consideration for our problems."

Veronique smiled. "I would not be going out in company with another—with a man at this time, dear Sylvie. I am not in the mood."

"But you mustn't let their sorrows concern you."

"Let whose sorrows concern me?"

"The dauphin died late last night, leaving only their four-year-old son as the royal heir. That's why the Abbé thinks he must be needed by the Family. But what about us?"

In her mind's eye Veronique suddenly saw the sad face of Marie Antoinette, so unlike the shallow creature who'd once graced the gaming houses of Paris and the extravagant balls given to entertain a woman easily bored.

"Oh, I *am* sorry! What a terrible thing for them! And with all their other troubles—"

"Well, I must say, Their Majesties are being quite maudlin about it. They've gone into deep mourning. They spent all last night at the bedside and now they've refused to attend any affairs at Versailles until after the funeral. And when all is said, the poor child probably was not even the King's son."

"Sylvie!"

"How can one be sure, my love?"

. . . The sooner I move out of this Versailles atmosphere the better, Veronique decided, which made her realize that she must also let Sister Thérèse of the convent know her decision.

During her first month at Versailles she had visited the Convent of Ste. Veronique in Paris twice, and both times known an aching sensation of loss as she realized that her love for Gilles meant surrendering the life of the convent.

From this Mother House much might be accomplished in the little nightmare world of hospitals, pesthouses and asylums. But she had chosen a secular love. Thinking of Gilles, she knew that, in fact, she'd had no choice.

She made plans to visit the Convent of Ste. Veronique again, so that Sister Thérèse would hear the news directly from her, but on the evening of July 11th she was astonished to have a visit from the Sister herself with disquieting news of Paris and much happier news for Veronique.

Fortunately, Sister Thérèse arrived at the townhouse some minutes after Sylvie and Alex had gone off to a soirée at the St.-Aubans' château, presided over by the beautiful young Duchesse.

"I know of your decision, Veronique," Sister Thérèse said once they were safe from eavesdroppers in the antechamber occupied by Marie-Josette.

"Sister, if I had never met Monsieur Marsan I might have been content. Believe me, I felt I had a real vocation for the work in the hospitals and all the areas where the Sisters of Ste. Veronique could be useful."

Marie-Josette brought Norman brandy to the nun, who responded gratefully, then said, "Things are so bad in Paris now. The food shortage is appalling! It is hard to believe people still live in this civilized fashion elsewhere. I often wonder if the king has any knowledge of what is happening. . . . Oh, yes, your betrothed came to see me today."

Veronique started, then felt an enormous relief, and then surprise. "He does not customarily visit the clergy. . . . I thought he disapproved of them. . . ."

"He does, or says he does." She smiled, the rare expression made her beautiful, somber face radiant. "I'm not concerned over the sentiments of passionate young men like Monsieur Marsan. In the ultimate hour they will come to God. It is those who no longer care. They are the ones whose souls I pray for. At all events, your betrothed said he had come merely to announce your decision. Unlikely on the face of it. Besides, I knew better."

Veronique and Josette looked at her anxiously. Veronique moistened her suddenly dry lips. "What do you mean?"

"He did not come to boast that he had snatched you away from the Church. He actually came to ask the blessing of Mother Church. I saw that at once, the way he genuflected when he thought no one saw. The look that came into his eyes when he stopped before the prie-dieu as he walked out of

Mother Superior's office with me. Man has disappointed him, not God."

"Then you approve our marriage?"

"The Church has always approved marriage between communicants. How else is mankind to be fruitful?"

Veronique was so relieved she drank down all her brandy, choking a little. "Did he say when we are to be married?" she asked quickly.

"Oh, yes. Although I have heard a rumor that I think you should know." She had given her plain black mantle to Marie-Josette, and the stark black and white of her coif and robes made her look nearly statuesque. She turned quickly now, glancing around.

Veronique followed her glance. The candelabrum on the elegant little Topino desk used as a dressing table lighted the immediate area and made the marquetry of the rare, pale wood glisten like gold, but the corners of the room were shadowed and Josette went to close the doors into Veronique's bedchamber as well as to check the foyer doors.

Sister Thérèse murmured, "I am sorry to say this, but I believe the Archbishop of Paris is being importuned to forbid the banns."

"Cousin Alex had lied to him, I daresay. But he certainly cannot force me to enter as a postulant, which is what my loving cousin hopes. Only papa could give such permission to forbid my marriage. . . ."

"Well, Veronique, I shall not aid them in their little schemes, though I need not tell you I would welcome you as a postulant. I think you were born to the work, if not perhaps the celibacy. What a pity one must be a celibate nun in order to organize and care for the sick, the despairing, and the dying!"

"But there are nurses," Veronique reminded her, "those women one sees occasionally and hires when no nursing nun is available—"

Marie-Josette broke in. "But they are mostly drunken, thieving old witches. . . . I wouldn't trust them—"

"Josette!"

"I'm afraid she's more right than wrong," Sister Thérèse said. "We need you desperately. But there, I apologize." She raised a thin, strong hand, very like Veronique's had been before she came to Versailles, before she began to take such care to make her fingers look delicate and soft. Suddenly ashamed of their softness Veronique buried her hands in her gown.

Sister Thérèse went on, "You must marry that attractive young man. I only came to deliver a message to you, and because Mother Clotilde needed a companion to Versailles. She is here to obtain new funds."

"You must remain here the night, Sister. I am, of course, deeply grateful to you for your message."

Sister Thérèse shook her head as she set aside the brandy goblet. "Much as I should like to remain in these comfortable surroundings, I will not. . . . It brings to my mind all the luxuries I knew as a child at St.-Hélier. It is not wise for us to enjoy too much of the world's comforts, as you will discover—as you would discover in taking your vows to serve our blessed Ste. Veronique." She accepted her mantle from Josette's respectful hands. "All the same, I am free to confess that I was glad to be quit of Paris in its present mood for even a day or two. There are bread shortages everywhere and prices have risen incredibly. Fourteen sous for a loaf of black bread that was seven sous only five months ago. The average workman's salary is less than ten sous a day, and you know that every family needs at least one loaf of bread a day to survive. Fortunately, the wine is still cheap."

Veronique was suddenly conscious of her own presumption. As a child, obsessed with the knowledge that she had been promised to Ste. Veronique, she had always believed she could solve whatever difficulties were presented to her. Her first sight of death from starvation had aroused her pity and outrage but did not reduce her opinion of her own capabilities, and she had begun at that moment to demonstrate those capabilities.

She got up to walk with Sister Thérèse to her carriage on the street below. It was then that the nun stopped in the foyer and seemed to study her features for a clue to her thoughts.

"Would you run away and be married by a simple parish priest?"

Veronique quickly took hold of the nun's hand. "You have another msesage for me . . . please, tell me."

Sister Thérèse smiled. "Indeed, yes. But I wanted to be quite certain." Within her mantle she found a small folded square of paper. There was no superscription. She placed it in Veronique's palm. "Read that, my dear."

Veronique unfolded the paper with fingers that shook slightly.

My Darling,

Be ready in your maid's, Josette's, clothing to-morrow shortly after nightfall. I will be Josette's lover, come to take her to a street fair. I will enter as I left, by the servants' stairs. My darling, that good Sister Thérèse will tell you how we are to marry as soon as Père Lefroy gives us his blessing. I adore you, my good angel.

Gilles

Veronique raised her head. She wanted very much to kiss the note. She was almost too excited to get out the words: "Gilles says you will explain."

With humor and warmth that contrasted with her cool exterior, Sister Thérèse nodded and said, "Your charming Monsieur Marsan will arrive here at darkness tomorrow evening, pretending to visit you maid. But he intends to take you back to Paris. There will be two friends to meet you in Paris. A gentleman named Desmoulins, I believe, and his betrothed."

"I know of Camille Desmoulins." She had been so excited by the news that she only now realized the implications. "But it is dangerous for Gilles to come to Versailles! Even if he cannot be arrested, my cousin's hired spy, de Gleeb, wouldn't hesitate to murder him."

"I'm afraid Monsieur Marsan is somewhat impetuous. He insists he will take you to the Church of St. Roch in the rue St.-Honoré and the formalities will be attended, the banns posted. I understand the priest there is a friend of the Corde-liers Club, or something of the sort."

"I mustn't let him come to Versailles. I will meet him in Paris where he is among his friends . . . except where in heaven's name can I find him?"

Sister Thérèse hesitated. "I learned something that may help you. Monsieur Desmoulins and your Gilles will be at the Palais-Royal at noon tomorrow to greet the finance minister, Monsieur Necker. They are to present him with a petition supporting his efforts to make our country solvent. They have collected some ten thousand signatures of substantial citizens. I suppose you could meet them there . . ."

"Oh, I do thank you. I'll go there, I'll make it appear I've gone riding in the opposite direction. Josette can manage that part—" In the midst of her sudden plans she felt a moment of regret that her parents hadn't yet replied, though heaven knew they'd had ample opportunity. Two packets of estate news had already been received from Vaudraye since she had posted hers. But she was determined to forget them, at least briefly, while she reveled in anticipation of becoming Gilles Marsan's wife. She hugged Sister Thérèse, who surprised her by affectionately returning the embrace. With Marie-Josette trailing behind them they walked down to the ground floor garden where the nun's coachman was flirting in the hot July night air with one of Sylvie de Vaudraye's parlor maids.

When the Sister was on her way, Marie-Josette asked Veronique anxiously, "Do you believe we can fool that de Gleeb? We know he is about here, and yet we haven't ever seen him. He is so clever—"

"Well," Veronique said impatiently, "it is certainly safer to meet Gilles in Paris than here under de Gleeb's nose. Come and help me pack. I will stay at the Convent of Ste. Veronique while the banns are read. I shall certainly not return to this artificial place. I was never suited to it. I haven't the manner, the air or the looks for it. Come!"

The girl followed her up the stairs with a light clatter of morocco slippers. "It really is so romantic . . . I never imagined I would be party to anything so exciting—"

"Oh, but you won't, Josette. You must wear one of my gowns and a big hat and hire a carriage that will take you in the direction of one of those châteaux we've visited lately. This should help confuse anyone who thinks to follow me."

Marie-Josette was disappointed but quickly allowed herself to be cheered by the prospect of playing a part in a romantic plot, and conveniently swept aside her misgivings.

7

ON THAT Sunday morning of July 12, 1789, Veronique knew how important it was to make her journey to the Palais-Royal without the knowledge of Sylvie, Alex, or their servants, especially the unseen but apparently ubiquitous de Gleeb, Alex's "Arno." She was regretfully resigned now to the fact that her father had deliberately, out of good but misguided intentions, sent Arnauld de Gleeb to Alex. And Alex and Sylvie—despite her assurances to her father, presumably passed on to them, that she had no interest in claiming her inheritance—clearly were less than convinced of her position and were collaborating with all efforts to see that she was safely in the convent—and out of Marsan's worldly arms— thereby safeguarding *their* position as principal heirs to her father's estates.

There was another reason for Veronique to make this journey in secrecy. With all the unrest in Paris it needed only the Vaudraye carriage and four, with coachmen and postillions, to spark bitterness and perhaps even violence in those slum districts. This would not be the first time she'd visited Paris since her arrival at Versailles, but this venture would be her first outside the aristocratic haunts of the faubourg St.-Germain, the Convent in the Marais, or the races at Vincennes. Sylvie could not conceive of anything worth venturing into the slums of the great city, and Veronique doubted if her cousin had ever really looked at the Bastille, or St.-Antoine Quarter, or the tangle of shacks and hovels crowded up against the enormous façade of Notre-Dame Cathedral on the island in the Seine.

When the Vaudrayes and the Abbé drove her out the rue St.-Antoine toward the racecourse at Vincennes, what Veronique saw along the way had come as a shock. From the grand carriage with the armorial bearings of Sylvie's du Plessis ancestors Veronique saw the filth and raw sewage that seemed everywhere, the thin, dirty and sullen faces of not just the old but the very young as well. Virtually all the lodging houses were centuries old and in such run-down condition that they looked as if they would not stand another year. Yet these were the homes of thousands of people, a half-dozen human beings in each room. When Veronique shared with Sylvie her horror and shock at what she saw, and what must be the fear and anger and hopelessness of so many of these poor, Sylvie could only comment on the foul stench, and there her concern ended. . . .

Immediately after Mass, having sent Marie-Josette off in clothes from her own wardrobe, Veronique went out secretly in her oldest summer gown, with a deep, concealing bonnet and green spencer. She found a fiacre for hire in the Place d'Armes, one of the new public transports which carried the less affluent members of the Legislative Assembly to Paris and back. The ancient, closed carriage was exceeded in age only by the nag that drew it. All skin and bones, with solid welts beneath the harness, it was spavined and undoubtedly had the heaves. The coachman, a dark man of middle years, with a brutish face and hands, shared one quality with his horse: both were crusted by layer upon layer of dirt. He accepted his passenger without the least surprise, explained briefly but with telling waves of his big hands that he was taxed double for carrying passengers who were from outside the customs barriers of Paris and he charged triple on holidays, so would mam'selle kindly pay in advance? He showed every sign of resorting to some unpleasantness if his passenger refused him.

Veronique, taking the measure of him, waved him on.

"But, mam'selle—" The coachman twisted his head to speak between the ragged curtains.

"We will settle this later, when we meet my father. He is investigating certain restaurants near the Palais-Royal."

"Investigating? Then mam'selle's father is—?"

"The Lieutenant-General of Police."

The coachman stared straight ahead, raised his whip, and laid it sharply across the wretched animal's neck. The coach lurched forward.

Veronique, relieved and feeling genuinely more confident now that her ploy had apparently worked, called out, "Coachman, I trust you don't ill-treat your nag. His Excellency, my father, is sending out men to report on such treatment. The Crown wishes to make a few examples. You'd do well to spread my warning among your fellows. . . ."

After that, resting her feet on her portmanteau that was on the dirty floor, she pushed aside the tattered curtains and looked out, preparing to take in the sights on her ride into Paris. As for the horse drawing the coach, he'd probably never known such gentle treatment as he was unexpectedly receiving now.

As they passed through several narrow streets, Veronique asked the coachman whether a particular building she pointed to had housed one of the royal tennis courts.

"Yes, mademoiselle, but now they say it'll be known as the birthplace of our new liberty . . . where Monsieur Mirabeau and the delegates stood up to the nobles. Only weeks ago it was, mam'selle. When the delegates were locked out of their regular meeting place they said they'd never disband until they got the people their liberty. . . ."

He looked back at Veronique. She found herself staring at a set of yellowed stumps of teeth. "You are not interested in the scene of such a moment, mam'selle?" He was surprisingly bold, considering who she'd said she was.

"I do not play tennis. Just drive on."

Even from the little she knew, her common sense made her doubt the event had been precisely as the coachman represented it. She knew only that the King, under bad advice, had behaved stupidly. The Third Estate under the wily Mirabeau had turned the royal mistake to their own account. And yet here it was more than two months after the first meeting of the States-General and nothing had been accomplished— prices were higher than ever, gold seemed to have disappeared from the face of the earth, and, to cap the situation, there were regiments being moved in from the countryside to barracks outside Paris. Clearly, they expected trouble.

Would the government actually use troops against Parisians? It was hard to think of a time when Paris had not been turbulent, given to riots at the slightest excuse, and often with no more justification than that used during the recent spring when they tore down a huge paper factory after a false rumor was started about a reduction in wages. The result of the riot was a hundred and thirty dead, and unemployment even more widespread.

Our world is collapsing over our heads and Gilles and I are marrying as though our happiness mattered more than all this misery around us. How selfish humans are . . . and how human we are. . . . Yet even thinking this, Veronique couldn't resist hugging to herself the prospect of her happiness. . . .

By the time they reached the elegant little customs barrier of Passy and entered Paris, Veronique began to sense that the atmosphere was far worse than the reports that had filtered out of the city from Sister Thérèse and others during the last few days. One of the customs collectors called out to the coachman, "You're from Versailles, is it true what we hear . . . that the Queen's party wants to have the members of the National Assembly arrested?"

"Not while Minister Necker holds the government together—"

A peasant driving an empty tumbril called out, "Ay, there's the truth, Monsieur Necker will know what to do. . . ."

Veronique wondered what would happen if all this confidence in the finance minister, or in his power, should collapse. She didn't believe that so much should depend on one man.

Inside the barrier all travel, commerce and economy came to a halt while tariffs on everything conceivable were paid, thereby raising the prices in Paris sky-high. Veronique noted that the crowds were much denser than in Versailles. The ugliness of the mood gathered around the fiacre like the customs walls themselves. No one touched the horse or the carriage, but men waiting here to pay their tolls or argue the fees, or simply out of work, glowered at the fine lady in the fiacre and made comments on her clothing which, though poor in Vaudraye eyes, was surely far richer than anything in this neighborhood.

As the fiacre and horse moved forward Veronique noted the area—filthy, overcrowded, smoky, with tenements seemingly ready to fall down onto the cafés at street level. Veronique had never seen so many of these new cafés, an invention borrowed from the Venetian Republic, and which had come into vogue during the last score of years. Most of the little cafés were closed for the Sabbath but now and then one of these social forums for all classes had stayed open in defiance of the clergy, whom they lumped into the noble class, not without some justification.

Suddenly, as the old horse clip-clopped onto the cobblestones of the ancient, serpentine rue St.-Honoré, a wineglass was hurled at the carriage. It did not break until its sour contents had sprinkled Veronique's pink and apple-green muslin gown and stained her short green spencer. She jumped, but being deeply aware that she was watched from the street, managed to control her panic and show no more than a quick flush of anger. She looked down and shifted the glass with the toe of her shoe. Fortunately, though broken, it had not shattered. The coachman, who'd pulled in the reins, looked around. A grin was hiding beneath the dirt that disfigured his face.

"You wish to turn back, mam'selle?"

"Certainly not."

She leaned over, took the largest piece of glass between thumb and forefinger and threw it out onto the cobblestones, just missing the boots of several individuals sitting at a small table outside a wineshop. The sly amusement on their faces froze, which gave Veronique considerable satisfaction. As the fiacre moved on, she brushed away any wine drops that had not already dried on her clothing. Despite her fine show she decided she'd do well to remain more discreet and out of view. She sat back now and gazed at the famous landmarks of Paris. She'd come into the fashionable center of the city and could see the glint of silk materials draped over a pattern doll, all faintly visible behind the shutters and bars that protected the mercer's shop on the Sabbath.

A few minutes later they passed into the quarter lined by narrow townhouses of the upper bourgeoisie, and Veronique noticed that the streets were deserted, as one would expect on a Sunday. Despite this she found that the desolate silence somehow did not follow naturally after the unpleasant excitement at the customs barrier. Was everyone at the barriers?

When they started across the rue Royale, which led into the enormous Place Louis XV at the western end of the Tuileries Gardens, they had their answer. In the distance Veronique saw a crowd on the swing-bridge leading into the Gardens. A company of cavalry was trying to scatter the crowd but had only succeeded in driving many of those wielding pikes, axes, knives and brooms into the area between the two winged stone horses at the opening of the Gardens. he screams, shouts and the noise of the horses' hooves tramping on the wooden bridge combined to suggest a massive explosion.

Veronique caught the sleeve of the coachman, who looked as if he might jump off his box. "Coachman, you'd best keep going. St.-Honoré seems to be safe."

But that proved impractical. The noise in the Place Louis XV had drawn the attention of those crowds around the now-distant customs barrier. Dozens of men and a scattering of women wineshop patrons running toward them blocked the rue St.-Honoré from both ends.

"Can you get to the next street before they reach it?"

"If you mean by cutting back toward the barriers through the Champs-Elysées, we can't . . . if St.-Honoré's busy, then the Elysées woods will be worse. They're directly opposite the swing-bridge. Best to go ahead and hope we'll find one of the other barriers open. We'll take that. No more business for me in this town today." He shook his whip without looking back at her. "I knew you were unlucky for me . . . well, if I get you out of this I expect you'll put in a good word for me with the Lieutenant-General—"

"Certainly. The moment we meet. That will be at the Palais-Royal Gardens just beyond the Louvre." She knew quite well she was not going to retreat from the city through some as yet untouched barrier while the man she'd come to marry would surely be moving closer into danger during the night.

Since the street ahead was crowded from gutter to gutter, it was necessary to go the long way around. The coachman took an alley near the half-empty palace of the Louvre, passing the busy stalls beside the Seine temporarily set up for the sale of second hand goods of all kinds. Even on this day it was swarming with buyers and sellers. The fiacre made its way carefully along the quai, keeping within sight of the three turrets of a great, sinister-looking building across the river, along the island's quai.

"What a horrid place," Veronique said. "Is it another palace? No wonder the royal family moved to Versalles."

The coachman laughed shortly. "Conciergerie Prison, mam'-selle. And at the side of it yonder, the Palais de Justice, where the trials are held."

"Then the bridge we just passed, with all the crowds on the island, that would be the Pont au Change."

"Pont Neuf, mam'selle. Pont au Change is the bridge ahead."

Somewhere in this quarter between the bridges was the Café Parnasse, where Gilles and his friends met, but they would not be here at noon. She must walk back to the Palais-Royal through this area and reach the gardens without being stopped by those mobs on the western fringes of the rue St.-Honoré.

"Coachman, it is still early for my appointment. Set me down here. I can walk up to St.-Honoré. This area doesn't look dangerous. . . ."

Citizens of the quarter sauntered over the bridge and along the quais, dressed in their Sunday best but prepared to argue the price of a used petticoat or a knife with a broken handle, or any other well-worn object that might still prove useful. Nor did the foreign soldiers look so forbidding . . . Swiss or German mercenaries in their fine Sunday uniforms, strolling in pairs, obviously on their first excursion into what they'd always heard to be glamorous, magic Paris.

Apparently no one was aware of the riot going on between soldiers and civilians at the Place Louis XV entrance to the Tuileries Gardens. It was a curious phenomenon that Veronique was beginning to notice for the first time. One quarter could often remain unaffected while another seethed with riots, until the news spread like a disease, insidious in its movement, spreading even wider.

As she paid what the coachman demanded, not troubling to bargain, she looked around. "Heavens! I've never seen so many uniforms in my life. And those who just passed us were the first *Gardes Françaises* I've seen today—"

"General Lafayette is in town," the coachman told her, importantly. "Trying to keep the militia together. There's desertions in all the French home regiments. They say if there be trouble, the *Gardes Françaises* won't fire on other Frenchmen. That's why those foreign soldier-boys are here. But Lafayette, he's for the people."

"What a pack they all are—nobles, court, people—all of them!" Veronique washed her hands of politics. "They've still got their precious finance minister, Monsieur Necker. The people keep saying he will save the nation. And God knows General Lafayette is on their side. So if anyone makes a move, I should think it would be the Court."

"That's as may be," the coachman said quietly, then threw

down her portmanteau and gave his horse the signal to be on its way.

Veronique tried not to allow herself time to feel lost or frightened among all these strangers. She started up the nearest street, which would be a mere alley in newer, more modern Versailles. It was so cluttered with animal and human offal that she made her way with difficulty. For all her care she barely missed being soaked by the contents of a chamber-pot hurled out over her head from the fourth floor of a wretched tenement. A voice sounded, too late: "Take care below!"

Once past this, Veronique noted that she'd fortunately escaped a good splashing and began to run as she saw the ancient rue St.-Honoré extending eastward across the street ahead of her. Turning west on the busy street she elbowed her way through the Sunday strollers, all of whom seemed headed toward the Palais-Royal, where entertainment of all sorts and at all prices could be guaranteed. With a rush of excitement she recognized the often-sketched portals by which Parisian, countryman and foreigner entered the great arcaded gardens of the Palais-Royal. The buildings themselves were a rectangular series, severely classic in style and surrounding the celebrated gardens, built to the specifications of Cardinal Richelieu, who at his death had bequeathed them to the King. Since then it had come into the hands of the Orléans family, one of whom disgraced but enriched his extravagant family by turning the entire affair into arcaded shops, restaurants, outdoor cafés and apartments above the arcades for the use of certain enterprising prostitutes as well as government offices.

As Veronique had always heard, the gardens were so crowded she thought at first that the riot had moved through the city to this tight-packed area between the tables and chairs of the outdoor cafés.

While she was looking about, hoping against hope to catch a glimpse of Gilles Marsan, she noticed an attractive young man who sat writing at a table under the trees, just outside the Café de Foy's arcade. His long brown hair, shaken out of its banding ribbon, caught the noon sun and glistened, giving his head a kind of halo of light. At his elbow was a charcoal sketch that looked very much like the work of Gilles Marsan, and, under his tricorne hat on the table, there was a copy of a book by the radical Jean-Jacques Rousseau. She felt he must be a friend of Gilles's. He certainly had all the marks.

He raised his head as Veronique approached him and she saw that the boyish look was deceptive. Although his face was unlined enough to give him a pleasantly ingenuous look, he was probably as old as Gilles. His hands were mature, and there were telltale signs, small crinkles, around his eyes.

"Monsieur . . . are you by chance acquainted with a Monsieur Gilles Marsan? A member, I believe, of the Cordeliers and Jacobin clubs? . . ."

The young man hesitated, looked her over. Then, apparently satisfied, said, "He is my f-friend, yes. And you, mademoiselle?" He surprised her then by getting up, making a great to-do over her. "But you must be Mademoiselle de Vaudraye, Gilles's b-betrothed. I've seen his sk-ketches of you. I thought they flattered you but I see that they do not." He pulled out a chair for her. "I s-seem to speak perfectly when I talk politics. Perhaps I s-should talk to my friends as if they were the government." He saw that she was still confused and remembered suddenly, with fresh apologies, "I am Desmoulins. But my father is Desmoulins. Please call me Camille. Everyone d-does."

Veronique now asked eagerly, "Will Gilles Marsan be arriving in the gardens soon?"

"Any minute, mademoiselle. We are to meet here or at the St.-Honoré entrance. He will be d-delighted to find you here. He talks of nothing but seeing you tonight. We are to witness your marriage, my Lucille and I."

"I know. I'm so very happy to meet you, monsieur—"

"Camille."

She laughed. He was irresistibly friendly. "Camille. May I wait here with you?"

"Delighted. We're expecting Mousieur Necker, the finance minister. That's why the crowd is here. Marsan and I are presenting these petitions to show him the thousands who support him. When Necker gives them to the King, we're sure His Majesty will support us against the Austrian and her crowd. . . . Matter of fact, just as you arrived I was going over my speech to Monsieur Necker. Well, it's not really my speech because I am not a speaker. I only write them. Yet it is strange for me to hear Max Robespierre get up in the Assembly with my words and my ideas. It's as if I were hearing them for the first time." He paused, seeing her look nervously about. "I think I have t-talked too much."

"Oh, no, monsieur, I was only thinking of how difficult it will be for Gilles to find us here in this churning mob."

"Don't be concerned. Gilles and all of us who work in Paris have become accustomed to crowds. A crowd is a place in which you can either stand out or hide . . . depending on where you stand politically. Let me assure you, Gilles will find us. . . ."

She nodded and looked around her again. Her familiarity with prostitutes did not extend beyond those women she'd helped to attend in the Norman hospitals and pesthouses. It took her several minutes to realize that three-quarters of the flashily dressed ladies parading the garden and between the café tables were of that profession.

She told herself she was not shocked . . . and remarkably they seemed to be more interested in politics and arguments than in their usual traffic. Groups of men and women were gathered everywhere, discussing the dangerous presence of foreign troops in the city, and rumors that the Court—the Queen's Party—might try to undermine Minister Necker's effort to solve the financial crisis. . . .

Beside the entrance to the popular little Café de Chartres stood several young men, together with a uniformed member of the Paris militia, the *Gardes Françaises*.

"What are they shouting?" Veronique asked Camille.

Camille stopped leafing through his papers and looked up. "It seems to be something about Monsieur Necker." Then, after a moment: "He must be about to arrive." Camille stood up. "Come, I'll present my petition to Monsieur Necker and then we'll both look for Gilles."

As Veronique forced her mind off the possible cause for Gilles not having arrived yet, she saw the anxious expressions on many faces. Worse, there was panic, and the beginnings of erupting anger. "It must be about the riot in the Place Louis XV this morning," she suggested, "or the trouble at the Customs Barrier. There was quite a turmoil when I came through—"

"I'm afraid it's bad."

The shouts and angry voices became general, sweeping toward the now-aroused crowd at the south end of the gardens. Among them, Veronique saw, thought she saw, a tall lumbering fellow in a wide-brimmed farmer's hat and a long greatcoat. . . . Arnauld de Gleeb? . . . perhaps . . . not unlikely . . . and then he was swallowed up by the rushing crowd.

More and more people began to pour into the garden, many pushing and shouting as they ran.

"Can you see what's happening?" Veronique asked Camille Desmoulins.

"Messengers from Versailles, I think, and the news must be bad."

One of the *Gardes Françaises* rushed toward Veronique and Desmoulins. "Necker is dismissed by the Queen's party. The Royal Swiss Guards are ordered into Paris—"

Camille looked stunned. "It c-can't be true—"

Someone in the crowd called out, "Necker is on his way to the frontier, ordered out of the country. . . ."

The cry was picked up . . . "The Swiss will march on Paris!"

The shouting increased. It seemed that everyone now was screaming for news and with each cry the tone of panic grew. No one could see anyone else, the crowd in the garden was too thickly packed. Instinctively Veronique backed away toward the arcade and the interior of the Café de Foy.

An instinct, or some other mysterious agent of transformation, had apparently taken hold of Camille Desmoulins. Looking at him, Veronique thought he seemed dazed, assaulted by this news that at first he wanted to disbelieve and now was momentarily stunned by, just as if he had been somehow shocked by a sudden swift blow. And then, still not seeming himself but another who had, perhaps, been lurking always behind that pen and beneath the skin, he slowly stood up on his chair, from there onto the table top, set his tricorne hat on his head and began to speak, without a trace of his damnable stammer, and in an almost eerily resonant voice that virtually could be heard from one end of the garden to the other.

"We have the news from Versailles. . . . Necker has been dismissed. The mercenaries are marching on us. . . . It will be another St. Bartholomew's Massacre. . . ."

As Veronique watched in astonishment, it seemed to her that whatever had transformed the notoriously shy, youthful Desmoulins had now begun to take hold of the crowd. They were strangely silent, clustering close around this slight figure whose words were like catalyst and release for fears and hates simmering unfocused in them for so long.

"Friends, patriots, they will march on the Assembly, they will imprison our delegates, and then they will spill our blood, our citizens' blood. . . ."

Pressed about him, seemingly mesmerized, the crowd was literally at his feet as it heard his now-fiery voice call out. . . .

"The time for speech-making is at an end. It is we, the citizens and patriots of France, who are left to stop the tyrants. It is our death they seek, let us make it theirs. . . ."

Now the crowd, shaken from its momentary trance, was as on fire as the slim young man before them. . . . "Our need is guns to defend ourselves and France. . . ." He paused momentarily, then . . . "We shall seek and take them wherever they are cached—in the Invalides, the Hôtel de Ville, the gunshops . . . the Bastille itself . . . we shall take up weapons and unite against them. . . ."

And then, in a crescendo of passion, his voice now a live thing apart from him and merged with them, his words came over them—only three, but each charged with its own explosive. . . .

"Patriots! To arms!"

Veronique, still drawn back from them, felt separated as well from the current of sound and movement that now began to gather momentum. Separated, yes, and yet not truly apart . . . for the emotion building and swirling about her had also touched her, strangely, irresistibly, as it must have anyone alive in that place, on that day . . . at that moment. . . .

And then she was startled from her own bemusement by a voice emerging from the massed crowd . . . "How will we know each other from those who support the tyrant? . . ."

Camille paused momentarily, then slowly raised his arm, and for an instant Veronique had the sickening feeling that he was about to point to her as a kind of terrible example . . . until she saw him instead reach up and tear off a leaf from a branch over her head. A leaf which he then waved before them.

"I say let a green cockade be our sign. The color of hope . . . to arms, citizens . . . *to arms* . . ."

At this they turned from him and rushed to denude the trees of every leaf, which they too waved as they broke up into groups and charged off to the armories of the *Gardes Françaises,* many of whose troops actually favored the people of Paris, and to the Hôtel de Ville, center of the city's government. Some shouted that the pavillions of the Invalides across the river held the largest cache of arms, but others said that everyone knew the largest quantity of arms was stored in the ancient and almost unused prison, the Bastille. The crowd scrambled to leave the gardens in both directions at once, causing massive confusion, with flailing arms and fists, and some swinging swords.

Through this excitement, the cause of it all stood on the café table, looking about him in a daze, scarcely aware of Veronique's importuning that he get down from the table before he was arrested. And he'd no sooner done so than a half-dozen Swiss Guards came in at a jog trot through the Montpensier entrance, the rattle of their accoutrements a rhythmic counterpoint to the sound of the mob dispersing at a run.

Still only partially aware of his danger, Camille Desmoulins yielded to Veronique's urgings and together they finally began to run toward the St.-Honoré entrance until, as though by a physical barrier, she was stopped by the sound of her name being called . . . and by a voice that for her could never be diffused even in the turmoil about them.

In a moment Gilles Marsan was at their side. "Gilles . . . I don't understand . . . it's impossible that you should be here when—"

"Not impossible at all. I happened to be on my way to our café to see Camille when I heard all the shouting and saw the crowd milling about. . . . A better question is what are *you* doing here? You should never have come here unescorted, and besides, I was to come for you tonight. Didn't Sister Thérèse tell you?"

"Yes, and you'd very likely have come to find Arnauld de Gleeb instead. . . . Oh, Gilles, you have no idea . . . your friend here really is in terrible danger. We heard of Monsieur Necker's dismissal and suddenly—"

"Yes, I heard of that myself a few minutes ago. But we intend to take the petitions to Mirabeau in the Assembly . . . he has an entreé with the King. More important, with the Queen." He looked at Camille, who was once more his old self.

"Gilles, m-mademoiselle came all the way in to Paris to m-marry you. You're indeed a lucky devil. . . ."

"Yes, I know, and she shouldn't have, but what is this business about your being in some danger? . . ."

"Darling, he incited a crowd of people with what I'm sure will be considered treasonous talk. I wouldn't be surprised if half Paris has heard of it by now."

"But that's nonsense," he said. "You don't know Camille. He doesn't make public speeches, he writes them for other people. He's much too shy to speak to crowds. Everybody who knows him knows that. . . ." And then he had her in his arms, and was kissing her, and she was responding, nearly unaware and, for the moment, wholly uncaring that it was in front of this strange young man she hardly knew.

When he finally released her, Gilles looked over her shoulder to Camille. "All right, my friend, now just what is it you've been telling Veronique to make her think—"

"I have not been telling her, Gilles. Actually, s-she has been telling me. But it's true. I honestly don't know how I did what I did, but something happened to me right after I heard the news about Necker, and the rest was almost like watching somebody else up on that table speaking my words through my mouth. It was I . . . and yet in a way it w-wasn't. . . ."

"It very much was you that the Swiss Guards nearly arrested, and will soon in any case if we stay here much longer," Veronique said impatiently.

"You're right, darling," Gilles said. "I still don't understand what came over our friend here, but apparently he lost his head. We must not allow it to happen again today, or I suspect it will be for the last time." He took the green leaf off Camille's tricorne hat and threw both hat and leaf to the ground. "Listen carefully to me, Camille. You are to play drunk until we get you to your lodgings. Say nothing at all. Whatever came over you hopefully has passed. Now please put your dramatic talents to use and stay between the two of us the entire way. We'll be supporting you, our drunken friend, to your bed. . . ."

The three trudged along the crowded street, Marsan and Veronique half-dragging Camille, who'd flung his arms around their necks and was indeed making a convincing drunkard. They were constantly buffeted by running men, and eyed with calculation by equally hard-looking men and women from the nearby fish markets.

Veronique, glancing back, told the two men, "Those Swiss Guards have come out of the gardens, they're looking up and down. . . ."

"Keep your face hidden," Marsan told his friend, whose tawny hair, hanging over his eyes, was half-blinding him.

"I s-still can't understand how it happened. Suddenly I felt like . . . Danton, m-maybe. Or Max Robespierre. I don't even remember how I started. . . ."

"You started," Veronique assured him, and said to Marsan, "You would not believe the effect of it when he called the city to arms and swore them all to the common bond of a green cockade—"

"Where did I put it—the green leaf from that tree in the

gardens?" Camille wanted to know, finally aware of the seriousness of what he'd done, that he could even hang for it.

"Don't worry," Veronique said calmly. "Gilles threw it away with your hat."

Camille raised his head. "He threw away my hat too? But I bought that especially to impress Lucille's family . . . I want m-my Loulou to—"

"Your Loulou will love you, with or without a hat. Not, however, with a rope around your neck."

Veronique looked around again. "The soldiers are coming this way."

8

"CAFÉ PARNASSE. On the right," Marsan ordered. Veronique and Gilles dragged Camille through a porte-cochère into a small street, scarcely more than an alley. The street ran toward the river and the busy quai. Beyond the river loomed the towers of the Conciergerie and the Palais de Justice. She saw it as a looming reminder to those who patronized the Café Parnasse, her Gilles included, that they might end their careers in those gloomy confines on the Ile de Cité.

Three patrons were seated at a table out on the cobblestones, one short little man and two women. Veronique also saw Yolande Berthelot, looking her loveliest in a shallow-crowned bonnet trimmed with tiny blue flowers that matched the sprigged pattern of her white muslin gown. Even on the day when Veronique hoped to make her marriage vows to Gilles, she'd not managed to outshine this dazzling woman. Well, so be it, she tried to console herself. There's no competing—or comparing—with perfection. . . . At least Gilles scarcely looked at the girl now, perhaps because he was accustomed to her or, more likely, because of his friend's immediate danger, she thought. The landlord of the café, a bulky, anxious man named Charpentier, saw the hurrying trio and pulled out a chair for the apparently helpless Camille. The other light-haired young woman, quiet and less spectacular than Yolande, rushed to take Veronique's place, putting Camille's arm around her shoulders.

"Where is he hurt, Monsieur Marsan?"

"Loulou, my adorable—" Camille said, "you'll not believe it b-but it seems I started a riot. Gilles's s-sweetheart was there. . . ."

Mademoiselle Lucille glanced at Veronique, who said ruefully, "I'm afraid it's true, mademoiselle."

Marsan was already speaking to the café owner. "Swiss Guards are likely after him now. Is he safe here?"

"So long as my good patrons agree that Camille Desmoulins has been here the past hour. Mam'selle Berthelot? Mam'selle Lucille? M'sieur de Robespierre?"

A narrow-shouldered little man with his hair carefully clubbed and his worn green suit immaculate turned around in his chair and looked up through small square spectacles that now suddenly seemed familiar to Veronique, as she remembered the two occasions when she'd seen him previously. He had been closely studying several papers full of corrected phrases, perhaps a speech.

Monsieur de Robespierre said in his chill voice, "Is our dear Camille in trouble? A pity. He had promised me a new ending to my speech. You are very thoughtless, my dear Camille."

Yolande Berthelot nodded to Veronique and turned her full attention to Marsan, who was explaining the matter to the other men. She interrupted him now by running her fingers over his cheek. "How heated you are, Gilles . . . so much hurrying on a hot July day. Charpentier, Gilles needs a cool glass of wine."

Marsan looked up long enough to smile and tell her, "The minute Camille's troubles are over today you may drink to us, if you like."

"Us?" Yolande echoed.

"Mademoiselle de Vaudraye and I are seeing Père Lefroy this afternoon. We are to be married as soon as possible."

Camille Desmoulins' Lucille looked over at Veronique with a warm smile, took her hand briefly and said, "I only pray that Camille and I may be as happy as you and Gilles."

Yolande seemed almost equally delighted. "And I, mademoiselle. I'm so pleased that the Vicomte has given his permission. I'm persuaded he desires only your happiness, but it would have been so difficult without it—fathers have such power. Why, if he'd chosen, the Vicomte might have had your marriage put at an end even now. Not, of course, that he would."

"Not, at any rate, after Gilles and I have been made man and wife. That would be beside the point," Veronique said easily.

"Very true, indeed. I only meant, if he happened to stop you before the ceremony, or were to change his mind—" Seeing everyone stare at her, Yolande let the matter trail off.

Veronique felt that the remarks about her father had been gratuitous, but she was also aware that her old jealousy might have affected her feelings. She put her hand up, conscious that her bonnet hung on her neck by its ribbons, as it so often did, and conscious too that her hair needed combing, her gown was disheveled . . . she could hardly have looked worse. While Robespierre referred Camille to the speech in his hand and sternly told him he must not jeopardize the cause of liberty by his antics, Veronique tried to smooth her hair and dress at the same time, and to stamp the dust off her shoes.

Her efforts were delightfully interrupted by Gilles, who took her in his arms. "Do you have any notion how wonderful you look to me?" He turned to the others. "Every time I am away from her I tell myself she cannot again look so delicious. And always I am wrong. She is unique among all the women of France—natural, lovely as nature and more unspoiled."

Diplomatic or genuine or both, Veronique had no time to question his fine speech as he immediately kissed her and once more she was indifferent to the audience to their affection as she returned his kiss.

"Remember the hundred gold louis?" he asked afterward, shifting his clasp from her arms and shoulders to her waist. "I earned it yesterday—"

The landlord Charpentier interrupted to say, "They're coming," and concentrated on polishing the table with the tail of his tight gray coat.

Veronique felt the muscles of Marsan's arm tighten around her waist but otherwise he seemed only mildly interested in the approaching Swiss soldiers, resplendent in their uniforms with the bandoliers so white they glistened like metal in the afternoon sun. The soldiers had come through the porte-cochère, slowing now from their brisk jog trot as they surveyed the table in the narrow street and especially its female occupants.

Their leader addressed the group around the table in excellent French, though with a Germanic accent. "Mesdames . . . Messieurs . . . we are looking for a young man who was preaching sedition in the Palais-Royal Gardens. We believe he took refuge here."

"Eh?" Charpentier came forward, hands on hips. "Not one of us. We are celebrating a betrothal. Those two. . . ." He gestured vaguely toward Marsan and Veronique.

"Quite true, monsieur," Marsan put in, slurring the words a little. "Let me present you to my bride and our friends. . . ."

The soldier paid little attention to the betrothed pair, being more impressed by Yolande Berthelot.

"And you mademoiselle? You are one of this party?"

Lucille pretended he'd addressed her. "But yes, officer. We have been here this hour at least."

"At least," added Yolande.

"You cannot believe one of us is guilty of inciting riots," Charpentier said.

The officer turned on him. "How do you know someone incited a riot?"

Before anyone could answer, one of the other Swiss dismissed Charpentier and Robespierre as unlikely candidates for a riot leader and whispered to the officer with a gesture toward Marsan.

"*Nein, nein!* The fellow was light-haired and smaller. Maybe more like this one." He took a handful of Camille's long brown hair, lifting his head with it. Camille swallowed painfully and stared at the soldier.

"No—please!" Lucille started, but Marsan quickly stepped in and said to Camille, "Tell them why you could not incite a riot, Camille."

"M-me? You wish a sp-speech from m-me? Certainly, m-messieurs." He tried to rise, fell back drunkenly. "With p-pleasure. On what s-subject sh-shall I address you?"

Only the Swiss officer retained his gravity, while his men joined the others in laughter. Even Robespierre seemed to join in, displaying his small, tightly packed lower teeth.

"Well then, friends, I leave you to your betrothal." The officer saluted the party, called his men together and they all made their exit onto the quai at the far end of the little street where the mob was still pouring along the river's edge. It took several minutes, however, for the "betrothal" party to recover from the fear that had gripped them all.

Except Maximilien de Robespierre. Brushing imaginary lint off his green coat, he addressed Camille. "Surely, now you have no further excuse for failing me, my boy. Come, pull yourself together and give us some choice phrase with which

I shall confound the National Assembly."

Pleased with his performance on all counts, Camille considered the final page of his friend Max's speech while Lucille smoothed his hair into a semblance of order.

Watching them, Marsan said to Veronique, "Will you be as obliging to me when I am in need, darling?"

"I devoutly hope you will soon have done with riots—"

He reminded her, "But it was you who were a party to the riot today, not I."

She conceded as much and he kissed her again, saying to the others, "We are off to see Père Lefroy. Wish us happiness, my friends."

The rue St.-Honoré was more crowded than ever. By this time clumsy cabriolets, barouches and gigs were attempting to make their way out of this general atmosphere of violence and seemingly unprovoked, sometimes murderous quarrels that had spread between classes, and between uniformed men and civilians.

"I'm afraid we chose the wrong church," Marsan said as they pushed through the milling crowds toward the exterior of the Palais-Royal. They were both flung against the gray stonewall. He protected her with his body but was almost knocked off his feet by a running soldier of the *Gardes Françaises* who was shouting something to the effect of . . . "for Lafayette and the people . . . the guards are going over to the people—"

Marsan remarked, "We may be grateful for that," while Veronique wondered. . . . "We either chose the wrong church, or the wrong day. I'm sorry, darling, but I'm not used to being afraid of people." She felt chilled, although the day remained sultry and the air was beginning to grow thick with dust and heat.

Marsan kept her close as they passed the great wasted hulk of the Louvre and were beset by more crowds. He maneuvered her around the barrier of hovels, shacks in a general state of dilapidation that shocked Veronique.

"Why do they allow the area around a great palace like the Louvre to remain in such a condition?"

"You should see the Palais de Tuileries beyond. Half those exalted halls are filled with would-be artists, camping amid the splendors of ancient kings."

"Why aren't the rogues put out?"

"I'm a poor one to ask, darling."

They hurried now along the rue St.-Honoré, avoiding cart-wheels and the even more dangerous flying hooves of cavalry and carriage horses. The ancient street, lined with tall, centuries-old houses, collected all the soot and dust of the neighborhood and was even worse now in the sultry afternoon.

A dense crowd gathered in front of the heavy, age-stained façade of the Church of St.-Roch. The church itself seemed too large for the narrow street and was often the scene of accidents when coachmen trying to pass some drunken young sprig tooling a high-perch phaeton would run their wheels over the protruding steps. A small, elegant landau had just overturned and the man and woman inside, gorgeous in satin, lace and powdered wigs, were the butt of ridicule by urchins and habitués of the local wineshops. Not satisfied with this amusement, some of them had begun to stone the church itself.

"They seem bad omens for us," Veronique murmured as she and Marsan went up the steps and into the church's dark interior.

Marsan stopped at the end of the nave and kissed her gently on the cheek. "Don't think of bad omens and superstitions. Remember, Veronique, before that altar I swear I will love you to the day I die."

"Don't speak of death, not here."

"I'm sorry, darling, but I wanted to tell you that what we do here is for a lifetime. . . . And from today on you are not going to have *all* the burdens of the world on you. . . . Everyone in Vaudraye has talked of your good works, your kindness . . . well, now you are in my care—"

"But Gilles, dearest, I like . . . being a part of life. I want to help you. . . ."

"And so you shall, only I'll see that you aren't forever taken over as you used to be by people with their endless problems." He smiled and kissed her. "Actually I'm being selfish. . . . I'll bring you my problems instead."

With a kind of urgent tenderness she returned his kiss, persuaded that she would be happy to devote her life entirely to her husband's concerns. They moved on now through the church, which appeared to be empty. Where was the sacristan? Or the priest?

"I wonder if that mob could have harmed Père Lefroy," Gilles said.

The sound of breaking glass and of furniture being hurled

about hardly reassured them. Gilles called out, "Père Lefroy, are you here?"

Veronique finally stopped him. "Please don't . . . he can't hear you, I'm sure, and heaven knows the echo is frightful. Hadn't we better search quietly?"

"The sounds seem to come from the alley behind the church. It's unlikely that they've broken in yet."

They crossed the nave to the church office. No one was in the austere little chamber. "Thank God for that!" Veronique said, "I thought he might have been injured by that mob."

Gilles nodded. The sounds outside the front of the church had increased. They moved out of the office along the wall, past a font, and then hurried toward the great doors that opened on the rue St.-Honoré.

A lean figure suddenly cut the sunlight that poured in through the open doors. Veronique grasped Marsan's hand— "Arnauld de Gleeb."

Clearly her ploy to have Marie-Josette masquerade as herself and thereby divert de Gleeb had fooled him not at all, or at least not for long. Despising someone, she thought ruefully, could also lead one to underrate his intelligence— however vicious.

And then there was no more time for regrets or thoughts as the impact of the situation made itself felt. She nearly started to run, but Gilles pushed her quickly into the darkness, placing himself between her and the doors.

De Gleeb's voice sounded now through the darkness. "I'm pleased we meet again, monsieur, and I assure you that this time the ingenuity of mam'selle will be of no use. It really is quite fitting, ironic even, that the Jacobin rabble-rouser and traitor will be reported stabbed by one of his own in a church during a riot provoked by his own friend. . . ."

Gilles knew better than to answer and betray their position, but Veronique found it impossible to control herself and before Gilles could silence her called out, "You will find that difficult . . . there are witnesses and—"

The only sound was not from the former gamekeeper but from Gilles, whose quick intake of breath preceded the sunlight flash on the blade of de Gleeb's hunting knife.

"You've led me on a considerable chase today, mam'selle, in fact ever since Versailles. I thought earlier that when I directed the *Gardes* to the Café Parnasse my job would have been done for me, but I am just as glad to attend to it personally. The Vicomte has just arrived in Versailles and his charge to me—at the peril of my own life—was to stop this marriage any way I found necessary. I find Monsieur Marsan's death the necessary way. Put your hands over your head, Marsan . . . and, mam'selle, if you should find it difficult to be discreet about these events, your cousin has His Majesty's authority to have you sealed in a convent whose rules won't permit you to emerge alive. . . ."

Veronique looked about for the witnesses she knew would not be there to help or back up her earlier threat. She could hardly believe it, her father in Versailles—this grotesque still apparently in his employ. . . .

Her thoughts were interrupted by Gilles quietly saying in measured words, "A pity I don't carry a weapon. A pistol would be just the thing."

And hearing him, Veronique suddenly realized that the words were not idle as they had first sounded but meant expressly and immediately for her . . . Gilles did carry a weapon, his sword, but of course he wasn't able to get at it with his hands held over his head, nor could she possibly draw it herself before de Gleeb would have killed him. Forcing down a sense of panic she felt the skirt of his coat, made out a pistol barrel in the large pocket, and drew it out as Gilles rushed at de Gleeb, whose knife was now concealed between their wrestling bodies. Veronique, feeling as though another hand was directing hers, brought down the steel barrel on the back of de Gleeb's skull. The man's head snapped up, then fell over to one side as if its weight were too much for the neck to carry.

Gilles disentangled himself from the unconscious man and got to his feet. Veronique had knelt to examine de Gleeb's body, but when she saw drops of blood on her gown she looked up anxiously. The blood had trailed between the fingers of Marsan's right hand. She could see the slash across the lower arm of his coat sleeve.

Before she could try to attend to it he had lifted her to her feet with his left hand and was saying, "We'd best not be found here, if this fellow has a Royal Commission for his crimes—"

She obeyed him without protest. She was in his world now. As they edged their way out into the noisy, crowded street and retraced their steps in an easterly direction, she removed the sash from her dress and insisted he wrap it around his

injured arm, which he did hastily and not too efficiently—
they could not find a moment to stop, swept along now in the
tide of the screaming mob.

9

THE SUNDAY riots did not end until early the following morning. It was well into Monday afternoon, July 13, before they could make their way to the relative safety of Gilles's lodgings in the Bastille—St.-Antoine quarter. As a temporary shelter, they had stopped at the Café Parnasse, where they saw some of the effects of the earlier violence. Veronique continued to be concerned about the cut across the flesh of his arm below the elbow, but Charpentier enumerated his previous injuries, as if to dismiss this one by comparison.

"This is nothing compared to the bleeding when you had that little argument with the Royal German Guard around All-Saints' Day last year," Charpentier reminded as Gilles straddled a chair and watched Veronique wash and powder and then wrap the wound.

Neither she nor Gilles had mentioned the body of Arnauld de Gleeb left behind in the church, though Veronique found herself haunted throughout the evening by the spectre of it. Had she actually killed a man, another human being? . . .

Several times, just as Gilles and Veronique were about to try once more to get out of this very temporary haven, the café was the scene of marching groups of men and women carrying what Veronique thought for an awful moment were human heads. Actually they proved to be busts of the Paris heroes, the Duc d'Orléans and that General Lafayette, who controlled the *Gardes Françaises* but was said to be in sympathy with the people of Paris against the throne. These wax heads had been borrowed from the wax museum of Madame Turgot.

Charpentier was busy serving wine to thirsty rioters when, at his suggestion, Marsan and Veronique made a supper out of a mutton bone, some broth and a bottle of red wine. At one time they were joined by Maximilien de Robespierre, who was remarkably curious about their marital status.

"Père Lefroy was gone, the rioters were all over St.-Honoré," Marsan told him. "Your glass is empty, Max. It isn't a bad vintage." He started to pour from the carafe but Robespierre sealed the rim of his glass with his thin, tight fingers.

"Not for me. A digestive upset. When I am to make a speech. . . . Some of that broth, however, if you please. That, or a citrus, often restores me. It is very important, my speech, you know. Its subject is of vital concern to the future of France—"

Since he seemed aching to tell them, Veronique politely asked, "And what is the subject, monsieur?"

"But virtue, of course. The virtue of the state and of the individual. That is the ultimate cause of all the disasters we have suffered. We have become a nation misled by debauched aristocrats, and are now ourselves hopelessly lacking in virtue. We must root out these impure influences, as one roots out the weeds in a garden. Chop them out with the good, sharp edge of a spade."

"Perhaps only God is pure," she said suddenly, recognizing her own sins very well. She had almost murdered a man—perhaps she had—and now she was spending the night in the company of a man whom she loved, and with whom she would, perhaps, commit a carnal sin as well—they had not yet been blessed by the priest.

She wished this pious little man would go away. She did not want to hear more about his plan for rooting out human impulses. Besides, what would remain? A virtuous few. And for the sinful majority, including herself . . . what did the so virtuous Max Robespierre have in mind for them?

Marsan added quickly, "Well, Max, perhaps you're right, except for my good angel here. Look at her. No beauty patches, no powdered wigs or frills and furbelows. . . ." He touched a strand of her now dusty black hair. "All real, and all true." His hand moved over the back of her head, caressing her hair and lingering on the warm nape of her neck. "And you may be assured, Max, we intend to make our vows the minute we find a priest who will marry us."

Robespierre adjusted his spectacles and bestowed a careful smile on them. "I never doubted it, my dear Marsan." The smile carried a chill in its wake.

When, near midnight, the street outside seemed to grow quiet, the three of them started down to the river with the hope that they could make their way out of this cul-de-sac, but the quai was closed to traffic by soldiers of the *Gardes*.

"Curious," Charpentier said to them when they'd returned, "a couple of the Guards were drinking here a few minutes ago. They call themselves a national guard. Claim General Lafayette has organized them to defend Paris from the royal regiments. Sounds as if we're in the midst of a civil war, I'd say. . . ."

Since Robespierre was suffering from a nervous stomach, Charpentier sent the delegate up to sleep in his own bed above the taproom. Gilles and Veronique spent the remainder of the night in the big cushioned chair, which the café owner told them was customarily reserved for his huge son-in-law, the lawyer Georges-Jacques Danton, currently directing his loud and strongly voiced opinions to his home province of Arcis-sur-Aube.

Marsan had brought in a three-legged stool from the still-room, borrowed the café owner's weather coat and started to settle Veronique in the chair, but she held up her hand.

"I love you, Gilles, and I do want to be with you, even in that foolish chair. It is very large, surely, but I doubt we could commit one of Monsieur de Robespierre's major sins without considerable effort—"

He burst out laughing, and Veronique, rather amazed she'd said spontaneously such a shocking thing, laughed with him.

So they huddled together in Monsieur Danton's chair, deeply aware of the tenderness, the unity, and, yes, the current of passion undeniably between them. Gilles explored every lineament of her face and throat and breasts with gentle, loving and skillful fingers. He taught her nuances of love she'd never known before, and which would be carried to their natural fulfillment when the priest had blessed them.

Monday morning Marsan escorted Robespierre to his austere lodgings in the midst of the riot-torn area of St.-

Honoré and on his return tried once more to locate Père Lefroy. He failed in this but did discover what had happened to Arnauld de Gleeb.

"Veronique, he didn't survive—"

"Oh my God!" Suddenly she felt deathly ill.

"The authorities believe he died at the hands of some rioter . . . now, darling, you don't want all the grisly details. He cracked his skull. I'm sorry, I know how it shocks you, but I think you must agree *no one* deserved it more—"

"But, Gilles, *I* killed him—"

"My love, it was as though de Gleeb's death was foreordained. Men who can be hired to kill others have already chosen God's retribution on themselves."

It was a fine speech, Veronique thought, but for the rest of the morning, while Gilles tried to find even a cart to get her safely out of Paris through some barrier that might still be open, she kept remembering the look of de Gleeb's head as it lolled over on his neck.

Could anything be more terrible?

Yes. If it had been Gilles who died in the church that Sunday afternoon.

All the same, it was not possible completely to thrust aside her convictions about the sacredness of life, any life. . . .

In the afternoon Marsan finally resorted to offering one of his precious gold louis to a butcher with a horse and tumbril who agreed to carry them to the faubourg St.-Antoine. Veronique had left her portmanteau in the Palais-Royal Gardens at the time the riots began, but that no longer mattered. Nothing that she wore as the daughter of the Vicomte de Vaudraye would in any case be suitable to the artist's wife who would be living in the faubourg St.-Antoine.

"From my lodgings," Gilles told her, "it should be easier to find a priest who will marry us."

"And that," she said, "must surely put an end to papa's plotting." But she knew that the Vicomte did not object so much to her marriage as to the man she had chosen.

Marsan lifted Veronique into the back of the tumbril, got in himself and restored the rear-gate that was made of stakes. The sides of the tumbril were waist high, and Veronique leaned on the uneven stakes, watching the street scene as the cart rumbled over the cobblestones through streets that had clearly been the stage for violence and burning.

"Not the most comfortable ride, I'm afraid," Gilles apologized.

"But the company is of the best." She looked up at him. In the harsh, dry sunlight he appeared a trifle older. The lines around his mouth and eyes were more noticeable, heightening the tenderness and concern that she loved but revealing also the tight muscles, the strong passions that excited her and yet also made her worry for his safe future. . . . He covered her hand with his, seeming to have read something of her thoughts.

"Please don't think about what you see everywhere. Litter, breakage, a few broken bones but no one killed, they say—"

"De Gleeb was killed—"

"Darling, my friends and I believe we are beginning the struggle for a better world . . . it is already a better world without the likes of de Gleeb."

She looked out over the briefly quiet street. In the long view perhaps he was right. It had never occurred to her before now how self-serving the long view could be. And, at times, how necessary for immediate survival.

In the tangle of streets around the usual congestion at the Hôtel de Ville there was a fusillade of shots. Marsan shoved Veronique down and shouted to warn the butcher driving the tumbril. The butcher hunched his head in upon his neck just as a bullet whined by, barely missing him and Marsan. Veronique had crouched on the floor of the tumbril. When she raised her head, humiliated at her own cowardice, she saw three members of the *Gardes* marching by, singing a children's song, *Ça Ira*. They called out to passersby, "Look at us . . . a national guard for the people, not for the Versailles Whore! You should be wearing cockades . . . where are your cockades?"

Veronique had flushed at the insult to the Queen, but knowing such crude slogans were used for this very purpose she chose to note the second subject, remarking to Marsan, "Poor Camille . . . his green cockade didn't last twenty-four hours. But where did they get those blue, white and red rosettes they are wearing?"

The butcher turned and looked back at his passengers. "They took the blue and red colors of Paris and joined them to the white of the Bourbons. We've no quarrel with the King, you know. Old Louis means well. It's the others who are rotten, who must go. . . ."

Fortunately at that minute they turned in at the westerly end of the rue St.-Antoine, where the traffic was severe enough to occupy their attention. Veronique had driven through this quarter with the Abbé de St.-Hélier and knew fairly well what to expect. The filth of the gutters, the crust of ages on the close-packed buildings, and the indifference or downright animosity of the street crowds didn't surprise her. But when, with Gilles as her guide, she leaned out over the side of the cart and got her first glimpse of the street's length, she gasped at the overwhelming presence of the ancient Bastille. In the mornings, she thought, those massive towers must cast the entire quarter in shadow, and even now in late afternoon there was no escaping them. The prison was the east barrier of the rue St.-Antoine. All activity, shops, lodgings, carts, carriages and the pedestrians moving along this street were sealed off from the faubourg beyond the enormity of this medieval fortress.

Marsan pointed out his own lodgings in a four-story corner building with windows in a mansard roof a half-story above the top floor.

"The two windows under the roof are mine. The front window faces St.-Antoine. The window in the east side faces—"

"The Bastille."

"But that is two streets beyond," he said, trying to reassure her. "Anyway, I'm afraid the Bastille is a fact of life for everyone in the quarter. But the other window . . . you can sit there by the hour watching the fish peddlers across the street, the glass-sellers strolling by, the water carriers . . . very colorful." He looked at her, then added slowly, "Not quite like the palace at Versailles, of course."

"I suspect I shall survive the comparison, never having myself lived at the palace."

He smiled in acknowledgment. At the corner two streets from the Bastille, Marsan lifted Veronique out of the tumbril, paid off the butcher, then asked him what the situation was in the rest of Paris.

"My partner saw them burning the Gobelins' Toll-Gate, and mobs were gathering at the Denfert Barrier." He leaned toward them from his perch to say confidentially, "Only a matter of time before they bring down the others. At every barrier our National Guards are waiting. Tomorrow, though, the Royal Swiss will try to reconquer Paris, but we have plenty of ammunition for that . . . our men have cleaned out every armory except the Bastille. . . ." He shook his whip in the direction of the great towers to the east.

The horse and cart swung around the corner past Veronique, who was trying to imagine how the inhabitants of this building reached their floors above the corner shop, which sold cutlery, tableware and even farm implements such as shovels and scythes.

Marsan led her some steps down the side street, which felt damp, chilly, and was deep in shadow even on this July day. He pushed a door open into flickering lantern light. When Veronique's eyes grew accustomed to the darkness around the storm-lantern set into a niche in the wall, she saw a staircase . . . or, rather, an endless set of wooden steps with a rail banister ascending toward the sky far overhead. The rain of centuries had rotted the timbers, which seemed to be replaced only when they reached the last stages of disrepair. The stairwell still contained rain-soaked refuse, garbage and other sewage.

Aware that Gilles was watching her face and understanding why, she laughed at his evident concern for her reaction. "May I lead the way?" she asked. "Just to show you that I am well accustomed to old houses."

"And older staircases?" But he now laughed too and started up behind her. The rotten, creaking boards had worn away in the center, and it was necessary to take each step with great care. On the third and fourth floors the landing occupied even less space, and the attic floor had such a low roof over the door that Marsan had to stoop as he put his key into the lock.

Meanwhile the attic door on the opposite side of the landing opened and a heavy woman with wild red hair and eyes to match came out to inspect them. Her breath carried the fumes of sour wine.

"Well, well, our handsome lodger brings 'em up by twos. And aristos, as well, or I'm the Queen of France!" Veronique didn't understand, she was too busy warding off the woman's touch to concentrate on the mystery behind her comment. . . . The harridan was reaching after Veronique and had grabbed a handful of her muslin skirts, rubbing them between thumb and forefinger. Veronique resisted her first impulse to pull away from those dirty fingers.

"Fancy English muslin by the feel of it. And fancy all the way to that aristo skin, I make no doubt. Well, *chérie,* you won't have it long—muslin *or* skin."

Veronique was too confounded to think of a fitting reply— it shook her to be referred to so scornfully by one of those people whom she thought she knew and had always gotten along with so well. She was still upset when Marsan stepped back out onto the landing to find out what was going on and the woman went clattering down the stairs in her wooden sabots.

But what *did* the woman mean by speaking of Gilles's aristocratic females in the plural? Undoubtedly the woman was thinking of Yolande Berthelot. . . . Had she visited here often?

Gilles's lodgings proved to be bright and sunlit, thanks to the two windows, although the roof slanted sharply toward the front of the room. Veronique thought the place held a good deal of charm, its rooftop and chimneypot view being exceptional even if the furnishings of the room were rather meager.

Then Gilles was calling her name with great urgency. She rushed in front of him to see what had happened. The only armchair in the room, in the front-window recess, was occupied by a fragile, lovely lady of a certain age. Her gloved hands clasped the arms of the chair, as if faintly apprehensive, and she also looked quite decidedly pleased with herself.

It was the other "aristo"—the Vicomtesse de Vaudraye.

10

VERONIQUE was momentarily too astonished to speak, as Gilles said quietly, "Good God!" and crossed the room to bow over the hand of the Vicomtesse and bring the delicate gloved fingers near his lips.

Veronique finally reacted with considerably less calm.

"Mama! Are you intent on getting yourself murdered? Don't you know there are riots everywhere? How did you get through the barriers?" As if to punctuate her warning, there was a shriek in the street below, followed, however, by a burst of female laughter.

"She's tired, and no doubt a little confused," Gilles suggested. "I'd think a small glass of wine should make her feel more the thing."

"Brandy, perhaps," the Vicomtesse said faintly, adding to Veronique, who was fussing over her, removing her gloves and mantle. "What very good manners the young man has. I am more than ever glad that I disobeyed my dear Claude and came on here—not that he knows I have gone beyond the convent!"

Marsan returned with a small glass from the alcove, which served as a cupboard and catchall. Veronique started to take it from him to give to her mother, but the Vicomtesse looked up at him with her large blue eyes and remarked, "So kind, monsieur," and drank from the glass as he held it to her lips. Veronique raised here eyebrows at Gilles, who grinned back at her over her mother's elegant head.

Having been revived, the Vicomtesse charmingly thanked Marsan and settled back in the chair. Veronique was ready to explode but held in her impatient curiosity long enough to ask, "Mama, what on earth are you doing here? How did you find this place? I warn you, if papa follows you—"

"Really, my love, do you think I'm totally a fool? Claude is the last man who must know. We arrived at cousin Alexandre's some hours after you must have left. I lay down at once, the journey had been unbearably fatiguing. We used our own linens on the beds in those wretched inns, but, my love, you cannot conceive . . . in some places there actually were fleas. . . . I was never so shocked. At all events, I lay down but fortunately I did not sleep. And I heard Claude and Alex speaking of this young man. You are Monsieur Gilles Marsan, are you not?"

He agreed that he was. The Vicomtesse patted his hand.

"I could not permit them to . . . dispose of you. It was not at all the sort of thing one abets, especially when directed against the man your daughter has told you she would give her life to. . . ." Looking at their startled expressions, she smiled briefly and went on, ". . . oh, yes, I may be old but not yet so old as to be immune to the appeal of such matters. Your letter made clear your feelings, Veronique. Well, at some moments a mother must simply take charge, even one in as notoriously poor health as myself. . . . I confess I was nearly panicstricken until I thought of consulting that good Mother Superior at Ste. Veronique's here in Paris, and by great good fortune I learned from your maid that Mother Clotilde was there in Versailles and intended to return to Paris this morning. You may imagine my state through last evening, knowing as I did that Claude and Alex were momentarily expecting Lise de Gleeb's husband to report he had done away with you. Such a bad fellow, as he has proven to be. Not at all worthy of Lise—"

Veronique evaded Marsan's eyes. "So today you came in to Paris to the Convent with Mother Clotilde. Is that how you got through the barrier?"

"Well, of course, my dear, they would not hold up Mother Clotilde. They were most polite to her. And I gave them fifty livres to drink the health of their General Lafayette. That did us no disservice."

"Fifty livres! Enough for a regiment. Mother, you are a born intriguer!"

"I did rather well, I thought. And it happens Mother Clotilde's brother is a member of one of those clubs to which I believe you belong, monsieur . . . the Cordeliers? He knows you and escorted me over to your lodgings here. A peculiar red-haired female obligingly used her key to let me in. She accepted a gratuity of two livres, by the way."

Small wonder, Veronique thought, the woman had spoken of her as one of Gilles's aristos!

Marsan took her hand, this time without its glove. "Madame, you are incredible. You came here to warn us—"

"Against Lise's husband . . . poor Lise, I cannot conceive that she knows what de Gleeb is about. Alex says they live just outside Versailles, but I do not think I will look her up."

Veronique busied herself making her mother comfortable while Marsan told the Vicomtesse, "You need no longer fear de Gleeb, nor need you fear for your daughter, madame. We have not found Père Lefroy, who was to have married us, but there are other priests. I'll be going out to find Père de Brissac, whose church is beyond the Bastille. The riots will soon be over. The city is in the hands of General Lafayette and he will treat with the Queen's party. They must bring back Necker—"

The window behind the Vicomtesse rattled under the impact of a crashing, rending noise in the rue St.-Antoine far below. Veronique responded with a start, but her mother merely clutched the arms of the chair until the knuckles of her hands seemed to push through her transparent skin. Marsan rushed to the window, where Veronique joined him. She could see a great muddle in the center of the street where a tumbril full of farm implements and sharp steel weapons had crashed into the door of an elaborate coach whose panel carried a ducal coat of arms. Obviously an aristocrat running away from the troubles. Coachmen, postillions, and the furiously gesturing driver of the tumbril were all screaming abuse at each other. The driver wore a blouse that reached his knees, and pantaloons with wide red stripes. Some other men in the crowd also wore pantaloons, Veronique noted—the outlandish costume seemed to symbolize a new ferocity.

"*Sans-culottes*," Marsan said, pointing them out. "The ones with pantaloons . . . they wear them in the markets and along the quais. They're very tough." He took her by the shoulders and drew her back from the window. "Take care not to let them see you—"

The Vicomtesse got up. "Because we are—who we are, monsieur?"

Veronique looked from her mother to Marsan, surprised that her mother recognized their particular danger as aristocrats before she did.

Preferring not to answer further, and obviously to change the subject, Marsan said, "We haven't eaten since that watery chocolate we had at Charpentier's this morning, and I'm sure madame would welcome something of a dinner. I'll try the café in the next street and see what's available. . . ."

Veronique, thinking of the *san-culottes* and the violence in the street, started to object, then stopped herself as she realized that she would have to accept this fear and this life if she were to live in this quarter. And she was determined to do that. . . .

Before he left, and unashamedly in front of the Vicomtesse, Gilles bent down and kissed Veronique, who, despite some unease, felt herself responding with the newly aroused feelings from that both awkard and delicious night in the chair of Charpentier's son-in-law. She did feel a trifle embarrassed afterward, not having, after all, ever been part of such a display before her own mother, but contrary to her expectations the Vicomtesse seemed not only to understand but even to be smiling . . . though a bit ruefully.

"I'm happy to see your happiness, my poor child, and it is something you should know and be grateful for the rest of your life. You will hold it all the more precious once you've made your vows and taken up your intended life of service. . . . I only wish you'd not misled this fine young man about marriage, which, of course—"

"But I did not mislead him. We *are* to be married. He will always come first for me and I for him, I will still do my work, as I have been doing, and—"

It was maddening to see her mother shake her head and smile in her infuriatingly calm, if sad, fashion. "Believe me, my love, my life . . . *life* bears witness to the contrary. We can count on nothing in this life . . . I only wish someone had warned me of this when I chose to marry your father instead of taking up *my* proper life work. . . . I loved Claude then . . . I love him now. How can I not, he is so good to me. But, don't you see, except for the glory of your birth, my darling— and how little I've been permitted to have to do with you since

—my life has seemed quite empty, in fact, rather useless. . . ."

Veronique went to the window to watch for Gilles's return, and it occurred to her that as the Vicomtesse Hermione de Vaudraye her mother was perhaps right about her own life, that as the wife of Claude de Vaudraye she'd lived pretty much a useless life as a semi-invalid, apparently suffering from imaginary ills.

She said now, without turning from the window, "Mama, I can't agree with you that my life must be the same as yours. . . . I even wonder now if you came here so much to warn Gilles about de Gleeb as to stop my marriage—"

"I can understand your feelings, my child, but try to understand mine as well. I did, I assure you, come to warn and save if I could this young man you so obviously have given your heart to. It would be cruel beyond imagining for something to happen to him now and for you to spend the rest of your life in mourning for something much better remembered than missed. . . . But that does not mean—" and her voice took on a tone of severity that set her daughter's teeth on edge—"that you will marry him or anyone else. If my words cannot convince you, then you will have to examine your soul. . . ."

Veronique was relieved to see Marsan in the street below the window, elbowing his way through the crowds with a tray containing a covered pot, a pan and an object that looked like a bone under a soiled piece of cloth. She went out to meet him on the stairs and they kissed over the delicious-smelling assortment of food as she defiantly assured herself, "He is my life. I feel it, I know it. He always will be. . . ."

Because it had been such a hot day the food was mostly cold—a slab of goat cheese, some dried ham, a small pan of stew made from eels and a pot of savory mutton soup that was still hot. Gilles apologized for the scarcity of the food, which surprised Veronique and her mother, who considered it ample, though privately they wondered if they would be able to eat some of the less appetizing portions.

"It may have to do through tomorrow," he told them. "There are riots in the St.-Marceau quarter, and the threat of some here. The most impatient want to collect more ammunition, and I don't like the way they're eying that farm-implement shop below us. They could do much damage if they ever got hold of the pikes and spades and axes, not to mention the scythes. Perhaps I shouldn't be telling you all this, nothing may come of it, but I wanted you to be prepared and understand in case I must get you out of here suddenly. Still, if General Lafayette and the National Guard can settle matters throughout the city, well, we've nothing to worry about. . . ."

"Thank you, monsieur, for crediting courage to us," the Vicomtesse told him as she straightened her shoulders.

He nodded, then said, "I'm afraid there's no bread. There have been too many riots over the price and now there seems to be none at all in the quarter. And the water problem is getting severe . . ."

Veronique tried to put on a festive tone. "Well, we may miss the bread, but we shall all promise not to ask for a hip-bath tonight. Then we won't need the water."

By pulling out Marsan's sleeping pallet and adding a wobbly stool they were all able to eat at the tiny table and found that though immediate prospects might be grim, the idea of having no food tomorrow made the lukewarm eels and the tough ham surprisingly palatable. They all felt the need of wine, which gave them a certain calm to face the night, and the women were surprised at how little was left in the bottle. But the evening air was so hot it dried their mouths as fast as they moistened their lips. And by the time they began to think of sleep, they found themselves wondering more and more about the water they had so easily dismissed as good for nothing but hip-baths.

The Vicomtesse was made as comfortable as possible on the sleeping pallet which, she pointedly told Veronique, "is precisely how I should have slept in the convent had I chosen the Church long ago." When it was decided that Veronique would rest in the armchair she caught Gilles's eye, read the tender amusement there, and whispered, "But I preferred last night."

She curled up in the chair inside the window recess. When Gilles kissed her goodnight, he said softly, "Last night was only the first, not the last, my darling."

She watched him pile two coats on the floor, one to lie on, one for his head, and after she complained at his discomfort he joked, "When I slept in the Tuileries I had only one coat."

For a few minutes after they settled down, presumably for the night, he lay on the floor beside her chair and raised his hand to take hold of hers. They said nothing. No words were necessary. Even the commotion in the street below seemed to have ended for the night. After a while, as she was dozing off, his fingers slipped from hers. She awoke and whispered anxiously,

"What is it?"

"Arm fell asleep."

She peered down at him in the dark. "I'm sorry."

He chuckled and began to rub his numbed hand. She lay there enjoying his nearness and finally went off to sleep.

She was awakened sometime after midnight by a low-voiced conversation. She sat up in the chair, resenting the tight lacing of her gown, and stretched to relieve the stiffness. She realized then that the door was open onto the landing and someone carried a storm lantern whose rays flashed briefly across the room, then were dimmed. She got out of the chair, stumbled over her skirts and reached the doorway. Gilles was talking with two men in the uniform of the old *Gardes Françaises* but proudly displaying the tricolored cockade of General Lafayette's new National Guard.

Veronique momentarily was afraid they'd come to arrest Marsan. He guessed her fear and gave her a reassuring smile, encircling her shoulders with his arm as he presented the soldiers to her.

"I'm complimented, darling. These men are from General Lafayette, who's asking a man from each of the political clubs to reassure the rioters in the various quarters. Messieurs, may I present my betrothed, Mademoiselle de Vaudraye?"

Considerably relieved, Veronique received the soldiers' good wishes but reminded Marsan anxiously, "You will be dealing with the roughest of every sort, you said so yourself—"

"Well, then, I'll be a *sans-culotte* along with them, wearing the widest pantaloons of them all and have by far the most stripes."

Because he expected her to laugh, she did so, and saw the soldiers politely turn their backs and tramp on down the stairs while Marsan kissed her goodbye. She felt the tension in his embrace, overwhelmed by her own response to the hard, demanding feel of his mouth upon hers.

It was only afterward that she was again afraid as she stood on the landing and watched his tall, lithe figure in the long, well-fitted black coat recede into the darkness. The last she made out of him was his hand, pale in the half-light of the lantern, as it slapped his high-crowned beaver hat jauntily on his head. A gallant gesture meant to reassure her? . . .

After the nervous, uneasy hours of the last few days, Veronique determinedly tried to adopt Gilles's optimistic view. The city's troubles had been solved—well, it certainly seemed quiet in the street outside—and tomorrow morning, July Fourteenth, Paris should be back to normal.

11

SHE DREAMED of bake ovens—the warmth and order of
the Vaudraye kitchens, but she awoke with her mouth bone-
dry and her head aching under a frightful assault from bells
somewhere not far enough away. Her eyes opened with difficulty, she became aware of her mother standing at the side
window, looking ghostly in the gray light that filled the room.

"Mother of God! What's that noise? It sounds like the
end of the world—"

"People in the street are shouting—it's a call to arms. They
say the Queen's party has sent troops against the city, the
Swiss Guard and the Royal German troops. The people seem
to be demanding ammunition. They say that without it they
will be massacred—"

Veronique pulled herself awake, learned with surprise
that despite the gray skies it was already past ten in the
morning, and went over to join her mother at the east
window.

The Vicomtesse said softly, "I know the governor of the
Bastille, the Marquis de Launay. A very decent sort of man.
I hope he is safe. He danced with me once when I was your
age. . . ."

The sky above the high towers of the Bastille was the color
of clay, relieved from its deadly monotony only by the King's

white banner, in which even the gold fleur-de-lis did not catch the light.

The towers themselves, below the Bourbon banner, were alive with activity. A few soldiers could be seen staring down the long western length of the rue St.-Antoine as they set cannons into the embrasures of the towers. Veronique returned to the front window, threw it open and looked out. The acrid stench of burning wood weighted the already heavy air.

She leaned far out, saw several fires in the ancient houses along the street, the smoke curling out of windows and chimney pots. The ringing of the tocsins had brought hundreds of St.-Antoine's residents into the street armed with knives, old muskets, pitchforks and even shears. Still more of the district's residents crowded their windows, like Veronique, to observe any new excitement.

Gradually she became aware of laughter, fingers pointing. She discovered that in the middle of a threatening holocaust the neighbors hanging out of other windows in this and adjacent buildings were laughing at her, at her gown unlaced and her hair disheveled. With a pretense of indifference she pulled her head in and started to dress, the Vicomtesse unexpectedly taking the laces out of her fingers and doing the job herself—something Veronique had not experienced since she was a child.

Afterward both of them stood watching the fury that swept through the two streets beneath the windows. Veronique spent most of the time at the side window, which faced the Bastille in the east. Workingmen of the quarter in pantaloons, rough women with skirts and sleeves fastened up, as well as men from other sections looking for trouble were climbing all over the roofs of the houses built against a long flank of the fortress's high walls. Governor de Launay gave the order to bring up the drawbridges, trying to shut off the trouble, but even as Veronique watched, some of the more agile men on the rooftops below the wall leaped to the nearest drawbridge as it was raised and were lifted with it. They would fall to their death in the dry moat below—one fellow wriggled at the end of a dangling chain, then lost his grip and plummeted down while the mob, pouring along the street toward the fortress, uttered a single groan at the awful sight.

Most of the fires in the neighborhood had been put out, but it seemed looting had started in a block of houses toward the west. Remembering the possibility of weapons in the cutlery shop on the corner below them, Veronique prayed that the shop would have some protection, that the looters would never get inside. The Vicomtesse fanned herself with one of Marsan's sketches but insisted she was perfectly well and, indeed, had never felt better.

"If only I could be certain this business would be over and done. I'm afraid I'm not very comfortable with the violence of mobs. . . ."

And yet, Veronique thought, these same people were part of the future Gilles believed in . . . his dreams and those of the seemingly childish Camille Desmoulins were perhaps not so far apart, after all, for all the other differences between them. . . . A loud crackling sound was repeated in the air, like the felling of a tree with rotten branches. And in that instant Veronique understood the few Swiss and other Royal Troops inside the Bastille had fired on those pouring across the drawbridge.

Into the St.-Antoine quarter from every alley and side street they came. The old house rumbled faintly now as the thousands of feet crossed the cobblestones. Veronique looked out over her mother's head at an enormous tide sweeping toward the ancient fortress and its defenders.

Outside, the thunder of movement stopped and for a while there was a stillness almost as nerve-racking as the noise. Apparently they were consulting among themselves . . . then a roar went up—word had been passed through the mob that jammed the streets from the Bastille's towers and west on St.-Antoine as far as Veronique could see. It seemed half of Paris had rushed here to be a participant in this moment.

Veronique was at the window in time to see the white banner with gold lilies of the Bourbons moving slowly down the flagstaff of the tower. This, together with the crowd's yell, announced that Governor de Launay, the King's soldier, had surrendered to a deputation of citizens representing the rule of the Paris sections. Veronique wondered if Gilles could possibly be one of that deputation. . . .

A perspective surely broader than any Veronique could possibly have had from her window would have revealed that midsummer a French society torn asunder. Not just in Paris but in the towns throughout the country the people rioted and overthrew the existing governments. Wine cellars and bakeries were looted, châteaux and castles were invaded, old scores were reversed as Frenchmen went hunting for the throats of

Frenchmen. In Paris Veronique de Vaudraye was aware of wild excitement during the night of July 12th, with people rushing about everywhere in search of arms. But what neither she nor any other observer at the time could know was that on the morning of July 14th a crowd of Parisians and French guards had broken into the Hôtel des Invalides, a home for retired soldiers, and an arsenal, and seized thirty-two thousand muskets and guns. Fully armed now, the crowd converged on the Bastille, the old fortress prison, manned by eighty retired soldiers and thirty Swiss Guards. When they tried to take it by storm they were fired upon by its defenders, thereby creating martyrs for the cause of freedom. The French Guards and a newly formed city militia were then brought out to help conduct a more professional takeover of the prison, and so when he was promised honorable treatment, the commander of the Bastille, the Marquis de Launay, lowered his banner and surrendered. Later, he and several of his troops were then killed, and the prison population of seven prisoners—five criminals and two madmen—were released. The hundreds of political prisoners rumored to be there were not discovered. Its dungeons were empty. Three days later the King gave his approval to the event by coming to Paris wearing the revolutionary cockade. . . .

The Vicomtesse looked very uncomfortable, dry and over-heated, and she had difficulty speaking. Her eyes seemed huge in her colorless face.

Veronique had to moisten her own parched lips to describe the events. "I worry that we have seen King Log, who does nothing, give way to King Stork, who destroys all."

Clearly her mother did not understand *Aesop's Fables*, but she seemed surprisingly practical. . . . "I only hope those people will honor the terms of the surrender."

Veronique said, "I suspect they would if it were up to men like the Marquis de Lafayette and perhaps even the Duc d'Orléans. . . . It's my guess, though, that they haven't the faintest notion of what they've released." And neither, perhaps, has Gilles, she thought. . . .

A blast, a roar, and the entire house was suddenly shaken, rattling Gilles's few dishes and glasses. Veronique said, "That will be cannon, and quite near." She looked out through the smoky afternoon air. As she'd suspected, the cannon-fire came from the besiegers. Apparently they believed the Bastille's governor would not deal fairly with them. Or was this their

way of announcing their triumph? On foot and almost unarmed except for a few National Guardsmen, this crowd had
attacked the symbolic might of France and won. The great
medieval giant of the Bastille was conquered.

"I suppose they've reason to be proud," Veronique remarked, making her voice casual, to take her mother's mind
off the nerve-racking business around the old prison. "They're
bringing men out now. Good God! The Royal Swiss are
prisoners. But that is impossible! . . .

It was not impossible. This day had proved that nothing
was impossible. As the burning sunset light cut through the
thick, brown, smoke-filled air, more *sans-culottes* led others
of the mob out across the drawbridges with their prisoners,
the handful of Royal Swiss in their midst. A child of ten,
giggling as he hopped and skipped, led a gigantic Swiss Guard
by a halter. The Royal Swiss could not see—someone had
stuck a bucket over his head and bystanders tripped or beat
his shins with sticks, broom handles and long, sharp-ended
pikes.

Veronique heard a kind of choked cry come from across
the room, and turned quickly. The Vicomtesse was pointing
to the street below the side window. Veronique looked down.
Several of the mob were dragging a waxen figure of a Swiss
Guard over the cobblestones. But the "wax" left a bloody
trail, and the waxlike body was headless.

Seeing the gray look on her mother's face, Veronique made
an enormous effort to remain calm. . . . "It's only one of
Madame Turgot's wax figures," she lied. "Come and sit down,
Mama. You shouldn't be standing for hours like this—"

"So thirsty . . ." The older woman formed the words with
difficulty, but she did sit down on the edge of the chair in the
window recess.

By evening the air seemed thicker than ever, full of the
roiling smoke, the shrieks and cries of the mob that had now
experienced its first taste of blood. But Veronique was too
concerned about her mother to take more notice of the bloody
scene in the streets. She went to the shelf where Marsan had
set the wine bottle. Only the dregs were left. She poured
them into a wine glass and tried to get the Vicomtesse to
drink it, but the older woman pushed it gently aside.

"Makes me more thirsty, dear."

Veronique became increasingly concerned about her, and
at the same time became aware af her own thirst. When it
was dusk the Vicomtesse got up a trifle unsteadily and made

her way to the door. Veronique followed her anxiously, but the Vicomtesse tried to reassure her.

"I thought . . . one of the neighbors might . . . a glass of water—"

"Sit right down, Mama. I'll do it."

She got a clean empty wine carafe from the shelf and went out onto the landing. She did not like to start the red-haired neighbor on one of her tirades but after a moment's hesitation she knocked. Apparently the woman was out in the streets celebrating. Veronique went on down the stairs, knocked at two other doors, and received only the drunken rantings from behind one door, nothing at all from the other.

The side street was deep in shadow, jammed with running figures, some of whom swung torches, the flame trailing behind them, some dragging dirty stained bundles in Royal uniforms along the street. She avoided speculating on the once-human remains that could now appear so like dirty laundry. She tried to look as far down the street as possible, but it required all her strength to keep from being swept up in the melée. She did see a small public fountain between two wings of a lodging-house and moved along with the crowd until she reached the fountain. She bent over the rippled stone edge, started to lower the carafe under the spray from a naked stone Bacchante . . .

And found herself staring down at something under the running water—a human head severed just under the chin. It peered up at her with a dull, glassy gaze, as if asking a question to which no one had the answer. The mouth sagged open. It was full of blood, which the water of the fountain had only partially diluted.

With enormous care Veronique raised the carafe from the fountain, concentrating upon what seemed the all-important effort not to break the glass, then was pushed over against a stone wall by the running mob and dropped the carafe. The sound of splintering glass was drowned in the roar of pelting footsteps. She began to make her way back up the street toward St.-Antoine against the torrent, but stopped once and pressed her face against a cool stone wall. At least it prevented her from vomiting. . . .

One of the Royal Swiss Guards from the Bastille came running out of the side street, dragging his long rifle with bayonet attached. He crashed into Veronique, sent her spinning backward and kept on running toward the nearest of the Bastille's eight St.-Antoine gates. Apparently he hoped to return and find refuge in the now nearly deserted old fortress.

A dozen men ran past her on the trail of the soldier. Veronique tried to recover her wits but before she could examine her own bruises her attention was caught by the chase toward the great fortress. The soldier's pursuers had caught him. For one moment he struggled. He was very young, all arms and legs. Then one of his pursuers had the rifle in his hands. He raised it high. Its bayonet glistened and then was plunged down into the boy's wriggling body. Impaled on the blade, his body squirmed and flailed the stones beneath him. After a few seconds, he was still. All looked alike, many of them commonplace for this district in their workingman's long striped pantaloons. They were likely the same friendly citizens of St.-Antoine Veronique had seen drunk and singing the night before, now, immune to pity. Veronique stumbled away from the sight, then saw something gleam within inches of her nose. It was the tip of a bloodstained bayonet.

Her throat was too dry for a scream. She raised her hand, struck at the blade, felt a cool, painless razor-cut across her fingers . . . and suddenly, as if all at once, the bayonet glittered and went flying across the cobblestones and one of the *sans-culottes* stood over her. To her disordered senses the workingmen of the district in their odd striped pantaloons and smocks were literally everywhere, milling around her, pushing their way past her to wave knives and rifles and even long pikes. . . . Throughout the wild, screaming din the *sans-culotte* who'd knocked the bayonet aside reached down to seize her. She was still struggling when he lifted her, his hair loose about his face, blood oozing out of a cut over one eye. She found an awful similarity between this unlikely, bloody version of her betrothed and those others who'd murdered the young soldier. . . .

"Gilles, I'm not helpless," she said as he elbowed his way to the door at the foot of the five flights of stairs. Still not reconciled to his appearance, or that it could really be him, she struggled to be free of him, which made him hold tighter to her.

Finally he let her down. "I believe I told you not to go out under any circumstance without me," he told her, his voice tight with anger. "I am not your good angel, please remember, you are supposed to be mine. My coming here just now was perhaps due to some special pact you have with the divinity, but it can't be depended on forever." His anger was clear in his voice, and Veronique felt shaken by more than the buffeting she'd received as she started to move forward, every muscle aching, her head whirling. On the fourth-floor landing he caught her under the arms and boosted her up the last flight. It was in this condition that they appeared before the Vicomtesse, who stood at the door, staring disbelievingly at the bloodstained, ragged pair.

"My God, is it really you?" She moistened her dry lips. "Monsieur, is that blood . . . ?"

Gilles seemed about to embrace Veronique, but her stiffness warned him and he said briefly, "We did hope to stop them, we've been at every barrier, every armory . . . it was only here, at the Bastille, that General Lafayette's orders weren't obeyed. We tried to get to the leaders of the mob by dressing like them but—"

"But you were too late—"

He ignored the bitterness in her voice and said quickly, "They're burning the bakery, it's in this block on St.-Antoine. And the farm tool shop in this building may be next. . . . I'm taking you to the Ste. Veronique's Convent until the street is safe again. General Lafayette will give madame a safe conduct to Versailles. Now please *hurry*, darling . . ."

As she went to find the green spencer that would cover the upper half of her torn and soiled gown she looked back at him. Beneath the bloodstains and his hideous red knit stocking-cap, his endearment reminded her, must indeed be the man she loved. . . . His grin, after all, was the same and the look in his dark eyes. She even managed a smile and felt momentarily that their world might somehow be whole again, in spite of the nightmare enclosing them.

The Vicomtesse, finding new strength in the idea of returning to the convent, quickly found her mantle and was ready at the door when Gilles opened it.

He stopped, then took her hand in his and kissed her fingers. "You are a very brave lady, madame." He turned to Veronique, but at the last moment, without intending it, she turned her face slightly and his lips brushed her cheek. Almost immediately she put her hand up, touched the cut on his temple with her fingers. She thought he looked paler than usual in the faint, flickering light from the staircase.

They'd started down the first flight when the street door far below burst open with a clatter. Gilles quickly pushed the women back farther behind him as Veronique wondered nervously if some of the assassins from the street mob had burst in. Now they heard the raucous, drunken voice of Gilles's red-haired neighbor coming up the stairs.

"Ah, you up there, found a friend of yours prowling the streets looking for you, Marsan. Smells like an aristo but pays like a decent citizen. . . . There he'll be, m'sieur, top of the stairs like I promised you—" She pushed her patron aside and staggered out into the street again in search of other sources of revenue.

The man had not spoken, but apparently, Veronique thought, Gilles could see him. . . . He started down quickly. Veronique and her mother exchanged quick, anxious looks, then followed him.

It was not until the visitor reached the first landing above the street that Veronique saw that the stocky figure in the dark travel cloak and ruffled, clubbed hair was the Vicomte de Vaudraye, nearly crimson with the effort to contain his furious indignation.

"Damn you . . . it's not enough that you ruin my daughter, you now dare to hold hostage my invalid wife—"

"Monseigneur," Marsan began quietly, "Madame and your daughter are not hostages and, as you can see, they are not harmed. It was necessary for them to remain here during the riots but now I'm taking them to the convent for safety."

The Vicomtesse called to her husband. "He is quite right, Claude. Please don't be so angry, you are upsetting me—"

She'd scarcely finished by the time the Vicomte raced up the stairs, breathing hard. "You will please not speak until you are addressed, madame . . . as for you, daughter, it's a cell for you until you've learned to behave like a proper daughter . . . as for this Jacobin filth—"

The Vicomtesse, without speaking, obediently passed Gilles on the stairs to join her husband, but Gilles put his arm out to stop Veronique. "Mademoiselle is my betrothed, I want that to be understood—"

The Vicomte glared up at his daughter. "He's an assassin, this fine betrothed of yours. He murdered Arnauld de Gleeb. Look at him, with the blood of loyal soldiers on his hands—"

"No, father . . . I'm afraid I killed de Gleeb, although he'd surely have murdered *both* of us—"

"So he has taught you to lie now. Is there no dishonor he's not capable of? . . ." His hand went into the inside pocket of his cloak as Gilles said, in a tight, controlled voice, "I don't spend my life in the rags of a *sans-culotte*. But I have just represented General Lafayette in stopping riots, where

I'd hardly have been welcomed in breeches and a white cravat—"

"You will come with me, daughter, and *this* time there are to be no more private meetings with bloody Jacobins—"

"If Veronique chooses, she may, of course, go with you. Not otherwise, though . . ."

"You damn—"

The Vicomte's hand came out of his pocket, holding a heavy-barreled dueling pistol, now pointed at Marsan. "You won't find me quite as easy to kill as poor de Gleeb—"

"Papa, good God, *no* . . ."

They all heard the click as the pistol was cocked. The next second Marsan had slapped the barrel aside. The pistol went off with a roar, the ball hitting the far wall. The Vicomte, looking near-apoplectic, dropped the weapon. It fell behind him down the stairwell as he now threw himself at Marsan.

Before Veronique could get between them, Gilles had struck the shorter man a glancing blow across the jaw, and the Vicomte's thick-set body was hurled backward against the ancient balustrade.

The splintering wood shrieked as it fell away under his weight. Marsan rushed forward, reached for the other man as Veronique fell across the landing and groped for her father's hands. He'd already slipped away through the broken rail, and his body plunged heavily down the narrow stairwell. He did not scream, but made strange grunting sounds that felt to Veronique like blows to her own body.

By the time she and Marsan had gotten down the last two flights of stairs, the Vicomtesse had her husband lying with his head cushioned in her lap. The left side of his head seemed crushed, though there was little blood. The Vicomtesse's own head was bent over his as she murmured brokenly, "My poor Claude . . . I was never the good wife you deserved . . . my dearest . . ."

With icy control, as if everything about her had died, Veronique knelt before her parents and groped for her father's wrist, trying to find a pulse. Finally she tried the pulse in his neck. When Gilles tried to help her, she drew her father's unnaturally limp hand away from his touch.

Gilles's hand now gently touched the crown of Veronique's head. Instead of comfort, it brought a pain that burst inside her. In that moment of her loss she became her father's image, with all his fury, his illogical hatred and bitterness.

She saw nothing but a red mist when she looked up at

Marsan. "Will nothing content you but more blood?"

She did not see him flinch, begin to speak and then turn away.

The only sound was from her mother, rocking gently back and forth, bloodstains on the bosom of her mantle. "He's gone. I waited too long . . . too late to tell him. . . ." She began to weep, silently, looking somehow deep into a past that could never be changed, or known again.

Book Three

July, 1793—July, 1794

The Torrent

1

VERONIQUE HAD soon recovered from her hysterical accusation against Gilles. He would not forget it, she was certain. All during the terrible business of removing the Vicomte's body to the Convent of Ste. Veronique for safety on that night, Gilles spoke only to the confused, grief-stricken Vicomtesse—he did not, in fact, again address Veronique.

Yet on the day of the burial in the Vaudraye plot at the Meudon family château outside Versailles, Marie-Josette told Veronique that Gilles Marsan had appeared in the graveyard briefly and then disappeared.

Veronique, now planning her entry into the Convent of Ste. Veronique, told herself it was, finally, for the best. And in following her father's wishes she was, in some way, offering up her life to pay for her own responsibility in his death. Her course of life had been briefly halted to include a bittersweet taste of the passions common to other women, but now she must resume that course prescribed at her birth, the life she'd been educated and prepared for.

Through her novitiate at the Convent she found herself confessing to the sin of having read the many revolutionary newspapers sprouting up after the victory of the People over the Court. She tried to tell herself that curiosity over the new politics of the people prompted her interest, but it was her heart that reacted to any mention of the brilliant propagandist Gilles Marsan, whose cartoons and sketches were as devastating as Georges-Jacques Danton's oratory or Camille Desmoulins's witty articles.

By the time she'd taken her final vows, however, and put on the habit and coif of Sister Veronique du Calvaire, she felt she'd nearly conquered the memories of the love affair she'd delighted in, suffered and renounced in the bright and promising summer of 1789.

Inded, it was the darker promise of that summer that was fulfilled four years later, when terror became the watchword of the gradually ascending party of the Jacobins and their Left-Bank rivals, the Cordeliers.

Sister Veronique had developed a theory that hard work not only eased the affliction of painful thoughts but was far more practical than the efforts of the revolutionary committees to improve the nature of mankind, whose sanity, the longer she lived through these Paris years, first as a novice, then as a nursing nun of Ste. Veronique, she was forced to question. As each of those four years passed since she'd uttered her cruel—and unfair, she'd nearly instantly recognized—taunt to Gilles Marsan, it seemed mankind was determined to sink lower into the abyss—and all in the name of some ideal that likely could never be reached. . . .

On a morning in July of 1793, the hand of one of the hospital's benefactors awoke Sister Veronique, who'd fallen asleep on a stool against the seamed old walls. She'd intended to sit up on a kind of death-watch with one of the shriveled old men on the straw pallet beside her, and was annoyed with herself to find she'd failed the old man. It also secretly alarmed her. The strength of Sister Veronique, her ability to remain on her feet for twenty-four hours in the wards without sleep, was well known at the Paris Hôtel-Dieu. It was also counted upon. She shook her head angrily to conquer the remnants of sleep and looked down quickly at her three patients crowded onto one straw pallet, covered by one stained and dirty sheet. The sheet would have to be washed again today, and how many others? Where to find help for the tasks?

The old man lying in the middle of the pallet opened his rheumy eyes. "Good morning, sister. Is it long now until our breakfast?"

She smiled. "Not long, citizen."

His eyes roved sideways. "I think Old Jacques-Henri is dead."

She was aware that a visitor's hand on her shoulder had awakened her, but she was too busy testing Old Jacques-Henri's heartbeat to see more than the visitor's wheeled invalid chair and to recognize that the paralytic Georges Couthon, of the all-powerful Committee of Public Safety, had wheeled himself up the narrow aisle to visit her and the patients of this central Paris hospital.

"Sister, if Jacques-Henri is dead," said the second patient on the pallet, "can I have his breakfast share? . . ."

Sister Veronique heard the visitor Couthon's sharp intake of breath and suspected he was shocked by this base display of greed. She found it very human. Under the circumstances.

"But he is not dead, Etienne. You wouldn't wish to deprive your friend of his breakfast, surely?"

From the look on Etienne's face, he would be perfectly willing to do just that, but shame, or the healthy respect with which most of the patients regarded the tall, dark-eyed nun with the capable hands and sharp tongue made him reluctantly agree. "As you say, sister."

Couthon murmured behind her, "Do you not sometimes feel they're unworthy of all the help you and the others give them?"

Veronique momentarily ignored this. "When you have made your prayers, Etienne, you and the others may have breakfast. And you have not made confession for almost a week. One of us will hear your confession this morning."

"What have I to confess, sister, lying here?" he grumbled, rubbing his pockmarked cheek. "Can't have any fun flat on my back in this place. And there's no use in confession without a little fun first—"

"Very true," she murmured, and the austere paralytic Couthon was newly shocked to hear her laugh. "We must see that you have a little fun so you will at least make a proper confession. Suppose I find you some playing cards and you and the friend on your other side can play at piquet."

"He cheats, sister," put in the third man sharing the straw pallet.

Veronique said, "Excellent. Etienne cheats and you tell tales, Marcel. You will both make healthy confessions. Let me know when Old Jacques-Henri awakens."

She got up, finding herself stiff in every joint after sitting for hours on the small, low stool. Standing there in her modified habit of homespun and a heavy apron that covered all of the habit but her sleeves, she stretched and then pushed Couthon's rolling chair away from the pallet of the sick and dying.

"Good morning, citizen. You must have a glass of wine with me to start the day," she greeted him as they moved rapidly along the aisle between endless pallets made up of straw and any material abandoned in the prisons of the city by those victims of the hungry guillotine. Every pallet and every bed was filled to capacity, and as she passed with the well-dressed paralytic, many voices called a greeting to her out of those endless, hopeful faces turned upward to see her.

"They call you 'sister,'" Couthon said as they reached a cross-passage leading to a side door over the river. "Haven't you explained that we're abolishing religious titles? And their prerogatives?"

"If they called me 'mademoiselle,' they would end on the guillotine," she reminded him quickly, though she didn't go so far as to say that he himself often called her "sister." "And they are much too well mannered to call me by my Christian name—there! I didn't mean to say Christian. Of course I meant . . . my name sworn to before the font of Citizen Robespierre's Supreme Being."

This forced a reluctant smile even from him.

"Let's hope we don't find it necessary to go quite so far. And then, too, I often commit the sin myself. I take it that you have no priests at present to hear confession. Does this mean there are none who will take our oath to the Constitution?"

"You've hounded them to exile or death, haven't you?"

Couthon regarded his thin, slightly twisted hands, then his useless thighs and limbs in their black breeches and pure white stockings, finally the buckles of the shoes on his motionless feet. "Priests prey on the ignorance and gullibility of the people. They are charlatans. And now they are traitors. Only you and a handful of others cared enough about the Republic to take the oath."

"Please understand, citizen, I took the oath because it was the only way anyone could remain to care for these patients. And because I did so, I am despised by my fellow members of the order."

His features tightened. She wondered if he was really angry, and unconsciously raised her hand from the back of his rolling chair to her throat. He glanced up at her, saw the gesture, and smiled. "I did not hear you, Sister Veronique. So be assured. Your neck is quite safe. Now. About your requirements for the next months, I promise you nothing. The war is draining us. We are everywhere attacked. When Danton's friend General Dumouriez went over to the Austrians after his defeat in Holland, it seems to have been a signal for all our appalling bad luck."

At his deliberate linking of the ex-defense minister, Danton, with the traitorous general, she found herself more genuinely terrified than she'd been over the possible danger to her own neck. She knew that Couthon, who had acquiesced in the execution of many political enemies was also, ironically, a humanitarian. It was most unlikely he would condemn a useful nurse. But if Danton was endangered, all who followed him would fall under the shadow of the guillotine, including Gilles Marsan and Camille Desmoulins and his wife Lucille. . . .

He looked at her, seeming to study her reaction. "Citizeness, I suspect you still hold warm feelings toward that damnable propagandist Marsan. . . ."

"Why do you call him damnable? It's men like Marsan who form the minds of your followers for you. His sketches posted on the walls of the city have helped Danton to mobilize Paris." She added the sharp reminder, "And without Danton and Camille Desmoulins and others like them we might very well have died under the heel of the Austrian Army—"

"That was last year. Now Danton can't seem to deal well with Robespierre. Have you heard? Danton wants to leave the Committee of Public Safety. Max will take his place . . . Maximilien, that is to say."

It seemed to Veronique that this correction was expressed with anxious haste, yet Couthon and Robespierre were very close politically.

"At all events," she said, getting back to basic matters, "we need more beds, quarters separated by age and by sex and above all, we need chambers for the contagious diseases. Yesterday two orphaned children whose parents had been executed last Wednesday were placed in beds with elderly dying women."

Seeing that her point had been made, she moved his chair to catch any air circulating off the river on this hazy August morning and started to the makeshift kitchen to order the serving of breakfast—which would consist of watered wine and soup with floating crusts of bread intended to give it some body.

Couthon called after her, "This Marsan, Camille's friend, asks about you on occasion. You were once betrothed to him, were you not?"

She had stopped at the name but straightened a moment later and said, "That was long ago. I have not spoken with him since the night the Bastille was taken."

"Well, please give my greetings to your gracious mother."

She nodded, amused that all these unsparing Republican idealists adored the *ci-devant* Vicomtesse de Vaudraye, who now supervised the preparation of foods in the hospital and was known as Citizeness Vaudraye. Not only had she found her useful place in life, but the Citizeness Vaudraye still exuded the gracious manner of the old regime and managed to make the Republic's most radical rulers like it.

On the execution of the King the preceding January she had served black bread to the patients, and herself fasted that day. But she'd recovered her old fragile-appearing charm by nightfall and was able to play games with the increasing number of children orphaned by the starvation or execution of their parents in these dark days of the Republic's birth.

Citizeness Vaudraye was quietly issuing orders to the orphans she'd trained to serve food in the wards, and she now shooed them off, two girls and a boy, as Veronique came in. "You're late on your rounds, my love, and you look dreadful. Did you get any sleep at all?"

"Yes, yes, Mama. Don't fuss." Veronique kissed her mother's smooth brow and explained, "Couthon is here. I am trying to get him to recommend more separate quarters. We cannot go on risking disaster with the contagious cases thrust in all helter-skelter among the orphans and the senile and the rest. You'd best go and charm him."

Her mother fluffed up her wispy still-beautiful red-gold hair. She wore the most delicate of striped silk pinafores over an old, well-fitted muslin gown and still moved about on tiny satin shoes popular before the Revolution, but she managed to get about so well her appearance was generally considered the one charm of this hideous old building, which loomed up across the street from the now empty and looted Notre-Dame Cathedral, in a district full of thieves, cut-throats and the wretched of the city. Even these had not yet molested her, or the few nuns and priests who remained in Paris to assist in the enormous work of the hospitals and other places of charity. They were all known to have sworn allegiance to the Republic, an oath that the Pope, the Vatican, and all of the Christian world shuddered at.

Seeing that all went well under her mother's aegis, Veronique returned to the all-important matter of wheedling more help from Georges Couthon. As she made her way through the maze of wards, some with beds enclosed in wood, and through endless tangled corridors, she made a mental note to go to see Camille and Lucille Desmoulins and their little boy Horace tonight. They must be warned that Robespierre and his friends would take full advantage of Danton's departure from the Committee of Public Safety. It was both pleasure and pain to visit the Desmoulins. She knew now that her present life was ideal for her in *almost every* way . . . if only one were permitted to do the tasks of the nursing nuns and still have the love of one man . . . and a family? No. It seemed clear that she could not conduct her work here and still rear a family. But Gilles . . .

Was *he* ever going to marry? What of his relationship with Yolande Berthelot, whose brother seemed to have become very active in the noisy councils of the Paris Commune, which controlled the riots in the city. It was difficult to remember her bitterness that July night in 1789 when her father died. Difficult to believe she could have, in effect, accused Gilles of his death and those other appalling massacres, yet her mother had an explanation for it—she insisted that it had been fated, that something was needed to bring Veronique back toward the life for which she had been born.

Veronique also knew now she would never cease to love Gilles Marsan. It was a knowledge that had made her do secret penance for years, but it did not make her care less for her busy, endlessly challenging life as a Sister of Ste. Veronique. But she sometimes asked the Holy Mother, in the dark hours of the night, why it was not possible for a woman to have both a life of love and a life of devotion to duty.

She wondered what the hour was. Everything in Paris had been made more difficult since the abolition of the church services. Throughout the centuries the bells of various churches had always tolled the hours. Now it seemed they were rung only when rousing the people to some new ferocity. . . .

Couthon was not where she had left him, having wheeled himself back to oversee the feeding of the women in the maternity sector, including one of the mothers whose child had been born two days ago and named for the recently murdered propagandist, Jean-Paul Marat. The child, a male, was to be called "Liberté-Jean-Paul-Victoire Pontneuf." The last name, as his mother explained to the puzzled Sister Veronique, had been for the place of the child's conception since the father's identity was not known. Veronique let him remain there without interruption for a few minutes, hoping Couthon would be influenced by the pain and desolation that he saw.

She was aware of a special tension as she watched Couthon, and when she heard her name whispered she fancied briefly that she had imagined the sound. She turned and looked along the cross-passage in both directions to the open doors, but whoever had called to her was nowhere in sight. She saw the busy river traffic and, on the island itself, crowds of out-of-work artisans, laborers and prostitutes milling around, looking lost and faded in the morning light. They were made-to-order prospects, easily recruited as rioters at a minute's notice by the Commune.

She knew she must return to see if the man called "Old Jacques-Henri" had awakened, and whether he was in pain or not. In this heat he would probably feel better after he had been washed. But again she heard the sharp whisper: "Veronique!" and a vague memory began to emerge. Before the Revolution she had known that voice as it spoke her name, one of the few men besides Gilles who knew her well enough to address her so intimately. She forced herself to turn slowly. Across the passage was an armoire contributed by Camille and Lucille, in which clothing left by the executed prisoners was collected for use by ambulatory patients. A man, slightly cramped, might conceal himself in the right half of the armoire. And the right-hand door was ajar.

Veronique looked around again. One of her mother's female orphans-in-training crossed the passage with an empty tray. Veronique moved along the passage in her most stately fashion, trying to betray no signs of haste. She waited until the girl was gone. Children might be the angels her mother claimed they were, but they possessed two less than angelic qualities. Like other human beings, they could observe and they could talk.

She stopped by the armoire, glanced toward Georges Couthon, who was at the far end of the west ward propelling his chair toward the contagious area closed off in curtained recesses. Satisfied that he could not see the armoire, she said in a low but distinct voice, "Are you aware that a member of the Committee of Public Safety is in this building?"

She had not spoken his name, but in the political language of the Republic he was known as the *ci-devant* Abbé François de St.-Hélier, proscribed emigré and an enemy of France. Penalty if captured—death on the guillotine.

He stepped out of the armoire, his once carefully tended face now browned and weather-beaten. His graying light hair was long, straggling about his face, and he had disguised his height with a convincing stoop, aided by the smock and pantaloons of a river bargeman. But for that old, ironic gleam in his gray eyes, she might not have recognized him.

"In heaven's name, François! Are you asking to lose your head?"

"I am very fond of this head, I assure you, *Sister* Veronique, and I devoutly hope I will not lose it." He glanced around again, then added, "*Chérie,* we need you. But I must warn you, this may cost your own head. When you are free to hear the details—"

She did not hesitate, and no Christian charity softened her hard-whispered, "Never! You must be mad. And, in any case, Prosecutor Fouquier-Tinville has a warrant out for your death.

"Now you must get out of here quickly, before Couthon sees you. . . ."

2

THE ABBÉ'S pretense of light cutting humor vanished. She'd seen him serious only once before, long ago in that beautiful hollow eggshell of Versailles. He took her hand, though she tried briefly to free herself.

"You owe it to the habit you wear to help us. When you swore an oath to obey the Republic you committed a sin against God and His Vicar on earth. The Pope is excommunicating those who take the oath to this heathen government."

"And was it better of you to betray our country? You see, François, I know you have carried messages between the Austrian armies and traitors in Paris. At least I've not betrayed France or my patients here."

With his smile and raised eyebrows he reminded her, "You and my saintly sister have betrayed God, my dear."

"And by playing the spy, you have found Him? How you have changed, François! Once you cared very little for the Almighty but you still had your honor. You hadn't sold out your country in those days."

"You call this your country, ruled by the rag-tailed bourgeois scum? That foul-mouthed Jean-Paul Marat, who was stabbed the other day? And Robespierre, the little worm, and worst of all this Danton, trying to negotiate a peace, like any bellowing coward? A brave man by your lights would surely have fought to the last Frenchman!"

"Hush! Don't raise your voice."

Too late. Out of the corner of her eye she saw Georges Couthon wheeling himself past the patients and toward the passage where Veronique stood with the Abbé. One of the maternity cases, the young woman who had already given birth to Liberté-Jean-Paul-Victoire, was being given her baby to feed and the nun, a nursing sister of another order, held out the infant for Couthon to touch. He did so, placing his hand on the strange little globe of flesh, cartilage and still mobile bone, patting the infant.

"As if he blessed the child!" the Abbé remarked. "And he is the greatest anti-Christian of them all. Religion means nothing to him."

"True," Veronique said, but added, with an edge to her voice, "yet no other man in Paris cares about these sick and suffering people, or the lunatics. He at least doesn't believe they should be chained to the walls. He believes many are curable if the cause of their lunacy is found out."

He shook his head. "You sound like a Jacobin yourself. You're worse than Thérèse. She, at least, agonized over taking the oath. But you—I believe it gives you pleasure to swear allegiance to this bloodstained country, and I think I know why. You still love that Jacobin, Marsan. It appears I should have had him arrested years ago when I had the chance."

Seeing that Couthon was near the doorway, Veronique coughed and snatched a bundle of clothing from a drawer in the left side of the armoire.

"I might give you these, Citizen, but we need them more than your barge friends, who play the highwayman with us when they deliver our coal and our fish and vegetables. Citizen Couthon!" With her strong sense that daring was a better protection than furtive creeping about, she startled the Abbé by urging Couthon to join them.

The paralytic Couthon propelled himself toward them, but before he could get close enough—just in case he knew François de St.-Hélier from the old Versailles days of the States-General—she thrust most of the clothing back into the drawer, giving the Abbé a worn shirt of excellent quality. Obviously it had belonged to a man of high bourgeois or aristocratic state, executed within the last week.

"Very well, then. As a good *sans-culotte* and an active

member of the Paris Sections, I suppose you are entitled to
it. But your friends will have to do better with their fish
deliveries. The carp was rotten yesterday. We had to make
soup of the lot of it."

He did not make the mistake of bowing but shuffled out
toward the river, mumbling his thanks, while she went to
Couthon and began to push him toward the ward she and
Sister Thérèse were trying to reserve for the dying, but which
was also crowded with homeless children as well as adults
suffering with contagious diseases.

The Abbé worried about souls and honor and the divine
right of kings. But all important to Veronique right now was
caring for these hundreds of suffering patients. No medical
supplies, scarcity of food. Why burden herself with François's fantasies of saving the old order?

Sister Thérèse was in the ward and took Veronique's place,
recounting in her quiet fashion the various heads of the
hospital while Veronique returned to old Jacques-Henri and
his two friends. They had all finished their breakfast. In
spite of the day's heat they were not at all averse to eating
a bowl of fish soup thickened by the dry crusts saved from
the last bread the hospital had received two days previously.
There was another bread shortage to protest the Law of
Maximum, which proclaimed stable prices for all loaves.

The men were still drinking their wine and seemed to
enjoy it. Most of the wine was still of very fair quality.
Jacques-Henri looked up and at Veronique.

"Fooled 'em, sister. They all thought I'd slip my cable, but
all's right and tight." He had a bad heart and one of the
doctors employed by the government to inspect the patients
was certain he would go at any hour, but every mug of wine
Old Jacbques-Henri drank semed to give him new zest for
life.

Veronique felt that his survival was a good omen and was
much encouraged for the day. When he requested to know
what the world looked like outside the closed, sealed windows, she described everything from memory, making up
what she couldn't quite put in its correct place among the
endless sights on the busy Seine. Old Jacques-Henri went to
sleep shortly after with a satisfied grin on his face. As a dying
man he received extra rations of wine, and his neighbors
regarded him jealously while he slept. In spite of the greed
of his friends, however, they shared Veronique's feeling that
every hour and every day in which one more patient survived

gave the rest of them an added omen of good luck.

Two of the nursing nuns who had taken the Oath to the Constitution and replaced their habits and coifs with *sans-culotte* costumes so that they looked like the fishwives from Les Halles, came on duty now, and Veronique went to wash and eat, and eventually to sleep. She found her mother teaching two orphans their catechism and felt a needling anxiety for the Citizeness Vaudraye who seemed to do so many things that were an offense against the government, though as yet apparently no one had ever reported her. Veronique prayed that such luck would continue.

Shortly before noon Veronique set off for the Convent, which, though officially unsupervised, was used as a dormitory for the few nursing sisters who remained in Paris against the threat of excommunication by the Pope. Several orders were represented and the clothing worn was as varied as the charity bags made it. To walk the streets of Paris these days in a nun's habit and coif was to invite abuse and sometimes even attack. There had been massacres, in September of the previous year and only a timely warning by Lucille Desmoulins, proceeding from Camille's friend Danton, had saved the Sisters of Ste. Veronique.

Veronique had adapted her habit very little. Over her gown she always wore a clean and all-concealing apron. Her worn sandals served her well as she hurried through the streets, and her hair, now grown out since the de-Christianization of the churches, was concealed by a homespun towel, skewered with a bodkin at the nape of her neck.

As she stepped onto the Pont au Change, the bridge beyond the Palais de Justice, she was careful not to look to her left, nor to dwell upon the trials conducted there every day. Far worse was the great dark medieval Conciergerie with its three distinctive capped towers. This prison had become the last resting place before the guillotine and the quicklime pits, and in one of those towers, at the moment Veronique crossed the bridge, she knew that the Public Prosecutor, Fouquier-Tinville, would still be at work after a night of gathering human fuel for the National Razor.

"Sister Veronique!"

She heard her name called and sensed the alertness of the other pedestrians on the bridge. It was hard to tell whether they were hostile or merely curious. She felt a shiver of terror as a tall thin man in a tricolor sash and a tricolor cloth rosette on his huge black bicorne had stopped to stare at her through the traffic—he looked like Raymond Berthelot, reminding her of her old dislike for that man. . . .

Sister Thérèse joined her—the good sister could never remember to be discreet in addressing the nuns publicly by their titles. She did not even seem aware of the danger. She said calmly, "Monsieur Couthon has agreed to furnish more beds. He tells me he is too frightened of you to refuse."

Veronique laughed. "To have put fright into one of the Committe of Public Safety is something out of the ordinary. But you know when you call him *monsieur* you are committing a crime, so do be careful."

"Very true . . . was my brother able to speak to you?"

"He did. And almost under the nose of *Citizen* Couthon. I told him he was mad to take such a chance. I hope he's safely away by this time. That is too handsome a head to leave in Sanson's hands."

"For that matter, any head is too handsome. Well, sister, what do you say? Will you help us?"

"Help you in what way?"

They reached the Right Bank and started briskly along the quai toward the Marais Quarter. Veronique was not really thinking of her friend's question but of the placard posted on the wall of a bakery they passed. She knew the hand of the artist responsible for the absurd but frightening giant painted with his brawny arms full of coins and the new paper assignats while poor skeletal figures crawled at his feet groping for crumbs of bread. To make the propaganda doubly clear the following words were printed above the giant baker's head: "DEATH TO THOSE WHO PROFIT ON HUMAN WANT!" Needless to say, the bakery itself had been closed by order of the Committee of Security.

Was Gilles Marsan actually as bitter as his work proclaimed him to be? Lucille Desmoulins said, "No," and the Desmoulins remained Gilles's good friends. Whenever Veronique visited the neat, cozy Desmoulins lodgings in the Cordeliers Quarter on the Left Bank, she tried to change the subject whenever Gilles's name came up, but ever since the power of the Church and the various religious orders had been broken, it seemed to Veronique that the Desmoulins were trying to bring about a meeting between Gilles and Veronique. Thus far she'd managed to leave early or arrive late, or turn away from the door when they had company. It was not that she did not care to meet Gilles, but rather that she cared too much.

Sister Thérèse said gently, "You are not attentive. What can you be thinking of? Not the extra beds, surely. We must trust in God. He has never failed us, even if Monsieur Couthon has."

Veronique fingered the ancient pumice crucifix that Gilles had given her long ago in happier times, and wondered if her face was flushed at her thoughts of Gilles, but her companion went on in her imperturbable fashion. . . .

"Did François explain his mission to you? It will be far more dangerous than the night of the massacre last September when we saved the Sisters of Petit Picpus, but you were so wonderfully competent in that affair. We must have you now. It will be a service to God—"

"I don't understand. What service do you mean?"

"But what more divine task than to rescue Her Majesty the Queen from that horrid Temple Prison?"

Veronique stepped on the edge of a broken cobble and slightly turned her ankle. She winced but hobbled on, too thunderstruck to fel the prickling ache across her instep.

"He *is* mad. And so are you, for listening to him. No one in France is more closely guarded. If you are caught—"

"If we are caught," Sister Thérèse corrected her in that maddenly quiet way.

The enormity of the idea was too much. Veronique asked sharply. "Don't you understand? We would destroy everything. They would murder every nun, every priest remaining in the city, and all to no purpose. They are going to exchange the Royal Family for the French Commissioners captured by the Austrians."

"The anointed head of that family has already been executed."

There was no answer to this except to refuse any further consideration of the subject. But the one quality about Sister Thérèse that Veronique secretly found most irresistible was her supreme faith in the most incredible events, and her serene persistence until she wore down all opposition.

. . . Yet this is the greatest madness of all, Veronique told herself, and was glad to reach the privacy of the monastic little cell in which she slept alone. (She had the incomparable gift of being able to sleep the moment her body touched the rough sheet covering the straw pallet.)

She awoke much refreshed in the cool of afternoon, and having eaten some fruit and drunk a glass of goat's milk she returned to the hospital on the Ile de la Cité to relieve the nurses there for three hours. Once she was relieved herself she threw a brown stuff cloak around her shoulders and went to pay a long-promised visit to the Desmoulins.

The walk began unpleasantly when two children playing with refuse in the gutter spotted her and followed her a few steps, calling, "Witch! Evil sorceress! Devil of the Church!" She'd learned to ignore them and to resist turning suddenly to swing her cloak in their eyes and with clawed hands make a horrible face at them (although she was tempted). Her instructions in humility went against her grain, however, when she was struck between her shoulderblades by a hard core of cabbage. The little ruffians then scrambled madly back down the street; so she tried to tell herself that such annoyances were an excellent penance for her many sins.

Walking through the dark streets of the Latin Quarter, she found that even the everpresent prospect of murder among these sinister alleys could not keep her mind off the preposterous dream of François de St.-Hélier and his sister. For six months since the execution of the King on the grounds of treasonable correspondence with the enemy, his wife and their two children and the late King's sister Madame Elizabeth remained imprisoned in one of the medieval towers built by the Knights Templar.

If only one of the Royal Family could be gotten out of that terrible death-in-life, it must be the Queen; for no one in France was more bitterly hated than Marie Antoinette, and if she were brought to trial on grounds of treason, there was little doubt of a guilty verdict. But surely she had suffered enough for her ignorance and the crimes of her ancestors!

. . . How would I rescue her if I were one of those madmen? And how smuggle her out of France? If I were . . .

Startled by her own thoughts, Veronique groped her way from the street under the dark archway and into the secluded little Cour du Commerce, where the Desmoulins had lodgings one floor above their friends, the Dantons. She mounted the stairs, led as much by the delicious, savory smells of a browning roast of veal and onions as by her knowledge of the address. Lucille Desmoulins, though the wife of one of the Revolution's heroes, usually planned and cooked her own meals when she invited the Dantonists and other political leaders to dinner. Unlike country custom, the dinners themselves were served after dark, for the guests were liable to be detained by business of the war or political trials, or the eternal problem of trying to rule a country that had been badly ruled for generations.

The door was opened for her by the huge figure of Georges-Jacques Danton, who, having arrived early for once, was already chewing on a succulent bone with which his hostess had thoughtfully provided him. He put Veronique so much in mind of a huge but friendly mastiff that she felt rather like patting him on the head and saying, "Down, Georges! There's a good fellow!"

"Ah! It is our good little Citizeness Veronique. Come in. Come in."

He was one of the few men in her world who might conceivably address the tall, slim Veronique as "little." But it was more than his size that made her intensely aware of his masculinity, and recalled to her unforgetful body the passion and excitement of those days when she had been free to love Gilles Marsan. Angry at her own memories, she bit her lip and forced herself to concentrate on the scene around her.

Lucille laid a steaming platter on the table in the dining parlor and waved to Veronique before going to fetch other savory dishes. Although the day's heat had cooled off under an evening breeze, the heavily furnished dining parlor seethed with heat from the food on the table. But the only sufferer appeared to be Danton, who wiped his free hand over his pockmarked face and bellowed, "Off with that wrap, Citeness! *Merde!* You make me sweat like a pig to look at you."

She had been in the orator's company enough to become used to his livid language, and when Lucille once apologized for it Veronique explained that the language of many patients at the hospitals made even Danton sound like a cardinal by comparison. She let him take her cloak and went to meet the others in the room.

Camille became aware of her only now. He had been reading his latest editorial full of polemic, sarcasm and some wit to an extremely young lady with an ingenuous face and big, wondering eyes. She must be Danton's new bride—the orator, who'd gone mad during a brief, terrible time after his first wife died, was a born family man. She'd heard of the pretty Louise Gely, and was pleased that the girl seemed as sweet as she'd been reported.

It was also clear to Veronique that the young lady understood only one word in ten of Camille's diatribe against someone or other.

He arose, started to greet Veronique but dropped his papers and scrambled to recover them while Danton presented her to the very young lady.

"Louise, my darling, this is Citizeness Vaudraye. Veronique, this angelic child is my wife. From her expression I can see that Camille has been haranguing her in what appears to be ancient Greek."

Looking ill at ease when hugged to the big man's breast, young Louise Danton protested anxiously, "No. He was very . . . enlightening."

Danton laughed and squeezed her again. It was good to see him happy, but Veronique suspected it must be a strain on a young girl to be thrown into such company with little education and even less knowledge of the world.

Danton asked Camille, "What luckless bastard are you skewering on your pen tonight?"

Camille's face lighted up as he became the hero of his own romantic drama. "I'm calling for the trial of the W-Widow Capet. A M-Messalina of foul corruption . . . how does that sound?"

Louise Danton peered out in a gingerly way from under her husband's arm. "Please, who is the Widow Capet? And who is Messalina?"

Veronique said dryly, "He is talking about the Queen."

"The *ci-devant* queen," Danton reminded her.

"I thought she was to be exchanged." She hoped against hope that this was true. The horror of some of the things Camille wrote very nearly blotted out for her the real warmth of his heart and her own knowledge that Camille actually faitned at the sight of blood.

"Unfortunately, those full bladders in Vienna talk of refusing."

Veronique took a breath, knowing that she must not interfere in their politics, and said carefully, "Then it would seem that you will oblige the Austrians if you ask for the head of Marie Antoinette."

Camille was flustered and looked to Danton, his mentor, for advice, but the latter hooted, "Ho! She has you there. The Widow Capet's death would certainly please the enemy. She will be a martyr and they imagine they will then get her crown."

"Th-then, I shouldn't have those printed? Max th-thought I should."

"Camille, do as you like, not what Max says. Or what I

say. Print your stuff . . . it can't hurt the woman now. In the end, we'll all be food for worms."

At this inopportune moment Lucille Desmoulins returned with a great bowl of vegetables, set it between the veal with onions and what Veronique knew from experience would be delicious river carp covered by a thick sauce. No one seemed to think it odd that when the bourgeois leaders and the laborers came to power they should eat well, just as some of them had always eaten. But Veronique did wish that she might bring some of these foods back to the undernourished charity patients at the Hôtel-Dieu.

Being human, however, she enjoyed every mouthful of her own meal.

Later, she heard the men talking about the Queen once more, joined by late visitors of the Quarter, while Lucille and Louise Danton and Veronique cleared the table of its second full course and the two young wives talked about their children. Louise Danton was very proud of her husband's two infant boys, who had already accepted her as their mother. During this time Veronique could not for a moment force the Queen's danger from her mind. She tried to eavesdrop. They might give her some hope that she could use as a weapon against the mad dream of François and Sister Thérèse to rescue the Queen, but the more she heard, the worse Marie Antoinette's prospects appeared.

Two of the Dantonists, Fabre d'Eglantine, the playwright, and an ex-aristocrat named de Séchelles offered to walk back to the hospital with her. They waited for her while Lucille beckoned her and Louise Danton to a small adjoining bedchamber, and the three women stood over the cradle of young Horace Desmoulins, whispering their admiration of the child. He was a cherub with a sweet disposition and a contagious smile.

"He looks like Camille, but he will not need me as Camille does," Lucille said. "He is *very* independent—"

While Veronique put her finger into the tight-clutching hand of the child and found herself returning his happy laugh, Louise Danton asked suddenly, "Citizeness, if your husband needed you, and your child needed you, which choice would you make?"

Veronique and Lucille stared at her in surprise, but Lucille did not hesitate. "I pray I need never make such a choice. Though it must be Camille. In many ways he is younger and more helpless than our bold Horace here—"

She had certainly shocked Louise Danton, but Veronique suspected she was right, all the same. The small boy looked up at her boldly, grinning. He likely needed no one but could depend on his own strong instincts. As for his mother, she glanced through the open door into the next room where Camille was reading his inflammatory article to his friends. He always seemed like a child play-acting. . . .

". . . a M-Messalina. An old harridan. Send her to the National Razor—that p-purifier of patriots and . . ."

Danton had reached for his young wife and kissed her playfully on the nose. He was not listening to Camille, but the others were listening all too well.

"Camille does not mean it, you know," Lucille assured Veronique softly (she had never allowed herself to speculate on possible consequences of her husband's scribblings—as she thought of them). "He just loves to *say* startling things but he's gentle as a lamb."

Veronique released her finger from the child. She said, "I am expected at the Hôtel-Dieu. I must go."

The women embraced and said goodnight but Veronique was secretly wishing she had not come this evening. She could think of nothing but the wretched family imprisoned in the Temple.

Perhaps she was not the only one who had been shaken by Camille's theatrical performance. The men who were to escort her had just applauded Camille, but she noted that Danton did not join them. She heard his weary remark to his uncomprehending wife. . . . "Still the killing. Still the blood. Is there never to be an end until we are bled white?"

His friends avoided his comment, shocked at this heresy; yet no one dared to contradict him.

A depression had fallen over the company by the time Veronique and her escorts left the Desmoulins lodgings. Fabre, a nervous, highly volatile man, shook his head sadly.

"I don't like it. Next Danton will ask clemency for every traitor in the Conciergerie. And that's the surest way to the blade. The Incorruptible Max is already hinting that Danton isn't a purist."

"That's because he knows women. Or his wives, at all events. Such normal ways of life have always annoyed Robespierre."

They descended to the dark little court and started toward the street, where distant lanterns illuminated the area beyond the archway. The court itself was still in heavy shadow but as a tall male figure appeared in the archway silhouetted against the light of the street, Veronique felt herself swept by panic. It *was* Gilles Marsan, walking with his quick light stride, and obviously headed toward the Desmoulins lodgings.

Fabre called out, "Marsan! You are late. We've cleared the platters. Is the Convention still in session?"

"Much good it does them," Marsan answered, and the sound of his voice brought memories flooding back to Veronique. "Robespierre and St.-Just are haranguing at the Jacobin Club, and in the end they will make all the decisions."

The group was near enough to make out each other's features now, and Veronique saw Marsan stiffen slightly. The pale starlight caught the glitter of light in his eyes. It was hard to tell whether he was angry or merely startled. Perhaps both.

He said coolly, "Fabre, if you hurry along, you may catch Max and St.-Just at the Café Procope."

"But the sister? . . ." Séchelles put in.

Marsan continued in this clipped and uncharacteristically chilly fashion. "I will take the Citizeness Vaudraye."

Veronique, for her part, was too astonished, if pleased, to say anything. To herself, though, she wondered if even as a generous gratuity of fate Gilles's appearance was not too deliciously convenient to be altogether accidental. . . .

She was, of course, right. Although he had not intended this particular meeting, Marsan alone knew certainly that it was far from a total coincidence, despite how it may have appeared—however improbable—to Veronique. It had been his practice to come by the hospital in the afternoon or early evening in the hope that he might manage a glimpse of her. At no time, though, did he want her to know he was near, let alone speak to him—that would have been far too painful. He only wanted to see her and to know that she was safe. He feared if they were to meet that he might speak to her in anger; she had thrown their future away all because of a sequence of events that no one could have prevented. No one was responsible; no one was to blame. That spring and summer of 1789 was a part of history that had roared up into their lives and swept everyone and everything along in its path. The small tragedies of so many lives were only part of a larger design and not to understand this was to suffer needlessly—which did not mean that he was able to avoid the pain of her memory. She was as much a part of him today as she had been then. She appeared constantly in his dreams . . . at times in a nun's habit seemingly infused with forbidding purity and making her appear remote and inaccessible . . . at other times in tattered clothes, exhausted by her work with the sick and the destitute. Seemingly ignored by all others in his dream, he would rage both at those who would not help her, and at herself for needlessly denying them both what they had, in a fashion, so miraculously discovered in so short a time.

Their eventual meeting, however, was as unexpected as it was inevitable.

3

VERONIQUE'S TWO escorts exchanged what struck her as knowing glances, indicating they were aware of her former betrothal to their friend. Fabre ventured, "I did want to discuss the Second Act of my "Maltese Orange" with St.-Just, who has a pretty turn of phrase and can sense a good rhyme. . . ."

They begged pardon of Veronique, received her permission to leave her in what they referred to as the "good hands of our friend Gilles," and went off toward the tavern lights of the popular Café Procope.

"Please come along, Citizeness," Marsan ordered her, offering his hand. It was a lean, hard hand that revealed none of his emotions—if indeed, she thought, they still existed so far as she was concerned.

"You are very kind, Citizen."

It took all of Veronique's willpower to keep her own fingers from trembling in his, but once she found herself moving rapidly down the street toward the Seine with him, she was able to recover somewhat. She felt she'd won a small point when she became aware he was watching her keenly.

"You've changed," he said after several minutes of uncomfortable silence.

"I am older. I have seen more. But you are—" she had to

clear her throat to finish— "you are the same."

"They tell me you are a remarkable woman, Citizeness. But I knew that long ago."

"Thank you. As I said, you are very kind."

"I don't mean to be——"

She would try to sort *that* out later . . . when the effect of him on her nerves had been diminished . . . the sooner they reached the hospital the better. . . . She kept remembering a patient in the lunacy ward near the Hôtel-Dieu. While still a novice of the Magdalenes this girl was actually found in a brothel in the St.-Antoine Quarter. She knew nothing of her normal life in the convent. Her nature was so split between these two radically opposite characters that she might have been two separate people. . . .

. . . Am I a little like that? Veronique thought in her confusion, and concentrated on wearing the safe, confident mask of Sister Veronique du Calvaire. . . .

A burly fellow in a blouse and pantaloons had been loitering in the courtyard of an old mansion abandoned by its aristocratic owners. He lurched now out across Veronique and Marsan's path, but Marsan's hand went to a pocket of his coat where the silver butt of his pistol protruded. The *sans-culotte* shuffled on and crossed the street, but the sight of the pistol brought back unfortunate memories to Veronique.

Was it this pistol with which she'd taken the life of Arnauld de Gleeb long ago?

After a painful few seconds, and to get her mind off the past, she said, "You have risen in the world. I see your work everywhere." Immediately after she'd spoken she hoped he didn't think there was an edge to her words. He thanked her without reaction.

She began again. "Do you . . . are you . . . how is Mademoiselle Berthelot? I thought I saw her brother this morning."

For the first time she detected the beginnings of a human warmth, but he corrected her in that same cool voice. "Citizeness Berthelot, you mean. Take care or I may report you. Remember, you are in the company of a dangerous, *blood*thirsty Jacobin."

"I doubt that."

"To answer your question, Yolande is still in Paris. We often meet. She is a very consistent friend—not too common a quality among women, I have observed."

She disliked the sarcasm, but she also felt ashamed at his reminder. "Yolande was always lovely. I meant that I supposed she would be married by now."

He lifted her over a rivulet of slops running down the center of the street as they started toward the bridge connecting the Left Bank to the Ile de la Cité.

"Perhaps Yolande shares my distaste for marriage. I was once betrothed to a lady quite out of my station, an aristocrat, as a matter of fact, but nothing came of it, and it was perhaps for the best, all considered. I find I'm not a marrying man."

She had several cutting things to say in agreement, but knew she couldn't manage any of them without giving away her true feelings. She said nothing. After all, he was undoubtedly right. It was impossible, of course, that there could be anything more between them. Too late . . .

He left her at the Hôtel-Dieu opposite the gutted and forsaken giant that had been known for over five centuries as the Cathedral of Notre Dame. She thanked him. He made a slight gesture suggesting a bow and started to bring her fingers to his lips, then, with his smile that she thought revealed more of his feelings, he let her hand go.

"That was very nearly a treasonable offense, but the temptation was too much. Long ago I had greater powers of resistance. You will not credit it, but I once had a desirable girl in my lodgings for two nights and resisted temptation. Of course, her mother's presence provided an obstacle . . . Still . . . times have changed. Goodnight, Citizeness Vaudraye."

He turned and started across the island toward the Pont au Change and the Right Bank. She was about to go inside, stopped, called, "Gilles?"

He looked over his shoulder. By the lantern's light in the street she read the years and the hard, stern set of his features. "Yes, Citizeness?"

She recovered herself. "Goodnight, Citizen." Despite his coolness—was it as contrived as her own?—she wondered once again, as she stepped inside the hospital, if he hadn't ever tried . . . or at least wanted . . . to see her before tonight and why even mere chance would not have brought them together at least once in all those years. . . .

Sister Agathe met her at once and gave her a brief report on the conditions in the wards. "All quiet. I do believe Old Jacques-Henri is going to get through another night. I always feel that we are waging a battle with Satan, who wants to snatch away these poor souls. I suppose most of them are sinners, as you and I, but . . ."

Veronique quickly removed her cloak. "Was there enough dinner to go around?"

"Quite enough, thanks to your wonderful mother. What a woman and a blessing the Vicomtesse has proved to be! We should never have solved our food problems without madame and her young orphans."

"It is the one wonderful thing for which I daily thank the Revolution," Veronique agreed. "Mama was very nearly an invalid; yet now, look at her. If only her heart remains strong. She had palpitations in the old days."

They made their way between the small, boxlike cubicles in which the more contagious patients lay, two and sometimes three to a bed. Sister Agathe lowered her voice as, at the same time, she snuffed many of the lights.

"Sister, have you heard of Her Majesty's condition? Fed so poorly, they say, that her blood has thinned to a dangerous degree. And the unfortunate lady is losing her sight."

"Dear God!" Yet in spite of her shock, Veronique decided it was an extraordinary coincidence that everyone tonight seemed to be concentrating on the plight of the Queen. It did not make the idea of her rescue any less wild or impossible, but it certainly explained the frantic activity of a royalist like the Abbé de St.-Hélier.

"We have been excommunicated, you and I and Sister Thérèse," Sister Agathe remarked abruptly, and looked at her. "His Holiness believes we have sinned against God in taking the oath of allegiance to the present government. . . . Do you believe we are damned?"

"God is just and merciful, Sister Agathe, and Jesus believed in good works. *They* will never condemn you, no matter what the Holy See may do. Look around you. Could you desert these people?" And she added something that surprised herself. "That woman on the far side of the cubicle. She suffers as much with the lung sickness as that poor, unhappy daughter of the Habsburgs in the Temple." She continued, "I am sorry for them both."

Sister Agathe bowed her head and clasped her thin young hands. "You are quite right. One sometimes forgets. I will do penance tonight for my thoughtlessness and lack of charity."

Veronique longed to tell her to get some sleep so she

could better serve these people, that it would do the world more good than for her to scourge her shoulders raw in self-punishment. Besides, she had a greater guilt on her own conscience—the sin of carnal thought—and she knew that no amount of scourging or starvation would wash it away. Only constant physical labor served to modify it, or displace the hunger beneath it.

Having talked quietly to the patients who couldn't sleep because of pain or the flickering glow of the night lamps, Veronique went to her mother's province, the stillroom and the newly improvised kitchen. This latter was rather too near the stairs to the morgue below, where the dead charity patients were laid out prior to burial in the charnel pits, but the hospital was lucky to have the kitchen at all, in times like these.

Her mother had returned to serve night potions to those who required drugs, and seemed in excellent spirits. "None of my orphans spilled a drop. Mulled wine—well, mulled wine with water—has proved nearly as potent as laudanum for the sufferers, and is much nicer."

"Much nicer, indeed, Mama." Veronique kissed her still unlined cheek. "So we are out of laudanum again. Sister Agathe calls you a blessing."

The Vicomtesse blushed. "What nonsense you children talk!"

"All the same, you must not work so hard. When the day porter goes home in ten minutes you must let him take you to the convent. Don't wait for me."

"I have never felt better. Why, when I think how I used to suffer agonies from the migraine, I can only say work agrees with my health!"

"It does indeed." Veronique stacked up the wine mugs and put them into a bucket. From here they might be taken out to the quai and washed in the river during times when water was short. Seeing an empty wine bottle, she fingered it with tenderness, remembering one who had loved his bottle with dinner.

Softly she asked, "Do you ever think of papa?"

The Vicomtesse, who was removing her pretty pinafore, asked, "Who, dear? Oh, your father. Yes, indeed. Very often. Only a few days ago I was up in Les Halles bargaining for the most wretched leg of mutton and a man went past me wearing a waistcoat that was an absolute twin of the one Claude wore when we dined at the house of the

King's Lieutenant in Rouen some ten years ago. Such bad taste to wear a satin waistcoat to Les Halles! Of course, it was badly worn and abominably stained. . . ."

Veronique's memories of her father floated away under her amusement at her mother's resilient powers. Poor Papa, he had loved his beautiful Hermione so very much. Yet so had she loved him . . . in her special fashion. A remarkable woman, indeed.

The Vicomtesse agreed to leave when the old porter Taddeo came in to fetch her. He had a wooden leg, which he found useful in numerous ways, but he seemed to take special pleasure in stumping through the long, crowded wards at midnight, arousing many of the patients who had just gotten to sleep. Veronique offered him his customary payment for this chore—a mug of unwatered wine.

"You will protect my mother, won't you, Taddeo?"

He poured down the contents of the mug at one long gulp, wiped each of his moustaches and swore, "I will guard the Citizeness with my life, and better than my life. My leg." They laughed but he assured them as soberly as his state permitted, "One twist and my leg unscrews. And what a flail it makes!"

Veronique watched the two leave the hospital but did not go from the doorway until she was sure they had passed the unsavory hovels around the cathedral, where the very worst of the Paris criminals semed to gather.

It seemed to Veronique that some of the finest qualities in human nature were demonstrated during the hours after midnight. The smiles of those patients still awake were always gentler, their pain eased for the most part by drugs or alcohol, their fears not yet aroused by the worst hours to come, the time just before dawn. Though it frequently was in the night that it became necessary to assist at one of the crude operations performed by any surgeon the Sisters could obtain, Veronique found that those hours seemed devoted to God . . . often the results of the surgery supported that feeling because of their being virtually miraculous.

As everyone knew, surgery was a final resort, and it had taken some of the paralytic Couthon's best arguments to persuade the hospital's religious authorities that advances were being made in the art of cutting open the human body. Couthon was the most paradoxical man of Veronique's acquaintance. He could be taken straight from a meeting of the Committee of Public Safety or the Revolutionary Tribunal, during which the lives of five hundred suspects in the city prisons had been bartered away, to the city's hospitals, where he bent all his efforts to bettering the condition of one charity patient. . . .

In the silent hours, while Veronique was concentrating on her beads, young Father Neu, who'd also taken the oath to the new Republic, came to report a mystery. "There are some strange sounds in the dead room, Sister."

She looked up. It took several seconds for the idea to penetrate her deep, self-probing thoughts. "Why are they strange?"

"But there are no corpses in the room tonight . . . so no one is down there praying, none of the Sisters or the priests, not even a porter."

She wondered if this modern, eighteenth-century priest could fear ghostly visitations from the dead. It seemed absurd, but then Father Neu was young and from the country. She rose from her knees. The Crucifix swung in mid-air and she caught hold of it. "I should think it must be a beggar or some homeless soul off the quais looking for a place to sleep. I'll go and see. You follow with a lamp."

Privately she thought the young priest a poor reed if she got into trouble . . . she'd not blunder down into the morgue at this hour if the intruder looked dangerous, she could see most of the cellar room from the top steps. . . .

She opened the ramshackle door and made her way down a few steps while Father Neu, moving behind her, held a storm lantern high over her head. Hardly a night had passed without the sound of a mob attacking some citizens who seemed suspicious to them, the telltale signs for them of decadence and aristocratic tendencies being clean clothing and neatly clubbed hair. . . . But it seemed clear now that there were no mobs waiting in the death room to make a cadaver out of her. Perhaps, she thought sardonically, "because my clothing is never spotless and only the cloth I use for a coif keeps my hair neat."

At the far end of the bare and gloomy chamber with its disconcerting piles of sacks awaiting future corpses, Veronique made out a figure that looked most familiar—a bargeman, tall but stooped, in blouse and pantaloons with a dirty red rag around his uncombed and disheveled light hair. She suppressed a reaction at the persistence of the lunatic Abbé and said quickly, "Father Neu, you may return to your work. I know that old fellow. He's harmless."

She went slowly down past cabinets and tables where

corpses were occasionally dissected for purposes of educating Citizen Couthon's friends, the surgeons. She looked up the stairs, waited until the young priest had set the lantern down and disappeared, looking relieved. Finally she pounced upon the Abbé de St.-Hélier.

"François, what if that boy had been older, a sympathizer with the government? You'd be on your way to the Revolutionary Tribunal, and I needn't tell you where you would journey from there."

He kissed her hand elaborately as he might have at Versailles, ignoring her businesslike mood. "Come. Behind these shrouds on the table. Now, Veronique, there isn't much time, and we do need you." He placed his hands on her shoulders. "We must have a woman who will not fall into the vapors, who can think and act in a crisis. We are going to attempt to rescue the Queen. You are our best hope and we will not take your refusal."

"My friend, consider!" She admired what he was trying to do, but there were a hundred very real and practical reasons why he could fail and bring down Thérèse with him, as well as herself and God knew how many others. With help so hard to find for the hospitals, even the loss of two nursing sisters might close an entire ward of the Hôtel-Dieu.

"You are not a coward, Veronique. I know that. You would not be afraid of failing. What is there to hesitate about?"

"Because the Baron de Batz made two attempts, and they say there was an attempt by the Queen's lover, Comte Fersen."

"Her admirer, not her lover."

"Yes, yes"—she impatiently swept aside this delicate correction—"but all have failed. There have even been several escapes planned by members of the Commission that guards the Royal Family."

"What remains of the family. Do not argue. Hear me now. . . ." He sat down on the edge of the table, but she would not join him, feeling that if she did so it would be a tacit agreement to his plan, whatever *that* might be.

"Well, then," he went on, "her majesty has lost considerable weight . . . several months have passed since she was issued new sets of undergarments, fichus and shifts and petticoats."

Veronique nodded, fascinated in spite of herself by what she considered a remarkable non sequitur.

"There were even discussions in the Convention recently about that very subject. Now I propose to have some ragtag women arrive in their *sans-culotte* costumes to take her measure, while I play the mercer whose materials will create these garments. When we leave there will be one more of the *sans-culotte* women than entered. Of course, we will have passes for each woman—"

"But it sounds so ridiculously simple."

"Exactly the beauty of the plan. It is simple, but not ridiculous. It is based on the notion that one only sees what one looks for. Those guards are prepared for a queen that looks like a queen and a rescue that, if attempted, would look and sound large and noisy. If the Queen is dressed like one of the *sans-culotte* women that the guards are accustomed to seeing every day, she may well go undetected. The event will be quiet, routine. The closer something is to one, the less likely he is to look carefully at it. The best place for a queen to pass is precisely under their noses."

"And after?"

"That will be your problem."

"Of course. Perfectly simple. I don't know why I didn't guess it at once. I am just the person to smuggle out of Paris, and France, the most sought-after woman in the world. What could be easier?"

"That is precisely why you are so necessary. You customarily visit the Paris Quarters at all hours to console the dying, or to help the sick—"

"Yes, but I do not go alone. Are you going to bring the entire staff into this conspiracy?"

"Thérèse will be the other Sister, until you reach the Temple Quarter and pass the Municipal Guards on duty. You separate afterward and Thérèse, who will be wearing her *sans-culotte* clothing beneath her habit, will join me and a royalist agent, one of de Batz's men who didn't have an opportunity to work on the other escape plan—"

"That failed."

He ignored that. "The fellow masquerades quite successfully as a wretched market woman who wants to stare at the so-called Austrian Bitch. He will manage the Queen's second guard."

"And I wait on some dark corner trying to look inconspicuous."

"You visit a patient in the quarter, making certain you spend only ten minutes."

"What patient? And what ten minutes? I don't carry a clock or church bells with me."

"You will visit a woman who has rented a room in the rue Nueve du Temple within sight of the first door to the Temple Keep. The woman is one of our sympathizers. The de Batz man has arranged this with her. Now the minute we pass the Municipal Guards inside, reach the street, and then pass the National Guard on street patrol, one of the *sans-culotte* women with us will join you. She will be the Queen. It will require but thirty seconds for you to drop a homespun gown over her striped costume, and another shirt to conceal Her Majesty's hair by a cloth or towel such as you wear. Over that she will have the hood of her weather cloak. You will then begin to walk with her toward the Hôtel-Dieu, as Veronique and Thérèse."

"Thérèse is known in the hospital."

"You are only to appear to be returning to the Hôtel-Dieu to anyone watching. Your actual destination is the lodgings on St.-Honoré, quite near the Duplay House, where Robespierre lives. Our little private joke. Certainly no one will look for her there. You leave her with two of our friends, and she will be removed as soon as the excitement quiets."

"And the rest of the Royal Family?"

"None of them is in immediate danger, my informants tell me. I visited them twice as the mercer who took their measure for the garments. But every day that Desmoulins and Hébert and others publish their scandal sheets the Queen moves nearer to the Conciergerie. There is even talk of separating her from the new Dauphin, little Louis Seventeenth . . . which I'm afraid can only mean they intend to bring her to trial."

"But she will go with you and leave her children? Leave the late King's sister, who has been so loyal to her?"

He looked at her coolly. "*She* is our anointed Queen. She must come first. After, there is a plan forming to get the children out as well, or to bargain for them. The Queen *must* come with us. It is her only hope. Ours, too. By now she has been informed of the details."

She was sickened by the cruelty of separating the Queen from her children, whether this was done by the Abbé's men or by the Convention, but felt something of her own guilt at having remained so friendly with the Desmoulins. Perhaps the thought of it would make it easier for her to fall in with the Abbé's plan. . . .

"Do any of the Municipal Guards inside the Temple recognize you by sight?"

"Only as the mercer. I have the list of those on duty. Read their names. Do *you* know any of them?"

She did not.

"Who are the others involved?"

"Thérèse, of course, and two members of the National Guards. I have been cultivating a few choice souls for this purpose."

Veronique left him briefly as she went to examine the steps and the door above. No one seemed to be anywhere nearby, which was hardly a surprise, considering their meeting place and the hour, all of which the Abbé had doubtless taken into account. Still, the bit of action did help relieve the tension, if only momentarily.

When she returned she questioned him on every point. She did not believe the Queen could be disguised so quickly in the Temple and that her constant guards would not notice the change, even if she were masked from them by the presence of the pseudo-mercer and his associates.

"One of her guards is with us. The other in the room must be dealt with. . . ."

"But one extra woman departing with the others would be instantly detected."

"Not so. They depart at different times and by two gates. . . ."

Sister Agathe now appeared at the top of the steps to see what had detained Veronique. As they went back to the wards together Veronique was so nervous that even the innocent Sister remarked: "Dear Sister, you have been working far too long on this watch. You are so pale."

"Nonsense. It is this bad light."

And fear. And a premonition.

4

A FEW HOURS of sleep did not, unfortunately, raise Veronique's confidence in the Abbé's scheme, but it at least made her mind more active on the subject. The first thing she said on meeting Sister Thérèse was to suggest they rehearse the changing of a *sans-culotte* into a nun within sixty seconds.

"But I myself must change in reverse, and I can do it in thirty seconds."

Veronique pointed out, "You are not the Queen of France. I must do it for her. They say she is not well."

"She can move rapidly and she is an intelligent, quick-witted woman."

"Thank God for that." It was also a relief to know that the Queen's physical condition was not yet so grave as reported.

The two women made rapid changes, discovering that the Abbé's description of dropping the gown over the loud, gaudy *sans-culotte* costume was easier then stepping into the robe. The hair was rapidly covered and the cloth skewered at the nape of the neck with a bodkin.

"Where does the change take place?" Veronique asked, aware that she'd been told once and shouldn't forget it.

"Inside the dark porte-cochère on the rue Neuve du Temple. You will have only a few steps to go. It is below the lodgings of the woman you will visit on your 'errand of mercy.' She is Madame Leplon. She has done a few small favors for our cause. . . ."

The former Vicomtesse de Vaudraye came through the ruined cloister, humming a tune that sounded suspiciously like the revolutionary "*Ça Ira.*" Thérèse shook her head, smiling. "Any day I expect to hear her singing that frightful march the Marseille Guard brought to Paris." She shuddered. "I have never heard anything to equal it."

The thought of martial music prompted Veronique to consider the possibility of her mother's safety if matters went wrong that night. "Mama," she began, "the times are very uncertain, but you do well, don't you?"

"Yes, my love. As I once told you, I never really felt myself to be of any value . . . until—" she laughed—"I suppose, until this horrid revolution."

"Then if something . . . my work, took me away from you, what would you do?"

"Oh, dear! You aren't going to emigrate, are you? In spite of all the bad things one hears, I feel so happy here at the hospital. So useful. Of course, if anyone threatens my orphans, then I will have to make other arrangements."

"Other? Mama, dear"—she hugged the older woman—"you are a born survivor. Bless you."

"I and my orphans can do very well, thank you. I only hope, none of our acquaintances makes trouble for us. I've seen so many lately. Do you remember Edwige? Emigrated with a wretched Marquise, they say. Sly creature. However Lise de Gleeb is still about. Marie-Josette told me."

Marie-Josette. Veronique remembered the girl with pleasure. Heaven knew she had few enough friends left in Paris.

"What is Marie-Josette doing now? Where did you see her?"

"At the Café Egalité, on St.-Honoré. She and her husband own it. You may remember a very respectable young country lad called Jeannot? He is active in the Paris Commune. Those wild creatures who, I believe, go about making trouble in the gallery during the meetings of the Convention. Now he owns the Café Egalité. Marie-Josette waits on the patrons."

Veronique knew that her gift of 10,000 francs to Josette at the time she took her vows as Sister Veronique had made it possible for Josette and Jeannot to buy that café. But because of Jeannot's politics she thought it best to avoid their place, and a possible encounter with people openly hostile to former clergy and members of religious orders. And she could not always count on her friendship with the Desmoulins—or her former one with Gilles Marsan—to protect her. She'd heard the rumor more than once that in some quarters of the city former priests and nuns were sometimes murdered, for no other reason than that they represented an old private hate for certain people. . . .

When she heard her mother had apparently been to their café she was considerably upset. "Mother, I hope you won't go there again—you know I don't think it safe. You worry me when I learn that you go about the city like that."

"Now, now, I am just fine. Anyway, no place is truly safe unless it is where you do the work of the Lord and there your safety is not really important. . . ."

All the while her mother continued to talk cheerfully about her work and her children Veronique kept thinking that nightfall would arrive long before she was ready for it. . . .

In spite of the day's warmth she was chilled all day and found excuses for not going near the death room, where she would be certain to recall in all too vivid detail her harrowing meeting with the Abbé de St.-Hélier.

She was to leave with Sister Thérèse at dusk. The only time during the day when she'd felt at ease was during an operation performed by one of Couthon's ambitious young surgeons. It had appeared for a few minutes that the patient, a boy of sixteen, would die with the steel point of a bayonet broken off in his chest. Veronique, working to staunch the blood while her other hand was held in the tight grasp of the wounded boy, felt that all her unspoken prayers were answered when the boy survived the knife and showed signs of recovery.

But now it was dusk. She had changed aprons and found an extra towel that would hide the Queen's hair and give her face a different look. Sister Thérèse always persisted in wearing her coif and it was necessary now to persuade her to wear the towel instead.

"It is always possible someone opposed to the Church will see us and we certainly don't want Her Majesty arrested as a nun who's not taken the oath."

Satisfied that Veronique's reasons were sensible, Sister

Thérèse agreed, but she would not discuss what might happen to her if she could not get out after the Queen had gone.

"I count upon God," she said, and it was not a bit of use reminding her that the Almighty might appreciate some aid and common sense from Sister Thérèse as well.

The Vicomtesse arrived as the two Sisters were leaving. Veronique said sharply, "I thought you were off duty tonight. Mother, how could you come through the streets alone after all I've told you?"

"My love, one of my few compensations for not having taken vows to the Sisterhood is that I need not always obey my daughter. As a matter of fact, my orphans and I are going to have a little class in manners tonight."

Veronique groaned. "Please, Mother, *please* do not let anyone see you teaching them to curtsy, or something else that is forbidden. Why not go back to the Convent?"

"Yes, dear. Just leave it to me. I'll have the porter take me back to the Convent as soon as we are finished here. You run along to your poor sick people now and I'll see you in the morning."

Veronique said a silent "Amen" to that and embraced her mother, who laughed, protesting she was being squeezed to death.

As the two young women started out, the last radiant glow of the sun was gone from the western horizon. The river, flowing under the bridge as they crossed to the Right Bank, was murky and green. Night had not yet turned it to silver.

Sister Thérèse, clasping her hands together, said, "By tomorrow at this hour she will be safe, and with her the future of our monarchy—"

"Hush!" said Veronique. "There are too many people around."

"Very true. Forgive me." All the same, her excitement in their mission could be plainly read in the exaltation on her pale features. Veronique, on the contrary, was busy repeating in her thoughts the exact address of the lodginghouse on the rue St.-Honoré where she was to escort the Queen. At first it seemed to her that every citizen on that crowded street would have to recognize the Queen, but then she recalled that often old acquaintances meeting her hadn't recognized her because of the covering of her head and the austere look this headdress gave to her high-boned face. She prayed that it would be the same for the Queen.

The city was more than usually restless tonight. Little groups arguing on nearly every corner, waving their hands, no doubt discussing the Law of the Maximum, which had put a price on bread that no baker could exceed. . . . Most approved, though the merchants were bitter. There seemed to be more arguments over the "Maximum" than over the Austrian enemy at the borders of France.

They reached the Temple quarter in the twilight. Like the now destroyed Bastille, the castle towers and main keep of the great quadrangle built by the Knights Templar in the middle ages hovered over the entire section of the city. Until the five members of the Royal Family had been delivered inside the main keep the previous year, the area within the Temple boundaries was full of hovels that housed the poor and a good part of the criminal element of the city. All of this had been cleared away during the year.

From a distance Veronique could see four of the dark-capped towers. As the two women reached the first gates, and the door in front where a detail of the National Guard patrolled, they saw that the men were in a jolly mood from drinking. As the guardsmen passed them Veronique smiled and nodded to the nearest young recruit: "Good evening, Patriot."

"Good evening, Citizeness. Death to tyrants."

"Death to all tyrants," she repeated, "of whatever party."

The moment they had rounded the corner Thérèse quickly took off her robe and cowl-coif and clapped on a wig of greasy black ringlets to fit her loudly patriotic blue, white and red costume. She looked to be a rough-tongued market woman. Veronique wrapped the robe and towel in a bundle as she and Thérèse were joined by two more *sans-culotte* women, one of whom was actually the man the Abbé had mentioned. The third party was a mincing fellow with a mercer's shears and measuring cloth dangling from his waist, the Abbé de St.-Hélier.

"Do you have Thérèse's robe? The head covering?"

She nodded.

"Good. Across the street are the lodgings of Madame Leplon, above the porte-cochère. Wait until we've rounded the corner, but get there before the Guard starts up this street again."

She was in the shadow of the wall, which marked one

boundary of the enormous territory once claimed by the Knights Templar when they were all-powerful at the times of the later Crusades. A second after the motley rabble had vanished noisily around the corner, she started to cross the street.

She must now rely entirely on herself. She looked around. The Guard Patrol she and Thérèse had passed originally was not yet in sight. She hurried across the street and into the darkness under the big archway of the porte-cochère. There was a small courtyard beyond, all uncared for, with grass growing between the cobbles; but from the small patch of green she saw a light in the window above the nearest staircase. She started up.

As Veronique stepped across the tiny passage and started into the lighted room she did not recognize immediately the woman who stood behind the door.

"Please snuff the light. We can be seen here," Veronique said.

The woman called Madame Leplon came in behind her. The moment she spoke Veronique knew.

It was Madame Lise de Gleeb.

"Ah, a pity you have not changed, mademoiselle." Her voice was cold. "Still the daughter of the manor, I see. You walk into a strange room and give orders immediately. But I think they will be your last."

My God, of all people to be an ally . . . Veronique looked across the room at the woman with her sparse topknot of pale red hair, her large teeth and her busy little eyes. Veronique would have no compunctions. The head of a queen was literally at stake. She would do anything necessary to keep Lise from exposing the effort to save Her Majesty . . . except, thinking about it, she realized it was even more likely that Lise had already betrayed the plan. In which case it was a matter of life and death to deceive her effectively.

"Are you threatening me, Lise? You, who masquerades as *Madame* Leplon, an antirevolutionary title which will not sound at all well to the Public Prosecutor. I, on the other hand, am here on a mercy mission. I arrive here and find not a Citizeness Leplon but a royalist sympathizer named de Gleeb."

The woman moved toward her. Time was passing. She must be on the street again in ten minutes. Lise had been only momentarily shaken by Veronique's quick reversal of the accusation.

"I notified the Committee of Public Safety as soon as I was asked to join your plot. An agent of the Committee will be here any minute, he'll arrest you and stop whatever you and your friends are planning on the Temple grounds. . . . And how dare you wear robes of mercy when you and your lover murdered my husband—"

"Then *you* must know that while your husband was serving an aristocrat he attempted to murder a representative of the People's Government, one of Citizen Robespierre's friends, as a matter of fact. . . ." But even as she spoke, she was also aware, from the woman's own words, that Lise de Gleeb didn't know precisely what was to occur in the Temple tonight, and thank God for that! But it was also clear that she must get away before the agent for the Committee of Public Safety arrived.

"You conspired with a royalist agent, Lise. You admit it. You will now come with me to the leader of the Temple Section—"

"You—you don't dare. . . . I left my message with Citizen Danton's office."

She was moving away from the door, however. Perhaps the agent's tardiness was somehow due to Danton's resignation and the consequent turmoil in the Committee. . . . Veronique was now past her and had reached the door.

Madame de Gleeb now appeared quite rattled as she said aloud, though mostly to herself, "In the Tuileries office they said I was to remain here, that an agent would come to arrest my visitor, *you*, mademoiselle. . . ."

Without turning around Veronique asked casually, "And what did the so-called royalist plotter tell you originally? Don't you realize now it was a trick? . . ."

"A trick? I don't believe you—"

"To get you to behave as you have. Poor Lise . . . Fouquier-Tinville must have his quota of traitors every day —one way or another. Well, I'll be pleased to see this agent myself." She moved to the stairs, then started down, in a hurry, gambling that Lise de Gleeb was by now uncertain enough of her position to let her go.

Evidently she was. Veronique reached the bottom of the stairs and rushed across the courtyard. The porte-cochère, black and cavernous, loomed up ahead. She'd just stepped under this archway when she realized she was not alone here. She made out the figure of a man silhouetted against the streetlamp, juts as a hand caught her wrist in a vise.

5

SHE WAS PULLED into the light, blinked for a moment to clear her vision, and then, astonished, believed she had not. It was doubtless a momentary trick of her mind, her own wishful thinking having somehow created out of the excitement and unreality of her involvement in this scheme its own deceptively real fantasy. . . .

Gilles Marsan was a mirage of the moment, of her perfervid desire . . . except could an illusion also have a voice, on a street in Paris, at night? . . . "My God . . . I can't believe it's . . . you . . ." Not her imaginings, not illusion or delusion, no more than the grip on her wrist that only now was loosening as Gilles recognized her, and shared equally her astonishment at their meeting.

"Yes . . . me . . . and I'm afraid I'm not on a very pleasant mission."

"And I'm afraid I know of it . . ." Gilles was the agent from the Committe of Public Safety, feared now throughout Paris, more powerful than the National Convention that had created it. . . . She'd not realized he was so deeply involved . . . had not wanted to think about it. . . .

"And do you also know that I was told a Citizeness Leplon had arranged to meet a traitor in her lodgings tonight, to trap and hand over this traitor? . . ."

"You or your office may have been told that," Veronique answered quickly, "but they were lied to. Her name is not Leplon, it is de Gleeb, the widow of a Royalist assassin. . . . I believe you've heard of them."

He looked up at the room above the courtyard, whose light had been snuffed out, and imagined Lise de Gleeb nervously waiting for the arrival of the Committee's agent, wondering what would happen to her without the "traitor" in hand as promised. . . . "Well," he said, "I suppose we can at least be thankful for that. She'll hardly be in a position to betray anybody, having already misrepresented herself and her sympathies." He looked at Veronique, still disbelievingly, and shook his head. . . . "When she tells me about you I'll say your being here was coincidence, that you'd undoubtedly been called to the lodgings as a nun to attend a sick person . . . that the actual traitor must have been frightened off or hadn't arrived yet—"

"I've already told her the same thing," Veronique added quickly. "And how do you know this isn't so?"

"Please, darling, you seem to have gotten yourself into an incredibly dangerous situation. Don't make it worse by trying to deceive me as well. Now I must go up and see her and convince, or if need be threaten her. . . . But this time" —he ignored her growing impatience and put his hands on her shoulders—"you will not leave me. Promise me, promise me to stay here and not move until I come back and take you to the convent. . . ."

She remembered how once before he'd taken her to the Convent in the Marais, on the night her father had died, and with his death, seemingly, their plans for marriage and a life together . . . she wondered briefly if he too were remembering . . . and then brought her attention back to the urgency of her situation. Could she wait for him and jeopardize what chance there might still be to do her part in saving the Queen? Could she ask him to help her in something she was certain he so deeply disapproved—?

The decision was made for her. Before she could answer or Gilles could take a step the night exploded with the sound of musket fire, coming, it seemed, from the direction of the door leading to the main tower of the Temple. And followed immediately by the sound of running footsteps coming toward them. . . . Veronique suddenly broke away from him, and by the time he'd caught up with her in the middle of the street, he was also face-to-face with the Abbé, who'd come abruptly out of the shadows.

There was none of the suave courtier about him now. Dazed and breathing heavily, he took in the presence of Marsan, whom he quickly recognized, and said, "Please, monsieur . . . don't stop me, not now . . . I at least must lead them away from Thérèse and the others . . . they've recognized her—"

"But in God's name, what *happened*?" Veronique said.

Shaking his head as if to say no time for explanations, the Abbé could only answer, "Lamplighter . . . had to brain him . . . found us at the top wicket gate . . . near Royal Ladies' quarters . . . otherwise might have worked out . . I *must* go . . . please, Marsan? . . ."

The shouting was closer now. Gilles could see the lights from the on-coming torches. "Go ahead," he told the Abbé. "I'll divert the guards."

As the Abbé, after a brief nod, rushed off, Veronique tried to convince Gilles to leave too, at least to say nothing that would involve and endanger him. "You've done enough, Gilles, you must not—"

"I must, as a matter of fact. I owe that man my life. He might easily have turned me over to your cousins and the guard when he discovered me at their château in Versailles. He did not. . . . Besides, I told you, I have no intention of leaving you again, especially alone in the street to be assaulted, probably arrested. . . . There's no time for argument. Do exactly as I say. Take that covering off your head and kneel down over me. Be very solicitous. I've been badly hurt, knocked down by an escaping traitor . . . *quickly*, damn it."

Understanding his meaning and the urgency, Veronique pulled the cloth off her head and let her hair tumble about her shoulders. As she knelt down over Gilles, now stretched out on the cobbled street, more rifle and pistol shots were fired from the nearby entrance to the Temple compound, apparently municiple agents from inside the Temple area again signaling to the National Guard that had been patrolling the street. . . . And now four guards were in sight, running toward them.

"One of the traitors attacked him," Veronique quickly said to the officer of the Guard as he came up to bend over Gilles —he wore the black-plumed bicorne hat with the official tricolour ribbons across his chest . . . apparently the commander of the Royal Family's guards inside the Temple.

"What the devil? . . ." he said, seeing Marsan's face and apparently recognizing him. "Is it you, Citizen Marsan?" Gilles fumbled to get out his identification papers, then handed them to the officer who examined them briefly, carefully noting the great seal at the top of the paper. "You tried to stop them, I see . . . seems they were actually trying to free the Austrian . . . a lamplighter caught them by one of the wicket gates. What direction did they take?"

Marsan waved vaguely to the north—the Abbé had actually gone toward the east—"Those alleys, found five of them. Nearly knocked down my betrothed here as well."

The officer of the Guard glanced at Veronique, saluted, and waved the young National Guardsmen on to spread out through the alleys to the north of the area.

"Would you recognize them again, Citizen?"

"Possibly." Marsan got to his feet with Veronique's help. "An ugly, stooped fellow seemed to be the leader."

"Two were women, we're told. One was a nun—she was recognized."

Veronique's fingers clawed into her palms nervously but she was relieved for the moment by Marsan's warm hand over hers.

"You will oblige by coming along with us, Citizen Representative. Your identification could save us time."

"Very well." He looked at Veronique. "Can one of your men—" he caught himself—"you will need all your men. They are a vicious lot . . . let's go."

Veronique understood he'd been about to ask one of the soldiers to accompany her home, which would have led them to find out she was a nun. And their knowledge of Sister Thérèse's identity would make the presence of still another nun in this area highly suspect on a night when the slightest irregularity might provoke summary execution without even the Revolutionary Tribunal's charade of a trial.

Being pleased to play out their role of a betrothed couple, Gilles kissed her quickly on the lips, looked closely at her for an instant, then went off with the officer and the remaining soldiers. Veronique touched her lips. How long it had been since that had last happened?

She waited until the area was clear, then glanced at the lodgings across the street, to find Lise de Greeb at her open window, watching the excitement in the distance. She must have seen the talk between Marsan and the guards, but had

she been watching earlier, during the meeting with François de St.-Hélier?

No time to worry about that now . . . she needed to get
away from here as soon as possible. She walked rapidly in
an eastward direction from the Temple, then south toward
the Seine. Ahead of her, and directly in her path, she presently made out two men squatting on the cobbles sorting
out what appeared to be their loot from a robbery. Too late
to turn back—they'd seen her. She walked toward them,
catching a glimpse of silver coins, some coppers, and a few
of the paper assignats the government had begun to issue
against expropriated properties of nobles who'd fled the
country. The two thieves had found little use for the paper
money, whose face value went down daily. They'd cast it
aside and the night breeze was already scattering it.

She approached them, carefully avoiding their hoard. The
nearest one looked up.

"Good evening, Patriots," she said pleasantly.

"Good evening to you, *Sister*," said the one who'd looked
up. "Glad to see they've not forced all you good ladies out
of Paris. Let them butcher all the priests they've a mind to,
but they'd best not lay a hand on you ladies—"

She bowed her head to both men and went on. But his
seemingly friendly remark alarmed her. This quarter of the
city was famous for its anticlerical feelings, as was the St.-
Antoine close by, and she realized the danger of being recognized by someone less friendly. Without her severe towel-coif
she'd taken it for granted that she would go unrecognized.
Now she realized how unlikely that was. . . . She was, after
all, rather well known. . . .

As she approached the rue St.-Antoine she noticed an
angry throng haranguing against the Church, and soon discovered why the thieves had mentioned butcheries. Making
her way through the crowd, she could hear pieces of what
was a rabble-rousing speech from an unseen orator:

"They're guilty of living off the fat of the land for centuries . . . a quarter of Paris they used to own . . . no wonder
they tried to rescue the Austrian Whore tonight."

So they already knew of the business at the Temple Prison.

"Every priest we find . . . death! . . . Every one of them
that bled us white . . . death!"

It was clearly no place for a nun, even one who had taken
the Oath to the Republic and was abandoned by her Church.
It was the September Massacres of the previous year all

over again. She had a strong impulse to run but maintained her stride, which rapidly brought her away from that mob and into the Marais district, where the silence of the deserted streets was almost unearthly. Where was everyone? Had they all hurried to the riot in the St.-Antoine? Or were they here in the ancient Marais, watching behind those closed shutters and darkened houses?

One other thing seemed clear. Because Sister Thérèse had been recognized, the city already associated the attempted rescue of the Queen with the Church. It could be disastrous to the hospital work as well.

She crossed an alley in whose deep shadow a dozen men were apparently sleeping off a bout of drinking, each bundled in his sole extra possession—a worn cape, a stolen greatcoat . . . she could even see some of the silent figures covered by a woman's full skirts. They'd chosen what was virtually the back wall of the convent's Mother House. She moved on, turned the corner and came on the severe, classical front of the convent, silent as a grave, though the lamp above the portal was alight. The stillness was not unusual; yet there was an ominous, waiting quality everywhere.

It struck her then—could those sleeping men she'd seen in the alley be . . . dead? And were there women under those full skirts . . . *dead* women?

Mother! My God, I told her to be sure and go back to the Convent tonight! I told her . . .

She began to run. Since old Sister Sophie-Marguerite, the portress, had emigrated the previous year there'd been no one at the great weathered doors. Veronique recovered her calm long enough to open one door quietly. Before she could step inside a woman's voice whispered urgently to her. She swung around, looked back into the dark of the lonely street. She vaguely recognized the voice but could not place it.

"What do you want? Who is it?"

The light overhead glistened on golden hair as Yolande Berthelot stepped into its flickering glow. "Don't go in—" Her face was twisted by an anguish that easily conveyed itself to Veronique.

The door was ajar. There seemed nothing unusual occurring inside. Officially, the building was empty. No religious services had been permitted for many months, though the Sisters who remained found effective substitutes in their own crucifixes and the austerity of their sleeping cells. A taper always burned on a small mahogany tea table, placed as if by chance beneath a dim, dusty portrait of Ste. Veronique wiping the brow of Christ on the way to Calvary.

Veronique saw that another candle burned somewhere at the far end of the ruined cloister, but amid all the greenery that the Sisters had tried to keep alive in the deep, green quadrangle she could see nothing moving. Yet there was no mistaking the panic in Yolande Berthelot's voice and manner.

"My mother. Is *she* in there? Tell me, for God's sake—"

"I'm not sure, but—don't!"

Too late. Veronique was in the doorway, blinded briefly by the dark after the lamplight over the street entrance. She felt her way inside, past the end of the cloister, needing to find out if her mother was still in her cell . . . she'd decorated it as a charming miniature bedchamber.

She'd nearly reached the cells when she became aware of scuffling noises, like rats scuttling into their holes, at the far end of the cloister. The open sky above the greenery of the cloister was faintly visible, dotted with stars, cold and far away. Clearly the Vicomtesse was not in her sleeping cell and Veronique felt sure now that somehow the convent was a trap and Yolande's warning was well meant. . . . If there were men waiting in the darkness beyond the faint illumination of the cloister, they would expect her to leave as she had come, by the big double doors. Instead she moved past the other cells toward the little side door opening off an empty stillroom.

A faint but nauseating odor. Something sickly sweet. While she concentrated on getting to the stillroom door unnoticed, she found herself trying to identify that odor. She reached for the latch of the door and then, with a scream, dropped the latch as a length of her hair was seized and twisted around the knuckles of a huge male fist.

Lights appeared everywhere from storm lanterns that had been muffled. Hell must have been filled with faces like these, the mouths slavering for her blood, the eyes bulging in the light of suddenly flaring torches.

She'd escaped the prison massacres a year ago, only to walk into this horrible trap. In a brief haze of confusion and terror she let herself be pushed along from hand to hand. A stout bare leg in a wooden sabot tripped her but she clawed at the smock of another nightmare creature and held herself erect.

No one else molested her. She heard a familiar voice call out curtly, "None of that. We are here to judge and punish, not to torture. The Republic has abolished torture."

It was Raymond Berthelot, now apparently a member in good standing of the bloodthirsty Paris Commune. How neatly he measured the difference between trial and torture! She fought to keep her dignity in front of them, those terrifying figures lining the four sides of the cloister, as she was brought politely to the long dry fountain in the center of the dead and dying shrubbery.

She stepped on a slippery substance and looked down. The marble base of the fountain was spattered with blood that had collected in the worn cup of stones around the fountain. Her knees weakened and she tried to reach out for support. She heard giggles . . . female sounds. She was held firmly by two men. The ragged cuffs of their pantaloons were sodden with blood.

Had her mother's blood flowed over those stones?

"Mother!" She heard her voice speak the word, bringing laughter from these seemingly demonic faces, whose eyes reflected the lantern light like a hundred little fires of hell.

". . . she calls on the good Mother Mary to save her—"

The sound of that voice was a whiplash. All her in-bred pride came to her. Her face set into a calm mask, her body straightened to full height. Her brain no longer seemed paralyzed by the horror of approaching death. She at least could die in Christ.

Father, forgive me, she prayed silently. I have sinned . . . in the hour of Thy Judgment, forgive me. In Christ's name . . .

"Enough!" Berthelot said to the taunting voices around him. "We are not here to mock this wretched person but to judge her for her sins committed against the people—"

Her eyes came open. "I do not ask your mercy, but I remind you I have been a friend to the people. Ask the people of Vaudraye. Ask those at the hospitals in Paris. I tried to feed the hungry when you fed them only speeches—"

"She has you there," someone called out as others snickered.

Berthelot bit his lip, managed to resume sternly. "The crimes of the Vaudraye family are well known. General Alexandre de Vaudraye is a proscribed enemy of the Republic. His wife, the heretofore Comtesse du Plessis de Vaudraye, is likewise a proscribed enemy. They give aid to the Austrian Emperor against the Republic. And, Veronique de Vaudraye, you are a representative of the Church, the greatest enemy of all."

"I took the oath to the Republic," she reminded him, knowing she would not gain by her defense but determined not to die like the luckless sheep who went before her under Dr. Guillotin's blade.

"She swore the oath," someone ventured . . . "she is excommunicated by the Church . . . maybe this one is a Patriot—"

"The last one took the oath as well," snapped Raymond, "yet she tried to rescue the Austrian *putain* tonight. What greater crime can there be against the Republic?"

So Sister Thérèse was dead . . . after the debacle at the Temple Prison she must have gone back to the convent, hoping to find safety . . . oh, God . . .

Berthelot shifted his foot and momentarily flinched, not wishing to step in the blood. Gaunt-faced, his lean body clad as always in an unadorned black coat, Raymond was revolted by blood. Annoyed he'd betrayed this quirk, he now reached for Veronique's neck. She stood stiff and resistant, expecting his bony hands to close about her throat. Instead, he jerked away the rosary and Gilles's crucifix and waved them over his head.

"See what she wears. Is this idolatry the act of a true Republican? Guilty or innocent, Patriots?"

It was only for a moment, but as the air was flailed with knives and a sword and the sharp point of a broken pike, Veronique thought she detected among the faces one that seemed to look on with revulsion, a strong peasant face. She could not place it. . . .

"Guilty!"

She was immediately struck down by a heavy blow from the fist of the peasant she thought she'd recognized. Thick cloth of a man's coat smothered her. At the same time a man's body fell across hers and the fellow was shouting, "Let me do it, let me—" But though his knife sliced through the cloth of the coat and cut across the flesh of her shoulder, she felt only the weight of his body on hers and under the wild scuffle and shouts overhead she thought the man whispered, *"Courage, mademoiselle . . ."*

It was Jeannot, Marie-Josette's husband.

Knocked breathless when he deliberately fell on her, she gradually comprehended what was happening. Other knives struck at her, only partially deflected by the coat Jeannot had dropped over her before he fell on her in the frenzy of his pretended attack. A pike's point now stabbed into the flesh of her lower thigh, and she tried to draw her trembling legs under the protection of Jeannot's body.

"One more thrust, and that's *done* it. . . ." he called out, wiping his knife on the dark material of the coat. "Let me dump her in with the rest of tonight's garbage."

Some of them protested but Berthelot called, in dry disgust, "He struck the death blow. It is his privilege. He may throw her into the cart."

With her head still wrapped in his coat, Veronique felt herself lifted high, her hair and bleeding arms and legs dangling. A sudden quiet followed as she was thrown partly onto wet straw that stank of blood, partly onto the cold flesh of other bodies that had preceded hers. And again she was knocked breathless, this time by the weight of a human corpse upon her body. The cart started forward. Jeannot called out, "I'll see these aristos driven to hell. They'll need no passports with me to guide 'em."

Veronique held her breath and prayed in the dark confines of the coat Jeannot had thrown over her. "No!" Berthelot said. "You have done enough. Get to your lodgings, all of you. The National Guard will be here at any moment. You on the tumbril, be off. If the Committee catches you with that meat in your cart they'll be serving your heads to Madame Guillotine—"

The cart moved with a jolt. A lifeless arm fell across the cloth covering Veronique's face. She lay there among the dead, trying to convince herself that she still lived, feeling nothing in her numbed legs and arms. It was too soon for pain. She shifted her head. Jeannot's coat slipped off and she saw a pale yellow glow in the eastern sky. The sun? It was only the moon. All the horrors of this night had occurred before moonrise. She prayed disjointedly. "Do not let mama be here . . . please let Gilles understand how much I love him . . ."

The two drivers on the board seat of the tumbril were arguing about the route. "Cemetery of the Innocents, it's got to be. Since they removed all the bones, there's pits everywhere."

"Then we're near enough. Turn across that alley. Make it fast. I can feel that damn razor on my neck—"

"I see the vaults ahead, we've made it all right . . . that's the cemetery. There's a pit at this end. They'll all fit into it, right and tight."

Veronique raised her head. Feeling began to creep into her fingertips.

"Have you got it?" one of the drivers was asking, only to be answered by, "Listen! You hear something? Riots in Les Halles, you think?"

"Who knows? . . . Anway, there's no time to lose here . . . well, have you got the quicklime—"

To Veronique's battered senses the word was meaningless. She numbly repeated it to herself . . . quicklime . . .

"Got it, wouldn't forget that—"

"Damn you, hurry! There's still too much noise off toward Les Halles—"

Quicklime.

Veronique felt for the rough side of the tumbril. Her numbed fingers slipped off. She made noises in her throat but could not get them out.

One of the men leaped to the ground. The other shouted at him, waving a knife in the moonlight.

"Look . . . headed this way . . .four of 'em, I think . . . no friends of ours!"

"No time! Get it ready. Destroy the whole damn cartful just as it stands—"

Veronique raised both arms. Someone was screaming terror into the night. The sound was deafening. But only to her.

6

IF, ON THAT July night, she had believed herself to be in a hell presided over by the demons of Paris, she now found herself in a state very close to heaven.

It semed a miracle, this new life—this *life*—that began wondrously new each day, day after day, through the late summer of 1793 as she recovered from her injuries.

Miraculous, too, was the seemingly inexplicable appearance, as she now remembered it, of Gilles's face in the moonlight that awful night, as he and Jeannot and two National Guardsmen rushed across the abandoned graveyard at the men beside the tumbril. . . . That had been her last conscious moment for days, and so it was nearly a week later before she was aware enough to ask . and understand how that miracle had come to pass . . . how, after leaving her alone in the street rather than risk exposing her true identity as a nun, Gilles had gone off with the guard to make his report, then as soon as possible had sent word to Jeannot at his café to go immediately to the convent and make certain that Veronique had arrived safely and to report back to Gilles as soon as he had . . . how Jeannot had gotten there to find Raymond and his fanatical mob, been forced to join them or risk his own death, and how once dismissed by Raymond had found Gilles and with two guardsmen managed to get to the Cemetery of the Innocents only moments before it would have been too late, as had happened at the convent. . . . Life and death in most delicate balance for Veronique de Vaudraye, all in the space of hours on that terrible moonlit July night. . . .

And yet even with explanation, it seemed to Veronique no less miraculous to wake up throughout the day or night and find Gilles nearby, either watching her or holding her hand tightly, or asleep in a chair near her bed.

When she'd first awakened she'd whispered his name and then asked about her mother. Consciousness faded, but when she opened her eyes again, the Vicomtesse was sitting beside her bed, playing piquet with Gilles and seeming very pleased with herself over having just won a bundle of paper assignats.

"Mama . . . thank God you didn't go back to the convent as I told you—"

"No, my love, the convent semed likely to be a dangerous place that night. I thought it best to come here to Marie-Josette's and her most accommodating young man's quarters." She smiled. "A good thing, I agree, that I did not obey you, my dearest."

Gilles now went to bed, which lay beside two long, narrow windows that opened on the crowded rue St.-Honoré two stories below. He leaned over to take Veronique gently in his arms and kiss her on the lips, as her mother looked on with evident pleasure and approval.

Veronique closed her eyes and said Gilles's name softly. When he took hold of her hand she made an enormous effort and somehow managed to close her fingers over his hand, as though securing and taking for herself its strength and love. It was her first of many small physical triumphs, and before she went back to sleep she was encouraged by Gilles's excited remark to her mother. "You see? She *is* coming around . . . soon she'll be walking. . . ."

"Of course," the Vicomtesse said calmly. "I told you so. Veronique is of good stock. We were all quick to heal, except, of course, for my dreadful migraine that plagued me for years. Strange! I haven't had a migraine in some time. It used to catch my head just about . . . here."

Managing a trace of a smile, Veronique drifted off into dreams that mingled the horror of that unforgotten night with the joy of Gilles's presence, to be awakened more than once by the sound of her own scream, with Gilles nearly always there to give her comfort and love.

Love. It was born new, natural as life, during one of those nights early in her convalescence when she dreamed of that ride in the tumbril with the dead. She woke herself by a sharp catch in her breath and sat straight up, stretching every painful muscle as she stared around her in panic.

Gilles, who usually slept on a pallet against the wall, had not yet gone to bed and was standing at the window looking out over the rooftops. In the moonlit dark she saw the white of his shirt against the dark breeches and trim muscular flesh of his legs.

He is truly what I dreamed of, she thought, pushing back her fears of the present dream that had been a nightmare, and wondering again that he had come to love *her*. . . . She wanted him, wanted to be part of that splendid body of his as well as part of his heart and his thoughts. It seemed the most natural desire in the world.

As if he shared it, he turned from the window and saw her eyes caught by the moonlight. He moved to her bed and took the hand she held out to him. Slowly, never taking his eyes from her, never being able to, he knelt on one knee beside her. He pushed the coverlet away and leaned over her, touching her cheek, her throat and the warm hollow between her breasts. She raised her arms, her fingers closing around the dark hair curling at the nape of his neck, drawing him to her.

Under his gentle onslaught she lay back among the pillows with his body both protector and invader upon hers. She welcomed his strength and felt the joyous sensation of winding her body about his as they locked together.

The release of passion, of a union so exact and so perfectly shared even in this instant, should have astonished them, but it did not. It was as if the years apart had somehow prepared their bodies for perfection together.

Later in the night, when they had become light-headed and laughed at their repeated joy in this bed together, they lay and talked occasionally of the past. They never mentioned the future; it was too precarious. . . .

"Were there many women in your life while we were apart?" She knew the question must sound fatuous, and yet her lover's curiosity demanded it.

"Hundreds. And what did *you* think of at night in your convent cell?"

"I thought of you, and then I scourged myself. I've the marks yet on my shoulders."

"You have beautiful shoulders." He turned his head and kissed the top of her shoulder, above the new bandage. "Lovely, clean flesh. No one ever had flesh like yours—"

"You talk like a cannibal."

"It's how I feel about you, how I felt when I would see you scurrying about Paris as Sister Veronique. Oh yes, I wanted . . . even then. Veronique . . . we've wasted so many years. . . ." He raised up on one elbow and looked down at her. "Life, it seems, is always too short."

In near panic she raised her arms to him. There was *now,* she told herself. They would live now.

But the world intruded upon now. . . .

One afternoon she awoke just as the wheels of a heavy cart ground over the cobblestones in the street below her windows, accompanied by cat-calls and yells and the sound of stones striking wood, and once again she lived the night-mare of that July night in the convent cloister.

She was alone for the moment—and had to force herself not to call out to Gilles in the hope he might be nearby. She looked about the sunny little room. The bed was decorated with a frilled coverlet of deep pink that put her in mind of clothing she'd worn in her girlhood, delicate fine-sewing accomplished by Marie-Josette.

She glanced out the window, saw the narrow buildings and mansard roofs across the street from her refuge, this house owned by Jeannot and Marie-Josette, who'd made these quarters available to her over their corner café. How fortu-nate . . . how wise, really, the two of them had been in ac-cepting their love from the start and building a life around it. And how good they'd been to her, singly and now to-gether. Jeannot had actually saved her life. Twice. The last time from butchery and . . . well, except for him, she'd be a handful of bones in quicklime now. . . .

But she would not think of that . . . only of the nights with Gilles, the love and special intimacy they now shared. At least from this moment on she'd devote her life to him, to *them.* . . . Her thoughts were interrupted by the growing noise in the street. Despite the considerable pulling of muscles in her right leg, she got up, opened the windows and looked out. Other heads also lined the windows as far as she could see down the slightly curving street. It was as if they all watched a festive procession.

One tumbril had already rattled past, filled with the daily

assortment of condemned bound for the guillotine set up in the great Place Louis XV . . . no, she corrected herself, trying to override the horror with dry facts—now it was called the Place de la Révolution. She looked down at the condemned in the second tumbril, so many of them cringing, begging—not like the customarily more stoic victims. Even the women among them were different, their hard faces distorted by fear now as they variously begged and screamed. . . . "I'm a patriot, Citizens . . . don't let me die . . . patriot . . . only did what I was told, that's all . . . only what I was . . ."

Veronique began to understand their difference as she made out the black-clad form of Raymond Berthelot, crumpled now against the stave sides of the tumbril. This empty, dry man was actually weeping.

"God forgive you," she whispered automatically, but her heart was not in the prayer. She kept seeing his eyes with their fanatic demand for her blood, so long as it didn't touch him, and the blood of those other bodies she'd seen in the alley back of the convent. And out of those who shared the death cart, she suspected she recognized at least two as having been among her worst tormentors. All her religious training, the deep basic teachings of Christian forgiveness, seemed to have been numbed, thrust back by the events of that July night.

She turned away and would have closed the windows, but Sanson the Executioner's procession had passed and the usual activity had resumed in the street below. She decided to take in the cool early autumn air as it drifted in. She tried to think of other things, to concentrate on getting her body back into its normal healthy condition. She limped across the room. Marie-Josette's nightrobe, which was too short for her, made Veronique look thinner than ever in the looking glass set in the armoire against the opposite wall. Her dark eyes appeared huge against her rather sallow skin, and she scarcely could see her pale mouth reflected at all. She looked ghastly, she decided. How could Gilles possibly love her?

Except that she no longer seriously questioned that he did. With the Church gone, the convent now desecrated and herself excommunicated by the Holy See, she belonged only to Gilles now as, perhaps, she'd always belonged to him since their first meeting.

She heard the latch rattle on the door and being unable to

get back to her bed, hurriedly limped around to the shadowed corner beside the armoire. A heavy knock came after the opening of the door.

Its authority made her fearful, momentarily, as if the Revolutionary Tribunal had sent its agents after her, legitimately this time . . . perhaps they'd uncovered her part in the attempt to save Marie Antoinette. She thought of how absurd she would look in the prisoner's box, in a nightrobe too short for her and with arms and legs a mass of scars. . . . Poor Gilles, he'd rescued her for nothing.

She watched the door open.

"Anyone about?" A booming voice challenged what appeared to be an empty room.

A big ugly man with the pockmarked face and the coat with flying triple capes seemed to fill the little room. He could only be Georges-Jacques Danton. She peered at him from around the armoire, thinking that he at least seemed friendly.

"Good day, Citizen. If you came to see Gilles Marsan I'm afraid he's out just now—" He'd seen her and obviously was amused at her ridiculous position. Embarrassed, she tried hastily to turn his attention to other matters. "Perhaps he's at the Tuileries, they're holding debates in the National Convention—"

"Including the announcement that I've stepped down from the Committee of Public Safety of my own will," Danton said with a sudden ironic tone that made her stare at him, "I will remain the head of the Cordeliers but I am *sick* of the stink of human blood. . . . Here. . . . Why are you hobbling about?"

While she was thinking of an answer, he reached for her and in a matter-of-fact way caught her up in a kind of bundle, bandaged arms and legs waving frantically in his arms, before he dropped her on the bed, her gown up to her knees and half off her shoulder. She pulled the coverlet over herself as calmly as she could while he strode to the windows and remarked, "More fodder for Sanson. This time, at least, on good account—yours and those other poor devils. If you have a taste for revenge, you might enjoy the sight. I'm sure your friend Marsan would on your behalf . . . those wretches took our *law* into their hands—though one wonders if perhaps it weren't more his anger at their presumption. The verdict was unanimous, of course. At least these will never set up their own tribunal again—nor many others, I suspect."

"Revenge," she murmured, "not a very satisfying pastime."

"Do you know that when I was Minister of Defense there were only thirty executions in all those months, and they were traitors and speculators?"

Was he defending himself to her? It was not like him. Perhaps his doubts weer greater than she'd suspected. "I sometimes think speculators are the more wicked of the two," she said.

He appeared surprised, but not disapproving. "Matter of fact, I tried to get it into our Declaration of the Rights of Man. The price of bread should bear *some* relation to the wages of the poor, I said. But Max and St.-Just and their crew insisted something they call 'virtue' was more important than the price of bread. Hell and damnation! They are the same. To Max Robespierre virtue is some kind of unreal purity. How is France to survive on Max's purity? To me virtue is devotion to my wife at night. To Max, it's devotion to him and what he wants. You may remember . . . no, I doubt you followed the politics of the Assembly that closely . . . but Max refused the Girondists' request to allow the question of the King's guilt to rest on a plebiscite. I quote him, 'Virtue is always in a minority.' In other words, if the people voted to save the King, it would be a vice, disagreeing as it did wtih the virtue of his desire. Clearly such vice should not be allowed, much less encouraged."

He walked up and down, unable to rest or settle anywhere. She found herself watching his movements and his face as it passed through sunlight, shadow, and sunlight again. It was said that those two terrible scars that split his nose and his face came from two—apparently one wasn't enough—encounters with bulls on that farm in Champagne where he was born. How unfitting that such a man should be brought down by the sting of wasps like Robespierre and his Angel of Death, St.-Just.

"Do sit down. It is wearing, just watching you."

He looked around. "Thank God you aren't my mistress. You give orders like Father Troyes, who taught me my Latin."

"I am afraid it is a natural result, Citizen. I was Sister Veronique, as you perhaps know."

He had stopped in front of the armoire's looking glass. "I knew a woman like you. Strong and clever, though not too intelligent."

Her chin came up but she made no protest, curious to

learn what he was thinking about as he studied the reflection of his face.

"Manon Roland was a little like you. I tried my damndest to get along with her when I was Minister of Justice. If we had combined her moderates, her Girondist party, with ours, we might have saved France this bloodbath. And do you know why that woman would not take the olive branch I offered? Too ugly. My manners offended her. But most of all it was my face." He struck his broken nose with one hand. "The bull that forked me has a great deal to answer for."

"To be ugly is not to be unattractive," she told him. "Nor is its absence necessarily a recommendation. For example, I do not find Citizen Robespierre ugly, yet—" She left it there.

He stared at her reflection in the glass and then burst out with his hearty laugh. "You are a discerning woman! I withdraw my criticism. Too bad Manon Roland didn't share your good sense. She might not have ended in Max's prisons, or chosen a husband whose only suggestion was that *he* flee Paris."

He sighed and paced up and down again, going to the door, which he had left partially open, and thereby almost frightening Marie-Josette out of her wits as she came up the stairs.

She reached the landing and staggered back before the sudden appearance of Danton. He grinned at her terror, helped her over the doorsill to get her out of his way, and called to Gilles Marsan, who was hurrying up the stairs two at a time.

"You there, Marsan! You are none too soon. I've been making love to your pretty mistress."

Veronique was jarred by the title as much as by the joke, but acknowledged the latter was an honest one. When she took the oath to the Republican government the previous year she repudiated her vows to serve the needs of the patients at the Hôtel-Dieu. Now that her work was taken from her, she could no longer serve those needs. She had been brought back to Gilles Marsan, and it was his needs she now vowed to serve. Here, she belonged. God—or fate? —meant it to be so.

Gilles smiled at Danton's reference to Veronique but came directly across the room and took her in his arms. To her intense relief she felt no embarrassment now, though Danton and Marie-Josette were watching them closely. To be with Gilles seemed wholly natural, as if they had always been together.

If the Holy See had excommunicated her—which meant no priest could marry them—she would still regard herself as free to love, if not to marry, Gilles.

Danton began to speak but for one of the few times in his life he was drowned out by Gilles's rapid questions addressed to Veronique.

"How are you feeling, darling? You look better. You do very well with this shoulder, but don't move it too much." He looked at her intently as he mentioned her shoulder. She understood.

"But I'm perfectly well. Really, I am. See?" She hugged him and he pretended to wince.

"An Amazon. Darling, I meant to come back earlier, but the sessions have been running night and day. They are arguing the fate of the Austrian." She raised her head. He squeezed her good shoulder as a warning.

Danton threw up his hands. "This domesticity is contagious. I'll go across the river and throw myself into the arms of my little Louise. I am taking her home to Champagne. I want to introduce her to that beautiful country life I was fool enough to leave once. In my present mood I want to remain there forever."

"It is only a mood. It will soon change," Gilles reminded him. "We need you here."

"Need me! I've been thrown out. And I'm tired." He looked at his large fists as he brought them down. "Christ knows I am tired of the fight. Good day, my children. I'll see you at the Café Parnasse before the journey. One more bottle with a few friends, eh?"

He did not wait for their farewells but went out past the tongue-tied Marie-Josette, and they heard his footsteps rumbling on the old stairs.

"I never thought to be so honored!" Josette said in some awe. "Citizen Danton in my own house! Wait 'til I tell of it to those Duplays with their precious Robespierre sleeping in their lodgings. Him with his Commune! And Jeannot will be pleased. Oh, mam'selle, after what nearly happened to you, he's sworn he'll never have any part of them. He testified against them. Did you know that?"

Dreading the answer, Veronique chose her words with care. "But the nursing sister! When those . . . when they attacked me they mentioned something about Sister Thérèse . . ."

Gilles said gently, "I'm afraid, darling, she was with those they intended . . . for the old cemetery pits."

"*My God* . . . those corpses in the tumbril with me . . ."

Marie-Josette came over to the bed and began a curtsy, but Veronique embraced her before she could complete the gesture.

"Your Jeannot really saved my life. I surely can never thank you enough."

"There was another," Gilles said, "who did her part."

Veronique looked at him questioningly.

He hesitated a moment, then went on. "Yes, after I'd come back to the Committee headquarters that night from the search for the Austrian's would-be rescuer" . . . he took her now into the circle of his arm . . . "I found Yolande waiting for me. You remember Yolande Berthelot, darling . . ."

"Very well," she said a bit sharply, and then quickly relented as she recalled Yolande's attempt to save her that night, even warning her, if cryptically, against her own brother. "Yes, I do remember," she said, "how she told me not to go inside. I wouldn't pay attention, though . . . I thought my mother might be in there. But why didn't you tell me this earlier? I might at least have thanked her for trying—"

"Darling," Gilles said, "can you blame Jeannot and myself for not wanting the heroes' roles all to ourselves for as long as possible? . . ." He didn't add, nor did he need to, that her long unease about Yolande was the reason they'd thought it best to wait until she was further along in her recovery. Veronique merely looked at him, half-smiled, and turned to Marie-Josette, who continued to be proud of her husband's part that night in saving Veronique from Raymond's outlaw tribunal. Later, at the trial before the Revolutionary Tribunal at which Jeannot identified Raymond and eight others from that night, it was explained that Jeannot had heard a disturbance and then gone to see the scenes of horror in the cloister and the alley behind it. It was thought unwise for both Gilles and Veronique to elaborate on his actual reason for being there. . . .

Now that Veronique had begun to walk about, being naturally active, she quickly recovered her normal mobility, and with a little encouragement from Gilles was soon taking her meals down in Jeannot and Marie-Josette's corner Café Egalité. And it was there that Georges Couthon came to her one brisk evening in early fall to tell her she might return to work at the Hôtel-Dieu.

"It is understood that you return as Citizen Marsan's mistress, not as Sister Veronique. Sister Thérèse's recent treason nearly destroyed all the good we've tried to do in the hospitals, but I have been permitted to use your services because of your association with a good patriot like Marsan."

It was ironic but welcome, so long as her work did not interfere with her relationship with Gilles. It also relieved her of a fear for her mother's safety. The Vicomtesse had a dangerous habit of continuing to teach her orphans all the religious history they could hold, as well as the manners of what was rapidly being referred to as the Old Regime. No amount of warnings, even a hint from Couthon to Veronique, disturbed the serenity of the Vicomtesse. So it was arranged, to Veronique's satisfaction, that she should work in the wards at the Hôtel-Dieu only during those hours when Gilles was with the Committee and in the National Convention. Her home, now and forever, she and Gilles agreed, was with Gilles in the second floor front lodgings on the rue St.-Honoré that they rented from Jeannot.

On the first night that she was able to walk beyond Jeannot's corner café, she and Gilles strolled through the street in a westerly direction and came on a small neat man in green glasses that, perhaps unconsciously, carried out the shade of his dull green coat. On anyone else his collar and cuffs would have been considered conspicuously fine, almost aristocratic, and he might have found himself fodder for the busy guillotine. It was unlikely, however, that anyone would suggest that Maximilien Robespierre had aristocratic sympathies.

Robespierre was accompanied by the elder daughter of his landlord, Duplay the carpenter. Robespierre smiled his small tiger smile as the four met by the desolate, deserted Church of St.-Roch.

"A beautiful evening. Warm and pleasant, is it not?"

Gilles and Veronique agreed. Citizeness Duplay said nothing. She was too busy studying her escort with eyes glazed by adoration. A moment before Gilles started to speak again Robespierre added in his gentlest voice, "How good to see you up and about, Citizeness Vaudraye. I am persuaded the Committee did right in overlooking your regrettable antecedents. After all, every one-time aristocrat is not necessarily an enemy of the Republic, any more than a one-time nun is an agent of the Papal enemies of France. But there"—he caught himself, laughed softly—"Citizeness Vaudraye was both nun and aristo. No matter, we trust our dear Danton's friends. By the by, tell Camille I will be coming to see little Horace one of these evenings. My godchild, you know. A delightful creature. Goodnight to you. And"—as they were passing each other—"peaceful dreams."

By the time they were beyond Robespierre's hearing, Veronique whispered, "What is there about that little man that terrifies me?"

Gilles did not appear to share her fears. "I suppose because he works rather deviously, through others. But he does get results, darling. He's an important part in this revolutionary change we're going through—"

"For the better?" She was thinking of this very street, where, every day, Sanson drove his tumbrils to the Place de la Révolution.

"There are terrible things, of course, and sometimes . . . many times . . . I admit I ask myself—and then I'm reminded of the great mass of the people, how *they* feel . . . and that there can be *no* comparison with conditions before the Revolution . . ." And she did not argue further. She loved and needed him too much. They must always be together. *Nothing* would ever separate them again. They repeated this vow to each other every night.

7

WITH THE CONVENT a desolate ruin the Vicomtesse had changed her residence to a charming little room on the first floor above the Café Egalité. She found little difficulty in paying the modest rent, for the simple reason that she usually forgot it. Marie-Josette considered such forgetfulness perfectly reasonable. Remembering the beauty of the Vaudraye château and the elegance that had everywhere spoken of ancient wealth, she could not make herself believe that her one-time employer and benefactor had no more money that whatever she could raise from the sale of her old trinkets. The jewelry had long been confiscated when the château and lands were taken over by the revolutionary government. But Marie-Josette's generosity could not help to pay her own expenses as prices mounted on virtually everything in the capital. Most merchants simply ignored the Law of the Maximum.

Such matters as money were scarcely any more in Veronique's consciousness than her mother's, and so when things became critical. It was Gilles who paid for the Vicomtesse's room as well as for most of her food. Veronique, however, became upset until she saw the honest pleasure with which Gilles made these payments, and realized how topsy-turvy the world had become.

"My dear Citizen Marsan," she informed him mock-seriously, "you are thinking of those day in Normandy."

"Exactly." He struck his chest, playing the pompous bourgeois. "Behold! The prosperous townsman at last." He stopped pretending. "You know, I suspect my overriding ambition when I returned to Vaudraye that day in the spring of '89, with all my dreams of overturning the structure of the Old Regime, was to bestow largesse with Vaudraye ease."

"And now you bestow it upon the Vaudrayes themselves."

He kissed her and looked into her eyes. "Do you mind so much?"

"Terribly. But—" she added with a mischievous grin— "mother doesn't mind in the least."

Gilles also took care of the clothing, with the not inconsiderable aid of Marie-Josette. By the time Veronique was on her feet again she felt luxuriously prepared for any situation, having two gowns for summer and two for winter, all of them secondhand but adequate, and beautifully fitted for her by Josette's skillful fingers. She even found herself with a hat that once belonged to an aristocrat, long since departed by the Place de la Révolution. It was an elegant, low-crowned leghorn hat with a wide brim. To relieve it of its aristo look Gilles adorned the crown with a blue, white and red rosette.

Now they were able to go about Paris like any other good Republican couple. The fact that Veronique was generally known to have been a nun and now lived as mistress to a popular Dantonist made her acceptable nearly everywhere, and it helped her that Gilles shared her knowledge that their marriage service would not be performed, even by the few priests who had taken the oath to the Republic.

The Vicomtesse never alluded to the matter. It became her beautiful pretense that Gilles and Veronique were husband and wife. It was not until she began to make frequent allusions to a mysterious religious figure in Meudon, near Versailles, who frequently visited Paris and often performed marriages that Veronique realized how very much her mother did care about the life of mortal sin in which her daughter was living.

The mere idea of her indiscreet mother being connected with a man who might be an enemy of the state gave Veronique fresh nightmares. To make matters worse, while she was working with the patients under her care in the Hôtel-Dieu, many of them believed they were giving her pleasure by boasting about the religious teachings of the ex-Vicomtesse.

Old Jacques-Henri, the dying man who had outlived his two bedmates, freely confided that only the strong and persistent prayers of the Vicomtesse at his bedside had healed him. Veronique pleaded with her mother to make her prayers silent ones, in Veronique's own fashion since the anticlerical laws had swept France. She pointed out that it would do her mother no good at all if she were guillotined and could not pray any longer, even for herself.

The Vicomtesse answered sweetly, "Quite right, my love. You are always so sensible," and went on behaving as if she enjoyed flirting with the guillotine. All the law needed would be her connection with some mysterious priest who, likely as not, was an enemy spy. . . .

On an autumn day Veronique saw Gilles coming toward her and, as always, ran to meet him with joy and relief, continuing on into his open arms, pretending his tight embrace had crushed her ribs, and went off with him diagonally across the Ile de la Cité to the Pont Neuf.

"Danton and Louise are leaving for Champagne," he told her, "and we want to give them a proper farewell. You don't mind, do you, darling? You like the Desmoulins, they'll be there."

"I like your Danton too. He once carried me in his arms." He looked at her, a little jealously, she hoped.

"Only to be rid of me. He didn't want me limping about while he was waiting for you. And as far as the Desmoulins, remember that's how I happened to meet you again after all those years. . . ."

"Do you actually imagine I arrived by chance that night? I'd waited an hour in the Cour du Commerce for you to start back to the hospital. And then you insisted on leaving with Fabre and Séchelles."

They exchanged glances, she pleased that her suspicions at the time had proved more accurate than she'd dare to hope. They made their way across the always crowded bridge toward the Café du Parnasse in its hideaway corner behind the quai.

Veronique was a trifle shaken out of her good spirits when she saw that although the Dantons had not yet arrived, the familiar big table near the doorway was occupied by Citizen Robespierre with his handsome acolyte, Louis St.-Just, and the Desmoulins. As always, Lucille watched her excitable husband with an almost maternal concern. It was she who first saw Veronique and Gilles with a quiet pleasure that had long ago made all who knew Lucille Desmoulins love her.

While the two women embraced, the tall St.-Just, with a graceful wave of the hand, offered Gilles a place between Robespierre and himself. Suspicious, Veronique wondered if the two men wanted to make it clear that Gilles Marsan was on their side rather than Danton's, should the schism between Robespierre and the Titan, as Danton was called, ever become public. Gilles took the chair but immediately became interested in the conversation across the table between Veronique and Lucille about young Horace Desmoulins, and St.-Just was obliged to address him twice before getting his attention.

"I was saying, it's perhaps wise of our friend Danton to get away from Paris at this time, wouldn't you agree?"

Gilles seemed to be listening with unlikely attention as Lucille described young Horace's ability to digest the tainted fish the family had eaten the previous day, then finally turned to St.-Just and with noticeable coolness said, "Well, I'm interested to hear your opinion, Citizen."

St.-Just glanced at Robespierre, got no help there and reminded Gilles, "He's not yet balanced his accounts but he is leaving Paris. I make no doubt he is adding to his holdings in his own province by moneys from the public accounts. When he was at the front he repeatedly demanded boots for the soldiers as though they were made of—"

"Paper?" Gilles asked.

Camille, ever indiscreet, laughed. "He's got you th-there, St.-Just. Danton says our boys were m-marching barefoot, leaving bloody footprints on the ground. We hear, though, that w-when he joined them, they had new fight in them."

Robespierre moved his head ever so slightly. His colored spectacles slipped along his nose and Camille found himself under the scrutiny of what appeared to be four motionless green eyes. He subsided and groped for Lucille's hand. Veronique filled in the awkward gap.

"You said young Horace was your godchild, did you not, Citizen Robespierre?"

Trying to restore an easier mood among the celebrants, Camille put in, "Max stood up with Lucille and me at our wedding. Why, we've known each other since time out of mind—"

"Indeed, yes," Robespierre agreed in his dry, quiet fashion.

"Those were good days. When my dear Camille worked with me on speeches at the States-General. You even once went so far as to tell me you admired me more than any man in history, isn't it so, Camille?"

Camille quickly answered, "Oh, I d-did. I did! I used to s-say it everywhere——"

At this second gaffe Veronique watched the faces around her at the table. St.-Just looked disdainful. Gilles frowned slightly at Camille, who didn't catch his hint, and Robespierre removed his glasses, carefully polished them on his napkin.

"Yes. I believe that is what you used to say, dear boy. I fear I have lost my influence over you. Time, I suppose. And perhaps questionable influences at work. . . ."

It was too much, even for Camille. He started to rise. "Now, s-see here, Max. You can't talk about my friends like that. Danton is not a questionable influence just because——"

"Dear, dear, what heat, my boy!" Robespierre said, restoring his spectacles. "I leave it to all of you. Have I mentioned any name? Not I."

"Damme!" called a voice behind them. "I am either too early or too late. Too late to hear the bad, too early to hear the good. Here, Charpentier, a chair for me. A stout one. My Louise will sit on my lap. Won't you, my adorable one?"

It was clear to Veronique from the way young Louise Danton clung to him lovingly as he balanced her on one knee that she was now more in love than in awe of her overpowering husband. He had found the way to her heart by his own boisterous warmth. The idea made this farewell celebration a little less sad; Veronique shared Gilles's fear that without the shield of the Titan's power on the Committee of Public Safety, France faced more terror. The daily loads rumbling down St.-Honoré to the Place de la Révolution had already tripled. But in spite of Danton's bluster and jokes, one could see that he was tired and disillusioned. He should rest and restore himself in his beloved Champage countryside, for she was certain he would eventually be needed to save what was left of France.

St.-Just remarked to Gilles, loudly enough to be overheard, "Forever late. Forever the actor striding in to take stage center."

"Yes," Robespierre agreed, smiling at Danton. "He will be late for his own funeral, I daresay."

Everyone pretended not to notice the quality of the silence which followed this and preceded Danton's laughing: "Always first at dinner and last at funerals. That's a happy motto, wouldn't you agree, Citizens? . . . What? Has no one finished a single bottle of blood-red yet? Gilles, Max, Camille, you must help me kill this one." He began to pour the red wine, whose quality Charpentier managed to keep high in spite of conditions elsewhere.

"And St.-Just," put in Robespierre, "I believe you forgot his glass."

"To be sure." Danton poured, passed the glass to the younger man. "Here's your wine, St.-Just. I thought that, out of habit, you would be drinking the blood-red from Max's glass."

St.-Just sprang up, knocking his chair over and thereby directing the attention of other patrons to this table. "You go too far, Danton, by God you do—"

"I thought you boys had abolished God," Danton remarked jovially.

Gilles touched St.-Just's arm, advised him, "Sit down . . . it was a joke, can't you see that?"

"I don't like jokes, damn you! I am not a man to be made sport of—" But St.-Just nonetheless began to pick up his chair, and Robespierre smoothed over matters by sipping from his glass and saying, "I propose a toast, citizens. We are here to do honor to our friend Georges-Jacques. Not to forget his charming young wife"—he tapped the glass on the table. "I give you—Georges-Jacques and Citizeness Danton."

Everyone drank while the Dantons sat with glasses raised, a trifle awkward, waiting for Robespierre's toast to be completed. "May Georges-Jacques and Louise devote their lives from this moment to the happiness and prosperity of that beautiful countryside called Champagne."

It was clear to Veronique, and undoubtedly to the others, that the little man further implied by his toast that the couple should remain there, far away from Paris. It may have been good advice, despite his motive, but Danton was hardly known for courting safety.

Veronique had raised her glass with the others at the table when she caught Gilles's expression over his glass. He was staring at her with that somber, dark look relieved only by his faint smile, altogether a guarded look such as she'd seldom seen from him. She gulped down the wine, understanding that far more than words were being flung back and forth on this brisk fall day. She had just witnessed the preliminaries in a mortal duel. It remained for the witnesses, the seconds in this duel, to choose their champions. They could no longer cling to both sides with the battleline being drawn up.

She was enormously relieved when Robespierre frowned up at the autumn sunlight coming in through the open doorway and said, "I fear I must leave this delightful gathering and be off about my work. So much unfinished business in the Committee these days. . . ."

Which was obviously addressed to Danton, who merely waved his refilled glass in the direction of the Incorruptible.

"Farewell, Max . . . until we meet again."

St.-Just had gotten up with Robespierre, who held out his hand, its nails deeply bitten, and Danton, momentarily disarmed by this unexpected display from his old comrade, took his hand—"remember always my letter to you on the death of your beloved Gabrielle. I said then, and I say now . . . whatever trouble our enemies may make between us, I love you more than ever, and I shall continue to love you, my friend, even unto death. . . ."

And he left them, with St.-Just following grimly behind him.

"But whose death?" Danton asked no one in particular, and then shrugged.

The others sat there looking at each other. No one said a word. The afternoon had grown more chilly, with a wind off the river.

8

IT SEEMED to Veronique that Robespierre and his adherents had planned their next bloody moves step by step, with infinite care. Thanks to the whispers, the lies that were impossible to trace to their source, and the machinations of St.-Just and others, they had brought down the Titan, Danton, carefully removing him from official power. Through all of this Robespierre's name appeared in only the most obscure way, until one morning Paris, and therefore France itself, woke up to find that it was entirely in the small, almost petite, hands of the Incorruptible.

On September 17th the Convention and its all-powerful Committee of Public Safety decreed a Law of Suspects, depriving all those arrested of a defense in court. And it was on this day that Gilles came earlier than usual to collect Veronique at the Hôtel-Dieu. He found her busy assisting a young surgeon as he reset the leg of a ten-year-old boy who moaned repeatedly and would have tossed and turned but for Veronique's firm hands, which held him while she murmured softly, "Sleep, little one."

"Is there no laudanum for the poor little devil?" Gilles asked as he came quietly into the ward behind Veronique.

She nodded. "But I don't dare give him any more, and he

cannot forget what he has seen. His mother and sister were in Sanson's cart this morning."

Gilles nodded grimly. "Well, at all events, I'll never have *any* connection with any of it again—"

She'd secretly hated his work with the Committee of Public Safety, but life was so precarious these days that the slightest deviation from the prescribed could mean terror for him or her mother—the two who were now her whole life.

"Darling, what do you mean?" she said hopefully.

"I've resigned from the Committee. After today no man who cares anything about France can go on working with those butchers—"

She glanced at the young surgeon, whose hands had stopped wrapping the splint—she'd no doubt he would report this conversation to Robespierre's friend, Couthon. She also doubted if her own credit with the paralytic was great enough to save both her mother and Gilles from suspicion. She felt the terror even in her fingertips.

"Please keep talking, mam'selle . . ." the boy whispered.

With an effort she recovered her calm and resumed in her soothing voice, "Sleep now, boy. Rest and sleep . . ."

He closed his eyes eventually and let the laudanum take him.

Veronique said quietly to Gilles, "Another orphan for mama. Just when I'm trying to send her away from Paris . . . but she's so stubborn."

"Well, have you ever tried to cut a bit of silk with a sword? Your mother is like that silk. She offers no resistance. And nothing is harder to break with a sharp instrument."

"The sharp instrument I'm worrying about is the National Razor. . . ."

The young surgeon must have heard her . . . she was as bad as the Vicomtesse when it came to indiscretion, she told herself severely, and as she left the hospital that night with Gilles she was again disturbed when she saw the surgeon hurrying to meet Couthon, who was carried into the hospital by his two bearers. She wondered if she only imagined that Couthon's eyes avoided hers nowadays.

The struggle between the Girondists and the supporters of Robespierre—called "The Mountain" because they sat on the high seats on the rostrum—focused on the War. For some months it went well, and since the Girondists were its sponsors their popularity stayed high. Soon the enemy was cleared out of France and the revolutionary armies took the offensive to carry the Revolution to the Rhine and over the Pyrenees . . . and as a practical matter the government in Paris also wanted the army out of the country—to live off the enemy land and because they still feared some unknown French Caesar crossing the Seine to take over the government. Madame Roland's husband expressed this fear well when he said, "The thousands of men we have under arms must march as far away as their legs will carry them; otherwise they might cut our throats."

And so the French armies moved, overrunning the Rhineland, Belgium, Savoy and Nice, freeing, so they claimed, these people from their tyrannical rulers. But after Louis XVI's execution in January of 1793, the armies suffered defeat after defeat in Holland, and finally the Girondist General Dumouriez not only surrendered to the Austrians but advised them on their plans to invade France. It was the death blow to the Girondists. In June, the Mountain purged the Assembly of thirty-one Girondists, and ordered their arrest. In October both Marie Antoinette and the Girondist moderates with Danton's ex-nemesis, Madame Roland, were brought before the Revolutionary Tribunal. No genuine defense was permitted and the verdict for both Monarchist and Republicans was foreordained.

It was also during these bright fall days of 1793 that Parisians began to take notice of certain posters on the walls, wild sketches in which a few faceless individuals held the squirming masses of men, women and children in their hands as blood dripped between their fingers. No one could identify these monsters who devoured the citizens of Paris. They might, of course, be the Austrians, or the Prussians and English, or the rest of Europe with which France was at war . . . or could it be, some dared suggest, that "these monsters represent St.-Just, or Couthon, or Hébert, or . . ." Not the Incorruptible—no one mentioned *that* name.

The first time Veronique saw one of these posters she examined it closely. Here was the only voice in Paris calling out against the horrors of excess, and for clemency and moderation. But would others recognize the hand of the artist as Gilles's? She thought the style looked somewhat forced, a bit crude, less artistic than his, but still, all the same, unmistakably. . . .

After that she took care to avoid such placards and posters wherever they appeared. She was too much afraid someone would read the truth in her face.

On the day of the Queen's death the city went about its work as usual. There was none of the suspense, the unspoken fear of divine wrath that had gripped the citizens nine months earlier when Louis XVI was taken to the place of execution, as befitted a King, in a closed carriage and warmly dressed against the mists of a January morning. Marie Antoinette of Austria and France rode on the plank of a vegetable cart, in a bloodstained, ill-fitting white dress. Her long hair had been hacked off in scallops by the busy Sanson, but there remained enough for passersby to see that the hair of the thirty-eight-year-old Habsburg Archduchess had, in a matter of weeks, turned snow white.

Veronique had sworn to herself that she would not watch the Calvary of this proud, unyielding woman, but when the hour came and Marie-Josette stood looking out and describing the sight, Veronique could not remain away from the window.

"Oh, mam'selle, how old she looks! Do come and see. You would never believe she was the beautiful lady we saw in the procession that day at Versailles. What a long while ago it seems now . . . and yet, only four years. I wanted to be her that day. I wanted to wear those great white plumes and all those jewels." She looked around at Veronique. "Who do you suppose has all that finery now?"

Veronique shook her head in anger and wondered why the Queen's tragedy struck her so hard? No . . . not the Queen's— the woman's.

The Queen looked to be sixty, with all the careless charm and all the loveliness gone. What remained was the diamond-hard core. Veronique thought that in spite of that Habsburg jaw and the ugly mob cap, Marie Antoinette had never been so beautiful. . . .

Gilles was busy all day at the printing press of one of Camille's friends, and did not discuss the execution until Veronique mentioned the passage of the tumbril. He too had been affected, and only nodded briefly.

Jeannot was more talkative. "The Austrian's arms were bound behind her, you know. When she mounted the steps to the plank and lost her balance, she stepped on Sanson's toe. Do you know what that woman said to him? 'Pardon, monsieur, it was not deliberate.'" He sighed. "Incredible woman, that Austrian."

The Vicomtesse had worn unrelieved black and remained in her lodgings all day, but she seemed curiously serene when

Veronique and Gilles called on her that evening. As they were about to leave after routine conversation about the weather, the war and high prices, she leaned nearer Veronique and confided, "My love, she was at least able to die at peace with God."

There was no question about the identity of "she." Veronique asked, "But how can you know?"

"Because there was someone in the crowd along the way to give her absolution——"

Veronique caught her hand. "Not someone you know! Mother, in God's name, don't let yourself become involved with enemy agents——"

The Vicomtesse freed herself and said with dignity, "Men of God are not necessarily enemy agents. Do you know, there is a little gatehouse on Alex's property in the Meudon Woods that would be perfect for me and my orphans."

"Mother!"

"All the neighbors there, around Versailles, are against this dreadful government but they mind their own affairs. They would never betray anyone. Neither would they call attention to themselves by foolish efforts to overthrow those friends of Gilles——"

"Promise me you will do *nothing* foolish!"

"Of course, dear."

It was poor comfort but the best Veronique could extract at the moment.

The Revolutionary Tribunal had scarcely crossed the name of the Widow Capet off the docket when it addressed itself to those members of the moderate Girondist Patry who had once been the hope of the new nation. By the end of October, twenty-two of the Girondists rode in tumbrils to the guillotine, singing the blood-stirring march brought to Paris by the soldiers of Marseille, followed the next month by their mentor Madame Manon Roland, dying as she had lived, with a superb sense of theater and a dignity to match the Austrian's.

Veronique made it a point to be far from the scene of this near-daily butchery, although she shed no special tears for the erstwhile Duc d'Orléans, who had finally worn one mask too many and took the road of his royal cousins to the Place de la Révolution.

Marsan and Camille conferred often these days, discussing propaganda aimed at a return to clemency. It was highly secret from everyone except Lucille and Veronique, who'd become fast friends and soon found themselves exchanging some of their most intimate confessions. . . .

It was on a rainy winter morning in the comfortable Des-moulins lodgings off the Cour du Commerce that Lucille was knitting her son Horace a jacket as Veronique untangled a ball of yarn that she'd tracked through two rooms and under innumerable articles of furniture.

Lucille looked down at her work, her cheeks tinged pink as she said, "It's strange to say, I suppose, but when Camille has worked unbelievably hard on one of those anonymous articles he and Gilles are forever discussing, he comes to me and we . . . we have never loved so deeply, so fully."

Veronique smiled at her own conceit in thinking that she and Gilles were the only lovers who had been affected in this way. "It's the same with us. I think life, the closeness of love . . . ours and yours . . . seems even more important when around us—"

"Death is everywhere," Lucille finished.

Both women looked across the room at the men they loved. Camille and Marsan were dovetailing some of Gilles's pre-liminary sketches with the editorials in a newspaper of Camille's, *The Old Cordelier*. They were creating this paper in order, literally, to give voice to Camille's sharp, witty views against the policies of the Paris Committee of Public Safety. Camille was always at his best on paper and still often seemed unaware of the dagger-edge to his own editorials. At the moment, as nearly as Veronique could discover, theirs were voices crying out in the wilderness of Paris—no one else dared utter a word in criticism of the regime.

"What does Danton think of the execution of the Giron-dists?" Veronique finally asked.

Lucille shrugged. "Well, we've not heard, but I'd think he is against all this blood-letting. Camille even blames himself for some of his old writings . . . says he went further than he meant . . . he says Robespierre is daily getting more and more power by executing all his political opponents, that nobody any longer dares to stand in his way. . . . We miss Danton sadly. We need the Titan. We could rally round him. God knows, we might even defeat this monstrous terror that seems to have us all by the throat—"

"Who would have believed that little man could have gone this far?" Veronique said.

"Camille feels that even Max is carried along by the tide. You know, he was Camille's first friend in Paris. And I honestly believe he loves his godson" . . . She looked toward the room where little Horace was. "Max will be faithful to that old friendship . . . I know him."

Veronique did not pursue aloud her own skeptical beliefs. Instead she asked to see Horace once more and was impressed as always with the child's self-sufficiency, his adult look that made him seem older in so many ways than his father. Much as she liked the appealing Camille, it often terrified her to think that Gilles might find himself involved with Camille's well-intentioned but wilder actions.

The two were arguing now. . . . "You can't say that publicly until we have more strength behind us. We must build gradually," Gilles was saying.

"I can't wait. My head is full of ideas. C-crowding it!"

"If you aren't careful you'll find it full of sawdust. Camille . . . we're playing this game with our lives. Do you understand me?"

Shaken, Camille seemed to retreat while his wife's hand groped for Veronique's. The two women felt the coldness in each other's fingers, but there was some consolation in the fact that they shared their fears.

"Couldn't we invite F-Fabre to join in the editorials?" Camille ventured after a time. "He's on the third act of his play . . . what the d-devil does he call it?"

" 'The Maltese Orange.' But I saw him last week at Jeannot's, and it will be months, he said, before he finishes the play."

"Then he won't do. And Séchelles . . . can we trust him not to b-betray us? Oh, God! What I'd give to have the Titan back . . ."

Veronique had to return to the Hôtel-Dieu by mid-afternoon, when Gilles had some private business in the St.-Antoine quarter. The rain had stopped by the time they dined at the Desmoulins, good company making up for the meagerness of the meal itself. Lucille sighed over the stewed hare, which she thought was tainted, but the turnips were filling and the bread and cheesecakes were eaten with pleasure. When families were invited out to dinner in these grim days, they brought food with them to help out—if the bread was fresh and the wine not too sour, life became bearable.

"Veronique, how long did you wait at the bake shop for this bread? It's the best I've tasted in weeks," Lucille said as she broke off a chunk to clean her plate.

"I was at the door just after dawn. But even so I was lucky. They ran out before they reached the end of the line.

I thought for a while there was going to be a riot."

It was plain to Veronique that Lucille wanted to prolong their visit, which was understandable. When she and Camille were alone, it must have been easy for her to visualize the danger to her husband fighting the greatest power in France. Indeed, Veronique knew that fear as all too familiar.

In the midst of dessert Camille got up and looked out at the sky. "A good s-sign. Seems to be clearing. There will be people in the streets so you won't be so n-noticed in that area—" He stopped as they all heard the heavy, booted steps on the stairs outside the door.

Lucille's hand went to her mouth. "Mother of Heaven! Is it soldiers?"

The men stared at the door, but Veronique thought there was something familiar in those ominous, heavy footfalls on the stairs. Then the two men turned to each other, half smiling, as if to confirm silently what they both now suspected.

"It's Georges-Jacques! He's coming back!" Camille said.

The gloomy day full of foreboding suddenly sparkled with light. Veronique found herself laughing in all the excitement, a laughter picked up by the Titan, who had raised his palm to slap the door just as Camille opened it wide.

There was much embracing, both Danton and Camille being openly sentimental in friendship.

"Certainly I am back . . . to cage the tigers. And now let's get to work," Danton said in his customary ear-splitting tones. He began to tear the travel gloves off his fingers, and Veronique, greatly relieved at his arrival, thought him capable of caging the tigers this minute, in Lucille's dining parlor. While he shook the raindrops off his big coat, spattering everyone in the room, he bent over Camille's desk.

"Where is this celebrated newspaper of yours? I hear you've named it for this dear old quarter."

"I named it for you, Georges. You are the Old Cordelier. But how the d-devil did you find out? That cursed printer?"

"Not the printer," Gilles put in. "When the Girondists went, I decided we had to have Georges-Jacques home again—"

"That idiot Séchelles had already sent me the news about the Girondists. Said I'd be glad to hear it! Glad! Do they think I stand about wishing everyone underground who disagrees with me? I knew then that Max must have run mad. I was half-packed to return when I got Gilles's message." He shrugged. "So here I am! Now, to clip the tiger's claws." He studied Camille's top handwritten sheets, abruptly slapped the desk. "Camille, you go too fast. Save this business about the Suspects Law for a future number. Attack that foul-mouthed Hébert first, for example. He deserves it, if for nothing else than what he did as principal witness before the Revolutionary Tribunal against the Queen, accusing her of incest with her son. . . . A filthy man!"

"But Max himself wants me to destroy Hébert."

Danton laughed. "Then why not oblige him? Jacques Hébert certainly doesn't much resemble the once great revolutionary journalist. . . . When he set up his damned whoring worship of the Goddess of Reason—*his* reasons, of course, to compete with the Virgin Mary . . . even Max couldn't swallow *that*. Not pure old Max. But mark me, we must have the Convention behind us before we say things like—" he read from the sheet—"A withered soul with neither pity nor love for his countrymen cannot love his country. . . .' Camille, my friend, any but a blind man would recognize Max in that. Wait until I talk to him. See if he can't be made to understand where he's taking the country. In which case we can cut his claws and save our old tiger. As to Hébert, he has simply gone beyond the pale of humanity, there is no hope for him. . . ."

In an admittedly selfish desire to cling to her belated happiness with Gilles, Veronique hoped he would not now become further involved in this deadly business. But Gilles was reminding Danton in a quiet voice, "Does it ever occur to you that Robespierre has two rivals for power—you and Hébert? And that if we rid him of the rabid Hébert crowd we do him an enormous favor?"

"Gilles . . ." Camille joined in, "you don't mean we should sp-spare Hébert—"

"I think we should involve Robespierre and St.-Just in his downfall."

There was silence while they considered. Finally Danton shook his head. "That's devious. Too much like Max's thinking. I say there may still be hope for Max. We are, we were, friends, after all. A clipping of the claws, yes. I came back for that. But you still can't compare Max with that vile excretion—Hébert." Gilles got up to leave. "Where are you going? Not angry, Gilles! Damn, I meant no offense. You know me well enough."

Gilles explained that he was escorting Veronique to the

Hôtel-Dieu and then had to see a printer about copies of a political sketch.

Danton and Camille declared a sudden desire for a bottle of wine, and then the four of them left, Veronique saying nothing at all as they walked along. Her fear was deep and quiet.

It seemed remarkable to her that after such a grim discussion the three men could stride through the Latin Quarter laughing, exchanging jokes, and hailing nearly everyone in sight. They reached the bridge at sunset, and Gilles boosted Veronique around a broken water jug with which someone had been drawing up water from the polluted river.

Danton remained behind the others, studying the river as it flowed under the bridge. Even hushed as his powerful voice was now, he could be heard at the other end of the bridge.

"Look at that, Camille. The Seine is flowing blood."

"It's the s-sunset," Georges said.

Danton shook his head. "I've been asleep too long. Camille, take up your pen. Marsan, your brush. Make your appeal to them. The Terror *must* end. I'll back you, here's my hand on it, my friends. . . ."

Veronique forced herself free of the river's mesmerism and breathed deeply. The clean night air, washed by the rain, invigorated her, and cleansed her, momentarily, of the thought of further bloodshed.

After all, the Titan had returned.

9

DURING the bright sharp winter days of 1793 and '94 Veronique, along with other Parisians, began to hear the first stories of monstrous cruelty practiced in such provinces as Brittany and various cities, especially Lyons, to put down rebellion against the authority of the Convention. The wholesale murder of hundreds of citizens picked at random in the rebellious cities followed in most respects the advice printed in Jacques-René Hébert's own newspaper. The details of how to rape and murder were so vile that even Parisians who might favor such obscenities discussed them only in whispers. And since the Hébertists had always resented the popular influence of Danton, they timed a new attack on the Titan just as news of the horrors at Nantes and Lyons drifted into Paris. It was a serious miscalculation.

The first edition of Camille Desmoulins' new paper appeared at the right time, striking at the wholesale cruelty in the provinces, which had been compounded by the praise of that cruelty among Hébert's followers. There was little that Camille's one-time mentor Robespierre could find in the first issue of *The Old Cordelier* with which to disagree. At the same time, as Veronique watched the Incorruptible, she couldn't doubt that he was enjoying the battle waged between his two rivals, Danton and Hébert.

Veronique saw Robespierre again when the cruelty of the commissioners in Nantes was discussed over a café table in the Palais-Egalité, formerly the Palais-Royal Gardens. Under cover of an argument between Danton and Robespierre that seemed to have been carried to these gardens from the debates that night in the Jacobin Club, she whispered an aside to Gilles.

"I can't believe it . . . he seems to see nothing wrong in tying men, women and children together alive and sinking them in a river—"

Gilles nodded, but before he could answer her he was interrupted by Robespierre speaking in a shrill and uncharacteristically loud voice:

"You harp on these thousands dead in one place or another. You demand justice, clemency. Call it what you will, but not one *innocent* man, woman or child has ever been executed under this regime!"

Patrons at other tables turned to look, as everyone stared at Danton for his reply. He smiled. A terrible smile. In his stentorian voice, he asked, "What, Max? Not *one*?"

After which he got up, shoved his chair back and walked out of the Gardens. He had given the lie to every death warrant on which Robespierre's precise little signature had been placed. Veronique glanced at Max, whose sallow face now appeared green in the light of the garden lamps.

A short while later, when Gilles and Veronique had walked with the Desmoulins as far as the Pont Neuf, Gilles said, "You will notice that Robespierre hasn't spoken against your new editorials, Camille. It seems he doesn't want to discourage you yet?"

"Discourage me?"

"From calling on Paris to condemn Hébert and his methods, even though privately they obviously please him."

"I'll do more," Camille said. "Danton is going to speak for clemency again in the Jacobins. I'll report his speech to the whole of Paris—"

Lucille whispered suddenly, "Oh, Camille, *no*!"

Veronique understood her fears very well. Still, she felt somewhat heartened since the campaign for clemency had begun, the effort to wean the majority of the Convention from terror to clemency as a better, saner way of governing. Since the day of Danton's return, she could almost feel the change in the air of Paris. She thought of it as a sprig of hope appearing between the blood-soaked cobblestones. . . .

As Gilles and Veronique passed Jeannot's café on their way up to their lodgings that night, Marie-Josette hurried out to ask them, "Have you spoken with the Vicomtesse? She is very late—"

Veronique quickly looked up but saw no flicker of light between the worn shutters of the Vicomtesse's room. "But she was not at the hospital tonight. She was to have come home before sunset."

"I'd best go back for her, darling. You wait here with Josette."

The dread she'd almost succeeded in dismissing came back in force. "No, please, Gilles, let me go back with you."

He didn't argue but carefully pulled the hood of her cloak forward over her wind-blown hair, and they returned rapidly to the Ile de la Cité and the hospital.

In the cold, windy night the streets were surprisingly full of people. Some of the fanatics who'd been dispersed after the massacre at the Convent of Ste. Veronique had now joined with the Hébert terrorists against Danton's call for clemency, but to Veronique's astonishment, when she and Gilles walked off the Pont Neuf and into the crowded Place Dauphine, these people were being shouted down by the moderates.

Gilles had Veronique's hand in his, and even at this moment of tension and worry she wished they might go on forever with this feeling, this sense she sometimes had that his blood flowed in her veins as his life forces joined with her body.

"The Titan is right," someone shouted, "there's been too much blood . . . first thing you know it'll be our turn to be shaved by the National Razor—"

That hit its mark and several in the fellow's audience agreed, though another protested. . . . "We must purify the nation of its rotten blood, murderers like Carrier in Nantes and thieves like Fabre d'Eglantine with his stock swindles. . . ."

"But Fabre is Danton's friend—"

"So much the worse for him. Danton must disown him."

As Veronique and Gilles cut across the Place Dauphine toward the Hôtel-Dieu near the left bank of the Cité, Veronique asked anxiously, "Is it true about Fabre?"

"Probably. God knows we would all be better off if he would keep to his 'Maltese Orange.' Bad playwrights aren't usually as dangerous as bad stock manipulators."

"But can't Danton free himself of the fellow?"

"You know the Titan. He never turned his back on any friend."

"Then this Fabre gossip is dangerous?"

He did not answer.

They reached the hospital, only to find it full of guardsmen. Veronique was sure that what she'd feared most had come to pass and tried to run ahead, but Gilles held her back.

"Careful. Act normally. . . ."

Inside the building they saw Couthon seated in his rolling chair, watching as guardsmen searched every cubicle in the contagious ward. Veronique tried to camouflage her fear and went up to Couthon.

With an effort he reached for her hand—his fingers already showed signs of the paralysis that was rapidly spreading through the rest of his body. "Citizeness, it's good you weren't on duty tonight."

"Why is that? Am I to understand that you and I no longer can work together against death—"

"Someone is working against the state, my girl! Not a very healthy occupation."

Gilles had gone at once to the stillroom of this hospital wing, as Veronique suffered in fear for her mother's safety. Now he appeared and *with* the Vicomtesse, smiling and looking faintly surprised.

"My love," her mother said, "you should have been here. Such excitement . . . one of the nurses reported to the guard on duty that she'd seen a Royalist—in this place! Can you imagine? Dear me, how we laughed!"

"A Royalist priest, Citizeness," Couthon corrected her. "And in disguise, naturally. His description seems to fit closely the enemy spy who organized the attempt to rescue the Austrian last summer."

"The fellow I chased?" Gilles said. "Yes, I remember . . . where did you get the original description?"

"From a Citizeness Leplon who lives near the Temple prison."

Veronique held her breath while admiring the ease with which Gilles dismissed the "Citizeness Leplon."

"I remember questioning the woman. I wondered about her possible Royalist antecedents. Well, no matter. But I felt that she disliked me intensely. No doubt she worried I might discover something in her past. . . ."

Couthon turned his head painfully, watched Gilles. "You

may be right. She did seem antagonistic to you. . . ."

Gilles and Veronique took care not to look at each other.

The guardsmen returned with nothing to report except the discovery of a curious bit of evidence from the Dead Room, a heavy weather cape obviously belonging to a tall man, and a satin pillow filled with herbs. A "headache pillow" of the kind used by ladies with migraine.

"Must have slept in the Dead Room with this stolen pillow," one of the guards suggested.

"Stolen?" Couthon repeated thoughtfully. "Or given to him?" He became aware of the silence in the long ward with its many closed cubicles. Still aware of the sick, Couthon lowered his voice. "This can be discussed elsewhere. And you, Marsan, take these ladies to their lodgings. The streets can be dangerous these nights."

Gilles took the hand Couthon could not extend as the two men told each other goodnight. As Gilles, Veronique and her mother were leaving, Couthon made a great effort and rolled his chair toward them.

"Gilles? You Dantonists are working hard to rid us of Hébert and his cutthroats."

Gilles agreed.

Couthon's fingers scrambled nervously at the wheel of his chair. Finally he said, "Have you thought what will happen when Max finds himself with only one rival?"

"You underestimate Danton's popularity with the people. . . ."

Couthon smiled wearily. "Marsan, are you still so naive you believe the people choose their leaders?"

In spite of Veronique's warning hand on his arm, Gilles turned and said, "Couthon, why you remain with men like St.-Just and Robespierre I don't pretend to know, but if Danton were to go down I tell you this—Max would not last six months. In fact I give him three!"

Couthon looked at Veronique. She felt she could sense a flicker of sympathy in his eyes, but when he answered Gilles it was without the slightest warmth: "You're a fool . . . Robespierre is still the hope of this nation—"

"Then this nation is in a worse state than I had suspected."

It was all very well to have the last word, but Veronique remembered how close the intellectual Couthon was to the chill, intellectual master of the Committee of Public Safety.

On the way home Gilles tried to inspire the Vicomtesse

with some kind of discretion, but she merely fluttered at his concern, complained about the beginnings of a headache and sighed. "I do need my headache pillows. What a pity! However—"

"Madame!" Gilles began again desperately, "do you so much want to die on the guillotine?"

Veronique could not help interrupting. "It's my opinion there isn't a sou to choose between you two when it comes to indiscretion. Gilles, you know how close he and Couthon are—"

"My apologies to you, madame," Gilles said suddenly, kissing the hand of the Vicomtesse. "We both hate hyprocisy."

Veronique could only be relieved that they'd reached a dark stretch in the road and no one could hear them. During the rest of the walk along the quais, where men and women were busy unloading during these midnight hours, they did manage to keep to harmless subjects. When they'd reached their lodging and seen the Vicomtesse safely to her room, Veronique and Gilles went on up to the room in which they'd known their greatest joy.

Veronique watched him push the bolt on the door. "What a pity we can't lock out the world!"

He came across the room to her, and she realized that the events of the evening had affected his mood as they had hers. He was fully aware of how dangerous the situation was. She saw it in his strained features, his somber eyes, and their sudden, open plea to her. She held out her arms to him. To comfort him. To love him.

For these brief hours they actually could banish the dangers outside their door, the fear for the Vicomtesse, for Gilles, for the Dantonists. . . . When they loved each other that night Veronique was certain they would remember these hours the rest of their lives. . . . It was in the timeless blue hours before dawn that Gilles said it for both of them. . . . "Do you realize that no one in Paris loves as we do?"

She smiled, touched his arm with her warm lips. "No one," and was surprised when he laughed. "You find me amusing?"

"Only the thought of Max in bed with the Duplay girl."

She too laughed at the unlikely picture, but wished he hadn't mentioned Max Robespierre. Suddenly he said, "Our children will probably never know anything like this—"

"Never know love?"

He stared at the high, pale ceiling. "I mean they'll never

know times like these, and be a part of them as we are. . . .
What can come after this, to match what has been done
here?" He turned his head, followed the bridge of her nose
and her mouth with his forefinger. "But they will have you
for their mother. I can see my daughter now. She looks
exactly like her mother. Long ago I memorized all these
features, this nose, this mouth and—"

"What nonsense! Our firstborn must be your son. I want a
child who looks exactly like you."

He leaned over and kissed the lips he'd so often sketched.

She slept in his arms and did not awaken until someone
had knocked repeatedly on the staircase door.

It was after dawn and the street was full of the raucous
sounds of the water seller, the old man with firewood, the
knife sharpener and the wine peddler calling his wares in
time to deliver for breakfast. Gilles went to the door, asked
who was there and Veronique began to worry again when
she heard Camille Desmoulins' panicky voice.

"Let me in. I m-must talk to you."

Gilles threw the bolt, then stepped back to get into breeches
and shirt, while Veronique pulled a nightrobe over her gown.
Camille rushed in, his bicorne hat over one ear and his heavy
winter greatcoat buttoned crookedly.

"They've arrested F-Fabre. They came and took him during
the n-night."

"How did you find out?" Gilles asked.

"His m-mistress. She came to tell us after they questioned
her."

"Good God, she led him right to you—"

"N-no, he was arrested because of that damned worthless
East Indies Company stock. We Dantonists had n-nothing
to do with it."

"And you can thank God and Lucille for it. You would
have been up to your neck in it if it weren't for her."

"But F-Fabre! What shall we do?"

"Above all, don't connect Danton with him. I'll try to warn
Séchelles and some of the others."

Camille took note of Veronique for the first time, bowed
politely to her and wiped his face—though the gutters of rue
St.-Honoré were running with a rain that appeared to be half-
sleet, Camille was sweating.

"Gilles, you were r-right. Fabre's mistress says they arrested
Hébert late yesterday. I guess that's why—"

That was why today Robespierre could begin to destroy, one by one, those who had supported his greatest, and last, rival, Danton.

10

DURING the last days of winter, before the trial of Hébert, Veronique saw less and less of the hospital. She understood only too well the importance of swaying the public to Danton and moderation as other one-time powers in the Convention mounted the steps to the guillotine, often in groups of five, ten and even twenty. Each day Sanson's procession of tumbrils grew longer, usually rattling its way along the rue St.-Honoré, turning at the unfinished Church of the Madeleine and dumping its human cargo into the enormous Place de la Révolution, where there was a choice of last views: the fresh, budding greenery of the Champs-Elysées, or the crowded Tuileries Gardens; the river, or the cold exquisite stone of the Gabriel architecture bordering the square on the north.

To the Dantonists time was everything these days. They were being ripped away from their friends. Every day another friend arrested, and every day Danton's voice heard in the Convention and in the infinitely more powerful Jacobin Club, calling for an end to the Terror. While Camille wrote his cutting editorials, Gilles made his equally devastating sketches and Veronique spent much of her days going from the printer to the men and women who posted the sketches on the Paris walls.

The most effective of Gilles's drawings appeared as the first

signs of a green and lovely spring began to be seen everywhere
in the city. One could almost forget Sanson's now daily cargo
in studying the first budding trees along the Seine or in the
woods surrounding Paris. . . .

Veronique had just delivered copies of Marsan's latest,
most provocative sketch to the Auvergnat water seller for
posting on walls in the Honoré quarter near the Louvre when
she met Marie-Josette coming from the markets carrying a
basket of odds and ends with which, as she explained to
Veronique, "I'll be making a savory stew. With herbs one
can do wonders to disguise bad meat. . . ." She looked anxiously over her shoulder, a gesture common to everyone
these days. "Mam'selle, have you seen the placard on one of
the Louvre gates?"

"Really? What sort of placard?"

"A dreadful thing. It shows the executioner Sanson, or one
of his men, holding up a human head in one hand, and the
other one points straight at me. And beneath the placard
there was just one word—'NEXT!' " She bit her lip nervously.
"Isn't it horrible?"

"Horrible," Veronique took a breath and added, "unfortunately, it seems to be true."

Marie-Josette stared, then banished all such unpleasantness.
"Do come and have dinner. You and M'sieur Gilles never
eat our food anymore. Always busy, busy, not like your dear
mama. Bless her! She has such an appetite these days! One
wonders how she retains her youthful figure. . . ."

"Mama with a great appetite? How very odd. It must be
because she insists on working so hard."

As the two women walked to Jeannot's busy corner café,
Veronique persisted, "I've never known her to eat like that.
Is it often?"

"That I can't say. She usually has Jeannot or the scullery
maid bring a tray to her room. But she eats every bite. When
we collect the tray it's always empty."

Veronique said no more. The crowds had already gathered
along the street to watch the passing of the tumbrils led by
Sanson.

"Somebody important is to die today," whispered Marie-
Josette.

"Hébert."

"Dreadful man. But heavens, he was only condemned this
morning, wasn't he?"

"Speed appears to be Max Robespierre's watchword—"

"Careful, mam'selle."

The café's open doors were jammed with eager crowds, women stretching on tiptoe to see over the heads of men in front of them, a few youngsters jumping up and down. . . . Veronique hurried up the stairs to her mother's room, tried the door. It was bolted on the inside, which meant that her mother was home—strange . . . at this hour she was almost always at the hospital overseeing whatever supplies could be obtained for the patients' one genuine meal of the day.

"Mother! Are you there?"

The Vicomtesse didn't answer. Veronique tried the door again. "Let me in, I want to talk to you." Someone was inside. She could hear footsteps that hesitated at the door. Her worst suspicions were confirmed by those sounds. They were not her mother's light steps. She rapped on the door again. "Open the door. I know you're there—Mother!"

The bolt grated as it slid back and the door opened. A hand reached out, took hold of her wrist, pulled her inside, and she instantly recognized the lank, middle-aged street sweeper, complete with smudges on his aristocratic face and curved broomstraws in his free hand.

Veronique was wild with fury, and fear. "It seems that all my mother's food was for you, François! And of course you are the man who used my mother's herb pillow, and very nearly got her into Sanson's cart—"

His smile was still better suited to Versailles. "The Vicomtesse de Vaudraye is well bred. Surely, my dear Veronique, you would expect no less of her. She, at least, hasn't forgotten my martyred sister."

She looked at him, stunned by his seeming lack of awareness of his own part in his sister's death. She started to remind him of it, then realized that for him the guilt would always belong to those who'd destroyed his gilded world of Versailles, a world that was lost forever . . . as was his sister.

"I want you to leave here immediately," she told him, "and if you refuse I'll not hesitate a moment to report you to the Tribunal—"

"And send the Vicomtesse to keep me company in the tumbril? I doubt it . . . Veronique, listen to me. You may have turned *sans-culotte* for your precious Gilles Marsan, but you at least know me well enough to accept my word if I give it to you."

She was shaking with anger but forced herself to hear him out.

"I think you would be happier if the Vicomtesse were out of Paris. There are four orphans that we wish to get out of Paris as well."

"Mama's orphans."

"Exactly. Two of them are the children of distinguished aristocratic families. In the Meudon Woods they could be under the care of the Vicomtesse, until this regime is overthrown." He waved the broomstraws at the closed shutters over the window. She heard the roar of the mob rising in the street below, as Sanson's procession approached.

What had Couthon hinted? And Gilles as well? . . . *With his rival, Hébert, gone, Robespierre would be free to destroy Danton and clemency . . .*

"After Hébert's head," the Abbé reminded her, "will come Danton's. Then even Robespierre's. After that, the people will open their arms to us when we sweep in with the Austrian armies. You will see."

She turned her back to the spectacle in the street below. "François, do you really think the people of this country will return to the conditions of 1789?" But she could see that he did, or that memory of the worst of the Royalist rule had been wiped out and colored by the present horrors of Republican excess.

"Will you give me that precious word of yours that you will never see my mother again if I help get your orphans—and mother, of course—to Meudon?"

"My word as a gentleman."

She was inclined to believe him. But as she considered how to get passports to leave through one of the customs barriers, she asked him suddenly, "How long have you been in mama's room?"

"I assure you, it was quite proper. The good lady arranged a pallet for me in the alcove beyond that armoire—"

"Don't be ridiculous"—she forced herself not to smile—"I did not imply that I thought you were behaving immorally, my dear *abbé*." All the same, she had to get this thing done as soon as possible in order to keep anyone else from discovering the connection between a proscribed enemy of France and the one-time Vicomtesse de Vaudraye.

Her new problem at least blunted the apprehension with which she read Camille Desmoulins' third and fourth editions of *The Old Cordelier*. Borrowing from Danton's speeches in the Jacobins and the Convention, he called for an end to the omnipotent power of the Central Committee of Public Safety

—a direct attack on the triumvirate directing the government
—Robespierre, St.-Just and Couthon.

Veronique knew that Gilles and the others believed they
were swaying the people, and perhaps they were. But as
Couthon had reminded Gilles—did the people have any power
so long as Robespierre's triumvirate was in control? Gilles's
answer was: "We simply must work faster to change the
government." Whatever, their very lives, and those of hundreds of others depended on reducing Robespierre's awesome
power. . . .

It was several days before Veronique received her passports, and when she did they came unexpectedly, before she
asked for them. She had refused to make any move until the
Abbé left Paris, but when she received a sheet of paper from
Nantes, folded and sealed and bearing the Abbé's single
phrase . . . "Either Brittany is much changed or I am" . . .
she set about questioning Gilles on the matter of passports.
He agreed with her that the Vicomtesse would be safer outside
the city but it had become more and more difficult to get past
the barriers. She did not mention the Abbé.

On the last day of March she said goodbye to Gilles as
usual in front of the Hôtel-Dieu. They embraced, and, as
always, she stood there a minute or two watching him cross
the bridge. He looked back once and waved before he was
swallowed up by the busy Latin Quarter. In a short while he
would be working with Camille's printer, and afterward he
would eat at the Café Procope, and after that he . . .

"You love him very much," Couthon observed.

She had been so engrossed in her thoughts of Gilles that
she failed to hear the rasp of Couthon's rolling chair as he
moved up behind her.

"Citizen, I only wish I had known long ago how much I
loved him. We would not have wasted four precious years—"

"Wasted? As a Sister of Mercy?"

"I mean I should have married him then and become a
nurse as well."

"One of those drunken women who call themselves nurses?
I don't believe you. There's only one class of women who
should have the sick and suffering in their charge. The nuns.
I have never seen a genuine nurse who was not a nun—"He
stopped abruptly.

"Is there something wrong, may I help you?"

He tried to raise his hand, to wave aside her concern, but
he could sarcely do more than move his fingers. He did take

his condition with remarkable courage, she thought.

"I'm perfectly well, thank you. In my condition, to feel pain at all is to cheat my ailment. Veronique, despite your mother's past loyalties, I have, I confess, come to respect and admire her for her work here. As, indeed, I do you. Now, as you know, your mother has four children she cares for here. The orphans who sleep in the wards at night."

She was startled at his bringing up the subject but tried not to show it. "It does seem to be an unfortunate place for children . . ."

"I want you to remove these orphans from Paris. And your good mother with them." She tried to mumble her thanks, scarcely believing what she'd heard. He said sharply, "There is one provision. You must remove the children, and your mother immediately—today. Unlike you, she can be indiscreet. She could be in danger. . . . The passport papers. My pocket. Take them."

She touched him with an unsteady hand. Any second she expected him to retract his offer. Instead he added, "How far can you go? Your mother spoke of the Meudon Woods."

"Yes . . . and I could return tonight—"

"No, that's not necessary. Tomorrow will be fine. Or, better yet, remain at Meudon until your little family is settled." Then he added, suddenly, "And speaking of families, you are pregnant, are you not?"

She almost dropped the precious papers.

"Certainly not, so far as I know." She glanced down at her figure, which was thin as a lath. "What nonsense!"

"Perhaps. I have seen it before, that look about the eyes. A certain expression. No matter. Go this morning. Spend the time you need."

"I must let Gilles know I'm going to be out of the city today."

"I expect to be seeing him. I will convey your message. Those papers are dated today. Do not delay in leaving Paris."

"Thank you, my dear Monsieur Couthon, *thank you*." She kissed him quickly on the cheek. He made no sign that he'd felt her touch. Perhaps he hadn't. She squeezed the papers tightly in her fingers. "When Gilles returns for me, tell him I love him and I will see him tonight—"

"Tomorrow," he gently reminded her. "Tonight you will be returning too late to get past the barriers."

"We will see."

She hurried inside to gather up her mother along with the

three boys and a girl who made up the orphan group. Surprisingly, they were all ready for her. The Vicomtesse had bundled them as well as she could for the cold clear March day. The youngest boy was about eight, the oldest could not be more than twelve. The girl and the middle boy were slightly under twelve, Veronique thought, and it was the middle boy, green-eyed, mischievous-looking and prepared to enjoy the trip, who proved to be the only nonaristocrat of the group. He seemed proud of this.

"He's called Tavi—"

"Short for Octave," the boy put in.

"And a naughty boy, but we like him anyway, don't we, children?" the Vicomtesse went on, then presented the "young Duc de Castries, and this is the daughter of . . . Comte and Comtesse de la Platière, and the little nephew of Duc and Duchesse de St. Roche."

Veronique acknowledged the introductions impatiently and was about to go to look for a horse and carriage of some kind when the Vicomtesse assured her "that good Monsieur Couthon has provided us with a delightful cart and a highly intelligent beast to draw it."

It came as a shock to go out one of the small rear entrances of the hospital and find a horse harnessed to a cart that might have been, and probably was, one of Sanson's line-up of tumbrils.

"You had best sit with me," Veronique suggested to her mother. "And the children can play on the straw in the tumbril."

This suited everyone, and besides, all except young Tavi were too frightened of the world around them to make any arguments. Veronique had not handled the reins since she'd left Normandy on the last day of April in faraway 1789, a lifetime ago. It felt good to do so now.

"François is wrong to think he can ever turn the clock back to the old days," she said, breaking the silence imposed by the difficulty of maneuvering through traffic to the Right Bank.

Her mother remarked airily, "Do you think so?" And Veronique realized that the Vicomtesse also still lived, at least partly, in her own world . . . an old world that in her rosy remembrance still was possible . . . even though it had never really existed.

As Veronique had hoped, they reached the barrier at a time when the Customs Officials, awe-inspiring in their huge black-plumed hats, were busy discussing the list of the day's condemned. Seeing Georges Couthon's signature among those on the passes, they saluted Veronique, called, "Good day, patriot," and let her go on.

In the early spring countryside Veronique breathed more freely. Everywhere she looked, from the burned and deserted great houses to the fields that had lain fallow, spring was beginning to spread the bright green look of new life, and with it she felt surges of hope for the future.

The children got into a tussle and began to throw straw at each other, which the Vicomtesse assured Veronique was a sign of their happiness at the notion of living in the Meudon Woods, far from the tensions of Paris. Like the children and her mother, Veronique was finally conquered by the bright country atmosphere. Optimism always came to her with spring, she thought. Hadn't she met Gilles in the spring?"

By mid-afternoon she was in such good spirits she allowed the boys to take their turn at the reins and sat back, enjoying their pride and gaiety, wondering too if Couthon had been right. *Was* she to have Gilles's child? Since her excommunication more than a year ago, the Church considered her dead to salvation. But while her life was hedged by Gilles's love, she could banish all fears of damnation.

It was different with Gilles. He talked often of their children, who would be a living proof of their unity, and would exist long after their parents were dust. It was Gilles who would never allow their children to be illegitimate; yet how could they expect a priest to imperil his own position with the Holy See by performing their marriage? She had known when she was excommunicated that she would never be permitted any comforts of the Church, but Gilles . . .

. . . We'll have to discuss it when I return home tonight, she thought—perhaps they could find a Protestant clergyman one day, but not while the anticlerical Terror ruled in Paris. . . . Gilles's child. A magic thought. She hugged herself.

Late in the afternoon they reached the gatehouse, where the Meudon Woods met the ancient Vaudraye property near Versailles, and the children went wild with delight at the prospect of roaming those secret forest paths. The little two-story house was stocked with winter vegetables, salt meats. The Vicomtesse smiled at Veronique's surprise—and at a pale young woman with blond hair swept severely back and knotted on the nape of her neck—Yolande Berthelot.

Veronique was stunned at the changes in her. She quickly

recovered and said, "I had no chance to thank you that night you tried to save my life—"

Yolande waved away her gratitude. "I want no part of their vileness in Paris. They made a monster of my brother and then executed him for playing his part too well. I had some bad weeks, I can tell you, after that. I loathed his friends. Then your mother found me at Hôtel-Dieu. There had been no work. Nothing. The Vicomtesse saved my life. Well, now perhaps we are all quits. . . ."

"She will be the housekeeper, my love," the Vicomtesse put in proudly, "and *I* shall be the cook. We intend to teach the children manners and the habits of a gentleman, or a lady. The dear Abbé arranged it all before he went off to fight for the rebels in Brittany. . . ."

Yolande put in, "There are a few neighbors, but those are discreet."

Veronique showed them Couthon's signature on the passports. "We have his approval for you to live here. It counts for a great deal."

The two apparently so different women seemed to get on very well together. Pleased by this, and as it was growing dark, Veronique went out, enticed the good-natured horse away from its fodder and left for Paris in a mood of profound gratitude. Half of her worries had been cleared away, and when she returned to Paris the other half of her nightmare fears would likewise be lifted. It was springtime, a time of new birth. Everything was possible.

With a much smaller load, the horse now trotted along over the roads still muddy from the winter rains, and Veronique found herself at the Paris barriers just as they were being closed for the night. The magic name of "Couthon" provided instant entry into the city, after which she called to the horse, "Hurry, Lad, we've no time for dallying!"

It was late. The supper hour was long gone but every café she passed seemed to be crowded with patrons. The doors of wine shops stood open, as if inviting in more of those groups wandering aimlessly through the streets. The lamp laws had provided for illumination so that there were no pools of light between long curtains of darkness. Chronic complainers said it was also easier for thieves to see their victims. Tonight each bit of lamplight seemed filled with groups of men and women speaking in low, hushed voices.

As Sister Veronique she had walked all over Paris at the darkest hours and never seen the phenomenon she noticed this night. A curious desire for company seemed to have swept over people. They drank but remained quiet, talking furtively, with nervous glances at each other and their neighbors—even during the worst of the September Massacres in '92 life had generally gone on much as usual.

No, she had never seen this before, as though a kind of stupor had gripped people who at other times were the most volatile individualists in the world. She called out to the horse. The cart rattled through the streets, past the Place de la Révolution, where men with broomstraws and cloth were cleaning way as best they could signs of the day's work. She avoided their long, grotesque shadows, gave the signal over the reins and turned up toward the rue St.-Honoré. She knew it would be necessary to return the horse and cart to the stables near the hospital but hoped to catch a glimpse of Gilles as she passed Jeannot's corner café.

Their room was dark. The café, though filled with patrons, seemed very quiet. Gilles had probably gone to the Cour du Commerce to spend the evening with the Desmoulins .or the Dantons.

At the stables she mentioned Couthon's name, and was given a quick look and a nod. She started to the Left Bank and up through hushed, dark streets to the Cour du Commerce. It was not until she raised her hand to knock at the Desmoulins' door and found it standing ajar that she suddenly knew what had happened.

Lucille came running blindly across the room. She saw Veronique and stopped, trembling. "I beg your pardon. I thought they might have released him. Max was always very fond of him, you know . . ."

The agony of that attempt at self-assurance caught at Veronique's throat. She whispered, "Arrested? And the—the others?"

Lucille nodded, reached for Camille's desk and caressed the surface with her eyes closed. Tears trailed out beneath her lashes.

"Oh, Veronique, they wouldn't even let me go with him! And my Camille put such a bold face on it, even though he was so frightened . . . so terribly . . . terribly frightened. . . ."

Veronique stood there staring about the warm comfortable room. She had the sensation of being somewhere far off from the world. She was caught in the tentacles of a nightmare and could not seem to free herself until Lucille's voice called to her.

"Do you feel faint? Veronique!"

"I'm quite well, it was the warm room . . . after the cold outside." She fought to pull herself together, frightened of her weakness just when strength would be most needed. "How did it happen?"

"You mustn't worry too much, Veronique. Max will help them. He only wants to frighten them."

"Yes. How did it happen?"

"Your Gilles was trying to persuade Danton to leave Paris until they had enough votes in the Convention to repeal the Law of Suspects. But you know Georges-Jacques. He wouldn't hear of it. Then the soldiers came. And they came here afterward and took Camille too. I tried to follow them but they wouldn't let me near him. . . ."

Veronique touched her arm in a vague attempt at consolation she did not believe in herself. "Gilles and Danton are with him. They will keep up his spirits. Do you think the people will stand for this? There isn't a man in France that the people love as much as Georges Danton. . . . And everyone knows Camille was the man who first lit the torch against the old regime that day in the Palais-Royal. . . ."

Veronique looked down at her own twisting hands. The knife scars had begun to ache. She could not remain in this suddenly stifling room. There must be something. Someone who could help. There were Danton's friends in the Convention. And her own friends, those people who were grateful for her help in the hospital. . . .

"I'll go to Couthon, he helped me only this morning . . ."

. . . and that night joined in signing Gilles Marsan's death warrant. . . . Not knowing, she could not allow herself to think the worst of him, or his motives—no doubt kind ones, in *his* view—in trying to get her out of the city and keeping her out long enough for . . . If she did that, he was lost to her as an aid . . . lost to Gilles. Gilles . . . oh, my God . . .

Encouraged by Veronique's show, Lucille said, "I might be able to reach Max. Think of it—Horace's godfather . . . surely he would never allow anything to happen—"

Veronique stopped at the door to ask, "Who signed the warrants? Does Robespierre's name appear?"

"Everyone on the Committee signed. But I'm certain Max didn't want to, he signed very small, I'm told, in one corner."

How like the little man, thought Veronique, but she did not say so aloud. She turned. The two women embraced. "You'll see," Lucille said, "it must all go well. . . . My parents

have Horace with them and I shall go and talk with Max.
. . . Do you know, the soldiers who arrested Danton were
afraid of him? If Georges hadn't gone with them I do think
they might well have turned and run—"

"I wish to God *he* had run. And Gilles with him. . . . I
must go, there's so little—" She broke off, feeling icy terror
at her own thoughts. *So little time.* Under the law of Suspects
they could be condemned in the morning and executed the
same day. Robespierre would never dare to give Danton time.

11

WITH EMOTIONS numbed, Veronique stood against the gallery railing in the "Hall of Liberty" of the Palais de Justice, almost smothered by the press of fascinated citizens around her. Sometimes it was difficult to see the room below, ill-lit in part by the window that looked out upon a passage in the Conciergerie, that ante-chamber to the guillotine. At the far end of the hall and facing her were the judges, each of whom owed his promotion to Robespierre or his henchman, St.-Just. Beside the judges' bench was the tiered prisoners' dock, and across the room sat the jury, hand-picked for their known opposition to Danton or clemency.

Perhaps the most dangerous man the prisoners had to face was the public prosecutor, Fouquier-Tinville, whose lean, saturnine face was well suited to his costume, the severe black robe and the black hat with its great funereal plumes. Staring at this man who was a cousin of Camille Desmoulins, Veronique wondered if Camille remembered that day long ago when he asked Danton to "give Fouquier, my poor, unemployed cousin, some kind of job. . . ."

Before the prisoners were brought in, the audience around Veronique buzzed with the gossip of the previous day. While she had been vainly searching for Couthon and then others who had given her help in the hospital, the city had begun to collect stories about their hero. It was as if they hoped to expiate the crime of their own cowardice by reminding the world of their leader's quick tongue.

"Our Danton actually wanted to appear before the Tribunal. He said last night, 'Now we shall see the figures these fellows will cut when they appear before us.' You see? It's really the judges—the Incorruptible's men—who are on trial."

Veronique heard the laughter spread through the gallery. A woman matched the first voice: "I hear that when he met his friends in the cells the old Titan said, 'I hoped to get you out. Instead, I got in myself. . . .'"

Another voice: "And he told them . . . but he meant all of us . . . 'If common sense doesn't win, this is nothing to what you will see. The river will run with blood.'"

There was a sputter of laughter but most of the Gallery was frightened. This struck too close to their own necks.

A woman beside Veronique whispered to her, "They do say, citizeness, that if Fouquier-Tinville and the president of the judges don't get convictions, there's a warrant already signed for their own arrest. . . ."

Veronique looked around, raising her voice. "The people have the power to stop it. Don't they know they will be next?"

She got blank stares, dull eyes, anxious little nudges. Silence.

The prisoners were escorted in: Danton first, then his followers, with Camille looking outrageously young and boyish between Gilles Marsan and the Dantonist general, Westermann. The tiers of the dock were filled with speculators and stock manipulators—a clear effort to bring the Dantonists down to the level of common thieves. The idea of their being charged all together fooled no one in the gallery. A dozen hands pointed out Danton's motions, his grin, head high, the fact that he actually was telling his friend Delacroix a joke at this moment of life and death.

"What an ugly devil! I do like an ugly man!" one of the market women confided to her neighbor.

Veronique's eyes were on Gilles. He looked calm, slightly pale, and was saying something to Camille with the help of Westermann, who had lost a battle against overwhelming numbers of the enemy and wound up in the dock to defend his life.

Camille nodded, his lips twisting nervously.

When the prisoners answered the roll, he shouted with a

surprising defiance, "Name? Camille Desmoulins. Age? Thirty-three. The age of the *sans-culotte* Jesus Christ when he died. It is a critical age for patriots." Still wonderfully, hopelessly vainglorious . . .

The gallery's roar of delight was cut off by the row of black-plumed judges facing them. Like so many crows on a fence, thought Veronique.

"Georges-Jacques Danton? Address?"

"Soon it may be the beyond. And my name? Consult the pantheon of history. I daresay you will not find yours there."

Were they all mad, Veronique asked herself, deliberately to joke at such a time? But she looked over at the jury and saw how soon even these men, sworn to do their duty by Robespierre's wishes, had come under the spell of the prisoners they were to condemn. Half the jury was nudging the other half, laughing, slapping a knee, nodding a head in sympathy with the remarks of the prisoners. It would be difficult to condemn men with whom they had laughed. And a man who faced death with a laugh was certain to be admired. . . .

The crowd's roar of approval was less easily silenced this time. They kept murmuring . . . "He's going to give us a show, our Old Titan, a show good as anything at the Theatre Feydeau . . ."

Veronique concentrated on somehow attracting Gilles's attention, willing him to look up and see her. He raised his dark head. Without realizing it, she'd pressed her knuckles against her mouth. He saw her and smiled. He understood, put his own knuckles to his lips and in that fraction of time she felt his presence, his touch, as vividly as if he were beside her.

"Gilles Marsan? Occupation?"

"A painter of walls."

The gallery had never had such a good time. They talked among themselves, not troubling to lower their voices.

"That placard of Sanson pointing to you and saying 'Next' . . . that's his work, gave you the chills . . ."

"I saw one before the Bastille days . . . a starving girl and the Austrian's diamond necklace . . . I remember—"

"Silence!"

The terror.

Fouquier-Tinville brought forth his evidence. St.-Just had gathered together against Danton a hodgepodge of charges in which the manipulation of India Company stocks appeared and were read in the most shamefaced way by one of Danton's acquaintances. Danton got to his feet.

"Do you actually believe we are traitors? Look at him! He laughs. Record it, you! Record that the witness laughed."

The Hall of Liberty was like a rope pulled taut as it would stretch. There were hums of agreement each time the Titan opened his mouth, and worse was to come for the public prosecutor. Danton began to name witnesses in his own defense, and in defense of his comrades.

Veronique gripped the railing until her fingers were stiff. She watched as Fouquier-Tinville looked up at the presiding judge, his forefinger against his throat . . . muzzle the dangerous orator . . . silence him legally or . . .

His pantomime was clear to Veronique and to most others present.

"Where is Robespierre? Couthon! St.-Just!" Danton was thundering. "I don't see them here. Miserable traitors! Show yourselves and I'll tear away your masks!"

The bell for silence rattled away, a tinkle against cannonfire.

The presiding judge tried to make himself heard.

Fouquier-Tinville tugged at the judge's sleeve, made the gesture to his throat again.

Veronique wondered if he were reminding the judge that signed death warrants waited for them both if the Dantonists were not convicted?

Her next thoughts were prayers—so close, so very close to acquittal. . . .

Danton was shouting. "In three months the people will tear my enemies to pieces!"

To the consternation of the judges, this was greeted with piercing agreement by the crowd. "Aye! It is so, count on it!"

The presiding judge scribbled a hasty note to Fouquier-Tinville. No mistaking the prosecutor's relief. Meanwhile Danton roared on, playing to the gallery and the jury—yet always with that truth they recognized through the joke.

"Me? A conspirator? Everyone knows I am too busy kissing my wife every night—" He looked up at the gallery. "You up there—*you* are the people. When I have presented my case it is you who must judge me."

Amid the cheers of the crowd the judges rose. The bell was rung for silence.

"Until the prisoner can continue in greater calm and tranquility, this Tribunal is adjourned."

"No!" Veronique cried out, her voice drowned by the

confusion around her, the predictions everywhere of what Danton would do to the Tribunal tomorrow when his witnesses were heard.

But Veronique was terrified. She had seen the looks and the note passed between judge and prosecutor. Could they afford to let Danton be heard again? Their own lives were in the balance.

When she got out onto the quai again she was surprised to see the bright April sunlight. Along the Pont Neuf everyone seemed to be talking of the trial. People—men, women, children—talked of the great distances from which they'd been able to hear the Titan's voice.

"I heard him from this bridge."

"I heard him from the end of the bridge."

"No. Farther. I was outside the Café du Parnasse and I heard him."

It was unbelievable, but so much about the Titan was unbelievable. Perhaps he could win, after all. And with him, the lives of Gilles and Camille.

Veronique stood on the quai and stared up at the towers of the Conciergerie with their own ominous dark caps. Somewhere behind those thousand-year-old walls Gilles would be talking now with Camille and Danton and the rest, going over the day, so near to victory that they might need only one more session to be freed . . . except perhaps the people would not rise to defend them. . . . They were human after all, and they were afraid. But their great voice would finally give them victory . . . all that was needed was a little time, one more hearing. . . .

Veronique whispered, I am with you every minute, my darling.

The crowd pushed her along the quai, and she thought of the hospital across the Ile de la Cité. Would Couthon be there now? It was still worth the chance. She began to run. Everywhere the city seemed to be in the grip of panic. She was jostled and knocked about but hardly noticed. She heard voices talking about the Dantonists. . . .

"Wait and see, the Dantonists can't be killed, not with the old Titan, wait and see . . ."

But it was this remark so often repeated that unnerved her. To wait and see was the danger. Robespierre moved fast.

She did not find Couthon at the hospital but was told that he and Robespierre and St.-Just would be working into the night at the Palais de l'Egalité, in former days called the Tuileries.

"Citizen Couthon wishes to speak with you privately tonight," one of the ex-nuns told her confidentially. If Couthon wished to see her, it could literally be the answer to her prayers.

While she counted the hours until she could see Couthon, she went up to find Lucille and tell her of her fresh hopes. The Desmoulins apartment was empty and still torn up after its examination by Fouquier-Tinville's agents.

Louise Danton had returned from a fruitless effort to see Robespierre. Her young face was mottled with weeping, but she said at once, "Georges told me I am very good with his little boys. I left them with a neighbor and I must go and get them now. They are all I have."

"And you don't know what has happened to Lucille?"

"We were both frantic when we tried to see Citizen Robespierre. We stood in the Duplays' little courtyard and screamed. Lucille even cursed him. She reminded him that he was Camille's friend, the godfather of his son Horace . . . the guards drove us away. I don't suppose he even heard us. . . ."

Veronique returned through the Latin Quarter. No one had seen Lucille Desmoulins since that hour in front of Robespierre's lodgings, but Veronique tried to tell herself there were a thousand harmless things that could have happened . . . she couldn't think of a single one of them.

By the time she reached the Tuileries on the Right Bank, the frantic comings and goings of all manner of men told her that panic had seized the Robespierre Triumvirate. Everyone in the Tuileries appeared to be terrified of an uprising by "the people." A Dantonist rally was expected within a day or two. . . .

"In a week we'll all be in Sanson's basket," one of the guards muttered as he and his comrade passed Veronique. "That damned Titan simply doesn't know how to die—"

"Work, work . . . I'd not be Couthon, to save my neck!" the other said. "Let's go and have a glass or two of the bloodred. By that time old Couthon may be willing to be lugged home."

It was, she told herself, the beginnings of good fortune, for a change. But as she started in through the great portals of the palace she saw the green-clad figure of Robespierre flanked by the tall, coldly handsome St.-Just, and two National Guards. She backed into the twilight shadows until they had passed. Others were patrolling the great hall, but when they had turned and started in the opposite direction she made her way up the wide staircase to Couthon's severely functional office. She had visited here on occasion to ask favors for the hospital, but never had so much depended upon her persuasive powers.

The guards had passed his door and she slipped in so quietly she was sure he'd not heard her . . . until he spoke, although she saw only his back.

"This would be Sister Veronique, would it not?"

"How did you know?"

"You'd been asking for me. And then, too, I know the faint slap of those convent sandals you always wear." With a grimace of pain he managed to manipulate the rolling chair around toward her. His face lacked that anxious, apprehensive look that seemed common to all of Robespierre's allies tonight. She also thought he looked sad, as he did when a patient unexpectedly died.

"Citizeness, you were mistaken to come back to Paris. I asked you to remain away."

"You knew! That morning when you sent me away——"

"I had just signed the warrant for Marsan's arrest, yes. But he . . . these men have plotted rebellion. They are a danger to the State——"

"A danger to Maximilien Robespierre and his dictatorship."

"I told you, he is the last hope of our Revolution . . . but no matter"—he tried to make a small gesture with one hand but failed to move more than his fingers—"it's important that you leave Paris very soon. I have stifled the Leplon woman, but others may not."

"The Leplon woman is actually Lise de Gleeb, the widow of a gamekeeper who shot and killed starving peasants and was hired to murder Gilles Marsan. Madame de Gleeb helped to place false evidence against innocent people. The citizens of Vaudraye will testify to it."

He looked relieved, somewhat to her surprise. Was he still her friend then?

"Good. That will serve. Otherwise it might be a trifle difficult to explain why you are not under arrest with . . . the others."

"The others?"

He paused. "Yes, the others. I cannot save your Dantonists. It is their lives or ours now."

"You *are* afraid, you're not different from the others . . .

you know that Georges Danton will win the minute his witnesses are heard—"

He tried to shift the wheels of his chair, studied them. "Can you tell me what there is left for me to fear? Please tell me . . ."

"I am sorry. I hoped for too much. I thought we might have remained friends . . . goodbye, *citizen.*"

"Stay a moment. There. Take that paper beneath my ink standish." She hesitated, then pushed the standish aside, picked up the folded sheet. . . . It's an order for Citizeness Zephine Fermeil, an agent of mine, to visit Gilles Marsan in the hope of extracting information about Dantonist plots to overthrow the government . . . there actually is a Zephine Fermeil, so take care that you are discreet."

"Why do you allow me to see him now? Do you worry they're about to win their freedom—"

"You ask too many questions."

He sat there, staring at the paper in her hand. "You are a woman of courage and great use to the state. France needs you. Whatever may come to your life, you and your child must survive."

"My child? Even if you are right, I can hardly think of that now—"

"Tell Marsan the truth. If you won't do so, then someone should. I have been a father. I know. It will mean more to him than any other news you *may* bring him at this moment."

"My God"—she forced back the tears—"what are they *guilty* of? You know they are good patriots."

"They are guilty of many things. Danton has spoken out against the Law of Suspects. Desmoulins has demanded clemency for prisoners in time of war. Your Marsan has produced antigovernment propaganda. They have associated with well-known criminal speculators such as Fabre and that tribe. . . ." His voice trailed off wearily.

"They can prove they are patriots, the only prisoners they ask clemency for are those who've had no trial and will be given no chance to bring witnesses to their defense. At least wait until you hear their witnesses."

He considered his nearly useless fingers. "It will be found impossible to hear Danton's witnesses in the Tribunal tomorrow. Their trial is over. Tonight a plot to destroy the Republic has been uncovered—a plot to empty the prisons and rescue the Dantonists."

"And where was this plot hatched? In the offices of the

Tuileries? In the brain of Max Robespierre?"

"In the brain of St.-Just, I believe"—his voice struck her as obscenely gentle—"it has been decided that a woman organized the plot, a person of great ferocity. Her name is Lucille Desmoulins. Needless to say she has been in custody since early today." He recited the outrageous account almost sadly, as if by rote.

"And when did the *plot* occur? While she was in custody?"

"St.-Just has been working out the details. A promising dramatist was lost when he chose the law."

She drew away from him. He seemed a living mask of death, coldly foretelling what was to come.

"So they are to have no defense . . . they are already condemned—"

"Officially, that will occur tomorrow. And afterwards, the penalty, as you are aware, is death within twenty-four hours." His image shifted and blurred before her eyes, but his matter-of-fact, dead voice brought her back to the present. "Remember this," he went on, only his eyes alive, "we can never go back. I know you cannot accept this, but what has been done, what will be done, is for France, for our Republic. It is terrible, yes. The past was worse. The future . . . I have done the only thing I can do to help you. Few could get you into the Conciergerie. Make the most of your few moments. . . . You and I will not meet again. Do not ask to see me. This will be *our* farewell, Sister Veronique."

She took up the pass, went to the door and stopped. "When they carry you to the lunette—when *you* hear the blade fall—I will be watching. Farewell, citizen."

And she left him.

12

THE LONG wait was over.

"Your pass gives you ten minutes with the condemned. Enter, citizeness." The young guardsman was not unsympathetic as he sent Veronique through a half-door into a Conciergerie passage that blinded her after the hours of waiting in the April sunshine.

"Sanson will be here any minute with his shears," one of the gunners, a soldier, told her in a low voice. There were guards and soldiers everywhere throughout this honeycomb of tiny cells, labyrinthine passages and dark courts that smelled of mold and age. The gunner was grizzled and had a big moustache. He looked like many of the men she had helped to treat at the hospitals scattered throughout Paris, but he reminded her now, in a whisper, "You were good to me once, Sister. They wanted to saw off my arm after the street riots in '92 but you wouldn't let them. So you're Zephine What's-Her-Name, if you say so."

Guards had been collecting the prisoners in the shadows behind a wooden grill. There was a worn, three-legged stool that a *sans-culotte* in a red Phrygian bonnet brushed off with great flourishes.

"One of Sanson's men," the gunner told her. "It's where *they* sit while they're being sheared. Don't look that way."

She scarcely heard him. There was a familiar step behind her, the sound of Gilles's boots grating on the stone floor. As she started to turn, his arms caught her and she felt his cheek and his lips warm against her cold, trembling mouth. She clung to him, praying to die now. Time must stop. Let her world end with his. There was nothing after he had gone.

As always, he read her thoughts and, miraculously, he knew what she only suspected.

"My dearest darling—don't. This isn't the end for us. There *is* our child. In all of eternity God couldn't have given us a greater gift—"

She looked up, tried to gain that control which had been her great asset. "Couthon told you? He could tell you this, and not save you—"

"Sweetheart, would I have saved him? . . . I don't know. . . . One of his soldiers, a gunner, told me this morning and ever since I've been walking these floors in a daze, smiling like a madman. Our daughter. Our son. Don't you see? Our lives—my life—weren't lived for nothing. We did something for the world, for ourselves. And now we leave something for those who will come after us."

"I don't care a damn about the world and the future. . . . Gilles, I want to be with you."

He caressed her face, trying to bring his own warmth to her chilled flesh. "Veronique, try to understand. It can't die with me. You will go on, you will see what we have done. Darling, we conquered the divinity of petty kings, and one day, when this is over, the people will rule themselves. Danton believes in the future. I do, too—"

A steel door slammed somewhere. A voice boomed out, "Damme! It'll be big game today. Line them up. My shears, boy!"

For the first time Veronique felt Gilles's hands tremble as they tightened around her. "Sanson. It's time—"

"No! Listen to me, Gilles . . . I want to go with you. I need only say something . . . 'Down with Robespierre,' anything . . . let me go with you. *Please* . . ."

He raised her chin with his palm. She had never seen him as severe, not even when they had parted on the night of her father's death. "Veronique, in my heart you are my wife. *And you will obey me.*" His dark eyes seemed to glow in the dim light. "If you and our child live, I live. Can you understand that?"

Unable to speak, she nodded.

"Swear to me that you will pray for our child."

She knew he was asking her to let the child, and herself, live.

"Time, citizeness," the gunner interrupted, clearing his throat.

"I swear it," she finally said.

Gilles enclosed her in his arms. In her long hours of waiting she had pictured a kiss, a passionate union and then nothingness. But in the end, their last embrace became a different kind of unity . . . of his heartbeat—strong—and of hers. And of his kiss, full of his love, the kind they had known a hundred times at a hundred daily partings. There could be none better.

"Listen to me, my darling," he said as his name was called again and two guardsmen separated her from him, "When it comes, I won't be thinking of it. I will be thinking of you . . . *remember*."

The gunner faced her away from the prisoner, took her arm and walked with her along the passage. Behind her there were conversations, laughter, jokes going about at the wooden grill and around the stool where each prisoner sat for Sanson's barbering.

There was a harsh burst of laughter, and one of the prisoners called out, "Damn it, Danton, that laugh of yours will be the death of you—"

And Danton's reply: "What does it matter? I've drunk my fill, spent my money, known good women—it's time to get some rest."

More laughter. And then, as Veronique moved past a guardsman with his rifle at the ready, the gloomy halls rang with Camille's . . . "Lucille, Lucille . . . *help me*—"

Veronique stumbled. The gunner tried to get her to her feet, muttering, "They say his wife will be brought in after he's gone. Seems a shame, somehow. Why not let 'em go together?"

Veronique reached out blindly for the stone wall, pulled herself up, shocking the gunner with her words, said in an expressionless voice, "I envy her."

Staring up into the courtyard she saw three tumbrils ahead of her, the horses pawing nervously at the paving stones. A pallid little man in a red mob cap and a blue, white and red smock over *sans-culotte* pantaloons made his way through the crowd on the steps of the Palais de Justice and passed Veronique. I know that man, she thought indifferently, though not in that awful costume.

Someone in the mob on the steps hurled a stone over into the little passage where the prisoners would leave the Conciergerie for the tumbrils in the courtyard above. The stone brushed Veronique's face. She touched the bruise above her eye.

. . . If I might die now, before it is over . . .

Above her there were shouts, anger and scuffling. "Let be! There's no aristos barbered today!"

And a woman's cry—"They're taking *us* now, don't you see? The old Titan's one of *us*. They hadn't ought to send this batch. It's wrong. . . ."

Veronique raised her head, then her momentary hope was gone. She moved up into the courtyard as someone else called, "Be quiet. You'll rattle yourself into the basket if you talk like that—"

And others joined in. "No talk or they'll have us all. . . . Here they come. Danton! Desmoulins—"

"Desmoulins!" a girl called out. "I was with you that day in the Palais-Royal. You set us all on fire. . . ."

"Westermann. Séchelles. There's Marsan. He showed us the truth in his pictures—"

The guardsmen pushed Veronique back. Gunners came on the run. She looked over their heads. "I must remember everything about him, his face, the way he walks, the way his hand goes out to give me strength. I must never forget. Not any single detail. . . ."

Gilles looked strange and remote with his long queued hair sheared off above the nape of his neck. And she had forgotten that the prisoners would have their hands bound.

A nervous attendant had bound Danton's wrists too tightly behind him. Across his massive chest the buttons on his jacket were almost pulled out of their buttonholes. He was trying to calm Camille, who had struggled so desperately his coat was nearly torn off. Westermann talked quietly to Gilles, who did not hear him as he kept looking into the crowd. Searching.

Fabre d'Eglantine was saying, "I'll never finish my 'Maltese Orange.' . . . Such beautiful verses . . . that thief Billaud is sure to steal it and be acclaimed a great poet. . . ."

Veronique moved, struggled against the backs of the guards. Gilles saw her. His face softened with his smile. He continued watching her until he was pulled up into the last tumbril, and then he looked for her once again. Danton too was looking. He sighed, turned and tried to see over the crowd and out into the street. Camille had to call his name several times before he heard.

"You see? A lock of my Lucille's hair. Don't let it fall out of my hands when they—*promise*, Danton." At the end she was still his strength.

"Yes, old lad, I promise." For the first time the mob saw the man beneath Danton's bold front. He could keep his friends' courage up, but there were grim thoughts of his own that must occupy him. The cords in his heavy neck stood out. He closed his eyes and then, as Camille called his name again in panic, he opened them, looked out over the rooftops to the April sky. Was he remembering the blue skies of Champagne in autumn, the skies he had left to return to Paris and the fight? Those pleasant, dreamy days in Arcis with Louise and the boys?

He shrugged, laughed. "Here's a verse for you, Fabre. Rhyme this little ride."

Sanson got up on his plank seat, looked around. It was four o'clock. He waved his whip. His cart pulled away. Then the second. The third and last tumbril carried the friends— Danton, Desmoulins, Séchelles, Marsan and other Dantonists. The crowd did not leave until the third tumbril moved out.

Veronique reached the street, where she came once more on the pale man in the red mob cap.

"Sister Veronique?"

She looked at him blindly.

"Father Neu. I used to give a little help when I could in the Hôtel-Dieu. They found me out, I hadn't taken the oath, you see."

The little priest who had been afraid of François's noises in the death room of the hospital. "What are you doing here?"

"I promised Madame Danton I would follow the tumbril to the end, with prayers for the dying."

"Let me follow you, Father."

The crowd had thinned out on the Pont au Change, but lines were gathered on the Right Bank, up the alley past the Café du Parnasse, scene of so many of Veronique's well remembered days and nights.

All along the ancient twisting streets toward the long rue St.-Honoré the people watched. The priest walked rapidly, cutting through alleys as if anxious to have done with this task. There was a stillness about the movements of those who witnessed the procession, and then there were cheers for the Dantonists. The soldiers watched, noted, but did nothing as they marched between the crowd and the procession. Shutters in the houses along the way began to close as Sanson approached. Grim faces peered up from the crowd. Angry men and women were thrust back by rifle butts and bayonets.

Once Camille, his long tangled hair hacked short, leaned over the back of the tumbril and called to the crowd: "They are destroying us! They have lied to you! They—"

Gilles tried to calm him, said something to him quietly. He swallowed, nodded and braced himself.

Veronique and the priest cut through the crowd lining the rue St.-Honoré before the Duplay house, where Robespierre lived. The shutters were tightly closed.

The tumbrils moved slowly. One could have walked past them as they moved along the curving street. In the third cart, as they passed the Duplay house, Danton's voice reverberated against the shuttered windows:

"Max, it is useless to hide. You will follow me, *citizen* . . ."

The hum of approval through the crowd swelled. Did the little man hear that promise for his future? Veronique broke through the barrier of guards and ran beside the tumbril for a minute before a gun butt drove her off. She'd wanted to give Gilles some gesture, some memory, promise. . . . Too late. He could not see her.

Sanson in the first cart raised his whip. The procession turned in front of the unfinished Madeleine, and those in the tumbrils caught their first sight of the great crowded square that was the end of their journey, the Place de la Révolution. With a few others Veronique followed in the wake of the last tumbril. She was not certain Gilles had seen her, but he still looked back over the crowd, searching. The procession pulled into the Square over the moat bridge, Sanson whirling his whip overhead to clear the way through the massed troops and the mob behind them. Turning the sharp corner into the one-time rue Royale, Veronique saw the tall parallel shafts reaching into the afternoon sky behind Gilles's head. She called his name, raised her two hands, clasped them as in a prayer.

He had said, "Swear to me that you will pray for our child." She did so now.

The carts, one by one, were swallowed by the square of soldiers formed around the scaffold, but before the third tumbril rattled in to disappear behind the rows of uniforms Gilles saw her, and in that brief moment she was certain he understood the meaning of her clasped hands.

She heard Father Neu beside her. No one stopped him, though he was obviously praying.

It was nearly sunset. A single sound filled the Square. The rattle of wooden uprights. An instant of silence. The throng in the Square held its breath. The quick whirr of steel falling.

"One!"

Father Neu struggled to hold Veronique. She thought she heard Gilles call once. "Veronique—"

The square of soldiers cut off her last view as Gilles was pulled out of the tumbril. How many had Sanson counted?

Fabre . . . Westermann . . . Séchelles . . . Desmoulins . . .

Father Neu's lips were moving, his voice barely audible. "I, thy unworthy servant, Georges-Jacques Danton, have sinned . . . I have grievously sinned . . . Forgive me, O Lord . . ."

She whispered a prayer of her own, dictated by her own heart . . . "Dear Lord, be with Gilles now. Be with him . . ."

The last rays of the sun plunged suddenly behind the distant woods of the Champs-Elysées.

The Titan's voice carried across the great Square. "Sanson, show them my head. By God, it's worth looking at!"

The last rattle of the uprights. The last whirr of steel falling. . . .

And Veronique thought, "I don't even know when he left me . . . I will never know. . . ."

A sound like a great sigh spread through the mob. Someone shouted, "Long live the Republic!"

Others answered, "Danton gave us the Republic!"

And a few began to sing the Marseille soldiers' song. Then others took up the march as they poured out of the Square and dusk covered the place where life was now gone.

Epilogue

January, 1795

SHE HAD been here six months now. They had given her the east bedchamber upstairs in the gatehouse because even here in the Meudon Woods she could not bear to look at the sunset. Seared on her brain was the memory of the two visits she had made to the great square in Paris at sunset—when finally Couthon and the hated Robespierre had gone under the blade . . . as Danton had prophesied. And before, when Gilles . . .

"His boy will be a child of the morning," she told her mother firmly. "And if I am alive to say so, he will never set foot in the Place de la Révolution."

To all of which the Vicomtesse agreed. When Yolande Berthelot stood by after smoothing the bed coverlet and said rather sharply, "What if it is a daughter?" the Vicomtesse murmured, "Hush, dear," and shooed Yolande out of the room, which was most pleasant and had a dormer window and sloping roof.

Gilles Marsan's child came into the world a fortnight late, but gave its first cry exactly as the sun rose above the horizon east of Paris and streamed across Veronique's exhausted face. She smiled, feeling the golden warmth of the January day and whispered, "Is he very like Gilles?"

"The eyes," said Yolande, peering over the cloth at the lively bundle in the midwife's arms . . . "no one could mistake them."

Since Veronique's slim body was not built for motherhood. a wet nurse had been located in the village. Veronique did not see Gilles's child until hours later.

"Even though his family name cannot be Marsan, he *shall* have the name," she announced as Yolande very carefully carried in the child, followed by the Vicomtesse and all four of the orphans who had buzzed and whispered excitedly until

they reached her door, at which time they behaved with un-
accustomed propriety, all trooping properly into the little
room and surrounding the bed. "He shall be called Marsan
Vaudraye," Veronique said, and was startled when they all
suddenly giggled and exchanged glances.

"He is well? Nothing has happened to him?"

The Vicomtesse bustled to the bed between the boys. "Certainly she is well, my love. What a to-do! A healthier child
you will never see."

"She's funny. All red and ugly, but we like her," put in the
boy Tavi, though this description was indignantly denied.

"A beautiful girl!" Yolande insisted. "Her eyes are Gilles's
to the life. And her mouth is exactly the shape of—" She
caught Veronique's intent gaze but added without retreating,
"at all events, anyone would know her for Gilles's daughter."

"Daughter!" Veronique fell back against the pillows. She
had been so certain. To have his son would fill a small part
of the eternal, aching loneliness. "Well, let me see her."

The boys thought her attitude very reasonable. The Vicomtesse quickly said, "You will adore her. She is a delight, with
a lively disposition very like your own at her advanced
age—"

Veronique shook her head, smiled in spite of herself. After
that they all left her alone to get acquainted with her unexpected daughter. She looked at the child, put a finger into the
tiny fist and saw the smile, then the big dark eyes.

The Vicomtesse slipped into the room, rustled over to her.

"Is the sunlight too much for you, dear? I had better draw
the drapes so you may get some sleep—"

"No! I love to watch those trees, swaying in the wind,
against the sky. Even in winter there is so much life in them."
She said, after a moment, "By the way, mother, I don't believe
I want to go back to Turgot's Waxworks. I only did that because I hated life, hated the living. But I think I'm over that
feeling now. . . ."

"I sincerely hope so, my love. You used to smell dreadfully
of those acids she has in that horrid place. Incidentally, I had
a visit from that nice Monsieur Barras who seems to be running things in Paris. He says you are badly needed at the
hospitals. The religious orders are reorganizing, but you are
so wonderfully . . . administrative."

Veronique laughed. "Wonderful at giving orders, you mean.
But of course I can't leave this little one for a long time. . . .
I'd guess since Couthon's execution there's no one left in

authority who cares much about the hospitals." And then, remembering . . . "I said something to Couthon that last time I saw him. I wish now I could take it back. . . ."

The Vicomtesse leaned over, stroking the infant but speaking to Veronique. "You mustn't be sad, dear. There are beautiful things ahead for you, with this little one. Remember, I was never sorry I had a daughter."

Veronique looked up. "Mother, I do believe you are stronger than any of us. You are the one who will surely survive." Veronique took her daughter's fist in her hand, squeezed it gently and then brought it to her lips. "My gift from Gilles. My own Marsanne . . . may she be a little of you and papa, and a little of me. And I can see already that she is his child. Think of it, Mother! To live as Marsanne Vaudraye will, in this new world *he* left for her." . . .

FAWCETT CREST
BESTSELLERS

She was shaking with anger but forced herself to hear him